Whispers of the Wind

Includes Bonus Story of
The Scent of Magnolia

Whispers of the Wind

FRANCES DEVINE

BARBOUR BOOKS
An Imprint of Barbour Publishing, Inc.

Whispers of the Wind ©2012 by Frances Devine
The Scent of Magnolia ©2012 by Frances Devine

Print ISBN 978-1-68322-266-8

eBook Editions:
Adobe Digital Edition (.epub) 978-1-68322-268-2
Kindle and MobiPocket Edition (.prc) 978-1-68322-267-5

All scripture quotations are taken from the King James Version of the Bible.

Published by Barbour Books, an imprint of Barbour Publishing, Inc., P.O. Box 719, Uhrichsville, Ohio 44683, www.barbourbooks.com

Our mission is to publish and distribute inspirational products offering excep-tional value and biblical encouragement to the masses.

Member of the
Evangelical Christian
Publishers Association

Printed in the United States of America.

Chapter 1

Georgia, 1881

Abigail James gripped the side of the wagon seat with one hand and clutched her small, feather-tipped hat with the other. Determined to have something colorful to brighten up her drab traveling suit, she'd purchased the emerald green confection at Madame Genevieve's boutique before she left Washington, DC. She'd be doggoned if she'd see its tiny, bright feathers splattered in the muddy ruts of a Georgia back road.

"Sorry about this here bumpy wagon, Miss James." The stocky, dark-skinned driver, who'd introduced himself as Albert, reached under the brim of his hat and scratched his grizzled head. "Sure wish the axle hadn't broke on the carriage at the last minute."

Impatience tugged at the edge of Abigail's emotions. This was the fourth time the man had apologized since they'd left the train station. She dabbed her lace handkerchief on her forehead.

"It's all right. I'm not that fragile." To be truthful, she feared she might bounce right off the wagon any minute and land in the middle of the road in an unladylike pile of skirts. She darted a nervous glance at the red clay mud that splattered against the wagon wheels as they slushed through the ruts in the road.

"You must have had a great deal of rain lately."

"Yes ma'am. Gully washer after gully washer for the past week." He reached up and scratched his head again. "Don't know when I've seen so much rain in the summertime. And here it be the first week in June. We shore did need it though. We been sufferin' a awful long dry spell."

So why hadn't the rain cooled things off a little bit? Back home the temperature was still nice and springlike. If she didn't get out of this heat soon, she might faint. And she'd never fainted in her life.

"How much farther is it to the school?" The constant bouncing of her backside against the hard seat was becoming quite painful. Perhaps she was a little more fragile than she'd thought.

"Just about a quarter mile or so. I know you're going to be a welcome sight to Mr. Charles and Miss Helen. They haven't talked of much else since they heard you was coming to help out."

Abigail knew the other two teachers, Charles Waverly and Helen Edwards, had taught at the school for nearly a year with no help since the school's other teacher had married and moved away. She smiled. The bride's wedded bliss was Abigail's good fortune. She'd yearned for a teaching position of her own ever since she'd finished her courses. When she'd received the acceptance letter from the director of the school, Joshua Carter, she'd been almost giddy with joy.

"When will I meet the director?"

"Mr. Carter gone to Mobile, Alabama on business. Don't rightly know when he'll be back."

"Oh." Disappointment tightened her chest. She'd hoped to be able to discuss techniques before she began teaching. In the letter the director had sent her, he had outlined the methods of teaching she was expected to know. Sign language wasn't mentioned. Excitement coursed through her. They must not have anyone qualified to teach it. Professor Roberts—her mentor, family friend, and instructor—had taught her sign language for two years until she was proficient in it, and she hoped to begin utilizing this method of communication right away. Did she dare go ahead without permission from the director? She chewed her bottom lip in thought. Probably not.

Albert guided the horses around a bend and turned onto another road. Even narrower than the other, it was barely wide enough for the wagon to pass. Honeysuckle sprawled across a weathered fence, its fragrance delighting Abigail's nose. Wildflowers of every color and shape dotted the fields. Albert pulled up in front of a wooden gate that barred their way. While he got out to open it, Abigail read the sign hanging to one side. Cecilia Quincy School for the Deaf. A shiver ran down her spine as reality hit her. Could she do this? With resolve, she lifted her chin and straightened her back. Professor Roberts said she was ready. He believed in her, and she wouldn't let him down.

Albert climbed back up on the seat and drove through then went to shut the gate.

When he was once more in the wagon, he flicked the reins and guided the horses down the long, tree-lined avenue.

"What are these trees?" She waved a gloved hand at the thick, sturdy trees, some gnarled with age, that lined the road.

"Them there's live oak. They been standin' there for hunnerds of years I reckon." He squinted and frowned. "Ain't you ever seen no live oak?"

"Live oak? I've seen oak."

Albert leaned his head back and squinted before he nodded. "Well now. They's oaks and then they's live oaks. Live oaks stay green year round."

"Really? That's strange." She couldn't help but be intrigued, but the spidery wisps hanging from the trees intrigued her more. "What's that hanging from the branches?"

Albert chuckled. "Guess you ain't never seen no Spanish moss neither. It's mighty pretty, ain't it? The school's right around the next bend."

They passed a magnolia tree covered with large white flowers and rounded the curve. Abigail drew her breath in sharply.

The white frame, three-story house stood regally against a backdrop of thick woods. Balconies surrounded the upper floors, and a wide porch stretched across the lower, its pillars tall and stately. A grove of peach trees, pink and white blossoms still clinging to the branches, graced the area to her left. More blooming magnolia trees stood on both sides of the lush green lawn.

"Used to be a plantation house, belonged to a man named George Quincy. After he died, his widow freed all the slaves and give 'em all cabins and land. Said she figgered they'd earned it. And that was ten years before the war. She turned the big house over to her son, Thomas Quincy, to open this school."

"What a wonderful thing for her to do. I wonder why?"

"Heard tell she had a little girl who was deaf. The chile died when she was young from some disease she'd had since birth. The school was named after her."

"One of the names on my application was Quincy."

"Yes'm. That be Dr. Trent Quincy. He inherited the school and all the Quincy property a few years ago from his father, Thomas."

"Oh. Does he live at the school?"

"No'm, Doc Trent live in the house Mr. Thomas built. It not as big as the school, but it be mighty fine."

He drove around the circular drive and stopped the wagon in front. Before Abigail could move, the front screen door flew open and a thin, elderly black woman stepped out, her eyes smiling and her lips curved.

"And here you are, Miss Abigail." Her voice was soft and low. She stepped forward as Albert helped Abigail from the wagon. "You come right on in the house, now, out of this heat. I'm Virgie, the housekeeper." She turned a frown on Albert. "Why'd you bring Miss Abigail in that old wagon? You were supposed to fetch her in the carriage." Without waiting for an answer the tiny woman turned and opened one of the double screen doors.

Abigail stepped past her and into the house, breathing a sigh of relief at the welcome coolness of the room-sized foyer.

"Miz Virgie, Miz Virgie. Is she here yet?"

A small girl, maybe five or six years old, descended the wide, curving staircase. Abigail watched with awe as the child held on to the rail and took one careful step down at a time. Her glistening brown eyes darted this way and that.

"She sure is, Lily Ann girl. She's standing right here beside me."

Abigail stood frozen. She must go to the child. The precious angel stepped forward with eager steps, hands searching the air.

Abigail forced herself forward, every fiber of her being wanting to grab the little one's hands. But somehow instinct kicked in. She mustn't frighten the child.

She stooped down and extended one hand in front of her. "Here I am, Lily Ann."

The child took one more step and found her. "There you are. You're Miss Abigail. May I look at you, please?"

Confused, Abigail darted a questioning glance at Virgie, who ran both her hands across her own face.

"Of course you may look at me, Lily Ann. It's only fair since I'm looking at you."

Lily Ann giggled and nodded, her brown braids bobbing up and down. "That's right." Her small hand was gentle as it smoothed and probed Abigail's face.

"You're very pretty, Miss Abigail." She dropped her hand.

"Thank you. So are you. Very pretty indeed." She stood, but let her hand rest on the little girl's shoulder.

At the sound of the door opening, she turned. The man who stood there was tall with broad shoulders. He held her wobbling trunk on his shoulder, and his white shirt stretched tight over bulging muscles. One coal black curl fell across his forehead, and the blue of his eyes deepened as he stared at her with a startled look on his face.

"Dr. Trent, Dr. Trent, my new teacher is here." Lily Ann jumped up and down, a grin on her face.

Abigail's breath caught in her throat, and her stomach lurched. She sent a questioning look to Virgie, who smiled and nodded.

But this was a school for the deaf. They expected her to teach a blind child?

28

Trent Quincy grabbed at the swaying trunk and set it on the floor, hoping to gather his wits about him before he had to face the beautiful, wide-eyed young woman who stood in the middle of the foyer.

"Careful, Dr. Trent."

Virgie's voice bought him back to his senses and he straightened, clearing his throat. "I know, Virgie. I wouldn't dare drop a trunk on your shining floor."

He glanced at the stranger. Soft auburn curls fell below the atrocious feathered hat that perched atop her head, looking for all the world like a big, green bird. The warm brown eyes below the brim searched his face, which, from the way it burned, must be flaming bright red.

"Doctor, this is the new teacher, Miss Abigail James." Virgie gave him a fond smile. "Miss Abigail, this clumsy man is our doctor and the owner of the school, Dr. Quincy."

Miss James thrust her small gloved hand toward him, and he took it, hardly knowing whether to kiss it or shake it. He bowed slightly, pressing her hand gently before releasing it.

"Welcome to Quincy School, Miss James. We're like a family here, and I trust you will feel at home among us soon."

Her lips turned up slightly at the corners. "Thank you, Dr. Quincy. I'm sure I shall."

Virgie took Miss James's arm and began to walk her toward the staircase. "My lands, Miss Abigail. Here we stand making small talk when you must be wore out from traveling and probably thirsty, too."

Trent's gaze followed them as they made their way up the stairs.

"Here, Dr. Trent." Albert grabbed the trunk by its straps. "I best get this here trunk up to Miss Abigail's room before Virgie be hollerin' down the stairs."

Trent grabbed the strap on one end. "I don't know what she's got in this contraption, but it's heavy. Let's share the load."

By the time they reached the room assigned to Miss James, both men were panting.

They set it down beside the bed.

"I'm sorry it's so heavy." Concern clouded her eyes, and she glanced from Albert to Trent. "I brought a number of books with me."

Trent nodded. "That's quite all right, Miss James." He smiled.

"I'd better attend to my duties. See you at supper."

He headed downstairs and found Lily Ann waiting for him. He'd discovered long ago that she could recognize him by his footsteps.

"Dr. Trent. Do you like my new teacher? She's pretty isn't she?" Her smile lit up her face like sunshine.

Trent dropped to one knee and placed his arm around the child. "I like her very much, and there's no denying she's pretty."

"What color is her hair?" She frowned. "Miz Virgie took her away before I could ask. And her eyes, what color are they?"

"Hmmm, I'd say her hair is auburn. Do you know what that is?"

She nodded. "Of course I do. Sort of red and sort of brown. At least that's how Mr. Charles taught it to me."

"And Mr. Charles was absolutely correct. Reddish brown." He pursed his lips. "Or maybe brownish red would be more accurate in Miss James's case."

"And her eyes? Are they green? 'Cause Billy told me redheaded people usually have green eyes."

"Well, some do. But Miss James's eyes are a very lovely shade of brown. With a glint of amber deep inside."

"Oh." She stuck her finger in her mouth then pulled it out almost immediately.

Trent smiled. When she'd first come to the school, four fingers were in her mouth most of the time.

"But I don't know what amber is."

His heart constricted. Lily Ann had lost her sight two years ago. She remembered most of her colors. Amber must be new to her.

"Honey, the amber I'm speaking of is sort of orange and gold all mixed together."

She tilted her head. "Oh. Okay. I think I can picture that, sort of. Are they pretty?"

"Yes, but not as pretty as yours."

"Mine are brown, too."

"Yes, but yours are like chocolate cake."

She giggled. "Don't you try to eat my eyes."

"I'll do my best to resist, but you know how I like chocolate."

"Lily Ann." Virgie came down the stairs. "Mr. Charles is waiting for you."

Lily Ann's rosebud lips formed a pout, and her forehead scrunched up. "But I thought Miss Abigail was going to be my teacher now."

"Miss Abigail is gon' to read to you and teach you spelling. But she just arrived and needs to rest. You got to go to Mr. Charles's class now."

"Oh. All right." She started up the stairs, one tiny hand sliding up the rail. Suddenly she stopped and turned her head. "Good-bye, Dr. Trent. See you at supper."

"Good-bye, Miss Lily Ann. Maybe we'll have us some chocolate."

Her laughter trilled downward. "Not my eyes."

He glanced at Virgie. "Miss James is settled in? I hope she found her room satisfactory."

"Yes, but something else isn't so satisfactory. I think we've got ourselves a problem."

"Why? What's wrong?"

"Mr. Carter didn't say one word in his letter about her teaching a blind child. She scared to death at the thought."

Trent groaned. "Do you think perhaps she overlooked it?"

"No sir. She showed me the letter." She shook her head. "That man left it out on purpose because he needed a teacher and wasn't sure she'd come if she knew about Lily Ann. At least that's how I've got it figured."

"Why would you say such a thing, Virgie?"

She shook her head. "I shouldn't have said that, Dr. Trent. Don't pay any mind to me. Now I need to go see what's keeping Sally May. I sent her to bring clothes off the line an hour ago."

Trent looked after her as she headed for the back door. The

longtime housekeeper seldom found fault with anyone. If she had a concern about the school's director, it was probably worth looking into.

He went to the infirmary to check on Donald Atwood, one of the students who'd shown possible influenza symptoms yesterday. As a precaution, Trent had had him moved to the infirmary so others wouldn't be exposed.

A memory of the new teacher teased his mind. What he'd said to Lily Ann about her being pretty was true. The first sight of her had nearly knocked him for a loop. But the important thing was that they needed her. His main reason for hiring another teacher was for Lily Ann. The other teachers were too busy to give the child the personal attention she needed. There was a school in Alabama that would be more suited to her, but Lily Ann's parents refused to allow her to go so far way. He didn't really blame them for not wanting to be away from their child. So he'd arranged for Lily Ann to board through the week and go home on weekends. He only hoped the task of teaching a blind child wouldn't scare Miss Abigail James away.

Chapter 2

Abigail's trunk stood open beside the bed. Virgie offered to send someone up to unpack, but Abigail insisted she preferred to take care of her own things. As tired as she was, this was only partly true. But from what she'd observed, the school was shorthanded, not only in teachers but also household staff.

Supper would be served in the dining room at six. That gave her two hours to put away her things and perhaps rest awhile before freshening up for the evening meal. Virgie had told her the children normally ate at five and the staff at seven, but in honor of the new arrival and because the children were so excited to meet her, they'd changed the schedule for today.

Her thoughts whirled with the new turn of events concerning her duties, and her heart raced as it used to when she would run across the fields trying to keep up with her brother, Nat. She closed her eyes and took a deep breath then another, letting the air out slowly. Her heart began to slow down.

She could do this. She knew strides had been made in teaching the blind. She'd attended a lecture only a few months ago. A Frenchman had given a very interesting address about a method of teaching created by one of his countrymen that involved some sort of raised dots. If only she'd listened more closely. She snapped her fingers. Braille! It was called braille. Was it possible her new school was utilizing this method or something similar? Well, if not, she would write immediately to Professor Roberts and ask him how to obtain materials for learning and teaching braille.

She reached into her trunk and removed the dress she planned to wear to supper. She shook it several times then slipped it on to one of the hangers she found waiting in the mahogany wardrobe against the wall. A few passes over the satin with her hands and the worst of the wrinkles were gone. Her hatbox sat on one of the shelves with her new hat safely tucked away inside for her next outing. She took a deep breath, enjoying the scent of lavender that wafted from the wardrobe.

When the trunk was empty and all her things put away, she removed her dress and corset and sank into the softness of the feather bed.

If they weren't using modern teaching methods for Lily Ann, she'd simply have to do the best she could to help the child learn for now. Even if she had to read every lesson aloud over and over again to help her memorize the material.

But Abigail's last thought as she drifted off was not of Lily Ann's sweet smile, but of the doctor's deep blue eyes and rugged, handsome face.

She was still groggy when she awoke. She glanced at the clock on the small side table and sprang out of bed with a little gasp. Only thirty minutes until she was expected in the dining room to meet the children and staff. She went to the rose-and-white porcelain pitcher and bowl on the stand in the corner. Someone must have tiptoed in while she slept, for the bowl had been filled with water that was still warm to the touch. After a quick face wash and sponge bath, she donned her pale blue satin dress and rearranged her hair.

Feeling presentable for the first time since she'd stepped onto the train in Washington, she retrieved a fresh lace-trimmed handkerchief from a drawer in the wardrobe and stepped into the hallway. Now, if only the butterflies in her stomach would calm down.

Muted laughter and conversation drifted upward as Abigail walked down the wide staircase, and a wonderful, but unfamiliar, spicy aroma wafted up, reminding her she had skipped lunch.

She reached the foyer at the same moment Dr. Quincy stepped in through the front door.

Her eyes met his startled expression, which was quickly replaced by a friendly smile as he crossed the foyer and offered his arm. "May I have the honor of escorting you, Miss James?"

With a slight nod she took the proffered arm, and they walked through double doors into the dining room.

The happy voices stopped and silence greeted them. A long table, covered by a snow-white cloth, stood in the center of the room. Two men and two women sat on each side of the head place at the table. Five boys lined the men's side, and four girls were seated by the women.

With a flourish Dr. Quincy motioned to Abigail. "Ladies and gentlemen, may I introduce our new teacher, Miss Abigail James. You'll have an opportunity to introduce yourselves to her later, but let's allow her to be seated first, please."

Heat rushed to Abigail's face as the doctor escorted her to an empty space that had been left for her. She wasn't accustomed to being the center of attention.

A man seated across from her stood and gave a slight bow as she took her seat. "I'm very pleased to meet you, Miss James. I'm Charles Waverly, teacher of math, science, and geography. The lady next to you is Miss Helen Edwards, who teaches reading, English, and history. Next is Mrs. Felicity Cole, the girls' dorm mother. The gentleman beside me is Howard Owens, the boys' dorm parent."

As he and the doctor seated themselves, a pair of light blue eyes peered at her from Miss Edwards's face. "Please, call me Helen. And you might as well call us all by our first names. We don't have a lot of time for formalities here as you'll soon find out for yourself." Her smile softened the words, but her voice held a ring of truth.

Abigail liked Helen's straightforward manner. She returned the smile. "And I'm Abigail."

Helen relaxed and sat back in her chair. "We're going to be friends. I feel it in my bones."

Giggles emitted from the line of girls, and Lily Ann, who was seated next to Abigail, thrust her hand up high.

"Yes, Lily Ann?" Dr. Quincy's voice held laughter. "You have something you want to say?"

"You can't feel that in your bones, Miss Edwards."

Abigail looked on in amazement as the children erupted into laughter. Apparently the phrase "children should be seen and not heard" didn't apply at Quincy School for the Deaf. But how had the children heard Lily Ann's comment?

She turned to Helen and spoke softly. "I thought the children were deaf."

Helen grinned. "Most of them read lips very well."

Abigail smiled and nodded. Lip reading was good. But she had come to believe that adding sign language was even better. Her stomach tightened. She hoped Mr. Carter would agree.

She glanced at Dr. Quincy and met his eyes—deep-set, mesmerizing blue eyes. His lips curved, and she lowered her lashes then turned her attention to Helen.

"When do you expect Mr. Carter to return?"

"Not till next week." Helen's eyes crinkled as she smiled. "But don't worry. He planned your schedule before he left, so you'll have plenty to do."

The door opened and two women, wearing aprons over their dresses and colorful scarves around their heads, entered the room carrying soup tureens. As the younger one filled Abigail's soup bowl with a hearty, stew-like soup, the aroma tantalized her senses.

"Thank you." She glanced at the serving girl. "It smells wonderful."

The girl only nodded, but the corners of her lips tilted up.

Abigail looked at the stew, which contained pieces of chicken, tomatoes, and onions that she could recognize. She had no idea what the green vegetable slices were and wasn't about to ask.

Dr. Quincy bowed his head, and everyone at the table followed suit. He offered a simple blessing, thanking God for the food, asking Him to bless it and those who prepared it. He then offered thanks that Abigail had arrived safely.

His amen had barely left his lips when he turned to Abigail. "Being from the north, you've probably never eaten our Georgia gumbo."

"No, I haven't. In fact, I've never heard of it." She offered him a smile and hoped her words hadn't sounded rude. "But it smells delicious."

"I hope you like it." At that he turned his attention to his food.

She lifted her spoon and let the spicy, unfamiliar flavor roll over her tongue. After the third taste, she decided she liked it and gave the doctor a nod. "Very good."

The soup was followed by fried chicken, potatoes with white gravy, and an array of vegetables, pickles, and preserves. The bread baskets never ran out of hot biscuits and corn bread. Abigail hoped this was part of her welcome and not an every night's occurrence. She was hard put not to sigh with pleasure but careful not to eat too much.

When the meal was over, the children went to their dormitories to have a time of Bible stories and prayer before bedtime.

"Shall we go to the parlor and visit for a while?" Helen motioned for Abigail to follow her.

The parlor was small and cozy with a spinet piano in one corner and overstuffed chairs and a sofa arranged comfortably around the room. Virgie sat in a wing chair with a basket of mending on her lap. She laid the small garment she was mending on top and started to rise.

"No, no, Virgie." Helen said. "Why don't you stay and visit with us. I'm sure Abigail has questions, and you can help me answer them."

Virgie leaned back as Abigail and Helen sat on the sofa. "I don't know how much help I'll be, but glad to do anything I can."

Helen laughed. "Don't give me that. You know everything that goes on around here."

The elderly woman's lips turned up slightly. "I might at that."

"Actually, I do have a question." Abigail looked from Helen

to Virgie. "I was wondering—have you begun teaching sign language here?"

Helen and Virgie exchanged glances. Virgie picked up the basket and returned it to her lap. Her tightly pressed lips gave a good indication she had nothing to say.

Helen sighed. "Mr. Carter won't hear of it. He says he doesn't see the point since all the children read lips. We gave up suggesting it long ago."

❧

Trent tried to concentrate on the medical journal he was perusing, but fatigue threatened to overcome him. He turned the page and began scanning the next section. If only he could find an answer for Lily Ann. Somewhere, somehow there had to be a surgeon who could help her. He tossed the journal onto the floor with a stack of others when he came to the end of the article then stood and turned his head from side to side in an attempt to stretch the tight muscles. He might as well go to bed. He reached over to lower the wick on the lamp. Someone knocked on the front door, and he straightened, frowning. Carrie, his only full-time maid and also Virgie's daughter, had already retired to her apartment over the kitchen with her husband, Solomon, who managed the farm for Trent, and their three-year-old son, Hunter.

Trent headed to the door, his breathing quickening with trepidation. A knock this late at night usually meant an emergency.

Cal Walker stood with his hat in hand on the front porch. "Doc, you gotta come. My two youngest are burning up with fever."

"Are there other symptoms?" Trent shot out the words while reaching for the bag he kept beside the door.

"Lutie's been coughin' and complaining about her throat being sore." He swallowed. "May's skeered it's the scarlet fever."

"All right. Why don't you get back home to May and the kids? I'll be right behind you."

Ten minutes later Trent secured his bag to the saddle and mounted Warrior. The gelding nickered. Trent patted him on the neck then urged him down the lane. The mile to the Walker farm sped by. Trent tied Warrior to a tree branch and ran to the open front door where Cal waited.

May stood twisting her apron in the middle of the main room of the two-room house. Anguish distorted her face.

Moans came from a bed against one wall. Trent hurried over and stooped down beside the bed. As he examined ten-year-old Lutie and her younger brother, Sam, relief washed over him. Finally he stood.

"I don't think it's scarlet fever. The symptoms are more like measles. I should be able to make a more accurate diagnosis by tomorrow."

May collapsed into a chair. Her shoulders shook as she cried silently into her apron.

Cal shook his head, a grin of relief splitting his face. "Now ain't that just like a woman? Didn't shed nary a tear while we was wondering, and now she bawls like a baby."

"Don't misunderstand me, Cal. Measles can be serious, too. After I care for my horse, I'm going to stay for a few hours until I'm absolutely certain this isn't scarlet fever." He put a hand on May's shoulder. "You'll need to get some clean, soft cloths to wash their skin, May."

She jumped up. "I've got lots of old flannel I've saved, Doc. I'll go get it. Hot water?"

"No, barely lukewarm. It'll feel better on their skin. And I need a spoon."

"I'll get it, Dr. Trent." Bonnie, the oldest Walker child at fourteen, hurried into the kitchen after her mother and returned almost immediately with a clean spoon. "I'll take your horse to the barn, Doc."

"Thank you, Bonnie. That would be very kind of you."

They took turns washing the sick children's fevered skin. Trent administered a dose of paregoric for Lutie's sore throat and cough.

The two older girls went to bed on cots in the kitchen and slept soundly even with their parents passing by to get water and cloths throughout the night.

Cal sat and whittled on a piece of pinewood. The shavings piled up on the floor beside him. May didn't seem to notice.

Trent turned to Cal. "Have you heard of any other cases of sickness in the area?"

"Naw." Cal stopped whittling and stared at the pile of shavings as though noticing them for the first time. "Can't say I have. But we don't get out much. Too much work around the place." He stood and, without a word, retrieved the broom from the kitchen and swept up the shavings.

Trent returned his attention to his patients. He'd need to check around the county. Measles could be dangerous if not caught in time or cared for properly. And if by some chance it was scarlet fever, an epidemic could be disastrous.

By daybreak, Trent was confident his initial diagnosis was correct. He left instructions for treatment and a tiny bottle of paregoric to be used sparingly for coughs and sore throat. "And don't go anywhere until I say it's all right."

As he rode away from the Walker farm, he wanted nothing more than to go home and crawl between his cool sheets, but the thought of the nine children at the school was enough to give him a surge of energy.

He found the staff and the children just leaving the dining room. In a moment he found himself surrounded by excited children. He was relieved to see young Donald out of the infirmary.

"Dr. Trent, will you come to our class today?" Little Lena Sammons peered up with wide green eyes.

"No! It's our turn," Billy said.

"Now, Billy. Lena. Say good day to Dr. Quincy. It's time to get to our classes."

They marched up the stairs in a straight line, with Miss James bringing up the rear. Trent motioned for her to join him.

"Yes, Doctor?" She darted a glance after the children. "I really need to go with Miss Edwards."

"I know. I'll only be a moment." He looked into her unusual

but beautiful eyes and almost lost his train of thought. He cleared his throat. "I didn't want to say anything in front of the children. Will you please inform the other staff members there's been an outbreak of measles at a nearby farm?"

She gasped.

He held up his hand. "Please don't worry. It may only be an isolated incident. But until we know for sure, I think it would be best to keep the children and any of the staff who haven't had measles here at the school."

"Oh, but the children are so looking forward to their Sunday school class."

"I'm sure they are, Miss James, but it's better to be safe, don't you think?" His gentle voice softened the words.

"Of course, Doctor. I'll inform the staff." Her thick lashes nearly swept her cheek as she lowered her eyes.

"Miss James, have you had measles?"

"Yes, I had them when I was ten." A shadow crossed her face. "Will that be all?"

"Yes. And thank you."

She sailed up the stairs and turned to look back when she reached the top landing. As their eyes met, she blushed and hurried down the hall.

Trent grinned. She hadn't expected to see him still there—watching her at that. His heart thumped wildly, and he straightened his face. Why *had* he still been there watching her?

Consternation shot through him. Okay, she was very pretty and her eyes fascinated him. And although he'd managed to keep from entanglements since his disastrous engagement and subsequent breakup with Sharon, there was nothing wrong with being attracted to a young woman. Was there?

He went outside and mounted his horse. He was exhausted and not thinking straight. He needed to get home and rest. That's all it was. He nodded. Yes. That was all it was.

Chapter 3

The chalk in Abigail's hand shook as she wrote spelling words on the blackboard. An unnatural silence hung over the small classroom. She turned and looked at the six children who attended her combination reading, writing, and spelling class. The expressions on their faces were as morose and forlorn as she felt, although for different reasons. She hated seeing them so disappointed. Yesterday they'd been cheerful and eager as they talked about the Sunday school Bible verse contest they were each sure they'd win. Now they stared at her with sad eyes in varying shades of blue, green, and brown. But of course the doctor was right to quarantine them.

Mr. Carter's arrival during the night had set her nerves on edge. Especially when he'd sent word by a servant that he'd see her in his office after her final class of the day. The director hadn't appeared at either meal that day, choosing instead to have a tray sent to his office. So she'd had no chance to examine his countenance and perhaps get an idea of how to broach her suggestions.

She stepped over to her desk and stood in front of it, hands clasped in a tight grip. Clearing her throat, she attempted a smile. "These are your spelling words for next week. Write them down carefully. Through the week we will be learning how to speak them properly as well as write them." And if she had her say, they would be learning to sign them, too.

Heads bobbed and pencils wobbled as the students peered at the blackboard then bent over their tablets.

One by one, they laid their pencils on their desks to indicate they were finished. The thing that impressed her most about these children was that although they had fun times and could even joke around to the point of boisterousness, they were respectful to adults and orderly in the classroom and in every task they faced.

The bell clanged and she straightened. "All right. Time for your next class. Please line up at the door."

When she had walked them to Charles Waverly's class for geography, she went back to her classroom and cleaned the blackboard. After giving the room a quick pickup, she patted her hair and smoothed her skirt then headed downstairs to the director's office.

She'd been planning what she would say to Mr. Carter all week, and the words replayed in her mind as she walked down the long corridor off the foyer. She tapped on the heavy oak door, waited, then knocked again, louder this time.

"Come in!" The gruff tone of the voice seemed to say, "Stay out," instead.

Abigail took a deep breath and opened the door.

A strong odor of pipe tobacco permeated the air, and she was hard put not to wrinkle her nose. He frowned as he stared at her from the chair behind his desk with an expression Abigail could only imagine was distaste. Finally he rose and gave a nod, apparently all he felt she merited. He motioned her into the chair across from him.

She sat in the chair, her back straight and proper, and looked into his eyes, searching for some spark of agreeableness. He was a little older than she'd expected, probably in his sixties. His hair was white, but dull and unappealing, and his eyebrows were bushy over faded blue eyes. Frown wrinkles dug trenches above his nose, and his lips turned downward at the corners. She'd hoped he'd be open to her suggestions in spite of Helen's and Virgie's comments, but his countenance wasn't too promising. He looked to be a very unpleasant man.

"Miss James, I see this is your first position."

"Yes sir, my first formal position, although I did assist—"

"Yes, yes." He waved his hand in dismissal of further words from her, conveying the impression he'd like to dismiss her altogether.

A wave of heat burned her face. Did the man have no manners

at all? She pressed her lips together, determined not to ruin her chance to talk about the sign language.

He perused the application and rubbed his hand across his forehead. He lifted his brows and peered at her from tired eyes. "I'm sure Miss Edwards and Mr. Waverly have instructed you on your duties and our manner of doing things."

"Yes sir. They've been most helpful." She twisted her handkerchief with hands that wanted to fly off her lap and speak the words her lips did not.

"Hmmph." He glanced at the letters of reference and without a word about them, looked at her directly. "Very well, Miss James. I'm sure you'll do quite well. You're dismissed."

Her mouth dropped open, and she clamped her lips together and stood. "Thank you, Mr. Carter. I'm sure I'll enjoy working here."

At his nod, she started toward the door. Her head pounded with confusion and dismay. That was it? Suddenly she stopped and whirled around. "Mr. Carter, I wonder if I might speak with you about an additional teaching method. It's been highly successful for several years now."

Annoyance crossed his face. "Really, Miss James. You've been teaching for one week, and you think you know more than seasoned instructors?"

Abigail pushed down the anger that threatened to rise up. She took a breath and expelled it. "No sir. I don't think I know more than others. Although I have been teaching for some time, not just a week. And perhaps some things I've learned from professionals might be of some use."

He sighed. "Very well, Miss James. Clearly you are determined. Please sit down and explain to me this wonderful new teaching method."

She eased back into the chair and swallowed. "I'm sure you are familiar with the concept of sign language. It has been used in the larger schools for some time now. And I've been thoroughly instructed in sign language and several ways to teach it."

She took a deep breath, clutched her hands together in her lap, and waited for his response.

A grimace of annoyance twisted his face. "Sign language? I personally haven't heard a thing about this so-called teaching method that makes me believe it is more beneficial than the methods we are using."

That couldn't be true. Abigail personally knew dozens of students whose lives had changed dramatically, for the better, with the use of signing.

"Miss James." He stood again, and his expression indicated the meeting was over. "You are very young, and I'm sure your intentions are good. But Quincy School has been doing quite well teaching lip reading and oral language for many years. I hardly think we need to change because a young girl sails in with untried ideas and uninhibited ambition."

"But Mr. Carter. . ."

"That will be all, Miss James. I'm sure you can find something to do with your time, as I certainly can with mine."

Appalled at Mr. Carter's seeming lack of knowledge on the latest teaching methods, not to mention his horrible rudeness, Abigail trembled with humiliation and her fists tightened in anger as she rushed to her room. It was a good thing she had no more classes today. How would she have been able to face her students when she was near to tears?

Couldn't he have at least heard her out? She hadn't meant to imply they should do away with lip reading and oral language. But adding signs could benefit the children so much and make learning easier. If only she had chosen her words more carefully instead of blurting out the idea the way she had and making herself appear ignorant and foolish. And they hadn't spoken about Lily Ann at all.

Oh! She stomped her foot. The man was impossible. But she was determined not to give up her quest.

Trent rode his horse to the barn and dismounted. Albert stepped out with a smile on his face. "I thought you forgot about us, Dr. Trent. Where you been all week?"

"Been taking care of the measles outbreak." Unfortunately the measles situation was worse than he'd realized. He had to stay on top of it to prevent an epidemic. It was all he could do to make it home every now and then to change through the week. Today had been an unexpected but very welcome respite, with no new cases. He could only hope it would last. He clapped the older man on the shoulder. "I knew you'd look out for things and come get me if I was needed."

"You know I would've. But everything went along fine here." He frowned. "Mistuh Carter got back last night."

"Oh?" Trent handed over the reins. "You don't seem too pleased about that."

"I don't say nothing about no man. Not me." He shook his grizzled head. "But that man don't ever find nothing to smile about, and they ain't no denying things was running a whole lot smoother without him."

A pang of unease ran through Trent. What was it about Carter that seemed to rub folks the wrong way? The man seemed efficient enough in overseeing the school. Still, there was a different feel in the air when the director was gone. Less oppressive somehow.

Trent glanced toward the former plantation house. "So how are all the teachers?"

"They's fine."

"Good. That's good." Trent cleared his throat. "The new teacher working out all right?"

Albert cut a glance his way. "Ain't heard no complaints."

"Guess I'd better head for the house. Take care of Warrior for me, please. I'll probably stay for supper."

"Yes sir. I'll fix him up good."

When Trent stepped into the foyer, the first person he saw

was Abigail coming down the staircase. His breath caught in his throat as she reached the bottom step.

"Dr. Quincy. How nice to see you." She stepped toward him and offered her hand.

He wondered if the shine in her eyes was for him. Had she missed him? Of course not. They hardly knew each other. He must be more tired than he realized.

He pressed her hand gently. "Thank you, Miss James. It's nice to see you, too. Are you all settled in?"

She removed her hand from his and gave him a slight smile. "Yes, quite. Thank you, Doctor."

"Are the children all well?"

Before she could speak, Virgie came out of the parlor. Her face lit up at the sight of Trent. "It's about time you came to see us. You staying for supper now?"

"Yes, I told Carrie not to bother to prepare anything for my evening meal. Between my being gone treating the ill and the meals I take here, I fear that daughter of yours might get lazy."

Her soft chuckle fell like healing balm over his tired body and spirit. "You stop that teasing now, Dr. Trent. You and I both know Carrie don't have a lazy bone in her body."

"True words, and spoken by a true mother." He glanced toward the infirmary. No light crept out from beneath the door. A good sign. "Does anyone need my attention?"

"Everyone fit as can be." Virgie glanced at Abigail then back at Trent. "You two go on into the parlor and visit until supper is ready. The children already gone upstairs."

Abigail shook her head. "I'll help get supper finished. One of the cook's helpers didn't come to work today." With a rather abrupt nod for Virgie and a bare hint of one for him, she turned and headed toward the kitchen.

Trent watched her go. So much for that shine in her eyes being for him. She'd probably been rubbing her eye or something. He chuckled.

"What so funny now?" Virgie eyed him then glanced down the hall at Abigail's retreating form. "You could do worse."

Trent's face flamed hot. "I'm not looking for a wife, Virgie."

She squinted up into his eyes. "Well, you ought to be. Just because that Sharon gal turned out to be a gold digger, don't mean all women like that. Besides, you're not getting any younger you know." She tossed her scarf-covered head back and laughed.

His own laughter joined hers in the empty room.

Mr. Carter stomped into the foyer from the hall and stopped still when he saw Trent. "Good afternoon, Doctor. I didn't realize you were here. I thought some of the children were playing in the hall."

Trent narrowed his eyes. This was the first he'd seen of the man's temper. "And would it have been so terrible if they had been? I always think it's a delightful thing when children are happy."

Carter tightened his lips then nodded. "Of course, but we also must have order in the school, mustn't we?" As if that settled it, he turned to Virgie. "Please see that I have a tray in my apartment. I won't be down for supper."

Abruptly he turned and headed up the stairs.

Trent frowned and glanced at Virgie. "Is he always like that? Or has he had a bad day?"

She shrugged. "Not my place to say."

"I think I'll go say good night to the boys before supper."

"That be a good idea, Dr. Trent. Be sure to come down in time to escort Miss Abigail in to supper. It'll be ready in fifteen minutes."

He sent her a teasing frown and headed upstairs. But by the time the boys had regaled him with all their recent escapades and he'd said good night, he came downstairs fully intending to take Virgie's suggestion. As he stepped onto the foyer, Abigail was just entering the dining room with Charles Waverly. He followed them in and held Mrs. Cole's chair while Waverly seated Abigail. A slight pang of jealousy shot through Trent.

The meal was delicious as usual, but uneventful. Abigail was quiet and withdrawn, but he seemed to be the only one who noticed. After several failed attempts to start a conversation with her, Trent gave up and ate in silence, only half listening to the conversations going on around him.

Finally he'd had enough. He pushed his chair back and stood. "If you'll all excuse me, I've had a very busy week, and I think I'll go home and get some needed sleep. I'll be back in a few days. Send someone for me if I'm needed."

Abigail lifted her chin and glanced at him then quickly looked away. A jolt shot through him. He should have realized before. The shine in her eyes was from unshed tears. And if her expression was any indication, they were tears of anger, not sadness.

He hesitated, at a loss for what to do or say. What could he do? He couldn't embarrass her by inquiring about the cause of her distress. And she certainly hadn't indicated in any way she'd appreciate such an inquiry. Some things were best left alone. He said good night and went outside where Albert waited with Warrior.

On the ride home, the disturbing memory of Abigail's angry tears invaded his thoughts. Had someone been unkind to her? Or perhaps she'd had bad news from home. A thought jolted him. Perhaps she'd decided to return home. After all, rural Georgia was a far cry from the city life to which she was accustomed.

Chapter 4

Abigail went to her room after her two morning classes, determined to take the time to write to her parents. She'd been so busy, as well as distracted, since she'd arrived that she'd only written to them once. She loosened her corset and sat at the little writing desk in the corner. After several attempts to begin, she simply poured out her heart, telling them about the children and how wonderful they were. Then she wrote about Mr. Carter's resistance to sign language and that because of his attitude, she had yet to bring up the subject of braille for Lily Ann. By the time the letter was complete, she leaned back, spent, emotions drained. She cared about all the children. But she'd have to admit, at least to herself, Lily Ann was her favorite. The child was such a cheerful little thing, and bright as she could be, always eager to learn something new. She did well with her verbal lessons, but Abigail believed she deserved every chance available. She simply must convince Mr. Carter as well. After all, it wasn't as though Abigail was attempting to persuade him to add some untried teaching tool. Braille had been taught successfully in the United States for at least thirty years. Unfortunately, no one at the school, including her, knew anything about this written language for the blind. But Abigail was determined that Lily Ann should have her chance.

Making a sudden decision, she opened a drawer and drew out her recent letter from Professor Roberts. She stood, tucking it into her pocket. Mr. Carter might be angry with her, but she had to at least attempt to open his eyes. She retied her corset, straightened her skirt, and walked out of her room and down the stairs.

As she descended the staircase into the foyer, a passing cloud darkened the room. A shiver passed through her. She paused and glanced back up the stairs toward her room. Perhaps she should wait. With resolve, she took a deep breath and straightened her back. She could do this. What could he do but say no? The dark hall leading to the director's private office seemed to stretch endlessly.

She stepped forward and walked down the hall. She lifted her fist and rapped on the door.

"Come in."

The same strong smell of smoke hung over the room. This time worse than before. Apparently Mr. Carter liked his pipe.

"Miss James." His tone wasn't exactly rude, but she certainly wouldn't call it friendly. He didn't bother to rise, but motioned to a chair across from him. "How may I assist you?"

She stepped over to the chair and sat. His desk was neatly arranged—a stack of paper to his left, his inkwell and pens to his right. Good. A man who was neat had at least one good quality. Guilt rippled through her. She didn't know him well enough to judge him. For all she knew he had many fine qualities.

"Sir, I would like to present a sug— That is. . .a request."

He closed his eyes and sighed. "I thought we had already discussed the matter. There will be no sign language taught in this school."

Why was the man so against change? Had he never heard of progress?

"Yes sir. I understand. And although I still believe the children would benefit greatly from learning signs, they seem to be progressing, and I accept your decision." For now, at least. She wasn't ready to give up completely.

He gave a short laugh. "I'm very pleased to hear that. Then what is your request? An excursion into town to do some frivolous shopping? Or perhaps you wish time off already? I realize teaching deaf children can be difficult for some."

"No, I have no need to shop at the present, and I don't require time off." Her throat felt tight and she cleared it. "Sir, I'm concerned about Lily Ann."

A frown of annoyance crossed the director's face. "What could possibly cause you concern about Lily? We are doing what we can to educate her. She's a blind child who was granted admittance to Quincy out of pity, I would imagine. I believe her parents are acquaintances of Dr. Quincy."

That was news to Abigail. Perhaps she was speaking to the wrong person.

"I'm of the opinion there might be more we can do for her. I'm sure you've heard of braille."

"Of course. But if you are suggesting we teach braille to the child, I would like to inform you none of our teachers are familiar with it, and therefore cannot teach it."

She retrieved the letter from her pocket and offered it to him. "Sir, this is a letter from Professor Roberts at my old school in Washington. He has sent an address where we might request the materials needed to learn and teach braille. I would be more than happy to volunteer to learn in my free time in order to help Lily Ann." Her heart pounded against her bodice. *Please, God.*

"I see. And are you also prepared to pay for the expense of such a venture?"

"Well, I. . . That is, I would be glad to if I had extra money, but I don't. I thought the school would cover the expenses."

"So, after being employed here for less than a month, you would have the school go to the expense of buying the necessary supplies to train you to teach braille to one six-year-old girl." He snorted. "Please, Miss James. Attend to your duties and stop interrupting me with your impractical suggestions."

She gasped and stood. How dare he speak to her that way when she was only trying to help a child? She spun on her heel and hurried out of the room, tears of rage coursing down her cheeks. She ran down the hall and across the foyer. She pushed blindly through the front doors and slammed into a hard, muscled chest.

❧

Startled, Trent dropped his bag to the porch and gripped Abigail's shoulders to steady them both. Tears streamed down her cheeks, and her body shook.

Before he could ask what was wrong, Virgie rushed down the stairs and, seeing them at the door, hurried over, worry distorting her usually calm face.

"Dr. Trent. Come with me. Sonny burnin' up with fever, and he's all flushed."

Abigail gasped and pulled away, her face pale. "Where is he, Virgie?"

"He in his bed, Miss Abigail. Thrashin' around somethin' awful."

"I must go to him." Abigail took a step toward the stairs.

"Wait." Trent touched her arm and turned to Virgie. "Have him brought to the infirmary. I'll examine him there."

"I'll help you get things ready." Again, Abigail took a step, this time in the direction of the infirmary.

"Miss James, you need to stay away from him until we know what's wrong. He may be contagious. Or it could be something as minor as a summer cold. Children often run high temperatures."

A sound of exasperation escaped her lips, but she nodded. "All right. But I'm waiting in the foyer."

He nodded, grabbed his medical bag, and headed for the infirmary.

By the time Virgie came through the door followed by Albert, who was carrying eight-year-old Sonny in his arms, Trent had everything needed for the examination laid out on his instrument table beside the cot.

Albert laid Sonny down and left the room.

"Hello, Sonny." The boy didn't respond. Trent put his finger gently under his chin and tilted his face until he looked at him. Then he repeated the words.

"Hi, Doc." His words weren't as plain as usual, and Trent didn't care for the raspy sound of Sonny's voice. Or the pink flush on his face.

"Will you open your mouth for me and stick out your tongue?"

Sonny complied, and just as Trent had suspected, his temperature proved to be a few degrees above normal.

Virgie removed the little boy's shirt, and Trent examined him thoroughly, growing more concerned as each measles symptom reared its head.

"Well young man, looks like you don't have to go to school for a few days." He patted Sonny on the head. "Miz Virgie is going to make up a nice bed for you right here in the infirmary so the other boys won't be making a lot of noise while you try to rest."

"Ohay, Doc. I how owioca?"

Trent grinned. "Yes, you can have tapioca. And I'll bet Miz Virgie would even put some of her spiced peaches on top."

He glanced at Virgie. Worry clouded her face. And she motioned toward the hall.

"Sonny, I'm going out into the hall for a minute; then we're going to give you a nice cool sponge bath to make you feel better."

When they entered the foyer, Abigail stepped toward them. "How is Sonny?"

"Miss James, I need to speak to Virgie for a moment; then I have a request for you."

She nodded and turned away.

Trent took Virgie's hand in his. "What's wrong?"

"It's measles isn't it?" Worry shadowed her eyes.

"Yes, I'm glad we caught it as soon as we did. Still, I don't expect Sonny to be the only one. Watch for any sign of it in the other children."

"Dr. Trent, Hunter was here with me all morning. Solomon just came and got him a few minutes ago." She squeezed his hand. "He's been exposed."

"All right. Try not to worry." Her little grandson was Virgie's pride and joy. "Even if he's contracted them, he should be fine. I'll send Albert over to explain the situation to Carrie and Solomon so they can watch for symptoms. Unless he was exposed sooner, it will be several days before anything shows up."

She nodded. "I know you'll take care of my angel. Just like you do all these others. I'll go get some warm water and cloths to bathe Sonny. And I'll tell cook to make him some beef tea and tapioca."

He glanced after her. Maybe he should send her over to be with Hunter. But no. Hunter was fine for now. And if more children at the school became sick, she'd be needed.

Albert came in from the kitchen. "Virgie say you want to see me?"

Trent gave Albert instructions, and when the old servant had left, he finally turned to Abigail.

"Miss James, I'm afraid it is measles. Since you've had them, I'd appreciate it if you'd help Virgie get Sonny settled while I take a look at the other children. And please pray that we have no epidemic here at the school."

Before the day was over, two more children joined Sonny in the infirmary. Since the children were in close quarters together, Trent saw no reason to stop classes for the well children. But when three more became ill the next day, classes were discontinued.

Chapter 5

Abigail jerked awake and sat up straight. She stretched her neck. Sleeping in the rocking chair beside Lily Ann's bed comforted the child, but it didn't lend much to rest. Thank the good Lord the child hadn't contracted the measles, but she was frightened. And since Mrs. Cole was taking a turn in the infirmary, Abigail hadn't had the heart to go off and leave her alone in an otherwise empty dormitory. How unfortunate that her parents were away from home this week. Otherwise she'd more than likely have been sent home. But they'd be home tomorrow night, just in time to pick their daughter up for the weekend.

Abigail yawned and looked at the little round watch on the white ribbon around her neck. Five o'clock. Mrs. Cole would return any minute. Then Abigail could wash up and change into fresh clothing. After breakfast, she'd take a turn at nursing. Dr. Trent was hardly sleeping at all. An hour here or there. But then the rest of them weren't doing much better.

The door opened and Mrs. Cole tiptoed in, looking exhausted.

"Felicity, when Lily Ann wakes up, why don't you take her to the kitchen? Cook won't mind looking out for her. And Lily Ann will love it."

The kindly woman lifted a hand to cover a yawn. She smiled. "I just might do that. The girls were all restless through the night. I couldn't even get a catnap."

Abigail stifled a yawn with one hand and waved good-bye with the other. She went to her room and glanced with longing at her soft feather bed before turning to her washstand.

When she entered the dining room a short time later, the smell of bacon, which usually set her taste buds watering, didn't even appeal to her senses. She went to the buffet and poured a cup of coffee then sat at the table with Howard Owens, Charles, Helen, and the two boys who hadn't become ill. Mr. Carter had scarcely put in an appearance since the measles appeared. He spent his time in his apartment and office. Charles had laughingly said the man was apparently depressed by the enforced change in schedule.

Virgie came in and glanced at Abigail. Without a word she went to the buffet and filled a plate. She set it down in front of Abigail.

"Oh, but Virgie, I'm not hungry." She pushed the plate away. After all, she wasn't a child.

"Miss Abigail. You need nourishment to keep your strength up. If you don't eat, you won't be any help to those young'uns at all."

Her face heated. Virgie was right. She pulled the plate back to her and picked up her fork.

Virgie smiled and patted her on the shoulder as she walked past her. She filled another plate then carried it from the room. For Dr. Quincy? Probably. He'd hardly left the infirmary all week. Abigail was amazed at his dedication to the sick children. Every day he checked on the others as well so that no symptom could slip by.

She'd noticed a special concern in his eyes for Lily Ann and wondered why.

"Abigail, are you all right? I've spoken to you twice." Helen's brow was furrowed with concern as she gazed at Abigail.

"Oh, I'm sorry. I guess my mind wandered. Did you say something?"

"I suggested that you get some rest. I had a good night's sleep, and I don't mind taking your turn in the infirmary."

Warmth flowed through Abigail at the kindness offered by her new friend. Helen's shift was right after hers, so if she took Abigail's turn, she'd be there twice as long.

"Thank you so much. I appreciate the offer more than I can say, but I'll be fine. Truly I will. And I know you have things you need to do this morning."

"Well, if you're sure, but promise me if you get too tired, send someone to get me. I don't mind."

Somehow Abigail didn't feel quite so tired. What was it about kindness that lifted not only one's spirit, but even strengthened the body?

She found Dr. Quincy and Virgie feeding porridge to the children who could tolerate it. The doctor's plate sat untouched on a table in the corner.

She hurried to his side. "Here, let me do this while you eat your breakfast."

He glanced up and gave her a half smile. Weariness filled his eyes. "Thank you, Miss James. I believe I will."

He stood and handed her the half-empty bowl.

She took it and leaned over ten-year-old Molly Flannigan. "Good morning. Are you feeling better today?"

The little girl gave her a tremulous smile. "A little bit." She eyed the spoon in Abigail's hand.

"Here you go. Don't you just love porridge?"

Molly nodded and swallowed. "Peaches in it."

"Yes, I see that. Smells like sugar and spice."

Abigail spooned the last bite into Molly's mouth and handed her a napkin. Then she moved on to Jimmy Parker. When all six children had eaten, Virgie piled the dishes on a tray and left to attend to her household duties.

Sally May brought in pitchers of water and set them on the washstand then left.

Abigail spent the next hour bathing feverish skin and replacing damp clothing while Dr. Quincy left to change and tend to personal needs.

She was relieved to note that several of the children seemed cooler than before.

When the doctor returned, he took temperatures once again.

"Miss James, did you by any chance see Lily Ann today?" He shook the mercury down in the thermometer and placed it under Sonny's tongue.

"Yes, she was sleeping when I left the dormitory."

"No symptoms?"

"No, she seemed quite well, Doctor."

Relief passed over his face.

"Good. She has enough to bear without contending with sickness."

"Yes. As do all the children." She gave him a pointed look.

"Of course. It's just—you see, I knew Lily Ann before she lost her vision." His eyes clouded with pain for a moment. Then he shook his head as though to shake away a memory.

"An accident." He spoke almost sharply before changing the subject. "You seem to work very well with her. She likes you."

"And I like her. I only wish I could do more."

"I'm sure we all feel the same. About Lily Ann as well as the deaf children."

She sighed. "Yes, I'd hoped—" She stopped. This wasn't the time.

He took the thermometer from Sonny's mouth and examined it. He gave a nod and winked at the boy. "Much better, Sonny."

Abigail walked beside him while he checked the rest of the children.

"Continue, please, Miss James."

"All right." After all, he'd asked. "I'd hoped to be able to teach sign language."

He threw her a surprised look. "You know sign language?"

"Of course. It was part of my training to teach the deaf. I was surprised to find out it was not being taught here."

He lifted Molly's wrist to count her pulse then patted her as he walked on to the next child. "I broached the subject to Carter at one time. But he assured me our current teaching methods were more than adequate."

She opened her mouth to retort then clamped it shut.

He lifted an eyebrow. "You disagree?"

"I most certainly do disagree."

"Have you spoken to the director about it?"

"Yes. He basically told me he had no use for signing and that I should stop bothering him." At the thought of her meetings with Mr. Carter, anger rose, and she felt heat rising from deep inside. Her face felt as though a fire had seared it.

"He actually said that?" Incredulity filled his voice.

"Well, no, not exactly. Not in so many words. But that's what he meant."

Trent frowned. "I'm sorry if you were offended, Miss James. I'm sure Mr. Carter didn't mean it the way you took it."

She should have known he'd defend the director. She clamped her mouth shut and picked up a book to read to the children. Were all men obstinate?

"Miss James."

She turned. "Yes, Doctor?"

"If you don't mind, I would like to discuss the matter further when we have more time."

Caught off guard by his statement after her unkind thought, she blushed. "You would?"

"Of course. If you feel that strongly about the subject, I'd like to know why." His serious expression left no doubt he meant it. "The welfare of the children is always my number one priority."

◆

Abigail looked across her desk at the empty classroom. She'd come up here after supper to gather her thoughts. She'd done it again. When would she learn not to speak impulsively. She'd been totally wrong to criticize Mr. Carter to Dr. Quincy. He probably saw it as insubordination, and perhaps it was. If only she could be patient. But patience wouldn't help the children now.

She sighed. There she went again. She couldn't control her thoughts any better than her words. It would serve her right if Dr. Quincy should dismiss her. Or had Mr. Carter do it.

A shadow fell across her desk, and she looked up to see Dr. Quincy in the doorway. Fatigue was written all over him.

Fear gripping her, Abigail rose from her chair. "Dr. Quincy. Has one of the children taken a turn for the worse?"

"No, no. Nothing like that. But if you aren't busy, I'd like to have a word with you."

Dread spread though her from her chest up to her head. This was it then. She hadn't expected it this soon.

She straightened her back and lifted her chin, meeting his eyes. "Yes, Dr. Quincy? You wish to speak to me about something?"

"Yes. I know you must be tired after being in the infirmary all day, and I promise I won't keep you long."

"That's quite all right. I'm not tired." Her lips trembled, and she pressed them together while she motioned to a chair beside her desk. "Won't you have a seat, Doctor?"

"Would you mind if we talk on the front porch? There's at least a little breeze out there."

His shirtsleeves were sticking to his arms. She averted her eyes. If he only knew how women suffered, with skirts, petticoats, and corsets. Realizing her thoughts were heading down an unkind path again, she slammed the door on them and cleared her throat. "No, I don't mind." She stood and started toward the door.

He stood aside to allow her to pass, and they went downstairs. They crossed the foyer and stepped out onto the porch.

She took a refreshing breath, relieved that there really was a fairly cool breeze blowing tonight.

He motioned to the wicker chairs that stood at one end of the porch. It appeared he would behave very courteously all the way up to the time he fired her.

She walked over and sat on the edge of the chair, stiff as a board. He sat on a chair across from her.

"Miss James, I wonder if you'd mind telling me a little more about sign language. Before I speak to Mr. Carter on the subject, I'd like to know what I'm talking about."

Her eyes widened and the corners of her lips turned up. "I'm not dismissed?"

"Dismissed? Why would you think that?"

An audible sigh of relief escaped her lips. "Oh Dr. Quincy, it was so disrespectful of me to criticize your director, thereby indirectly criticizing your school. That was inexcusable. You see, although I am very qualified to teach, I'm a little headstrong sometimes. Yes, and I'm opinionated, too. And stubborn. It was disgraceful of me to think I could come in and run things."

Disturbed by her distress and remorse he started to take her hand but thought better of it.

"Miss James, I don't see you that way at all. I see you as a caring woman who wants to bring good things to the school to help the children." He smiled. "And although I generally allow the director to handle things pertaining to the school, there's nothing wrong with you making suggestions. And I hope you'll always feel free to tell me when you believe something relevant to the good of the children is amiss."

She nodded. "I'm grateful. But I still handled things impulsively. I've repented to God for that. I'm sure Mr. Carter cares about the children, too. Perhaps he feels it best not to change things that are working well."

"But change is good if it makes things work better. And that's what I need to find out." He leaned back against the cushioned back. "So if you wouldn't mind, I'd like for you to tell me all you know about sign language."

She pressed her lips together in an attempt to hold back a smile, but it escaped anyway. "It took me two years to learn all I know, but I'll give you a quick lesson if that's sufficient."

For the next hour, Trent listened intently as she told him the history and progress of signing and the great strides made in communication with the deaf.

"And while lip reading is wonderful in its place, it isn't always possible. Many people don't enunciate well enough."

Trent nodded. As long as he'd been involved in this school, sometimes he forgot to speak directly to the child.

"And when two or more people sign together, the communication is more satisfactory to them."

Trent, wrapped up in her explanations, nodded. "Yes, I can see where it would be."

She chuckled. "The funniest thing happened at the school where I trained. Two young girls were in a heated argument in signs. Finally one of them turned her back and walked away with her hand behind her still signing. She got the last word."

Trent burst out laughing. "That is a delightful story."

"Would you like to learn some signs?" She smiled, her eyes sparkling.

"Could I? I mean do you think I could learn?" Excitement sparkled in his eyes.

"Of course. Let's start by learning the letters to your name."

She made a fist and put her thumb between her first two fingers. "This is a *T*."

After several clumsy tries, he managed to make the *T*. "How's that?"

She smiled. "Perfect."

She continued with the letters in his first name then had him form the name. After several mistakes, he finally got it right without help. A heady sense of satisfaction washed over him. If he felt that good about spelling his name, how would a deaf child feel?

"Abigail, thank you for taking the time to teach me."

"It was my pleasure. Keep practicing your first name, and I'll teach you how to sign your last name next time. You already know one of the letters."

"So I do." He laughed and stood. "I'd better let you get your rest. Besides, I need to check on Warrior before he thinks I've deserted him." His lips turned up in a slow smile. "When I see you tomorrow, I'll prove to you that I've been practicing."

Her heart raced as she watched him round the house toward the barn. How could she have misjudged him so? Why he was kind and gentle, nothing at all like the stern man she'd pictured in her mind. Of course, they'd never really had a chance to talk before. Just a few words here and there and the little bit of conversation they'd had in the infirmary.

But he'd seemed as excited and happy as a child when he was learning to sign his name. And he hadn't even seemed tired when he left. A thrill ran through her as she remembered how his eyes had met hers as he said good night. And the slow mysterious smile he'd given her just before he walked down the steps. Something almost like a giggle escaped her throat as she turned and went inside.

❧

Trent's heart was light as he walked to the barn. He'd intended to discuss improving the condition of the children with Carter, but after listening to Abigail, he wanted to gather his thoughts together before he encountered the director. Questioning Carter about his decisions concerning the curriculum was out of the question until he had a chance to think things through clearly.

That he'd been affected by Abigail was obvious, but whether by her words or being so near to her physically was the question. He was undoubtedly attracted to her, and it wasn't merely a physical attraction. Or at least, he didn't think so. Her gentle administrations to the sick children had touched his heart. But there was no denying when she looked at him with those deep gold-washed brown eyes, he had trouble concentrating on anything but her.

Perhaps before he approached Carter, he should do some research on the subject of teaching techniques for the deaf, including signs. There must be someone in Mobile who could either help him with answers or direct him to someone who could. But surely Helen and Charles would have said something to him if they felt that Carter was inefficient in some way. Even though he'd always stressed the fact that Carter was in charge. Perhaps they thought that meant they couldn't approach him about anything that fell under Carter's duties.

One thing was certain. He needed to have a talk with his director.

Chapter 6

Sunrays filtered through the thick, leafy branches of sturdy trees, casting shadows on the ground, even at midmorning. Abigail had hesitated when Lily Ann asked if they could have her lesson outside. Did she want to give Mr. Carter something else to disapprove of? But the child's eager face had decided the matter for her. As they entered the woods behind the house, she was glad she'd acquiesced to Lily's request.

All the children had recovered, and classes had resumed a few days ago. Lily Ann's parents returned her to school as soon as they knew for sure the danger had passed. Abigail hadn't realized how much she'd missed her until she was back again.

She carried a book in one hand and held on to Lily Ann with the other, but the little girl tugged away, and with arms stretched out before her, made her way from tree to tree, bush to bush. Abigail watched in amazement as Lily Ann dodged a tree before touching it. Now how had she known it was there? Lily Ann stooped down and, with a trill of laughter, scooped up a small object enveloped in some sort of husk.

Abigail rushed forward. "What is that, Lily Ann? Not an insect I hope."

With a giggle, the child jumped up and offered the object to her. " 'Course not. It's a pecan. Too early to drop off the tree though." She pointed upward. "Can you see them up there?"

Abigail peered up at the towering tree. Small husked objects, similar to the one in her hand hung from the branches. "Yes, I see them. When are they supposed to fall off?"

Lily Ann shrugged her tiny shoulders. "Not in July. Sometime in the fall."

They walked on, Lily Ann finding different trees and flowers that grew in the woods. Most of the time, Lily Ann had only to run her hand over the bark before she began telling Abigail all about it.

Amused, Abigail listened closely. Who was teaching whom? Finally they found a level spot underneath a live oak and sat on the thick grass while Abigail read and Lily answered questions. Abigail praised her when she answered correctly, which she usually did, and encouraged her when she missed one. Lily loved the stories, and Abigail could only hope that someday the child could have the pleasure of reading them herself.

"I'm going to tell the story about the princess that had no grabaty to my mama this weekend."

Abigail nodded. "But be sure to say 'grav-i-ty,' not 'grab a tea.' "

Lily Ann laughed. "Grav-i-ty. I know it now. What's the name of the story again? I want to ask Papa to buy it for me."

"*The Light Princess*. By George Macdonald. It's rather new as fairy tales go."

Lily Ann's stomach growled, and she giggled.

Abigail smiled and closed the book. "Your tummy speaks for me, too. I think it must be dinnertime. They got up and brushed loose grass off each other's skirts then started back through the woods, emerging into the clearing behind the school. Abigail lifted her face to the breeze that drifted across her then smiled as she noticed Lily Ann doing the same.

"The wind is pretty today, isn't it, Miss James?"

As Lily Ann's countenance brightened with radiance from her smile, Abigail caught her breath. "Yes, I'd say it is. What about it do you find so pretty?"

Scrunching up her forehead, Lily Ann tapped her foot, and then another smile broke out on her face. "It has a pretty smell. And makes my skin feel good. The whispers are very pretty, too."

Abigail sniffed then sniffed again harder. This time she caught a faint smell of flowers, grass, and cows, but that was all. And whispers? She stood still and tried to listen, but couldn't hear so much as a faint rustle. The child's senses must be very acute. Did God do that to compensate for Lily Ann's inability to see? She breathed out a sigh of impatience. Well then, if that was the case, why did He allow her to be blinded in the first place?

Shock zipped through her and her breathing quickened. You didn't question God. Her parents had drummed that into her head over and over through the years. Beginning with the first time she'd asked them why her brother, Nat, was born deaf. And even more so after the accident that caused his death. Her heart beat loudly in her ears.

"Are you all right, Miss James?"

Lily Ann's small hand on her arm jerked her back into the moment. She dabbed her handkerchief at her moist forehead and took several slow breaths until she was breathing normally.

"Yes, thank you, Lily Ann. I really shouldn't have walked so fast."

She held out her hand to the little girl. They walked, swinging their hands, across the vast lawn to the back door.

"Mmm. I smell dinner." Lily Ann sped up her pace, pulling Abigail along.

They entered through the back door, into a large mudroom, and Lily Ann joined the other children who took turns washing their hands over the wash pan with a small bar of soap while Helen poured water from the pitcher.

Abigail was surprised when Mr. Carter joined them. He'd had supper with them a few times since the measles epidemic, but never the midday meal. Abigail had assumed he didn't want to eat with the children. She bit her lip. Obviously another misconception on her part.

ਂ

The sun was low in the sky when Trent dismounted in front of the school and tied Warrior to the hitching post. He'd hoped to arrive in time to join the staff for supper, but Clyde Ramsey, a farmer a few miles away, had broken a wrist.

The foyer was empty, but he could hear faint voices coming from the parlor, so he walked down the hallway and went in. Waverly leaned against the mantel of the huge empty fireplace, a cup in his hand. The smell of coffee tantalized Trent's senses.

Helen and Abigail glanced up from their seats on the sofa as he walked in.

Virgie jumped up from her chair in the corner. "Dr. Trent. You sit down, and I'll fetch you some supper." She smiled. "You have that hungry look all over your face."

"You know, I think I'll take you up on that, Virgie. Thank you." He sat across from the ladies, nodded at Waverly, and greeted the ladies.

"How are the children? Any sickness I need to attend?"

After being assured all was well, he leaned back and relaxed. The measles epidemic had been trying for all of them.

In a short time, Virgie returned followed by Sissy, who carried a tray that she set on the table by Trent.

The plate was piled high with fried chicken, mashed potatoes and gravy, greens, and corn, with a little dish of assorted pickles to the side. Two hot dinner rolls and a chunk of corn bread accompanied the overabundant supper plate and a slice of sweet potato pie for dessert.

Trent grinned. Virgie was always trying to outdo her daughter in feeding him up as she called it.

"Thank you, Sissy. And thank you, Virgie, but I can't eat all this."

"Yes, you can. I'll bet you haven't had a bite all day." She gave him a disapproving shake of her head.

Trent proceeded to prove her right, enjoying the meal while the teachers conversed about the day's classes.

When he'd eaten the last crumb of sweet potato pie, he threw a sheepish grin to Virgie.

"I was hungry, but just so you won't think evil thoughts about your daughter, she insisted on cooking me a huge breakfast this morning and practically stood over me while I ate it."

"Carrie's a good girl. She knows how to feed a man."

Shortly afterward, Charles excused himself and left the room.

"Oh my, look at the time." Helen scrambled to her feet. "And I still have history papers to grade."

Abigail rose, too, and Trent quickly stood. "Miss James, we never did have time for that second sign language lesson. I wonder, if you aren't too busy, if you'd mind catering to my whim."

"I'd be happy to." She flashed him a bright smile. "I don't consider a desire to learn a whim, Doctor."

"In that case, shall we have my lesson here? Or adjourn to the site of the last one."

She laughed. "If you think we have enough light to see, I'd rather go outside."

Soon they were seated in the wicker chairs on the porch.

"Well Dr. Quincy, I think the first order of business is a review." She gave him a teasing smile. "Can you still spell your first name?"

"Ah ha. I knew you'd ask." With a flourish, he raised his hand and made every letter in his name without pausing. "How's that, Teacher?"

"I'm very impressed. Someone has been practicing. Shall we go on to your last name?"

"Absolutely."

When she made the *Q* he groaned. "My fingers will never do that."

"Sure they will. It's easy. Go ahead and try."

He peered at the position of her fingers then tried to make the letter. After the fourth try, he growled in disgust. "Told you."

She shook her head. "Here, let me help you. May I?" She reached for his hand.

He sat perfectly still while her soft fingers positioned his. "There. See?"

Trent looked at his hand still clasped in her small one then glanced up into her eyes.

Suddenly she blushed and dropped his hand. "Well, that's how you make the *Q*. Now you try it."

He cleared his throat. "Yes ma'am, Teacher."

He made the letter perfectly. "Is that right?"

"Yes, now make it again."

After perfecting the *Q*, they went on to the other letters.

"I think you have a right to know I plan to speak with Mr. Carter about adding signs to the curriculum. I will, of course, give him an opportunity to present me with any reasons he believes we shouldn't."

She closed her eyes and breathed a sigh then opened them and smiled. "Thank you so much, Doctor. Whatever you should decide, I want you to know I appreciate your considering my suggestions."

"And I appreciate your passion for wanting what's best for the children." He leaned back in the chair. "If you don't mind my asking, what made you go into this field of teaching?"

Moonlight had fallen across the porch, casting strange lights and shadows over them both. So perhaps that was what caused the sudden ghostlike paleness of her face. But what caused her sudden silence?

"Forgive me for intruding. It's really none of my business."

"It's quite all right. There's no reason you shouldn't know." She drew in a quick breath. "My brother, Nat, was born deaf."

"I'm very sorry to hear that." Why couldn't he have kept his mouth shut? "Is he doing well?"

"He passed away when we were twelve." She stood and her sad smile twisted his heart. "I really should go in now."

He stood. "Of course. Forgive me for asking questions that cause you grief."

"As I said, it was many years ago." She nodded. "Good night."

"Good night."

He stood, mentally kicking himself for bringing up a subject that caused her pain. Even if he hadn't known. Still, he'd intruded into her personal business. She'd said her brother died when *they* were twelve, so they'd been twins. How terrible it must have been. He offered up a quick prayer of comfort for her before going to retrieve his horse.

Chapter 7

Trent would be the first to admit he hated confrontation. He avoided it when at all possible. Peace in his life was more important than arguing or accusing. Or even questioning. But his sense of concern and duty for the students of Quincy School far outweighed his reluctance to speak to Joshua Carter about his refusal to even consider adding sign language to the curriculum.

Hot sun beat down on him as he rode to the school. He reined Warrior in at the hitching post. Albert came around the corner of the house. "Dr. Trent, want me to take Warrior to the barn? It mighty hot out here in the sun."

Trent removed his pocket watch and glanced at the time. Almost noon. It would be at least an hour before he could talk to Carter, and he had no idea how long the meeting might take.

"Yes, please, Albert." Trent dismounted. "I've been riding him hard this morning, and he's hot. Rub him down and give him water."

"Yes sir. Be glad to." He took the reins and led Warrior to the barn, talking to him as they went.

Trent grinned. From the time Albert was a young man, he'd worked as a handyman and stableboy for the school. After the war, since the Quincy slaves had already been given their freedom, many stayed to continue working the land that Trent's grandmother deeded to them. Albert's parents were paid house servants with a cabin and land for their personal use. When his parents passed on, Albert stayed in the cabin and continued to work for Quincy School. He was part of Trent's earliest memories, as was Virgie.

As Trent stepped into the house, the aroma of seasoned pot roast wafted into the foyer, teasing his senses. The children were filing into the dining room. Mrs. Cole gave him a nod and smile as she followed them in. Knowing there would be plenty of food and that Virgie always made sure there was a place for him, just in case he showed up, he stepped through the door and took his place at the head of the table.

After he prayed a blessing over the food, he lifted his head, and his eyes met Abigail's. She smiled then blushed and turned to the server who was ladling soup into her bowl.

After the meal, the children and their teachers returned to the classrooms.

Carter rose and gave a nod as though he would leave.

Trent stood as well. "Mr. Carter, I'd like to meet with you if you have no pressing duties at the moment."

Carter shot him a surprised and not-too-happy look. "I suppose I could spare a half hour or so."

"I don't anticipate my business to last longer than that. Would you prefer your office or mine?" Trent's office, a small room off the infirmary, usually smelled strongly of disinfectant and medicine, so he wasn't surprised when his director chose his own.

When he followed Carter into the stuffy room, the stale tobacco smell was so strong he wished he hadn't given him a choice.

"Please have a seat, Dr. Quincy. How may I help you?"

Trent shot him a quick glance. Had he always spoken in such a haughty tone of voice? Funny, he'd never really noticed it before. He hoped he hadn't used that tone with Abigail.

Trent sat across from the man and eyed him for a moment.

"I'd like to discuss the possibility of adding sign language to the curriculum."

Carter's face reddened, and he pressed his lips together. He sucked in a breath then gave Trent a tight smile. "I believe we discussed this two years ago and decided against it."

"Yes, we did. But I was unfamiliar with the possibilities at the time and simply left the decision to you."

"Which I believe is proper, considering I'm the director."

"Perhaps. I've always had utmost faith in your decisions. But in this case, I believe you may have been mistaken. Would you be so kind as to give me your reasons for not wishing to at least give it a try?"

The redness in Carter's face heightened, and he sprang up from his chair. "Doctor, I hardly think it's proper for you to question my decisions."

Trent stood and faced him. "I think it is very proper to ask for your reasons."

"Very well! Verbal instruction has worked well in this school from long before I came here, and I see no reason to change what works."

"And that is your only reason?"

"I believe it is enough." He gazed stone-faced at Trent, and perspiration beaded his brow.

Trent studied him for a moment.

"I disagree. You are to inform the teaching staff that sign language will begin on a trial basis, starting next week, with Miss James as the teacher. If it works well, the rest of the staff will be expected to learn to sign in order to communicate with the students with signs as well as verbally."

He nodded. "As you wish. And will I be expected to learn this abominable practice as well?"

Surprised at the director's attitude and tone, Trent was silent for a moment. "That is entirely up to you. But I hope you will work on improving your attitude about the subject."

"Perhaps you would like for me to resign my position."

"Mr. Carter, I sincerely hope you won't choose to do that. You have been an excellent director in matters of business and finances. I don't know why you have an aversion to the teaching of something that can improve the lives of these children. If it's a personal bias, you need to get it under control." He took a few steps toward the door then stopped and turned. "But if you ever use that tone of voice with the children or any member of the staff and household, I will certainly accept that resignation. Good day, sir."

Disturbed at what had just transpired, Trent left the office and went in search of Virgie. Apparently the school wasn't running as smoothly or congenially as he'd thought. If Virgie wouldn't talk, he'd have a meeting with the entire staff. One way or the other he intended to get to the bottom of it.

He found Virgie in the kitchen going over menus with Selma, the cook.

Selma's eyes brightened when she saw him. "Dr. Trent. You ain't been in this kitchen since you was knee high to a grasshopper."

He laughed. "Now you know that's not true. I came in here last Christmas and snitched sugar cookies that were cooling on the rack."

She gave a belly laugh and snapped her fingers. "So you did. You just as naughty as when you was knee high though."

Virgie shook her head. "Dr. Trent, I know you didn't come in here looking for cookies, so I expect you're looking for me."

"You're right." He glanced at the long worktable. "And since I don't see any cookies, I guess I'll go. Do you have time to talk for a few minutes?"

"You know I always have time for you, Dr. Trent."

"Good. I'll wait for you in the parlor. Finish what you're doing if you like. I'm not in that big of a hurry."

He went into the parlor and shut the door then sat at the piano. He ran his fingers along the keys, wishing, not for the first time, he hadn't quit piano lessons when he was a boy. Practice just couldn't compete with fishing back then. He flexed his fingers and began playing, losing himself in music. Finally he sighed and put the lid down.

"I love hearing you play, Trent. Wish you'd do it more often."

He stood and smiled at Virgie, who'd come in and sat in her corner chair while he played. He leaned over and kissed her on her wrinkled brown cheek. "And I love hearing you call me Trent. Wish you'd do it more often."

She shook her head. "Now you know that wouldn't be respectful.

But maybe sometimes. Like now."

He sat on the sofa. "Virgie, I'd like for you to tell me everything you can think of, good or bad, about Carter."

She sucked in her breath. "Dr. Trent, I'd rather not, if you don't mind."

"Why not?"

"You know I don't like to talk about folks behind their backs."

He frowned. "You'd tell me if he was mistreating someone wouldn't you?"

"You mean like hitting them?" Her voice never rose a notch, but a fire burned deep in her eyes. "I hope you know I wouldn't wait to tell you or anyone else. He ever mistreated one of these young'uns, he'd wish he hadn't." She pressed her lips together and stood to leave. She laid her hand on his shoulder and gave it a gentle pat. "If it goin' to make you feel better, my sweet Hunter crazy about Mr. Carter. Lord only knows why. But if my angel boy like him, he can't be all bad."

⁂

The hours seemed to crawl by all afternoon. Usually Abigail's attention was riveted to her students and their needs. But today, her thoughts continually wandered to the meeting between Dr. Quincy and the director. She'd never have known about it if Helen hadn't whispered in her ear between classes. She couldn't help but wonder if they'd discussed the sign language class.

Tommy Findlay's hand popped up, and she went back to check his paper. "Teeher, did I do it wight?"

Abigail's heart swelled as the eight-year-old boy valiantly spoke the words he couldn't hear. She nodded and spoke directly to him as he watched her lips. "Yes, Thomas. You didn't miss a single one. But perhaps, you could practice making your *G* a little better. Remember how I taught you?"

He nodded and smiled, motioning that he'd try again.

When class was finally over, she dismissed the children and watched them file out. Eager to play after being inside all day, they were still orderly as they went to their rooms to change into playclothes.

She went to her room and checked her clothing for spots or tears. Finding a small tear in the seam of one of her skirts, she sat in her rocking chair and mended it then replaced a button that had come loose from her favorite blouse. Having finished that chore, she chose the clothing she would wear to church on Sunday. Due to the measles outbreak, the children hadn't been able to attend Sunday school for the past three weeks. The community had cancelled the Independence Day festivities, but planned to have a picnic later in the month that the children were very excited about.

Finally she couldn't handle the anxiety anymore and went downstairs in hopes someone would know something about the meeting. But no one had yet heard anything.

Lily Ann's parents arrived to take her home for the weekend, and with hugs for her teachers and promises to be good for Mama and Papa, they were off in their buggy. Lily Ann sat proudly between her parents, smiling with happiness. And her mother looked near tears from her own joy.

How difficult it must be for them to let her go, week after week. But how brave of them to do it anyway, for the good of their daughter. Now that Trent seemed in favor of sign language for the deaf children, Abigail determined to speak to him soon about braille for Lily Ann. As much as the family was sacrificing to give her a chance for a better life, they deserved the best for her.

When suppertime rolled around, Mr. Carter still hadn't come out of his office. Abigail wasn't sure she could stand the suspense much longer. He requested a tray be brought to his rooms and sent back a summons for all the staff members to meet in his office directly after supper.

Excitement rippled across the room during the meal. Abigail knew everyone was as anxious as she was.

"Abigail, if the news is what we're expecting, I want to say, my hat is off to you for succeeding where we've all failed for a number of years."

She smiled and shook her head. "It's not my doing. If Dr. Quincy has made the decision we hope for, it was quite an act of God that I had the chance to tell him about the benefits of signing."

They finished the meal as quickly as possible and trooped down the hall to the director's office.

Apparently hearing them, he opened the door before they had a chance to knock.

He offered polite nods to Charles, Helen, and both house-parents, barely glancing at Abigail. He didn't sit or invite them to, but stood straight as a rod.

"I wish to inform you that we will begin the instruction of sign language next week on a trial basis. Since Miss James is the only one qualified at this point, she will teach the class. If it proves to be successful, which I'm not convinced it will be, you will each be expected to learn signs so that the children can communicate with you in this way. We shall, of course, continue with oral speech classes and lip reading. That is all. You are dismissed."

He stalked to the door and held it open while they filed out then shut it firmly behind them.

By the time they reached the parlor, Abigail was about to burst with unreleased glee, and from the expressions on the other faces, she knew she wasn't alone.

Mrs. Cole and Mr. Owens sailed joyfully up the stairs to attend to the children.

Abigail followed Helen and Charles into the parlor where they found Virgie waiting.

Helen went to the older woman and took her hand. "It's done, at last. We have our sign language class."

Virgie's eyes filled with tears, and she clutched Helen's hands in hers. "Praise be to our blessed Lord. Thank You, Father."

As her words of thanks and praise rang out, they all joined hands and added their voices to hers.

Chapter 8

Abigail breathed a sigh of relief Sunday morning when she took a seat on one of the reserved pews near the front of the small church. Three little girls slid in behind her, followed by Helen and Felicity. Charles and Howard sat behind them with the boys in between.

Following the decision about the addition to the curriculum, the days had flown by this week. Abigail had lost no time in implementing the new class. Mr. Carter had left the following day, citing business appointments as the cause of his hasty departure. But with help from Helen and Charles, the class schedule had been rearranged.

The children were a little apprehensive about being introduced to something new, but when Abigail showed them her signing book and taught them how to sign their names, their interest overrode the fear.

On top of her new classroom schedule, Abigail spent most of her spare time handwriting worksheets for their individual use. But her tiredness couldn't detract from the joy of knowing she'd succeeded in getting them what they needed. Well, most of them anyway. There was still the matter of braille for Lily Ann.

Because a few more cases of measles had popped up in the community, the picnic had been postponed again. So the teachers planned their own for after church today. Dr. Quincy had promised the children he'd be there if he possibly could, so Abigail was secretly plotting to take him aside and broach the subject of braille.

She glanced over her shoulder, hoping to see Lily Ann and her parents. They hadn't been here for Sunday school, but she hoped they'd attend the main service.

Out of the corner of her eye, she spied Trent walking down the outside aisle on her side. She turned around to face the front.

"Is there room for me?" His whispered words seemed to resonate through the room, and she heard a giggle from Annie, who sat next to her. The little girls slid over, and Abigail moved to make a space on the end for Trent. At a twitter from someone behind her, she felt heat rise in her cheeks.

Why had he chosen to sit next to her when there was plenty of room on the row behind where the boys and men sat? He should know how people loved to gossip at the most innocent things. Fidgeting, she grabbed a hymnbook from the rack.

His arm pressed against her shoulder, and she tried to no avail to get the others to move down a little more. Apparently the pews were shorter than she'd realized.

Reverend Shepherd stepped up to the podium and bowed his head to pray. He thanked God that the measles epidemic had run its course, and no serious side effects had occurred because of it. He then prayed for the service. After his amen, he looked out over the congregation. "Brothers and sisters, I'd like to welcome you. The topic today is Christ's love to undeserving sinners. Our first scripture is Romans the first chapter and the eighth verse."

Abigail, who always looked forward each week to the reverend's message, heard very little of the sermon, and relief washed over her as they stood for the final hymn. The beautiful words of "Jesus Paid It All," touched her heart, and she wished she'd been more attentive to the sermon.

As the people poured out of the door, the group from Quincy school waited until the aisle was clear.

As soon as they stepped outside, the children surrounded the doctor, chattering with excitement about the picnic and begging him to go.

"I wouldn't miss it." His expression serious, Trent glanced around the group. "I have it on good authority that Cook has made one of her famous chocolate cakes for the event."

Oohs and aahs chorused through the children.

Helen laughed. In an aside to Abigail she proclaimed, "He could hardly go wrong on that one. Cook always makes a chocolate cake for picnics. Oh look, Lily Ann is here."

Sure enough, Lily Ann stood with her parents as they conversed with Reverend Shepherd.

Abigail started to walk past them, not wishing to interrupt, but Mrs. Parker touched her on the arm. "We'll see you at the picnic."

"Oh good. I'm so glad."

"Miss Abigail." Lily Ann reached out her hand, and Abigail enclosed it in hers. "Mama made lots of fried chicken and molasses cookies for the picnic."

"I'll bet they'll taste good."

The little girl nodded. "Uh-huh. Mama's the best cook in the world." She leaned toward Abigail. "But don't tell Cook," she whispered. "It might hurt her feelings."

"All right then. I won't." As she walked away, she shook her head in wonder at Lily Ann's sensitivity to others. She had seen this repeated in other children at the Deaf School in Washington. Not that all handicapped children were selfless. But perhaps the trials they faced made them more aware of the feelings of others.

Nat had been like that. Well, not so much when they were small. Sometimes he'd stand in the middle of a room and scream at the top of his lungs in order to get his way. And it worked for a while, until their parents caught on and realized they needed to be a little wiser.

Humor arose in her as she recalled the first time Mother and Father turned and walked away, leaving five-year-old Nat standing there screaming at the top of his lungs. When he'd realized they really were gone, he'd clamped his mouth shut and stared after them in disbelief. Of course, it took a few more incidents like that before he got the idea.

Abigail's heart lurched. Nat had grown to be an obedient son and a kind and funny brother and friend. A boy whom everyone loved and wanted to be around.

The picnic was held by the stream about a half mile from the house. Plenty of shade trees would offer protection from the late-July heat. While Abigail and the other women loaded the food and dishes onto the long picnic table, the boys dragged Trent into a game of marbles.

Everyone was hungry by the time the food was ready to eat.

Abigail sat on the ground beneath a live oak tree with Helen, her plate in her lap. She'd tried not to serve herself too much, but with fried chicken piled high on platters, fresh corn, sliced tomatoes, and cucumbers it was hard not to. And Lily Ann just might be right about her mother's cooking.

She kept darting glances at Trent, hoping to find a moment to speak with him, and several times their eyes met, but the boys and the other men kept him busy trading funny stories.

When the desserts were finished and Lily Ann's parents had left, the boys talked Trent and Charles into going fishing at the stream. She watched him saunter down the hill with Virgie's grandson, Hunter, on his shoulders, the child's tight black curls hugging his little head like a cap. He giggled at something Trent said.

Abigail played button and bowl with the girls, who laughed each time she missed the bowl, which was nearly every time she tossed the button.

Finally, tired but happy, they all trooped back to the house.

The boys begged Trent for a story, so he agreed to tell them one while Albert fetched Warrior from the barn. He sat on the top step of the porch while they lined the lower steps.

Abigail smiled at Trent's common sense in choosing a story that calmed the children instead of getting them too stirred up to sleep. By the time they followed their houseparents inside, most of them were yawning. Abigail knew they'd be given a light supper then sent to bed. They had school tomorrow. Trent stood to go.

Should she ask to talk to him? But it had been such a long and wonderful day. It would be a shame to end it with business.

Especially since she wasn't sure how he'd respond.

He smiled down at her. "I'd hoped to have a moment to visit with you, but the boys kept me busy all day."

She laughed. "They like you a lot, Doctor, and I think the feeling is mutual."

"You're right. They're all such great kids." He grinned. "Some of the most likable people I know."

"I agree. Well, I really should go inside. Perhaps we can talk another time."

He nodded. "I'll look forward to it. Good night, Miss James." His eyes gazed into hers for a moment, and then he mounted Warrior and rode away.

She stepped inside. Virgie stood in the foyer speaking to Mr. Carter. Little Hunter stood by her side, eyeing the golden eagle handle on the director's cane. Abigail stopped in surprise. Mr. Carter's lips were curved in a smile. When he noticed Abigail he pressed his lips together, gave her a nod, and turned toward the hall. But she would have sworn his eyelid drooped in a wink as he walked past the wide-eyed little boy.

❧

Trent whistled a merry tune as he rode up the drive to the stable. Leaving Warrior with the stableboy, he went inside. It felt good to be home, but he'd much rather be sitting on the front porch of the school with Abigail.

He probably shouldn't have been so bold as to sit next to her in church. He feared he'd given some of the old gossips fodder to talk and caused her embarrassment, but the chance to be near her was too much to resist.

The aroma of gumbo drew him to the kitchen, where he found Carrie dishing up a bowl for Solomon.

"Dr. Trent, I didn't hear you ride up. I'll set the dining room table for you right away."

"No, don't bother, Carrie." He sat at the table opposite Solomon. "I'll eat here with you and Solomon."

"All right, if that's what you wanta do." She grabbed a bowl and started filling it.

Trent had grown up with Solomon and Carrie. They'd been playmates, then friends. He'd taken part in the outlandish shivaree the night they were married, and Solomon had threatened to beat the tar out of him the next day. His years away at college then medical school could have changed that, but when he returned home, they fell effortlessly back into the old camaraderie. When they first agreed to work for Trent and live in his house, it was a little uncomfortable for all of them. But Trent needed the help and Solomon and Carrie needed the income, so they made it work.

There were those in the neighborhood who didn't understand the friendship, but Trent had never cared much about other people's biases.

Carrie placed the bowl of gumbo before him and set a plate of corn bread in the center of the table. "How was my boy when you left?"

"The last time I saw him, he was following Virgie into the house, trying to talk her into letting him eat cookies for supper."

A burst of laughter exploded from Solomon's lips. "That boy. If he ain't something else, I don't know what is."

"He's a humdinger, all right." Trent bowed his head and mumbled a short thanks for the food then spooned a bite of the spicy stew into his mouth. "Mmm. You make the best gumbo since Virgie turned the cooking at the school over to Selma."

"Are you saying Mama's was better than mine?" Carrie frowned and pouted.

"Your gumbo is exactly like your mama's," Trent said. "Think maybe she's the one who taught you to make it?"

She laughed. "That she did. Besides, she gave me all her recipes when me and Solomon got married."

The three of them continued the banter until the meal was over; then Trent went to his study to write a letter of inquiry to an eye specialist in upstate New York.

He stared at the stack of replies he'd received over the past two years. He simply wouldn't accept that there was no one who could help Lily Ann. The old memories forced their way into his mind once again. He'd sat on his front porch with Dan and Trudy Parker while Lily Ann, not quite four years old at the time, played with a puppy in the front yard. The horse seemed to come from out of nowhere. In an instant it was gone, and the tiny girl lay with blood streaming from her eyes, where the horse's hooves had landed on her face.

They'd found out later the animal had been struck by a rattler. It had seemed to go crazy, throwing its rider and ending up on Trent's property. Trent knew it was one of those things he couldn't have prevented, but his feeling of guilt was strong enough to continue to drive him. He must fix things for Lily Ann. Someday he'd find someone somewhere who could restore her sight.

છે.

Sonny squinted his eyes and stuck the tip of his tongue out the side of his mouth as he concentrated once more on making the *Y* sign at the end of his name.

"It's too hard, Teacher." With his other hand he pressed down on the wayward finger that kept popping up when it was supposed to bend down.

"I know the *Y* is a difficult letter to make at first, Sonny. You just need to keep practicing. You'll get it. I promise."

She straightened and moved on to the next child. The children, who had been so excited in the beginning, were beginning to lag now that they realized learning signs took a lot of work. But Abigail had learned patience while working with Professor Roberts.

"Abigail," he'd said, "it's like any other subject children learn. When it becomes difficult, they want to give up. You wouldn't let a hearing child give up learning to read and write, would you?"

Abigail walked to her desk. Lily Ann sat in the corner playing with shaped wooden blocks while she waited her turn. But she was only hitting the blocks together instead of building with them. Abigail rested her hand on the small shoulder. "What are you making, Lily?"

She tilted her face upward toward Abigail. "Ummm. I'm just thinking."

"Oh? Thinking is good. Would you like to share your thoughts with me?"

Eagerness crossed her face. "May I learn to sign, too?"

Abigail looked at her. "But Lily Ann, you don't need to learn signs. You can hear and speak."

"But sometimes my friends can't read my lips good enough. And I can't always understand what they say."

Of course. Why hadn't she thought of that? Furthermore, learning something new was good exercise. She made an *L* with her hand. "Here, Lily, feel my hand and fingers. See if you can do the same thing."

Lily began to examine Abigail's hand with her own. "Yes. I can do that. Look." She made the sign. "What is it?"

"It's an *L*."

A smile crossed the child's face. "Like in my name?"

"That's right. And what do you think this one is?"

Lily traced her fingers around the sign. "I'll bet that's the next letter in my name. An *I*."

"Very good. Now, do you remember how to make the *L*?"

When she got to the *Y*, she had as much trouble forming it as Sonny had.

By the end of the class, Abigail was ready for a break, but it was time for Lily Ann's spelling lesson.

She spent the next hour having Lily spell verbally then sign the word.

If Lily Ann wished to learn to sign, she'd teach her, even if it would be a useless skill for her to know when she was no longer among deaf children.

If she worked this hard to learn signs, how much better would it be for her to learn braille so she could read and write?

Abigail had been so happy about being permitted to teach signs that she hadn't pursued the question of braille any further, although she had thought of speaking to Trent about it. She hadn't seen him for a few days, since the day of the picnic. She'd be prepared when he came again.

Chapter 9

The minute Trent rode into the yard and headed for the barn, children came running from every direction. He dismounted and tried to decipher their excited speech, but with them all talking at once, it was next to impossible.

Laughing, he raised both hands. "Wait. Hold on! Albert, where are you?"

"Here I am, Dr. Trent." Albert came from around the barn and took the reins from him. "Here now." He made a shoving motion with one hand then leaned over closer to the children's level so they could see his lips. "You children back off and leave the doctor alone."

"It's all right, Albert." He glanced around at the excited children. "Now. One at a time. Molly, you first."

"Oh Dr. Trent, we are learning sign language." Her nimble fingers began forming letters as she verbalized her actions. "M-o-l-l-y."

"That's wonderful, Molly." He turned and focused on Sonny. "Can you show me your name?"

Sonny gave an uncertain nod. He began forming the letters. When he got to the *Y*, he hesitated and looked into Trent's eyes.

"I'm sorry, Sonny. I don't know how."

The little boy looked at his fingers, and taking a deep breath, he tried again. When he made the *Y*, a huge grin split his face.

"That's great." Trent squeezed Sonny's shoulder then glanced around. "Who's next?"

As soon as the last child had proudly signed his name, Trent thumped himself on the chest. "I can sign my name, too."

"You can?" Wide-eyed, Sonny gave him a doubtful look.

Trent laughed. Actually they all appeared a little doubtful as they watched his hand.

Slowly and carefully, he formed the letters of his first name then his last. "You know, if you learn to sign my last name, you'll know how to sign the name of your school."

"Show us," they chorused, jumping up and down.

He thought for a minute. Better not. Abigail might have a particular way to teach them.

He motioned for them to follow him to the house. They lined up behind him and he led them all the way around to the front and up the porch steps. Trent smiled, feeling rather like the pied piper. He turned to face them. "How about if we ask Miss Abigail to come outside and teach us a few signs."

"On Saturday?" Jimmy frowned. "We don't go to school on Saturday."

"Oh, but it's not school. First of all, we're outside. Second, we are asking the teacher to teach us instead of the teacher telling us to learn."

Jimmy nodded. "I guess that's all right then."

Seven-year-old Phoebe tossed her blond curls. "Lily Ann's going to be mad she missed it."

Trent quirked his brow. "Why should Lily Ann care? It's sign language."

"Miss Abigail's teaching her signs, too. She wanted to learn."

He supposed it was natural for a child to want to be included in what the other children were doing. If not for her injury, she would be having her lessons at home from a tutor more than likely. She'd probably be learning to ride horseback and perhaps have dance lessons as well.

The familiar pang shot through him. He turned to Molly. "Would you find Miss Abigail and see if she has time for us this morning or later in the day?"

Her eyes lit up at being chosen for the task. "Yes sir." She hurried inside.

Clouds covered the sun and Trent looked at the sky with an experienced eye. Hurricane season was just around the corner. Georgia seldom got hit, and the school was too far inland to worry about waves, but the rivers and streams often overflowed when a storm was near the coast. Not to mention the tornadoes that could spin off from coastal hurricanes. He scoffed inwardly. Not today. It was only late July. But a thunderstorm could very well be in the works.

The door opened and Abigail followed Molly onto the porch, a puzzled look on her face.

"Doctor, you wanted to see me?"

Their eyes met, and Trent felt as though he'd been hit by a falling tree. Maybe there was a storm after all. He took a deep breath and smiled in her direction without looking straight into her eyes.

"Doctor?"

He cleared his throat. "Good morning, Miss James. We have a dilemma with which we hope you can assist us."

"Oh?" An amused look crossed her face. "And what might that be?"

"It has come to our attention that by learning to sign my last name, the children would also learn to sign the school name."

The corners of her lips started to tilt, and she pressed them together. "Well children, it seems to me that Dr. Trent could teach you that himself. I know for a fact he has accomplished that skill."

"Oh, but I thought you might have a particular teaching technique for them. I didn't wish to confuse them."

She tossed him a skeptical look. "I see." She smiled at the children, who stood with hopeful expressions on their faces. "So you wish me to teach you how to sign *Quincy*?"

"Yes ma'am." The chorus of voices exploded into the air.

"Very well. You're in luck to find me with idle hands and feeling bored."

Trent couldn't keep the grin from his face. But when she cut a glance his way, he quickly clamped his mouth shut.

For the next half hour, Abigail taught each child to make the letters. Trent hadn't watched her teach the children before, and he couldn't help but be impressed. When any of them had difficulties with a letter, usually the *U*, she patiently took their hand and helped them form the letters, just as she had with him. Furthermore, she had them all laughing on several occasions with the wonderful sense of humor he'd only recently discovered. The children reveled in it, and he had to admit, so did he. Not only was her attitude good for the children, but it was having a very positive effect on him as well.

When the dinner gong sounded, Mrs. Cole fetched the children, and they hurried around back to wash their hands.

Trent eyed Abigail with admiration. "You are wonderful with them."

A blush tinted her cheeks. "Thank you. I feel that happiness is a great teaching tool."

"You must be right. They seem quite eager to learn." He offered his arm. "May I escort you to dinner, Miss James?"

They held back while the children filed into the foyer. Little Hunter trailed behind, holding on to Virgie's hand.

"Mamaw, wait." The little boy tugged his hand away from Virgie and took off in a run down the hall to Mr. Carter's office. His small fist pecked on the door. Then he pounded.

Carter stepped out into the hallway and looked down at Hunter, who grabbed his hand and attempted to pull him toward the foyer. "Eat."

Trent stood still, curious to see what the man would do and determined to intervene if he deemed necessary.

Mixed emotions washed over Carter's face. Reluctance? Joy? What was it? He cleared his throat. "I'm not hungry. I'll eat later." His voice held a hint of kindness.

Hunter frowned and tugged harder. "Come. Time to eat."

Carter sighed. "All right, Hunter. If you insist."

The director followed the child down the hall and into the dining room. Trent looked on in amazement.

He glanced at Abigail whose surprise seemed to match his

own. "Can you beat that?"

She shook her head and smiled. "'And a little child shall lead them.'" She took Trent's arm once more, and they stepped through the carved double doors.

❧

Should she or shouldn't she? Abigail was thrilled that the children were doing so well with their sign language classes. But the victory paled when she thought of all that Lily Ann was missing out on.

She hesitated to go over the director's head again, but Lily Ann was worth it. And this could be the perfect time to broach the subject to Trent.

She waited until Hunter had reluctantly gone with Virgie to her quarters for an afternoon nap and the other children followed their houseparents up to the dorms to rest.

Trent still sat at the table with her and the other teachers having a cup of coffee. She fidgeted, not realizing until she noticed she'd squeezed her napkin into a twisted rope. Quickly she smoothed it on her lap then folded it and placed it on the table.

Helen threw her a look, her eyebrows slightly raised in question. Abigail glanced away hoping Helen wouldn't bring up the subject. It wouldn't do to make him feel trapped by discussing it in front of the other teachers.

She wasn't quite sure how to ask for an audience, especially since they usually discussed school matters on weekdays.

Finally he arose and glanced at her. "Miss James, I wonder if I might speak with you for a few moments. I realize you are off duty, but if you wouldn't mind I have a few questions."

Thank You, God. "Of course. I don't mind at all." She stood.

Helen rose as well. "Abigail, would you like to join me in the parlor around three or so. I thought we could discuss next week's schedule."

Helen was almost as eager to get braille for Lily Ann as she was. Amused, Abigail nodded and stepped into the foyer with Trent.

"My office or the porch? We seem to conduct a lot of business out there." His smile reached his eyes and the corners crinkled.

"How about a walk to clear away my afternoon drowsiness?"

"Oh, forgive me. If you need to rest, our talk can wait."

"No, I'd rather not sleep in the heat of the day anyway. I'm still not accustomed to the heat. There's hardly any breeze at all."

He held the door for her to step outside. "You'll have breeze enough and more when storm season starts on the coast."

"You mean hurricanes?" Her pulse quickened.

"You won't need to worry. We're too far inland, but we do get strong winds on the rare occasion one hits the Georgia coast." He took her hand and assisted her down the steps. "Of course tornadoes are always a possibility as well, but God has spared us from ever being hit. And we have a good strong storm cellar. I shouldn't have brought it up. I didn't mean to frighten you."

"It's perfectly all right. I'm not frightened." But she knew her trembling hand said otherwise.

She took his proffered arm, reassured at his strength as the muscles jumped beneath her hand. Blushing at the thought, she withdrew her hand, allowing her arms to rest at her sides as they walked down the lane past the magnolia trees and the huge live oak. When they reached the gate, they turned and walked back to the bench beneath the live oak tree.

After they were seated, he said, "I guess that's enough walking in this heat. Don't you agree?"

She nodded, only half hearing, as she smoothed her skirt and tried to decide how to begin. But first she needed to listen to whatever questions he had for her.

He loosened his tie and cleared his throat. "Have any problems arisen with the sign language classes?"

She glanced up quickly. Did he think she wasn't competent to teach it? "Why no. The children are learning quickly. Of course there is an occasional problem with making a letter, but nothing serious." She shook her head. "Of course, sometimes they don't want to work at it, but that's no different from any schoolwork."

He nodded. "I can remember dreaming up every excuse imaginable to put lessons off."

"Can't we all?" She laughed. "We're about halfway through the alphabet and have tried a few simple word signs. They all know *boy* and *girl* and a few others."

"That's wonderful. Are they using the signs they know in their conversations yet?"

"Not really. They aren't quite sure enough, although I did see Molly calling Sonny a bad boy in signs one day."

Trent laughed. "That doesn't surprise me. These kids never cease to amaze me. By the way, I understand Lily Ann is learning to sign."

"Yes, at her request, and she's doing very well." *Thank You, God, for giving me this opening.* It should be easy now to lead into the request. "She's such a bright child. She learns everything well, even without her eyesight."

Trent flinched and pain crossed his face. Abigail bit her lip. Why did he suffer so? She hurt for Lily Ann, too, but his pain seemed out of proportion. Even if the little girl had been a sister or a daughter, he should have learned to deal with the tragedy by now. Perhaps it would help if he had the chance to improve her world with braille.

"Dr. Quincy, I am so excited about the new program for the deaf children. It's going to be so helpful to them. But there's also a wonderful teaching tool that could help Lily Ann."

He took a deep breath and focused on her once more. "Yes, Miss James? You know of something that will help Lily Ann?"

"Have you ever heard of braille?" She held her breath. Of course he hadn't heard of it, or he would have seen that Lily Ann learn it before now.

He nodded. "That's a reading and writing system for blind people. It was created by Louis Braille, a Frenchman, and consists of combinations of raised dots."

Surprised, she threw him a confused look.

"Well Doctor, if you know about it, I'm surprised you haven't already begun to utilize it for Lily Ann."

He smiled. "Of course, how could you be expected to know when I haven't yet discussed this with you? Lily Ann is only six. She has plenty of time to learn to read and write. And as you say, she's very bright. When her sight is restored she'll learn quickly."

Joy coursed through Abigail. "Her blindness isn't permanent? Oh Dr. Quincy, that is wonderful news. I had no idea. Is she to have some sort of treatment or surgery?"

"Yes. Of course. I constantly search for a specialist who will be able to help her. And I have no doubt that someday, with God's help, I'll succeed."

Confusion shot through her. Wait. What was he saying? "Dr. Quincy." Her words came out barely above a whisper. "Do you mean you haven't actually found someone to help her, but are only hoping?"

Anger flashed in his eyes. "And are you saying I should stop hoping?"

"Of course not." She snapped the words then swallowed past the lump in her throat. "You should never give up hope. But in the meantime, shouldn't you give her every chance to learn to read and write? It might be years before you find anyone to help her. And there is no guarantee, is there?"

He pushed up from the bench, and the glance he gave her seemed cool. "I'll think about it. Come. I'll escort you back to the house now. I have patients to see this afternoon."

They returned to the house in silence; then Trent bowed and headed around to the barn to get Warrior.

Abigail, dismayed at the turn of events, was near tears as she entered the foyer. She ran upstairs and washed her face then stepped to her window and pulled the curtain aside. She watched as Albert led Warrior out of the barn. Trent mounted and took off at a gallop. She composed herself and went down to the parlor, where she found Helen and Virgie.

They both glanced up, obviously eager for good news.

"Uh-oh. Bad news?" Helen's lips drew downward at the corners.

Abigail gave a loud sigh and shook her head. "I don't know what to think. You aren't going to believe this."

She told them about her conversation with Trent. "Did anyone know he was trying to find someone who could restore her sight?"

Helen shook her head. "This is the first I've heard of it."

"It almost seemed as though he was afraid if he allowed us to teach her braille, it would mean he had stopped believing."

Abigail glanced at Virgie, who silently rocked her chair.

"Virgie, do you know why he is so adamant about this?"

The old lady lifted her still-sharp dark brown eyes. "If I know anything, it don't mean I'm telling anyone anything."

"But Virgie. If I could only understand. I'm so angry right now. This isn't fair to Lily Ann."

Helen stood and gave her a sympathetic glance. "I'm going upstairs to rest awhile before supper. We'll just have to keep praying."

When the door closed, Abigail glanced at Virgie and met her waiting eyes.

Virgie sighed. "Miss Abigail, I'm goin' tell you something because I believe you care about Dr. Trent, and I don't want you thinking bad about him."

Abigail listened with tears flowing as Virgie told her the details of Lily Ann's accident and the agony of guilt that Trent had taken upon himself.

"But why does he think it was his fault? Have Lily Ann's parents blamed him in any way?"

"No, they beg him not to blame himself. No one could have done anything to stop that poor old crazy horse." Tears filled Virgie's eyes. "But my sweet Trent, he always been sensitive and for some reason he blames himself for that baby's misfortune."

Abigail fought back tears as she went upstairs to change for supper. Somehow she'd get through to Trent. She had to. For his sake. And for Lily Ann's. Because Lily's future was at stake here. She cast a quick prayer up to God to heal Trent's heart and to make him see how wrong he was to allow his grief to deprive the child of a better future.

Chapter 10

Who would have thought the first week of September would feel like the middle of summer? Abigail fanned herself with the cover of the fairy tale book from which she'd just read to the children. Realizing what she was doing, she shut the book and laid it on her desk.

Even the occasional whiff of air that blew in through the open windows was hot. The children didn't seem to mind at all. She wondered how these Southern boys and girls would handle the ice and occasional snow of the capital. Probably just fine. She shook her head. No extreme of weather seemed to faze children.

The oppressive heat bothered her far worse now than it had during the scorching July and August sun. Perhaps because she had looked forward to this month for a reprieve. September had always been one of her favorite months, heralding the beginning of cooler weather and drawing closer to the holidays. Why had she not realized the fall season wouldn't start as early in the South?

She couldn't help the grateful sigh that escaped when the bell sounded. Relieved that she had an hour before her next class, she went to her room and splashed some water on her face. Unbuttoning her top two buttons, she ran a cool cloth over her neck. She should go over the lesson for the next class, but the room was so stifling. She rebuttoned her dress and went downstairs and out through the back door. Perhaps the shade from the many large oaks in the backyard would provide a little relief.

Spying Albert near the barn, she headed in that direction and hailed him. "Hi, Albert. How are you today?"

"Just fine, Miss Abigail. How you be today?"

"Hot. And you look cool as a cucumber. How do you do it?"

Chuckling, he shook his grizzled head "I's used to it, I reckon.

Lived in these parts all my life."

She nodded and smiled at the good-natured old man. "I guess that explains it." She peeked around the barn door to see if Trent's horse was there. Ever since she'd spoken to him about braille for Lily Ann, he'd made himself scarce. When he did show up at the school, he avoided her like the yellow fever. Not seeing Warrior, she heaved a sigh.

Albert sent her a knowing glance. "You looking for Dr. Trent?"

Heat rushed to her face. "Why would you say that?"

"Humph. Maybe cause you craning your neck to see if his horse in the barn."

She bit her lip. "Albert, I am not. Anyway, he'll more than likely never speak to me again. I overstepped my place again about Lily Ann. But I didn't know the accident happened in his yard or that he blamed himself."

He gave a solemn nod. "That be a sad day. But don't you worry none. If Dr. Trent mad at you, he get over it soon enough. Don't you know he sweet on you, same as you be on him?"

Heat blazed up in her face again. "What a thing to say. I most certainly am not sweet on the doctor."

"Okay. If you say so." His knowing eyes belied the words.

Abigail blew her breath out in a huff. "I do say so. I have to get back inside. Have a good day."

"Yes ma'am. I sure will. You have a good day, too." He chuckled again.

"Oh, fiddlesticks." She whirled, stomped across the yard, and flounced into the house. She leaned against the door and fanned herself with her handkerchief. That hadn't been very smart. Now here she was perspiring like a racehorse. The lacy handkerchief became a blotter as she pressed it against her damp forehead.

The day passed slowly, and by suppertime Abigail's head throbbed and ached. She excused herself early and fell into bed with the cool cloth Virgie had pressed into her hand. By morning her headache had eased some. In the middle of her sign language class, the breeze picked up a little. Abigail's heart quickened at the welcome sound of raindrops on the roof.

The rain had stopped by the end of class, and the grass didn't seem to be so much as damp, so Abigail gave in to Lily Ann's pleas to have her lessons outside. With an armful of books, she took Lily's hand and started toward the woods behind the house.

A few drops of moisture clung to the branches of the trees as they made their way through the thick foliage to their special tree. Lily Ann squealed at the occasional drop that fell on her. Abigail laughed. She hoped the slight rainfall was the beginning of cooler weather.

She spread a blanket upon the thick grass beneath the huge live oak tree, and she and Lily Ann seated themselves. Abigail opened the spelling book. "All right, here we go. Spelling first." She read the first word to Lily Ann, and the little girl spelled it back perfectly. After the spelling lesson was complete, they spent a little while on signs. When they'd finished the last one, Lily Ann clapped her hands.

"Now it's time for Alice. Right, Miss Abigail?" Lily Ann's face glowed. Story time was her favorite. Sometimes Abigail felt the little girl would live in the fantasy lands she loved so well.

"Yes, but what is the full title of our story?" She had no doubt Lily Ann knew it.

"*Alice's Adventures in Wonderland.* And Mr. Lewis Carroll is the author." She gave a smile of satisfaction, confident she was correct.

"Very good. Do you remember what Alice was doing when we left off yesterday?" Abigail used every opportunity to exercise Lily Ann's memory. It would help her in every skill she attempted.

"She opened a tiny door with a key. And when she peeked through the door, she saw a garden inside."

"And did Alice go through the door and into the garden?"

A giggle trilled from Lily Ann's lips. "No. 'Course not. The door is too tiny, and Alice is too big."

"You're right. How silly of me. Are you ready to find out what happens next?" Abigail slid her finger in front of the blue bookmark and opened the book.

A gust of wind swept across the small clearing, riffling the pages of the book and blowing leaves and grass across their laps.

Abigail's hair came loose from her combs and blew into her eyes and face.

Lily Ann let out a little scream. "Miss Abigail!"

"I'm here." Abigail scrambled to her feet, gripping the book with one hand and reaching for Lily Ann's hand with the other. "Don't be afraid. It's just wind, but I believe we'd better get back to the house. The sky is dark overhead. We don't want to get caught in the rain."

The little girl squeezed Abigail's hand tightly.

"Hurry, Teacher. Hurry." Her voice shook. "I don't like the sounds in the wind. They aren't whispers anymore. They're very bad sounds."

Abigail put her arm around Lily Ann's small shoulders, and she guided her forward as fast as she could without risking her falling. "It's all right, sweetheart. It's only the wind you hear."

The child's body shook, whether with fear or chill Abigail couldn't tell. As they burst from the woods, the rain began to fall in torrents. Abigail tried to cover the child's head with her arm. The wind had increased until it was all she could do to keep them both on their feet. Small hailstones began to pelt the ground around them.

Suddenly Albert appeared before them. He swept Lily Ann across his shoulder and grabbed Abigail's arm. He hurried them to the back of the house, where Virgie held the screen door open with both hands. The moment they were in the house, the door slammed shut.

Albert placed Lily Ann in Virgie's waiting arms and steadied Abigail. Water poured from the three of them and onto the floor.

Virgie tossed her a towel and started swabbing Lily Ann down with another.

As Abigail wrung water from her skirt and dried herself off as well as she could, she turned to Albert. "Where did it come from all of a sudden?"

"Must have been a cyclone around here somewhere. I think it going right over us, but it just come out of nowhere with no warning. No time to even get the young'uns to the storm cellar."

He must be talking about a tornado, Abigail thought. "Is it gone now? Should we get the children to the cellar?"

"Too late. They all in the dining room with the other teachers, praying under the table." He glanced out the window. "Anyways, I think it's done gone."

The wind had decreased. Abigail could scarcely hear it at all, and the rain had dwindled to a light drizzle.

Felicity appeared in the doorway. Relief crossed her faced when she saw them safely inside.

Lily Ann had calmed down under Virgie's gentle hands and willingly followed her housemother upstairs for dry clothing before the midday meal.

Abigail followed, bunching up her wet skirt to keep it from dragging across the hardwood floors and carpet. At least her headache was gone.

❧

Trent dismounted in the Taneys' yard and stared in dismay at their demolished farmhouse. Sections of roof were scattered across the garden and potato patch, and only the wall with the chimney remained. The stark sunlight after the storm only made the shambles look worse. Jim Taney sat on a stump, his head in his hands while his wife, Lucy, who was heavy with child, huddled near him, their two small children clutched in her arms.

A wagon pulled into the yard and Jim's brother, Hal, jumped down. "Jim! Lucy! Is everyone all right?"

Jim looked up, his eyes bloodshot and agony on his face. "Do we look all right?" He waved his hand around. "Does this look all right to you?"

Hal hunkered down by his brother. "We'll get it rebuilt, Jim. I know it's hard to imagine, but this ain't the end. And you have your wife and children. Thank the Lord for that, man."

Trent stepped forward and ran a professional eye over Lucy. "How do you feel?"

She sighed and stood, rubbing her back. "I'm okay, Doc. Just a little aching here and there."

"You'll need to lie down and rest as soon as possible. What are your immediate plans? Do you have a place to stay?"

"They'll stay with me and Irma till their house is back together," Hal said. "Don't worry, Doc. My Irma will see to Lucy."

Trent nodded. Irma Taney was a midwife and had delivered most of the babies in the area until Trent opened his practice. And there were still some women who were more comfortable with her. "If you need me, send someone."

"I will, Doc."

Trent mounted his horse and took off toward the school, where he'd been headed when he saw the storm-damaged home.

God, please let them all be safe.

He'd spotted the funnel cloud when he was visiting one of his patients. It had headed in the direction of the school. But he had no idea how long it stayed on the ground or even if it continued on the same path. He could only hope and pray.

He didn't know he was holding his breath until he let it out in a loud whoosh of relief when he saw the house standing whole and solid, just as it always had.

He rode around back and dismounted in front of the barn.

Albert, who was puttering with something on the ground, looked up from his hunkered position.

"How's everything here?" Trent asked.

Albert pushed his old slouch hat back and looked up. "Everything fine here, Dr. Trent. No one hurt, but we had a little scare there for a while."

"What happened? Did you see the tornado?"

"Naw sir. But the wind and rain be awful strong. Couldn't hear myself think over the noise. It rained mighty hard and even hailed a little. Figured there must have been a cyclone going over our heads."

"Well, you're very lucky it went over your heads. The Taneys lost their house. The twister about blew every piece of it away."

"So that's where this here contraption came from." He scratched his head and stood up, half a harness in his hands.

Trent shook his head. "Gather up anything you see that you think might have come from there. I'll take it to them next time I'm over that way." He rubbed at a tight muscle in his neck. "I won't be here long, Albert. Warrior won't need anything but water." He gave a wave and walked to the front of the house.

No one was in sight when he stepped into the foyer, but he heard voices and the scraping of chairs across the floor coming from the dining room.

Mrs. Cole led the girls into the foyer. When they saw him, they smiled and waved but followed their housemother up the stairs.

The boys came next, following Howard Owens. When they saw Trent, they broke ranks and surrounded Trent, all talking at once.

"Boys, boys. Upstairs, please. Your teacher will be waiting." Owens gave Trent an apologetic smile and followed his disappointed charges.

Helen came out and gave him a smile. His own smile froze as Abigail stepped through the door.

He nodded in her direction then turned to Helen. "Albert said there was a little excitement here this morning. Everyone is all right though?"

"Quite all right, Doctor. Although Abigail almost drowned herself."

Trent's stomach tightened, and he couldn't help the concern that washed over him.

Abigail flinched then gave Helen a very brief smile. "Lily Ann and I were caught in the rain. That's all it was. We're fine. And now, I really must get some things ready for my next class." She gave a nod and was gone.

Trent relaxed as she disappeared from view. He'd avoided her for weeks because he simply didn't know what to say to her. He'd behaved abominably the last time they'd spoken. Although he'd meant what he'd said about Lily Ann not needing braille, he hadn't had to be so brusque with Abigail. She was only trying to help the child. And to his chagrin, he was beginning to have doubts about his reasons for withholding braille from Lily Ann. Was he being irrational about it? It couldn't hurt for her to learn braille while she waited for her recovery, could it?

Perhaps he should at least check it out.

"Dr. Quincy, good day, sir." Carter stood just inside the foyer from the hallway to his office. "I wonder if I might speak with you for a moment on a matter of some importance."

"Yes, of course. Shall we go to your office?"

When they were seated in the smoke-filled room, Carter cleared his throat. "Dr. Quincy, before I say what's on my mind, I'd like for you to know I've given the matter a great deal of thought."

Wishing the man would get to the point, Trent nodded and smiled. "Very well, Mr. Carter. I'll take your word for that."

"I want to assure you what I'm doing doesn't reflect on you or anyone in this school whatsoever. It is strictly a personal decision based on my desire to do what is best for both me and the school. I sincerely regret doing this so suddenly and without giving proper notice."

A pang of dread stabbed at Trent's stomach. Surely it wasn't what it sounded like. Surely the man wouldn't abandon ship without warning.

"I fear, sir, I must resign my position as director of this school immediately."

Chapter 11

Surely the man wasn't serious. Trent took a deep breath, determined not to lose his temper. "So you are leaving with no notice at all?"

Regret crossed Carter's face. "I'll be leaving in two weeks. My new employers wish me to begin right away. I can assure you I've made certain all books and records are up to date and in order. You should be able to handle things until you find a replacement."

Trent stared in disbelief, his lips clamped shut. This wasn't what he'd have expected from the proper and staid Joshua Carter.

"You haven't forgotten, sir, that you signed a contract?"

"Of course not." He rubbed his knuckle across a spot over his right eye. "I will, of course, return my recent wages for the last half of this semester."

For a moment Trent was angry enough to agree, but decided to ignore the comment. "Mr. Carter, can you give me a reason for this action? Were you that angry that Miss James went over your head about the sign language and that I agreed with her?"

Carter steepled his fingers and appeared deep in thought. "Not anger. But I suppose indirectly it contributed to my decision." He sighed. "Very well, Dr. Quincy. I suppose you deserve more of an explanation."

Trent leaned back in his chair and waited for the man to continue.

Carter closed his eyes and breathed slowly. Finally he sat up straight. "I had a son named Michael. A spirited and willful boy who could charm you one moment and try your patience the next. He was deaf in one ear. It didn't seem to affect him a lot. He'd sleep on his good ear, so noises wouldn't wake him." He smiled. "Of course it was a perfect excuse not to hear anything he preferred not to."

"He married young, when he was only twenty. He and his wife,

Jane, had two children. A daughter named Rose and a son they named Joshua, after me."

Carter stood and paced the floor behind his desk. Finally he propped both hands on the edge of the desk and stared at Trent with pain-filled eyes.

"They were coming over to our place one Sunday after church when, for some reason, their carriage overturned. Jane was dozing and it happened so fast she had no idea what happened. Rose and Jane escaped with only a few scratches. Little Joshua's leg was caught beneath the carriage, and he was left lame. Michael was thrown from the carriage. His head struck a rock, and he died instantly."

Horrified Trent sprang from his chair and placed his hand on the older man's arm. "My dear Mr. Carter, I am so sorry for your pain."

Carter sank into his chair, breathing deeply. "I'm afraid I didn't handle things well. I couldn't bear to remain where every memory included Michael. Every glance at my wife reminded me of our son. Every smile or tear from one of my grandchildren brought back thoughts of Michael. Especially Joshua. He's the spitting image of his father."

Trent frowned. "Of course. I understand. But surely you don't mean you abandoned your family."

"I'm afraid that's exactly what I did." He wiped his hand across his eyes, as if in doing so he could eradicate the memories. "Oh, not financially. I've always provided for them. And I visit once or twice a year."

"And now? Is something wrong at home?"

Carter sat up straight. "Only the fact that I've failed my family for the past seven years." Another sigh escaped his lips. "I thought by helping deaf children, I could somehow ease the pain of Michael's death. To my grief, it worked the other way. I came to resent the children here for not being Michael. I've held back from getting to know them. Surely you've noticed I had little to do with anything but the financial business."

Trent returned to his chair. "I'm ashamed to say, I didn't notice until recently. The school always ran smoothly, and the children seemed well and happy."

"Yes, well you can thank the rest of your staff for the latter." He drummed his fingers on the smooth surface of his desk. "The staff is first-rate, you know. Including Miss James. I must admit I was wrong about the sign language class, and I fear my decision to disregard her request to add braille to Lily Ann's studies may also have been in error."

"But Mr. Carter, I still don't understand what made you suddenly decide to leave."

"A number of things. When I saw the mistake I'd made about the sign language, I began to question my connection with the needs of the students. I finally faced the fact that I was here for all the wrong reasons." He smiled and something close to a twinkle flashed in his eyes. "Then Virgie's little grandson, by some miracle, took a liking to me. And suddenly, I realized I'd not only deprived my grandchildren of me, but I'd also deprived myself of them."

He took a deep breath. "Not to mention my dear wife and sweet daughter-in-law. So you see, I can't waste a moment. I need to go to them as soon as possible and attempt to make amends. I only hope I haven't waited too long."

"I'm sure you haven't, sir. And I don't blame you one bit." Trent smiled. "And of course, I wouldn't think of letting you return your wages. You have more than earned them through the years, I'm sure."

"That's very kind of you. But I'll feel better if you'll accept it. Perhaps it could be my contribution to the expense of braille supplies."

Trent turned and glanced out the window. There it was again. Braille. And now Mr. Carter seemed to feel it should be added.

He rose. "I wish you the best with your new job and reconciliation with your family. If there is anything I can do to help you prepare for your journey, please let me know."

He shook the director's hand and left. He sympathized with Carter's decision, but how in the world could he take on these added duties? He had no doubt the staff would help all they could, but the business and financial tasks would fall into his realm of responsibility.

Well, *c'est la vie*, as his grandmother used to say. And she was right. That truly was life.

❧

Abigail paid little attention to the delicious supper Selma had prepared. She listened in horror as Trent told them about the destruction of the Taneys' home. Lily Ann had been right. There were bad sounds in the wind. And from what Trent was telling them, it seemed likely the same twister that destroyed their neighbor's house and barn could have just as easily struck the school. Her chest tightened at the thought. *Dear God, what use is a storm cellar if the funnel cloud could hit us without any warning?*

Mr. Carter had joined them for supper and informed them of his imminent departure. Abigail sat stunned. Was it her fault? Had she been such a nuisance to the man she'd driven him away? She must apologize. But what could she say? She couldn't pretend he was right about the curriculum.

She turned and met a concerned look in Trent's eyes. Well, it was no wonder he was concerned. Who would take Mr. Carter's place as director on such short notice?

After dinner she followed the director to his office and cleared her throat before he could shut the door.

"Yes, Miss James?" His voice wasn't exactly kind, but at least it was less gruff than usual.

"Mr. Carter, if I've done or said anything that caused you to resign your position, I apologize and beg you to reconsider." Her voice shook as she spoke.

His face softened momentarily then he stiffened. "No, my

decision had nothing to do with you, Miss James. And I'm the one who should apologize. I spoke unkindly to you without cause. Even though I thought I was right about the signing class, I could have been more courteous. And as it turns out, I was in error. The sign language class is most beneficial. I've told Dr. Quincy as much, as well as my opinion that Lily Ann could most likely benefit from learning braille. Of course, the decision is entirely up to him."

Abigail blinked back tears. "Thank you for telling me that, Mr. Carter. It means a lot to me. And I know I could have been more courteous as well. I can sometimes be quite headstrong."

He gave a slight smile. "Well, I hold nothing against you. After all, you're young."

Peace flowed through her, and she smiled. "Yes, I am. Good night, Mr. Carter."

"Good night, my dear."

With lightness in her steps she walked back to the foyer. The sound of music drew her to the parlor where she found Trent seated at the piano. The tune he was playing was one of her favorites, so she tiptoed in and sat just inside the door. His hands were visible from where she sat, and she admired his strong fingers as they drew the music from the keys. Her glance drifted from his hands to his profile, and her fingers longed to run across his forehead and through the thick waves of his hair.

The music stopped, and she gasped and jumped up. He turned, surprise in his eyes as they rested on her.

"Abigail. Oh, forgive me." Consternation crossed his face. "Miss James, I meant."

"It's quite all right if you wish to call me by my given name. We're all informal here, you know, as long as the children aren't around. I don't mind."

"Then you must also call me Trent."

"Oh no, Dr. Quincy. I couldn't possibly. But perhaps Dr. Trent as the others call you."

"As you wish."

She was almost sure she detected a trace of disappointment in his voice.

"I didn't know you could play the piano. It was beautiful." She paused, suddenly embarrassed. "I hope you don't mind that I listened."

"Not at all since you enjoyed it." He smiled. "Would you like to hear another?"

"Oh yes. If you don't mind."

"Not at all." He pulled a chair up beside the piano stool. "Here, sit beside me and you can turn the pages for me."

"All right. I used to do that for my father. He plays, too."

As he played a familiar tune, she began to hum.

He nodded. "Let's sing."

She reached to turn the page of the hymnal, and so did he. Their hands touched, and a tingle went through her fingers and up her arm. She jerked her hand back.

"Sorry. I'm so used to turning the pages myself, I forgot." His eyes were warm as he smiled at her.

They sang song after song, their voices blending together perfectly. Suddenly the clock on the mantel chimed. She glanced at the watch on the chain around her neck and gasped. "Oh my, I had no idea it was so late." She rose, feeling a little dizzy. "Thank you for sharing your music with me, Dr. Trent."

He stood and took her hand. "It was my pleasure, Abigail." He looked deeply into her eyes.

"Good night." She turned and sailed out of the room and up the stairs, her heart pounding. What on earth was the matter with her? It was almost as if she were attracted to the doctor, and of course that was nonsense. She wasn't even sure she liked him.

But as she prepared for bed, the thought crossed her mind that this was the first time they'd been alone together and hadn't talked school business. And it had been very nice.

·❧

Trent hummed one hymn after another as he rode home, his heart lighter than he could remember it being for a long time.

Who would have thought the opinionated Miss Abigail James could be so charming. Quite beautiful, too.

He grinned as he recalled the blush that had washed over her as their hands accidentally touched. He'd been slightly attracted to her before, but tonight, he had to admit, he'd been dazzled. Her auburn curls, hanging loose across her shoulder, had brushed against his arm on more than one occasion, and the gold in her eyes had sparkled like stars.

He chuckled and urged Warrior to speed up. Since when had his thoughts become poetic?

Perhaps it wasn't going to be so bad having to spend more time at the school. Reality hit. The school. He'd need to begin a search for another director right away. His patients couldn't be allowed to suffer. He'd simply need to fit the school business in between his patients, because the patients had to come before business. Virgie would send for him if he was really needed at the school.

He sighed. Well, he'd had this evening to relax and enjoy himself. It might possibly be the last for a while.

His conversation with Carter ran through his mind, and sympathy shot through him. The man must have been in misery all the time he'd been director here. But there was a definite change in him today. He'd been almost kind and apologetic. And had admitted he'd been wrong about the sign language class. Of course, he'd also said he'd been wrong about adding a braille class for Lily Ann, but Trent wasn't so sure about that. He'd have to think about it. Perhaps, when he found a new director and wasn't so busy, he'd make a trip to St. Louis and check out that school. Find out firsthand just how beneficial braille might or might not be to Lily Ann. But he'd never give up on finding a way to restore her sight.

By the time he reached home, he realized his thoughts had

become such a jumble nothing was making sense to him. He went to the kitchen and heated up the coffee that stood waiting on the stove. Maybe it would help clear the fog away until he was ready for bed.

He carried a cup of coffee to the study and sat at his desk. Taking out stationery, he composed an advertisement for a new director. He'd send it to all the newspapers in the area as well as the universities within a reasonable distance. Georgia was still recovering from the war. People were more inclined to seek employment in the northern states. He mentioned the scenery and the peaceful countryside and indicated that the salary was more than adequate.

He wrote several copies. When he'd finished, he had a stack of envelopes ready to take to the post office the next day. He could only hope and pray that the right person would respond, and they'd be available in the near future.

Yawning, he climbed the stairs to his bedroom and got ready for bed. A long, deep sleep was just what he needed. Hopefully he'd awaken with a clear head. He drifted off to sleep with the thought of Abigail's pink-tipped fingers brushing against his, and her sweet voice singing praises.

Chapter 12

The next few days seemed hotter than ever to Abigail after the brief respite. Even the children seemed lethargic in the oppressive heat and the stillness of the air. Finally one evening as they sat in the parlor, Charles suggested a nature walk.

Helen's face lit. "That's a wonderful idea."

Charles nodded. "We can make it a science project."

"And combine it with a sign language lesson." Abigail glanced at the other two to see if they'd agree.

"And more." Helen laughed. "We can have them draw pictures and write an essay about the vegetation and insects they discover."

"We could make a group project." Abigail scrunched up her forehead in thought. "How about if they each make a little book with their essay and pictures, and perhaps some leaves pasted in, as a gift for their parents?"

"Yes." Helen sat on the edge of her seat. "They can present them when their parents come get them for the Christmas vacation."

"Oh." Abigail glanced from Helen to Charles. "I didn't realize the children go home for Christmas."

Helen nodded. "We usually put on a little program then have a gift exchange. We end the day with a special meal at one o'clock. Then the children go home with their parents."

"All of them?"

Charles scowled. "So far. Although one year, Sonny's family didn't show up for hours after the other children had left."

Helen placed a hand on his arm. "Calm down. At least they got here. And Sonny was so happy to see his mother."

"And his father?" Abigail hoped Helen would say yes.

"Sonny's father was killed in a brawl a few years ago. His mother lives with her brother, who doesn't seem to want to be bothered much with Sonny."

"Poor Sonny. Does he know?"

"I don't see how he could help it." Charles frowned. "But his mother is getting married this spring, and her fiancé seems like a good man. I think he'll treat Sonny well."

After this brighter note, they cheered up and scheduled the field trip for the following day, directly after the morning classes. They'd ask Cook to prepare a picnic basket, and they would eat lunch by the creek.

"We should probably get permission from Mr. Carter." Abigail's suggestion surprised her as much as it did the other two. Now that he was leaving, they hardly saw him except at the supper meal.

"You're right. Even though he hasn't involved himself in anything this week, he's still officially in charge until next Monday." Charles glanced from Helen to Abigail. "I suppose I'll see if he's in his office."

Abigail grinned. She should probably offer to ask permission of Mr. Carter, but Charles was looking at her so expectantly, she decided to make him do it. After all, she had already made her peace with Mr. Carter. She wasn't about to rock the boat.

"Oh. All right." Charles stood and left.

Helen giggled. "It'll be good for him."

"My thoughts, too. After all, we've all had our grievances with the director. Now that we know his story, we need to send him off in peace, with no hard feelings on our part."

Charles returned shortly, an expression of pleased relief on his face. "He was quite nice. Actually, I'd say downright affable."

"He's going home to his family." Abigail stood. "I wish I could be a fly on the wall when they see the change in him. I suspect it will be a very touching moment."

The next day proved to be every bit as hot and miserable as the previous ones. But when the children found out about the field trip, they cheered up and could hardly stay in their seats.

Abigail cast a few nervous glances out the window at the sky. The heaviness of the air reminded her of the day of the storm.

Although the tornado had gone over them, the thought of the Taney family's tragedy poked at her all morning. That storm had come out of nowhere. And it had been the same kind of thick, oppressive heat as today.

She glanced at Lily Ann to see if the child was nervous, but she sat smiling, playing with her blocks. Abigail stepped over to her and touched her hand. "Are you happy about the nature walk, Lily?"

"Oh yes, Miss Abigail." She threw a radiant smile upward. "I can hardly wait. My mama and papa will be so happy when I give them their Christmas present."

Relief shot through her. She was just being silly. After all, Lily Ann had sensed a change in the air last time. This was just a normal, hot Georgia day.

The classes went well, with the children behaving for the most part. When the signing class was over, they all lined up and went to their next class except for Lily, who stayed for her special lessons.

Finally the bell rang, and Abigail took Lily Ann to line up with the rest of the children. She followed them down to the mudroom to wash. Little Hunter jumped from one foot to the other, excited that he'd been invited to go on the nature walk.

She was glad Felicity and Howard had volunteered to go along on the walk to help keep the nine children together and out of the creek.

Sally May was waiting in the foyer with a large, cloth-covered basket, a basket with tableware, and a covered pail filled with cool milk.

The aroma wafting from the basket teased Abigail's senses and caused her stomach to gently rumble. There was fried chicken for sure in that basket.

Charles took the handle of the covered basket from Sally May and handed the other one to Howard. Sally May passed the pail over to Abigail.

They filed out the back door and across the yard to the woods.

Abigail drew in a breath of relief when she stepped into the wooded area. It seemed cooler in the blessed shade and darkness of the woods.

Each child held another's hand, except for Lily Ann, who clung to Abigail's as they navigated through the trees.

"Look, children." Charles had stooped beside a large bushlike plant covered with bright red berries.

"What do you think about these berries, children?"

Curious, Abigail drew closer. She wasn't sure what the berries were.

Donald leaned in closer and wrinkled his nose. "These are poison. We learned about them last summer before they turned red."

"Very good, Donald." Charles stood and looked around at the other children. "What's the number one rule about berries, leaves, or stalks?"

"Never put anything in your mouth unless you know for sure it's safe to eat." The voices rang out together.

By the time they reached the creek on the other side of the woods, everyone was famished. Abigail, Helen, and Felicity spread white cloths on the tables that stood beneath the shade trees. Soon the delicious food was all ready, and they filled plates for the children. Howard asked God's blessing on the food. Soon everyone was stuffed with fried chicken, baked beans, pickles, and peach cobbler.

Everyone pitched in and helped clean up.

Lily Ann, who leaned against Abigail and yawned, suddenly stiffened.

Sensitive to every move of the child, Abigail looked at her. "Is something wrong, sweetheart?"

"We need to go home." Her voice trembled.

Abigail took a quick look around. Except for a tiny increase in the breeze, which felt wonderful, everything seemed the same. She smoothed Lily Ann's hair. "It's all right. Everything is fine."

The little girl nodded, but as they started back through the woods, she stayed close to Abigail, clutching her hand, while the other children squealed with delight over new discoveries for the project.

Suddenly the woods became dark and Abigail shivered. Rain began to pelt them as they scurried the last few feet toward the clearing.

As they stepped from the woods, fear rose in Abigail as Mr. Carter came running toward them from the direction of the storm cellar. The wind howled, and she couldn't make out what he was shouting. She saw the twister just as he reached them.

"Twister!" He grabbed Hunter up under one arm and Lily Ann under the other and ran for the cellar. Abigail turned and looked at the black funnel cloud. It was headed right for them. She grabbed Molly's hand and ran as hard as she could toward the safety of the cellar. Children's screams mingled with the adults' shouting as they ran toward shelter.

Pain pierced Abigail's head as a hailstone hit her. There was no time to try to shield anyone. The cellar suddenly loomed before her. She shoved Molly in as Charles held the door open. Abigail turned to see if anyone else needed help.

"What are you doing?" Charles yelled. "Get inside. He gave her a shove, and she tripped down the steps. Howard caught her at the bottom and pushed her aside while he helped the others in then ran back up the steps to help Charles get the door shut.

Abigail glanced around. Virgie and the rest of the household staff huddled together against the wall of the dark cellar.

"Are we all here?" Mr. Carter could hardly get the words out as he glanced around, counting children and adults.

Virgie, holding on to her grandson with tears streaming down her face answered. "Yes, Mr. Carter, everyone is here, thanks to you."

Above them, the tornado howled and screamed while the hail and winds beat against their place of shelter.

Trent shoved the brim of his hat down over his eyes. The wind howled around him, and torrents of rain assailed him from all sides. The storm had seemed to come out of nowhere. "Eeyahhhh!" He whipped the reins and kicked against Warrior's sides, determined to make it to the school.

Suddenly a deafening roar came from behind him. His heart lurched when he saw the large black cloud spinning toward him. He kicked again. He had to get to the school and make sure they were all safe inside the cellar. The roar increased, and this time he knew it was almost on him. Leaping from Warrior's back, he slapped the horse and dove into the deep ditch beside the road. He grabbed a scrawny bush that grew in the middle of the ditch and held on, hoping its roots were strong, as the ferocious winds almost tore him apart. Rain and hail pounded his back, and he shielded his head with his arms. It seemed like hours, but he knew in actuality only a few minutes passed before the twister was gone.

He crawled out of the ditch and ran down the road toward the school, dodging downed trees and branches. An ancient live oak lay on its side in the field to his left, its roots exposed.

Dear God, please let them be alive and well.

He rounded the curve by the magnolia tree and saw the old white gate ripped off its hinges and in shambles. But thank God, the house still stood. He rushed up the steps and crunched through shattered glass as he hurried into the foyer, shouting for Abigail. Then Virgie. Anyone. The house was deserted.

He spun around and rushed outside toward the storm cellar, praying he'd find them there, safe and sound. A heavy limb lay across the cellar door and someone pounded from inside. Trent dragged the limb away and wrenched the door open. Charles stood there, a smile of relief on his face.

"Is Abigail here? And Virgie? Are the children safe?" He panted as he fired the questions that screamed inside his mind.

"We here and everybody just fine, Dr. Trent. Don't you be worryin' now."

At Virgie's softly spoken words, Trent sank to the ground and buried his face in his hands for a moment. He stood as the children came through the door, one by one, eyes large with fright and relief. Then the women stepped out and smiled as they saw the house still standing.

The last one out was Mr. Carter, who had insisted everyone exit before him.

Virgie placed her hand on Trent's arm. "This man here saved us all, Dr. Trent. He made us all get in the cellar; then he took off toward the woods to fetch the children and the teachers. If not for him, we'd of probably all been dead, it happened so fast."

"What? They were in the woods when it hit?" Fear wrenched through him at the very thought.

"No, they were in the cellar when it hit. Because Mr. Carter ran and grabbed young'uns and warned everyone about the twister heading this way. They made it inside just as that old devil cloud came roaring through."

Trent lifted a silent prayer of thanks upward.

"Look, Mamaw!" Little Hunter pointed toward the house.

Trent chuckled. It probably did look pretty bad to the little fellow with part of the roof hanging and several windows broken out.

"It be all right, my angel boy. Just need a little fixing up, and it be good as new." Virgie took his hand and walked toward the house with the others.

"Be careful when you step up on the porch," Trent called after them. "There's glass everywhere."

He glanced at Mr. Carter, who stood beside him. "Thank you, sir. You've done a good work today."

"No more than any man would have done, Dr. Quincy. Now I suppose we'd better see what damage is done. Hopefully all the records are still intact."

The major damage to the house was the windows and sections of the roof. But cleanup would take some time. Pictures lay on the floor, some of them ruined. The chandelier in the dining room hung from two chains and would need to be repaired before the room could be used. Trent locked the door so no child could wander in and perhaps get hurt.

Selma and her helpers went to work cleaning up the kitchen so they could prepare the supper meal.

Virgie came into the foyer with a broom and basket and started to sweep up glass fragments and leaves from the floor.

"Virgie, please let someone else do that. I'll need you to do an inspection of the house with me."

"Here, Virgie, let me do this." Abigail gently removed the broom from her hand. "You should probably rest awhile before you do anything."

"Lands, Miss Abigail. I can't rest with the house in this kind of shape." Virgie smiled and patted Abigail's shoulder. "But you can do this while I go with Dr. Trent."

Trent looked at Abigail in surprise. "Miss James, I didn't mean you. The maids can take care of the cleanup. This isn't your responsibility."

"Nonsense! A little work never hurt anyone. Certainly not me. And my family didn't have maids, Dr. Trent. Only one part-time girl who helped out on laundry days." Her smile softened the words. "Although, I'll admit there were times I wished we did."

"Then, thank you. I appreciate your willingness to help." He followed Virgie toward the infirmary where they'd start their inventory. Suddenly he stopped, a cold feeling in his heart. "Virgie, where's Albert? I haven't seen him."

"Don't you worry yourself. He went home early today, complaining with stomach sickness."

Chapter 13

Trent charged around the house to the barn. He'd have to take one of the carriage horses. He hoped they were both all right. He stepped inside and stopped. He chuckled. Warrior stood in front of his usual stall, saddle and medical bag intact and his bridle hanging loose. His nose poked through bars on the gate, and he nibbled loose hay.

Trent patted his flank. "Good boy. You knew your home away from home, and no storm was going to keep you from it."

Warrior raised his head and whinnied, perking up his ears.

Trent checked the horse over for cuts from flying debris, but he seemed fine, so he gathered up the reins and mounted. "I know you're tired boy, but we have to make sure Albert's all right."

Albert's cabin was on the east side of the property, about two miles from the school. Trent rode into the yard. The cabin stood intact, but debris cluttered the yard and a peach tree lay across the steps as though it had been yanked up and thrown there.

"Albert!" Trent walked around the cabin. The back door hung open. He stepped inside and checked the three rooms. Nothing seemed disturbed, but Albert wasn't in sight. He went back outside. An empty farm wagon lay upside down near the barn, and something seemed to be sticking out from beneath.

Trent ran to the wagon. An overalled leg protruded from under the wagon.

"Albert!" Trent lifted the side of the wagon and shoved it aside.

Albert moaned, and his eyes fluttered. "Trent, that you?"

Trent dropped to his knees beside the longtime servant. Albert hadn't called him by his first name since he was thirteen. "It's me, Albert. Lie still while I check you over, all right?"

"All right, boy. I be real still. Maybe you best get your pa over here though."

A pang of fear shot through Trent, but he knew he had to focus on what he was doing. Albert was obviously confused. And that could mean a concussion or worse.

He ran his hands gently over Albert's head. His fingers found a gash, sticky and wet. "I'm going to have to turn you over. You seem to have a cut on your head."

Albert didn't answer, but his breathing was even. Trent assumed he was unconscious again. When he turned him over, his left arm hung crookedly. Trent laid him down as gently as he could. But the gash had to be examined first. Especially as disoriented as Albert had seemed.

He retrieved his bag and removed the needed supplies. When he'd cleaned the wound, he was pleased to see that although it had bled a lot, as head wounds often did, it wasn't very deep. After applying disinfectant, he bandaged the cut then turned Albert over once more and set his arm. Albert woke up and yelled as he splinted and bandaged the arm.

"Albert, it's okay. You have a broken arm. I'm attending to it."

"Dr. Trent, how Virgie and all the little young'uns and everbody at the school?"

"They're fine, Albert. No one has a scratch. And the buildings are all standing." Thank the good Lord Albert was lucid.

"Glory be. I saw that old twister comin' from that direction, and I was scared somethin' fierce."

"So was I. But they're all fine. What happened here?"

"I was heading for the storm cellar when that old wagon come flying out of nowhere. That's the last thing I remember." He shook his head. "I don't see how it still laying there all in one piece. Wonder where the other three wheels be."

"That's a puzzle, but these things happen quite often with tornadoes. Or so I hear. Well, I'd better get you over to the porch, and you can rest until I get your horse saddled up. I don't want you staying here alone until I'm sure there are no side effects from that head injury."

"I'm sure I'm all right, but if you say so, I'll go."

Trent kept a steadying hand on Albert until the older man was seated on the porch then turned and started toward the barn.

"Where you going? Old Betsy tied up out front."

Maybe Albert wasn't as clearheaded as he thought. "Are you sure you left her there? I didn't see her when I rode up."

"Aww. She must have broke loose and run off."

"Well, there's no telling how far she ran. She'll more than likely come back. We can keep an eye out for her."

But how was he going to get Albert back to the school. He wasn't about to leave him here alone. "We'll have to ride double, Albert. Do you need me to get anything from the cabin for you?"

"No, I always keep a change of clothes in the barn at the school, just in case I need them."

"All right then, let's go." Trent helped him up and walked slowly around to the front. He helped Albert up then climbed up behind him.

He kept Warrior at a slow trot so Albert's arm or head wouldn't be jostled.

The sun had set when they rode up to the school. Trent slid off the horse as Virgie slammed out the front door and down the steps.

"Is Albert hurt? Oh sweet Jesus." She stood wringing her apron as Trent helped her old friend from the horse.

"I'm all right, Virgie. Don't you worry about me none."

"He has a broken arm," Trent said, "and a cut on his head. We'll need to watch that." Trent helped him up the steps. "Can you have someone make up a room for him?"

"I sure can. You just set him down on the settee in the parlor for now, Dr. Trent."

Trent grinned. Virgie could be bossy, especially when she was worried. "Yes ma'am, Miz Virgie, ma'am." He walked Albert into the parlor and made sure he was comfortable. "Maybe Selma could send a tray in for him, too."

"They just sounded the gong. I'll get him a tray myself and send

Sally May to make a bed for him."

"Good, what would I do without you?" Trent said.

"You do fine in some ways, and not so fine in others, I expect." Her eyes crinkled as she smiled.

He laughed. "I need to go home and make sure Solomon and Carrie are all right. I know you must be worried."

"They fine, Dr. Trent. I should have told you right away. Solomon came a little while ago because they were worried about their baby. He grabbed Hunter up in his arms and just about squeezed the breath plumb out of him." A soft smile touched her lips. "He took him home to his mama, and that little angel was ready to go."

Trent nodded. "I'm sure he was. Did Solomon say if the house or outbuildings were damaged?"

"No damage at all. He said tell you that twister must have been high in the sky when it passed them. They got lots of rain and wind though."

"In that case, I'll stay here and clean up the infirmary. It looks like you've already got the foyer in perfect shape." Even the floor was polished to a shine.

"Abigail in the infirmary sweeping up now. Wasn't too bad in there. Would you tell her supper is ready and both of you come eat? We've set the table up in the library. I'll get that tray now." She headed for the kitchen.

Trent stepped into the infirmary. Abigail stood on a stool dusting the top of a supply cabinet. Her hair was tied back with a blue bandanna, and her auburn curls cascaded halfway down her back. She turned and started when she saw him, but immediately she composed herself and her lips turned up into a smile. He caught his breath. He'd never seen anyone as beautiful as Abigail James was at that moment.

❧

Abigail was conscious of every stain and damp spot on her dress. She was a mess from straightening and scrubbing her classroom and cleaning up broken crocks of preserves, fruit, and pickles. She tried to compose herself as she placed her hand in Trent's and stepped down onto the hardwood floor. She'd thought he was gone for the day. Otherwise she'd never have come into the infirmary and let him catch her looking like this.

"Thank you, Dr. Trent." The laugh she attempted sounded more like a hiccup. "I hope you don't mind me intruding into your domain. If I'd known you were coming back, I'd have waited."

"On the contrary, I appreciate your doing this, although I certainly didn't expect it."

She blushed as he continued to hold her hand. Gently, she withdrew it.

"You must not have heard the supper gong. I think we're both expected in the library posthaste."

"The library?"

"Yes, because of the chandelier."

"Oh, of course. I'd forgotten." She gave a quick glance at her attire. "Please tell everyone I'll be there in a few minutes and not to wait. You must all be famished."

She slipped through the door and hurried up to her room, which had remained untouched by the storm. She unbuttoned her blouse as she walked toward the washstand. Bless Sally May. The pitcher was full of warm water.

Ten minutes later she crossed the foyer to the library in a clean, if slightly wrinkled, dress. Delicious aromas drifted through the door, but she was still flustered by the doctor seeing her dirty and unkempt and doubted she could eat a bite.

One table was set for dining, and the other held platters and bowls of food.

"Ah, there she is." Charles looked up from his heaping plate. "We took you at your word, my dear, and did not wait. Please help yourself to supper. The kitchen staff is busy trying to get things back in order and said we must fend for ourselves. Although, as you can see, they still managed to prepare us a feast as usual."

Trent rose from his chair and walked to the food table with her. He handed her a plate then got one for himself.

"Oh, you're late to supper, too, Dr. Trent?"

"No, Abigail. He waited for you." Charles sounded amused. "And I think he was rather upset that no one else did."

She looked at Trent and saw him flash an annoyed glance at Charles.

He turned and looked down at her with a smile. "Pay no attention to him. I think he's a little delusional tonight. More than likely from being frightened of the dark cellar."

She shook her head and focused on her plate. She'd heard the two men engage in friendly banter before, but this was the first time she'd been the object of it. Was Charles implying that Dr. Trent was interested in her? She blushed and returned to the dining table with her plate. She glanced at Charles. He smiled. She frowned. He chuckled. She frowned harder.

"All right, all right. I'll be good."

She certainly hoped so. He was behaving like a twelve-year-old boy.

"You'll have to excuse him, Abigail." Helen's eyes twinkled. "He's so relieved that we got by with little damage and all the children are safe. I think he deserves to behave a little silly tonight."

Helen was right. She felt a little giddy herself. It must be for the same reason—and not because of Trent Quincy's smile or his deep blue eyes.

She smiled. "I'm ignoring him. Why aren't Felicity and Howard here?"

"They're eating upstairs. Trudy's and Jane's parents sent word they couldn't help out tonight."

Abigail nodded. The two neighborhood girls helped out part-time and sat with the children at suppertime, but she could understand their parents keeping them home tonight.

"Besides," Helen continued, "some of the children are still frightened. Felicity wouldn't have left them anyway."

"I wonder if Lily Ann is all right. She didn't want me to leave her." Abigail bit her lip. "I had to force myself to go."

"I know. I noticed that." Helen threw her a sympathetic glance. "It's good that she feels safe with you. But you need to remember you are her teacher, not her mother."

"I would have thought her parents would have come to check on her. They don't live that far away." She cringed at the harshness of her voice.

Trent laid his fork down. "Perhaps something has detained them."

She bit her lip and nodded. "Of course. I didn't mean to criticize."

"I'm sure you didn't. But let me assure you, Lily Ann's mother and father love her very much."

"Yes, I know they do. My words were uncalled for." When would she learn to think before she spoke? What must he think of her?

"We all speak hastily at times. Please don't think I was reprimanding you in any way."

Oh dear, this was becoming very uncomfortable. One minute he was acting almost like a suitor and the next he was proving he owned the school. And everyone in it. No, that wasn't fair. She was being overly sensitive, as always. Maybe she was overtired. She should excuse herself and go to bed.

Helen pushed her chair back and stood. "Well, I don't know about the rest of you, but I'm exhausted. Good night, everyone."

As both men stood, Abigail rose. "Yes, I was thinking the same thing. I'm almost going to sleep at the table."

She walked to the door, but as she slipped through, her dress caught and she heard a rip.

Trent was at her side before she could see what was holding her. "Here, let me. I believe a splintered piece of wood is holding you captive."

He freed her skirt then leaned slightly toward her. "Abigail, I had intended to ask you to sit with me for a while on the front porch. Perhaps tomorrow?"

"Oh." Was he going to chastise her for insinuating his friends weren't good parents? Even though she'd apologized, and he'd said everything was fine? "Dr. Quincy, if you wish to speak to me about something important, of course we can talk now."

"No. It can wait. I know you must be very tired. As we all are. I'm staying tonight in order to go over some things with Mr. Carter. Perhaps if you have some free moments between classes tomorrow, we could talk."

"Very well. Good night then."

❧

Trent watched Abigail sail up the stairs. Or maybe she floated. She was the most graceful creature he'd ever seen. In spite of getting caught on splinters. Now what was he going to talk to her about tomorrow so she wouldn't know he'd been so desperate to spend another few minutes with her, he'd lied just to keep her there?

He brightened as a thought came to him. He'd ask to observe one of her classes. Lily Ann's. That would be a reasonable request.

Behind him, he heard a low chuckle and turned.

"Man, you've got it bad." Charles walked over and slapped him on the shoulder. "Why don't you just tell the girl how you feel and put the both of you out of your misery?"

Chapter 14

Abigail hid a smile as the class erupted with laughter. The children had challenged Trent to a signing contest, and they were far ahead of him. He'd just tried to finger spell *puppy* and had made the sign for *K* instead of *P*.

"You're funny, Dr. Trent." Sonny chortled.

Trent gave an exaggerated sigh. "I know. You've all beat me. I suppose you want to collect your prize soon."

"Yes!" The word resounded across the room.

"All right. An ice cream party at the creek on Saturday. But you all have to help me crank the freezer."

"Can we have chocolate?" someone called from the back of the room.

"No. Banana." Lily Ann frowned and plopped her hands on her hips.

Abigail stepped forward. Time to intervene before an argument broke out. "We'll take a vote. Everyone write your favorite flavor on a slip of paper, and I'll gather them up. Lily Ann, you may whisper to me." A thought came to her. "No. On second thought, whisper to Dr. Trent. I'm sure he'll be kind enough to write it down for you."

A strange look crossed his face then he smiled and bent over so Lily Ann could whisper in his ear. Good, it had made him think. At least for a moment. He certainly needed to think. It was ridiculous to make the child wait while he chased around trying to find a cure for her. That might happen tomorrow or next year or never. But in the meantime, there was a way for Lily Ann to read and write. Perhaps she wouldn't have to say another word on the matter.

She gathered the slips of paper and placed them on the desk, motioning for Trent to do the same with Lily Ann's.

Trent put the votes in four separate piles then looked up, a gleam in his eye. "Vanilla, two! Peach, two! Chocolate, two! Banana"—he held his arm up high—"is the winner with three votes!"

Lily Ann and two other children cheered.

Abigail felt something akin to joy as she watched him play with and tease the children. Trent was a good man, kind at heart. God would speak to him, and he'd do the right thing about Lily Ann. She was sure of it.

The bell rang, and she dismissed the class, except for Lily Ann. She took the little girl's hand. "Dr. Trent is going to be with us for our lesson today. What do you think of that?"

"To our special place in the woods?" Lily Ann frowned then nodded. "I guess that will be all right."

Abigail detected surprise on Trent's face as he glanced from Lily Ann to her. He was one of Lily Ann's favorite people. Abigail was sure he still was. But she and Lily Ann had a special student and teacher bond.

They walked across the lawn to the woods with Lily between them, holding their hands. When they reached the woods, she tugged her hands loose. She could feel her way from here. Abigail watched Trent's obvious amazement as she went ahead of them, making her way from one familiar tree or bush to the next.

"How does she do that?"

"Her sense of touch is very strong. It's as though she sees with her hands. Her senses of smell and hearing are extra sensitive as well. Hadn't you noticed?"

"Hmmm. I guess not. But we're usually playing or teasing each other when we're together."

She smiled. "Yes, I've noticed. She's crazy about you, you know."

"Well, it's mutual." He grinned. "She's my girl."

Abigail's heart did a flip-flop as his eyes sparkled. She glanced away. "Oh, here we are. And your girl is waiting by our special tree."

"Ah yes. This is probably one of the oldest live oaks on the property. I used to climb it when I was a boy."

"You did, Dr. Trent?" Lily's mouth dropped open. "I didn't know it was that old."

Trent laughed. "Well, it's much older than I am, Lily Ann, if you can believe it."

As Abigail began Lily Ann's spelling lesson, she sent a silent prayer up to God to open Trent's eyes without a word from her.

Lily excelled in her spelling and signs. When they were finished Lily Ann reached over and found Trent's hand. "Now it's story time. Have you ever heard of *Alice's Adventures in Wonderland*?"

"No, I don't believe I have. Is that the story Miss Abigail is reading to you?"

Lily nodded. "Uh-huh."

Abigail opened the book. "Do you remember what Alice was doing when we left off, Lily Ann?"

Lily Ann's face went blank then a frown puckered her forehead. "I can't remember. I'm sorry. It's been two weeks."

"Oh Lily, it's all right, sweetheart. A lot has happened to us since then. I'm not sure I recall very well either." She patted Lily's hand. "Why don't I read the last chapter over?"

Lily nodded. Abigail tried to make the chapter as alive as possible as she read it again.

Soon Lily seemed to forget her disappointment. After every paragraph she'd say, "I remember now."

By the time they returned to the school, Lily was laughing with Trent and seemed to have forgotten the incident.

After Lily Ann had disappeared into the dining room, Abigail stood in the foyer with Trent.

"Are you joining us for dinner, Dr. Trent?"

He shook his head. "I received a telegram inquiring about the director's position. I need to reply and let him know what information to include on the application."

"Well, at least you have one person interested. I hope it works out. Mr. Carter will be leaving in a few days."

"I probably won't be here tomorrow. I need to check on some folks getting over the measles. So I'll see you on Saturday."

"Oh yes. The ice cream party." She laughed.

"I'll ask Carrie to mix up the ingredients, but she'll probably make me mash the bananas." Suddenly he sobered. "Abigail, I want you to know I'm considering your request to teach braille to Lily Ann. But I still haven't made a decision."

She nodded. "Thank you for letting me know."

She smiled as he walked out the door. She had a feeling Dr. Trent's decision would be yes. And the sooner the better.

❧

Trent dressed and ate a quick breakfast. He'd seen most of his recovering patients over the past two days. He planned to visit the last two families today so that he could spend tomorrow at his office in Mimosa Junction. Once Carter left on Monday, he'd need to be at the school most of the time. Unless, of course, a medical emergency occurred.

Every attempt to find a doctor who was free to cover his medical responsibilities had failed. He sighed. When had life gotten so complicated? At least the telegram was on its way to this P. H. Wellington. He hoped the man would prove to be qualified and of good reputation. And that he could start soon.

His first stop was the Benson farm. All three of Hattie and Bob's children had come down with measles. They'd been well on their way to recovery when he'd visited last week. Both boys were outside playing and came running when he pulled up to the weathered frame house.

"Hi, Doc Trent." Five-year-old Tobe's gap-toothed grin met him at the front step.

"Hi, Tobe. You look like you're feeling better." He grinned at Tobe's older brother, Sam, who had hopped up onto the porch. "You, too, Sam."

The front door opened and Hattie stood there smiling, holding Mary, the baby, on her hip.

"Morning, Dr. Trent."

"Good morning, Hattie. I can see by your smile that all is well."

"That's the truth. Thank the Lord." Her smile faded. "But Bob's sister Nancy's been down with the miseries."

"Nothing serious, I hope."

"I dunno. We ain't seen them for a couple of days. Bob's been busy getting the harvest in, and I had the young'uns to tend to. She was feeling mighty poorly the day before yesterday though."

"Maybe I'd better ride by there, just in case."

Relief crossed her face. "That'd ease Bob's mind a lot. He worries about Nancy, what with that no-account husband of hers. Were you wanting to come in?"

"No, since everyone is well here, I'll be on my way and stop by Nancy's before I finish my rounds."

She glanced up at the sky. "Hope you don't get drenched. It looks like something might break loose any minute."

"Maybe it will pass over. See you at church on Sunday?"

"I'll try, Dr. Trent." She glanced away, avoiding his eyes. "You know how it is with three little ones."

"I understand. Well, I'll still hope to see you there." He smiled and walked back to his horse. "You boys help your mama, now."

He mounted his horse then waved to the boys as he rode away. He'd been praying for the Bensons since he'd taken over this practice. Although they were nice, friendly folks, as far as he knew they never opened a Bible, and he'd never seen them in church. If folks could only realize what a difference a relationship with God could mean in their lives.

He reined Warrior in when he reached Nancy and Tom Williams's cabin. Not seeing anyone in the yard, he stepped up onto the stoop of the porchless log house and tapped on the door. When he received no answer he tapped again. He heard a scuffling sound inside and something scratched at the door then a dog whined.

Concerned, he gave a push and the door swung open. Ten-year-old Frannie stood swaying in the doorway. Her bloodshot eyes peered at him imploringly. "Doc, we're awful sick."

He caught her as she fell. Her thin body didn't weigh much. He glanced around and saw that Nancy was asleep on the big bed against the wall, with Tom sprawled out by her side. At least he hoped they were both sleeping. The odor in the cabin was vile, and ordinarily Nancy kept the shabby little home nearly spotless.

He laid Frannie on her cot on the other side of the room. Her pulse was a little rapid and her skin warm to the touch. He covered her with the ragged blanket that had fallen to the floor and went to check on her parents.

A quick look at Tom confirmed his suspicions. The man was sleeping off some heavy drinking. He turned his attention to Nancy, who lay still and limp. Her nightgown was stained and damp, and her skin hot. Trent put a thermometer between her lips and held it there. When he saw how high the mercury was, he took a sharp breath. He was pretty sure Nancy had more than what the folks around here called the miseries. It looked like influenza. And in her worn-out condition, that could be serious.

He got a dipper of water and poured it over Tom's head. He'd need the man's help, whether he liked it or not.

Tom gasped and sputtered. "What the. . ." He looked bleary-eyed at Trent. "What'd you go and pour water on me for, you. . ."

Trent ignored the filthy words that proceeded from the man's mouth.

"Your wife and daughter are very sick." He shot the words at Tom. "I need you to sober up and help me."

"Aw, there ain't nothin' wrong with that lazy woman." He sneered then his eyes widened. "It ain't catchin', is it?"

"Yes, it's *catching*, and you've already been exposed. So maybe you'd better help me get them well. Otherwise you won't have anyone to take care of you when you come down sick." He knew the words were cruel, but he didn't really care at the moment. How could a man drink and sleep when his family was ill?

Tom stumbled out of bed and staggered outside. He was back in a few minutes. Not bothering to even glance at Nancy or

Frannie, he went to the stove in the corner and set a tin coffeepot in the center to heat.

By cajoling and threatening, Trent managed to get the man sobered up.

Apologizing profusely for getting drunk, neglecting his family, and numerous other sins Trent would have just as soon not heard, Tom turned out to be fairly helpful.

Several hours later, Trent rode away satisfied they'd be all right. That was, if Tom stayed sober enough to take care of them. Maybe he'd better not count on that. He turned and rode back the mile and a half to the Bensons' place. After being assured that they'd go every few hours and check on Nancy and Frannie, he turned and continued his rounds.

He discovered one more case of influenza that day, and when he went to his office the next day, he found there were several cases in town.

His part-time nurse, Wanda, stayed by his side as he visited patient after patient and left medicine and instructions. Two days later, just after sunset he packed up his medical bag, mounted Warrior, and headed home. His head throbbed, and he could barely swallow from the fiery pain that clutched at his throat. He was ready to drop off his horse by the time he rode up to the stable.

Solomon appeared at his side and grabbed him around the waist. "Steady there, now. Let me help you to the house. You're about to pass out."

Trent managed to mumble his thanks as he staggered into the house supported by his friend. The next thing he knew he was being carried up the stairs in Solomon's strong arms. The last thing he remembered was Carrie's soothing voice as she placed a cool wet cloth on his head.

"Don't you worry none, Trent. You gonna be just fine. Me and Solomon, we gonna take good care of you."

He closed his eyes and drifted away on a warm blanket of peace.

Chapter 15

What could have kept him from keeping his promise to the children? He'd seemed almost as excited as they had. As their disappointment rose, Abigail's irritation turned to anger. He could have at least sent word if he was too busy to come.

She'd about decided to prepare the mix and go ahead with the party without him, but the thought of keeping nine children safe and out of trouble alone didn't appeal to her, and the other staff members were too busy to help. She assured the children that Dr. Trent would more than likely do it another time and that if he didn't, she would, but they continued to mope.

A few at a time, they went outside, and before long their laughter drifted across the lawn and through the back door. She smiled in relief. She only hoped Trent had a good excuse for his abandonment.

She took a book onto the front porch and sat in one of the wicker rockers. The rain of the past few days had stopped, and a cool breeze blew across her face.

Around noon she looked up from her book as the sound of hooves came up the lane. In the next moment, Solomon reined his horse up in front of the porch.

"Miss Abigail, I got a message for you." He made no attempt to dismount.

At the worried look on his face, Abigail jumped up, concern stabbing at her heart. "Solomon, what is it?"

"Dr. Trent done got sick, ma'am. He so weak he can't sit up, and me and Carrie been tending to him for a day and a half."

He paused a moment to take a breath. From the horse's heaving sides, Abigail knew Solomon must have ridden him hard.

"But a little while ago, he woke up, clearheaded for a change. He told me to ride over here and let you know why he didn't come for the ice cream party. Then he passed out again. Just like that." He yanked the horse around. "Gotta get back."

"Solomon, wait, what's wrong with him?" Her words fell on empty air as he galloped off down the lane.

She rushed into the house and shouted for Virgie. Running into the parlor, she found it empty. When she reentered the foyer, Virgie was coming from the dining room.

"Were you looking for me, Miss Abigail?" Her soft voice calmed Abigail's pounding heart.

"Virgie, Dr. Trent is ill. Solomon was here and gone so fast I didn't have time to find out what's wrong with him. Do you think Albert would take me over there?"

Virgie's eyes bored into her. "What you want to go there for? If Dr. Trent sick, Solomon and my Carrie take good care of him."

Flustered, Abigail bit her lip. "I just want to make sure it's nothing serious."

"If it anything serious, Solomon would have told me to come." Virgie sounded very sure.

"Well, I don't care. I'm going to see for myself." Abigail came close to stomping her foot then caught herself. But her hands curled into tight fists. Her fingernails cut into her palms.

Virgie's lips tilted. "You think I don't know you be loving that sweet boy? Nothing to be ashamed of."

Abigail opened her mouth to protest then blinked her eyes against tears that had suddenly pooled there. "Oh Virgie," she whispered. "I don't know if what I feel for him is love or not. But I know I care for him, and I don't know why."

Virgie opened her arms and gathered Abigail into their soothing comfort. "It's okay, baby girl. You don't have to know why. I know you is confused." She patted Abigail's back then gently pushed her away. "You go on and get ready. I'll tell Albert to hitch up the carriage and wait for you out front."

"Thank you, Virgie!" Abigail ran up the stairs and changed into her best dress. Next she donned her little green hat with the feathers. If he woke while she was there, she wanted to look nice for him.

She sat on the edge of the seat as they drove down the unfamiliar roads. "Can't we go faster, Albert?"

"Yes'm, we can cut across the property like Dr. Trent does on his horse, but then this here buggy would most likely turn over and spill us out. Then how'd your pretty dress and fancy hat be looking?"

Abigail started to laugh at his droll sense of humor then stopped and cast a disapproving frown his way. "Well, I don't think it's very nice of you to make jokes when Dr. Trent could be lying on his deathbed."

He cut her a glance from the corner of his eyes. "Still ain't sweet on him, I see."

She glared in silence.

"Aw, Miss Abigail. I'm just trying to take your mind off your troubles a little bit." He gave her a sympathetic smile. "Don't you weary yourself none. Solomon and Carrie ain't gonna let nothing happen to Dr. Trent. They love him like he was their own brother."

"They do?" Abigail forced herself to calm down. "I didn't know that."

"Oh, yes'm. They growed up together they did. Use to run all over the countryside together like three wild pups." He grinned. "Oh, the pranks they used to play. But no one could stay mad at them three for long."

"I see." Another interesting side of Trent that Abigail wouldn't have imagined. But oh, how she wished she could have been around to know that mischievous young boy.

They pulled up in front of a beautiful three-story white house with a columned porch. Almost a replica of the school, except on a smaller scale.

Carrie, in a clean blue dress with a white, starched apron greeted Abigail and escorted her up the stairs, her voice calm and soothing as she spoke of Trent's condition.

"He come home in a thunderstorm two days ago, so sick he could barely sit on his horse. He'd been working night and day for two or three days. He burning up with fever and half out of his head. Told Solomon he had influenza then passed right out. We took care of him best we knew how till he woke back up. Then we managed to find out what medicine to give him. He ain't done much but sleep since. I got a little soup down him now and then. But this morning he sit straight up and ask me what day it is. Then he tell Solomon to ride like the wind and let you and the children know why he can't come." She sighed. "Conked right out again and been sleeping ever since."

Abigail sat on the chair next to the bed and gazed at Trent's drawn face. A glass and spoon sat on the table next to him. And a wash basin was on the floor with a cloth inside.

"Sorry 'bout the wash pan. I just finished giving Trent, I mean Dr. Trent, a cool sponge bath when you came." She bent over and picked up the basin. Turning, she smiled at Abigail. "He probably gonna be mad at me for letting you see him like this."

"Do you think he'll be all right?" Abigail had cared for sick children before, but never a full-grown man. His pallor beneath the black two-day beard alarmed her.

"Sure he will. He always been strong. Little fever and sickness won't kill him. Just make him feel like he dying."

She stepped out of the room and closed the door softly behind her.

Abigail looked at the shock of black hair that fell across Trent's face. Unable to resist, she reached out trembling fingertips and smoothed it back.

He moaned and turned slightly. She jerked her hand back, heat rising to her face. Goodness, what was she doing?

His eyes opened and gazed at her. Something like awe flickered there for a moment, and then his lashes fluttered down and a soft sigh escaped his lips.

Abigail smiled. He was going to be all right.

❧

Trent opened his eyes, blinking to clear his blurred vision. One small lamp burned on the corner table. Otherwise, the room was dark. He glanced around, and his heart lurched when he saw a shadowy form in the rocking chair across the room. Abigail? The figure moved and Carrie stirred in her sleep. Disappointment flooded him. It must have been a dream. Well, of course it was a dream. Why would Abigail have been sitting at his bedside while he slept? Still— He smiled. There was no denying it had been a beautiful dream. He sighed.

Carrie stirred and sat up, yawning. Glancing his way, her eyes widened and she stood and came over to his bedside. "You really awake or still out of your head?"

Trent laughed, a weak sound to his own ears.

Carrie grinned. "I knew you'd decide to wake up in the middle of the night when I was trying to get a few winks of sleep."

"How long?"

"Two days and three nights. You were a sick man, Trent." She poured a fresh glass of water from the pitcher.

He tried to sit up, but weakness caused him to flop back down.

"Here let me help you. You gonna be weak for a few days." She slid her arm behind his shoulders and helped him to scoot up then arranged the pillows behind him.

"Two days? I promised the children an ice cream party on Saturday."

"That's all right. Solomon rode over and told Miss Abigail why you couldn't make it." She gave him a keen glance. "You had some company yesterday."

"Who?"

She grinned. "Miss Abigail James, all dressed to a T and wearing a hat that looked like a big old bird on it."

"She was really here? I thought I dreamed it."

"She here all right. Made Albert drive her over, fussing at him all the way to go faster." She chuckled. "Albert say she sweet on you."

121

He cut her a glance. "Albert doesn't know what he's talking about."

"Uh-huh. I told him you sweet on her, too."

He started to sit up then plopped back down. Maybe he'd better lie there awhile longer.

"So you really think she likes me?"

"I didn't say it. Albert did." She flicked a thread off her skirt and started humming.

"But what do you think?"

"Ain't my place to think nothing. I'm just your cook and housekeeper."

Trent snorted. He closed his eyes and moaned. "I don't feel so well. I'm going back to sleep."

When he awoke the sun was streaming in his window. It must be at least midmorning. He sat up and swung his legs over the side of the bed, yawning. The door opened and Solomon came in.

"Trent. You sure you oughta be doing that?"

"What? Yawning?"

Solomon chuckled. "I reckon you must be feeling better."

"Much better. And starving." He stood and walked slowly to the washstand.

Solomon slid a chair over beside him. "Just in case you need it. I'll go tell Carrie to fix you some breakfast."

"A lot. Tell her to please fix a lot. And Solomon, would you bring Warrior around? I need to go to the school."

Solomon gave him a frown. "Carrie gonna have a fit if you ride out of here today."

"I have a lot to do. I promised those kids a party and didn't show up. I need to let them know we'll still have it. Besides, Carter is leaving today, and I need to be there to see him off." He poured water into the basin. "I'll be all right."

An hour later he mounted Warrior and rode away, an exhilarating sense of freedom washing over him after several days of being incapacitated.

He arrived at the school just in time to see Albert loading Carter's luggage into the carriage. He'd sent several boxes and a trunk on ahead the week before.

Carter came through the door followed by Virgie, who was holding Hunter's tiny hand. Carter bowed deeply. "Well Master Hunter, I'm sure you will be a good boy and make your grandmother and parents proud. It has been an honor to be your friend."

Hunter offered his free hand. "Good-bye, Mr. Carter."

Abigail stepped out onto the porch. "Oh Mr. Carter, I was afraid you'd leave before my class was over. Lily Ann and I wanted to tell you good-bye also."

Carter shook both their hands then turned and seeing Trent, nodded. "Once again, I do apologize for leaving before you have found a replacement, Dr. Quincy."

Trent shook the man's hand. "I have received a promising query and hope to hear back from Mr. Wellington this week. So perhaps it won't be such an inconvenience after all."

"I hope it works out. And now I'll say good-bye."

Carter got into the carriage, and Albert clucked to the horses and drove away down the lane.

"I'm happy to see you well again, Dr. Trent." A very attractive blush tinged Abigail's face.

"Thank you. It's nice to be out in the fresh air again." Should he mention her visit? Probably not. He had a hunch that was the cause of the blush on her cheeks.

"Dr. Trent, I'm sorry you were sick." Lily Ann tilted her head. "You know we didn't have the ice cream party yet."

"Yes, well, if no one has other plans, I thought we'd have our party after school today." He chucked her under the chin. "How does that sound?"

"Oh yes. Will that be fine, Miss Abigail?"

"I'm sure it will be, Lily Ann." The smile she turned on Trent about bowled him over.

"I hope Miss Abigail will come along, too, as we'd planned before."

"Sure she will. She was disappointed, too."

Abigail blushed again. "Of course I'll be happy to help out, Dr. Trent." She took Lily Ann's hand. "And now we need to go. We have lessons to do."

"Don't forget, Dr. Trent," Lily Ann called back over her shoulder.

"I won't. I've already asked Miss Carrie to mix up some good ice cream fixings for us. And I think she and Mr. Solomon are coming along, too."

Abigail looked back and smiled, her eyes glowing. "Then we'll see you later, Dr. Trent."

Trent watched them round the house. Maybe Albert was right. He hoped so. And one thing was for certain. Carrie had him pegged all right. He was definitely sweet on Abigail James.

Chapter 16

Trent handed his ticket over to the conductor to punch then leaned back, relieved to be on the last stretch of his trip from St. Louis and nearing home. The layovers in stations had been the most tiring aspect of the trip. A few had been comfortable but most had been a nightmare. The train was scheduled to arrive in Atlanta at 5:00 p.m. Just in time to check in to a hotel, take a hot bath, have something sent in to eat, and get a good night's sleep. Then tomorrow he'd pick Warrior up from the livery and head home.

He wondered if the new director had arrived yet. After several telegram messages back and forth, Trent had received a packet of references in the mail. Wellington's résumé sounded good, and after verifying the references, he'd hired the man sight unseen on a trial basis.

Once that was accomplished, he'd sent word to the school staff he'd be away on business for a week, and he'd left for St. Louis. The Missouri School for the Blind had been an experience Trent would never forget.

When he'd first arrived in St. Louis, he'd spoken with a skilled eye surgeon who had agreed to examine Lily Ann, but he'd cautioned Trent not to get the child's hopes up. From her medical records, it seemed unlikely there would be anything anyone could do to restore her vision.

The news had pushed Trent to the brink of despair. But the next day, he'd met Piper Allen. A seventeen-year-old boy, born deaf and blind, who had managed somehow to excel in both sign language and braille. The boy was cheerful and happy, and the staff at the school had high hopes for his future.

Meeting Piper had caused hope to arise once more in Trent's heart. If Piper could have a full and happy life with his double handicap, then Lily Ann could, too.

Trent's dread and fear since her accident had been that her life would be empty and filled with dreariness and grief. He knew now that didn't have to happen. Lily Ann was a strong child and a happy one. She'd more than proven her willingness and ability to learn even with limited resources.

He'd sent the box of books and supplies on ahead. He could hardly wait to see Abigail's face when she saw the teacher's manuals and equipment for teaching and learning braille. Of course, he'd also learned some things by observing and doing. He'd need to teach her these himself. He grinned. That might take a while.

A loud burst of the whistle announced their arrival in Atlanta.

With renewed energy, Trent bounded out of his seat and removed his luggage from the overhead compartment.

This time tomorrow he hoped to be seated on the front porch of Quincy School with Abigail. He'd watch the joy and excitement in her eyes as he regaled her with stories about his time in St. Louis.

And he hoped there would be a chance to talk on more personal things. Because he'd finally admitted to himself that Carrie was right. He was very sweet on Abigail.

≈

Abigail laughed as P.H. tossed her head, causing several blond curls to escape the tightly wound bun, and gave them the slam-bang finish of another funny escapade that had occurred at her last school.

"I can't believe you've been involved in education for thirty years. You look much too young." The words weren't flattery. They were gospel truth. Abigail would have guessed the new director's age to be between thirty-five and forty. But, with total openness, the woman had confided she'd turned fifty-two in March.

P.H. emptied her cup and set it on the table by her chair.

Immediately Howard was across the parlor and at her side. He picked up the teapot. "Here let me give you a refill, Miss Wellington."

Abigail pressed her lips together to hide the smile that threatened to break through. Both Howard and Charles were smitten with the new director, and they either couldn't hide it or didn't care to. Abigail and Helen had been hard-pressed not to tease them. Abigail was especially tempted to get even with Charles, who'd teased her about Trent.

"Thank you, Mr. Owens. That's very kind of you." The lady smiled gently as she had each time she was inundated with one of her admirers' attentions.

Abigail had worried ever since she'd laid eyes on P.H. this morning about what Trent's reaction would be when he realized he'd hired a woman director. She hoped he wouldn't send P.H. packing, because she had won them all over in the few hours she'd been here. But gentlemen in general didn't take too kindly to women in administrative positions. And she had a feeling Southern gentlemen were even worse. Of course they wrapped their attitudes up nicely in packages of chivalry and protection of the weaker sex.

Charles and Howard didn't seem to feel that way, but they were fascinated with the woman herself.

A huge box had arrived the previous day, addressed to Trent from Trent. Something he'd purchased on his business trip she supposed. She couldn't believe how much she missed him. Since yesterday she'd found herself peering up the lane every time she had an excuse to go outside.

She tried to tell herself she was simply eager for their doctor to be present in case of an emergency. But even she saw through that. After all, Dr. Lowell, who was retired, had agreed to take over Trent's practice while he was away. And Dr. Lowell was a very competent doctor.

Was it possible Albert and Virgie were right? Was this feeling she had for Trent love? Since she'd never experienced it before, she had nothing to compare it with.

The sound of her name drew her attention back to her friends and colleagues.

Helen smiled. "I was telling P.H. about your desire to teach braille."

"Oh." Abigail glanced at the director, who looked at her with interest. "Yes, I would love to teach braille to Lily Ann. But so far, Dr. Quincy hasn't given his approval."

"I see." Her blue eyes sparked.

Abigail almost cringed. She didn't want P.H. to have a negative view of Trent before she even met him. "Dr. Quincy cares deeply for Lily Ann. I've no doubt he'll change his mind when he realizes how much it would benefit her."

"And the former director's views on the subject?"

Abigail glanced around for a possible excuse not to answer.

Helen cleared her throat. "Actually, we've had a number of improvements in the school recently."

"Oh?" To Abigail's relief, P.H. turned her attention to Helen. "Please tell me."

"Until recently, you see, we taught only lip reading and verbal speech." Helen's eyes sparkled. "A couple of months ago, thanks to our former director and Dr. Quincy, we added sign language to the curriculum."

"I'm very pleased to hear that." P.H.'s eyes confirmed the truth of her words. "You'd be surprised how many schools refuse to change. I'm glad to hear that's not the case with this one. Perhaps I shouldn't have been so quick to judge your Dr. Quincy about the braille. We shall see what transpires."

She stood. "And now if you'll excuse me, I believe I'll retire for the night. I'm rather tired from the train ride and subsequent buggy ride on the rutted roads."

When she'd gone upstairs, Abigail glanced around at the other teachers. "I like her."

"Me, too." Robert's emphatic agreement set them all laughing.

"Oh dear." Helen wiped her eyes and laughed again. "It's been quite a day. I'm curious about Dr. Trent's reaction to our lady director."

So she wasn't the only one. Abigail nodded. "I've been thinking about that, too."

"I don't know what you two are worried about." Charles stood. "Trent will see her worth, the same as we do."

He walked out, and Helen rolled her eyes. "I hope he's right. But Trent's not going to be infatuated the way Charles is."

Abigail sighed. She knew she'd be saying a special prayer tonight.

She was the last one to leave, so she turned the lamps off and shut the door behind her. As she climbed the stairs, a feeling of loneliness came over her. Well, perhaps he'd be home tomorrow.

◈

Trent tossed and turned in the uncomfortable hotel bed. He should have been home by now. But he couldn't very well have refused to care for an emergency.

He'd awoken that morning, dressed, and walked downstairs to turn in his key and leave. But just as he reached the desk, a boy came running up beside him.

His face white with fear, the boy shouted at the desk clerk. "Ma needs a doc. I think she's bleeding to death."

The clerk turned a startled glance upon Trent.

"I'm a doctor, son. I'll go with you." He followed the boy across the lobby to the stairs.

They took the stairs two at a time. "Do you know what's wrong with your mother?"

"The baby's coming, I think. But it ain't time."

"Where is your father?"

"Don't know. He was supposed to get here last night, but he didn't show up."

They burst into the room, and Trent lost no time. A chambermaid stood helplessly wringing her hands, and three younger children stood crying.

"Get me some hot water and clean rags and sheets." Trent fired the words at the frightened maid. "Hurry. Don't just stand there. And tell the manager we need someone to look after the children."

By God's grace and Trent's skill, he'd saved the tiny baby and the mother. Afterward he had them transferred to the hospital. He'd left them in the care of the hospital staff, after promising the mother he'd see that her children got to her aunt's house about five miles from town.

The children were hungry, so he took them to a café then rented a wagon and mules for the trip to their great-aunt's house.

By the time he'd made it back to town, it was too late to start home on horseback, so he stayed at the hotel for another night.

Late the following evening, Trent rode up the familiar lane to the school. The house looked dark. Disappointment washed over him. He supposed he'd go home and return in the morning. He started to turn Warrior when someone appeared in the doorway with a lamp.

He dismounted and walked up the steps.

"Trent!" Abigail came out on the porch. "You're home."

His heart quickened at the lilt in her voice. He stood looking at her in the lamplight. "It's so good to finally be here."

"We've missed you."

"Has everyone else gone to bed?"

"Yes. Even the household staff. Would you like me to find something in the kitchen for you to eat?"

"No. I'm not hungry."

Moonlight touched her hair, and the gold in her eyes gleamed.

"Are you too tired to sit awhile and talk to me?" He had so much to share with her, but tonight he just wanted to hear her voice.

"I'm not tired at all." She blew out the lamp and went over and took a seat.

"Your box arrived." The corner of her mouth turned up. "The one you sent to yourself."

"Oh yes. I'll leave that here. I'd like for you to open it with me tomorrow morning."

"You would?"

He wanted to answer the question in her voice, but not enough to spoil the surprise when she saw what he'd brought.

"Yes. I think you'll be interested." He sat in the chair across from her. "I've been in St. Louis this week."

"Oh? You had business there?"

"Yes. I went to see a surgeon about Lily Ann. He wasn't very encouraging about her condition, but he did agree to see her."

"Oh. Well that's good. Did you make an appointment?"

"No. That, of course, will be her parents' decision." He paused before going on. "Then I paid a visit to the Missouri School for the Blind."

A sharp intake of her breath told him she understood the significance of his statement.

"Yes, I know you must have thought I was indifferent to your pleas concerning Lily Ann's education. But I did tell you I would think about it."

"Yes. Yes, you certainly did." She spoke breathlessly, but he could hear the hope in her voice.

"I met some very interesting staff members, as well as a few of the students." He drummed his fingers on the arm of the chair and wondered how to tell her about Piper in a way that would really impart the wonder of the young man.

He finally told her about the boy's amazing skills and the courage and joy that radiated from him, in spite of his double handicap. When he finally looked up, Abigail's eyes were swimming with tears.

She pressed a handkerchief to her eyes. "The man from France I told you about mentioned Piper. He'd met him when he visited the St. Louis school. I was amazed at what he told us about the boy's education, but you have brought his personality to life for me. Thank you, Trent."

"No, I should thank you. Your passion for doing more to help the children lit a spark in me, Abigail." He reached over and took her hand. She started but didn't pull away.

He told her how they'd allowed him to observe one of the classes in session. And about the little girl who was just learning to use a cane. He laughed. "She didn't want to use it at all. She felt she was doing perfectly well with her hands held out before her."

"Oh." Her eyes widened. "I hadn't thought of a cane. Why doesn't Lily Ann have one?"

"She does have one. Her father had it specially made for her. She doesn't like it either." He shook his head. "It's in the cupboard in my office."

"Hmmm. Would you let me have it, please? She really should start practicing with it. She got a thorn in her hand one day last week from carelessly grabbing on to a rosebush that was in the way."

"Yes, you shall have it tomorrow." He glanced into her eyes. "Abigail. . ."

"Oh my!" She jerked away from him and pressed both hands to her cheeks. "I've been so excited listening to you, I forgot the news."

"What news?" *Dear Lord, please nothing bad.*

"The new director arrived this morning. P. H. Wellington is all settled into her new quarters and eager to meet you."

"That's great news!" He stopped. And gave a little laugh. "For a moment I thought you said *her* new quarters."

She nodded. "Uh-huh. That's what I said all right."

A woman? He'd hired a woman? He pressed his lips together and breathed in deeply through his nostrils then let it out with a whoosh. "P.H. She deliberately deceived me. Well, I hope she hasn't unpacked yet, because she's going right back to where she came from!"

"What?" Abigail's brows furrowed. "Without even giving her a chance to explain? It seems to me you're being very unfair. And in case you've forgotten, we need a director. Badly!"

Chapter 17

A woman?" Trent exclaimed the words out loud as he rode to the school the following morning. How could he have made such a stupid mistake? He'd been berating himself most of the night until he finally fell asleep after midnight.

The woman had deceived him. That was obvious. P. H. Wellington, indeed. Using initials had been a deliberate attempt at subterfuge. He growled. And it had worked. Who would have thought a female would apply for an administrative position at a school for the deaf.

Well, she was in for a big surprise. This was only a trial. It said so right in the contract. He'd looked through it again this morning to be sure. Maybe when he sent her back to Savannah with her head hanging down in shame, she'd think twice before she pulled such a trick on anyone else.

A pang of concern ran through him. Abigail was right. They did need a director, and P. H. Wellington had been the only applicant for the position.

Maybe he'd at least give her a chance to explain herself before he fired her.

He rode around to the barn. Albert, avoiding Trent's eyes, took Warrior's reins and started to lead him away.

"Albert, wait a minute."

"Don't get me in the middle of this here ruckus."

Trent, a little taken aback, gave the old servant a surprised look. "I haven't said anything yet."

"You don't have to. Miss Abigail done told me what's going on with that director lady. I told her the same thing as I told you. I ain't getting in the middle of it."

"I guess you're taking her side though. I know you are." Trent frowned. "Do you want a woman running things around here?"

Something like a cackle emitted from Albert's throat. "I ain't sayin' nothin'."

"Fine, Albert." Trent stalked around to the front door and went inside.

A tall woman, with a twinkle in her eye that belied her severe bun and sensible black dress, stood in the foyer about to enter the dining room. She paused when she saw him. "Dr. Quincy, I presume." She held out her hand and flashed him a dazzling smile. "P. H. Wellington."

He took her hand and gave it a firm shake. If she thought she could charm him, she was mistaken. "*Miss* Wellington, may I speak to you in the director's office, please?"

Her eyes darkened, and she gave a short nod. "Yes. Of course. Is right after breakfast satisfactory, or is this an emergency?"

Feeling like a schoolboy reprimanded for rudeness, he stepped back. "After breakfast will be fine."

Virgie came down the hallway. "Dr. Trent, I see you've met our nice new director. Come have breakfast with the staff."

"Thank you, Virgie, but I've eaten already. I think I'll wait for Miss Wellington in her. . .or rather. . .the director's office."

Without another word, he turned and left.

By the time she joined him he had deliberately sat in the chair behind the desk. Instead of being flustered when she saw him there, something very akin to amusement crossed her face. Without comment, she sat across from him.

"Miss Wellington. . ."

"P.H. please."

"Miss Wellington, I believe I deserve an explanation." He tapped his fingers on the desktop.

"About what?"

"About why you misrepresented yourself." He scowled. "Pretending to be a man."

"I didn't misrepresent myself, and no one asked my gender."

"But you knew I would assume you were a man. P.H.?" He fired the accusation at her.

She sighed. "My birth name is Portia Hesbeth. Family names

that I've hated all my life. Why anyone would put such a hideous name on a baby girl I can't imagine, family name or not. So as soon as I left home to attend business college, I started going by my initials. But, yes, I suppose I did think you would initially think I was a gentleman. However, the letters of reference should have cleared that up. You did read my references?"

"Yes of course." Well, not word for word. Unease bit at him. Had there been something in the reference letters about her being a woman?

Her eyebrows lifted.

"Well, perhaps I didn't read them word for word."

"Then I suggest you do that. In the meantime I'd like to remind you we have an agreement. And since I wish to keep this position, I will hold you to it. So unless you find an actual misrepresentation in my application, I intend to fulfill my portion of the agreement."

He rose. "Very well, Miss Wellington. Then I hope you will remember that the children are the major concern in this school. And with that thought in mind, I'll leave you to your work."

"Actually, Dr. Quincy, today is Saturday." She smiled. "I hope we can consider this a truce. And to relieve your mind, if at the end of the trial period you don't wish me to continue here, then I will leave."

He nodded and left the office, stalking down the hall to the infirmary. The box of supplies sat in the middle of the floor. He turned at a tap on the door. Abigail stood there, looking like an angel in a soft print dress with her hair hanging softly in curls— except for the front part, which she'd pulled back.

"Come in, Abigail."

"How did your meeting with P.H. go?" She bit her lip, no doubt remembering his words from the night before.

He sighed. "I was rude. I made accusations before she had a chance to say anything." He motioned to a chair, and when she was seated, he pulled another one up for himself.

Sympathy crossed her face. "I'm sorry. And I'm sorry for what

I said last night. I know you must have been tired from your trip and shocked when you found out about P.H."

He nodded. She was making excuses for him.

"Well, she'll be staying for a while anyway." He stood and stepped over to the box. "I hope my attitude hasn't spoiled the surprise for you."

When he opened the box and began to remove the supplies, she clapped with delight. "Oh Trent, how wonderful." She picked up an object that was sharp on one end. "What is this?"

"That's called a stylus. It's sort of a pencil." He pulled out a flat, wide metal object with tiny holes. "This is the slate. The paper goes between these two parts. You punch the stylus through to make numbers and letters."

"Oh." Confusion crossed her face. "How can I ever learn this?"

"There are instruction books in here for teaching braille. Both reading and writing." He smiled. "They taught me the basics. I'll show you what I know."

Abigail went from one item to the next, awestruck. When they'd examined every object and riffled through the pages of the teaching manuals, they returned everything back to the box and Trent carried it up to her classroom.

"Trent, how can I ever thank you? Lily Ann will be so excited."

"Oh, wait. I almost forgot something."

He went back downstairs and retrieved the child-size cane from the infirmary then went back upstairs.

"Here you go. I hope you have better luck getting her to use it than the rest of us did."

She put the cane away and sat down looking a little overwhelmed. "Trent, I'm going to have to go slowly. There's so much for her to learn. Don't be disappointed if it takes a while." She bent her head and a ringlet fell across her cheek.

Trent reached over and brushed it back. "A little at a time. Of course. Step-by-step."

Just like his relationship with Abigail. One step at a time. There was no rush.

❧

Abigail had never had such mixed feelings. One moment, excitement and joy. The next minute, fear would overwhelm her.

Why hadn't she been content to teach what she knew? How could she have been so egotistical as to think she could take on such an enormous task. First she'd have to teach herself braille. Then she'd need to actually learn to read it. Then use the stylus and slate to write words and stories and lessons for Lily Ann.

It was too much. She should have taken off a few weeks and gone to the school to learn.

Finally she calmed down enough to think straight. What was it Trent had said? Step-by-step.

Of course. She arranged everything in the cupboard in the order in which she'd use them. Then she took the dreaded stylus and slate and put them away, too. She took out the *Learning Braille* book and carried it up to her room. She'd study it in her spare time. And as soon as she learned something new, she'd teach it to Lily Ann. They'd be learning together.

On Wednesday she and Lily Ann walked to their special lesson place and sat down beneath their tree. "Lily, the leaves feel a little damp today. Even through the blanket."

Lily ran her hand over the blanket. "It's not wet. Just cold. The ground isn't as warm anymore."

"Well, it is October." A few leaves had turned brown and fallen to the ground. But the live oaks were as green as they'd been in July. Apparently they really did stay green all year.

She pulled out a card containing the alphabet. "Look, Lily. I have something new for you to learn. She placed the card on Lily Ann's lap and guided her finger to a raised dot. "That's an *A*."

Lily's eyes widened. "Is it braille?"

"Yes. The key to your new world of adventure."

"When will you teach me?"

"I hope to understand it well enough so that I can begin teaching you the first letters in two weeks."

"So one dot is *A*?"

"Yes, but there is more to it than that. The placement of the dot is important, too. There are six places, you see. But I don't want to confuse you."

The expression on Lily Ann's face showed that Abigail had already confused her.

Abigail patted her hand. "Don't worry. Learning to read and write print is difficult at first, too. You'll learn. We both will. Soon you'll be able to read to your mama and papa."

"Oh Miss Abigail. They'll be so happy." She handed the card back. "Can we do our signs now?"

Abigail laughed. "Yes, we can. Now what am I going to do if the sighted children decide they want to learn braille just as you wished to learn signs?"

"Teach them, I guess."

"You guess? I guess, too."

Their laughter rang out across the small clearing.

After their lesson time was over, they gathered their books and papers and went in to dinner.

Abigail entered the foyer in time to see Trent offer his arm to P.H. She murmured something, and they both laughed as they walked into the dining room. Abigail's heart sank. Was Trent attracted to the new director he'd been so fired up against?

Oh. She chided herself. Why shouldn't he be? She, herself, certainly had no claim on him. And there was no denying the lady was very beautiful.

Her appetite suddenly gone, she stood for a moment, undecided about going in. Perhaps she'd go upstairs and study her braille for a while. She had no class for two hours.

The trill of P.H.'s laughter floated through the door. What was she finding so funny?

Abigail lifted her chin and stepped into the room. Trent rose as she approached her chair. He pulled it out for her. She glanced around, relieved to see P.H. seated between Charles and Howard.

How silly of her to imagine Trent was interested in the older woman. Why, she must be fifteen years older than he was.

"How is the braille coming along?" His eyes seemed to caress her, and suddenly she felt giddy.

"It's a little daunting, but I'm sure I'll be able to learn it."

"New things can often seem daunting, Abigail. I've no doubt you will conquer it in due time. Remember, one step at a time."

"I'm sure you're right, Dr. Trent."

"Doctor, I'd like to applaud you." P.H. glanced from Trent to Abigail. "As well as Miss James. When word gets around about how progressive this school is, I'm sure we'll have more students applying for entry."

Trent frowned and gave a short laugh. "I think we have about as many as we can handle for the present. Sometimes when quantity increases, quality decreases."

"Yes, sometimes it does, but it doesn't have to. More space and additional qualified staff can usually take care of that problem."

"You may be right." Trent took a drink of water. "But for now, I think we'll leave well enough alone."

"Even if there is a need? There aren't that many schools for the deaf or the blind in this state." She leaned forward, her face serious.

"I'm not sure there is a need. How many deaf or blind children could there be in this state?"

"Probably more than you think. But I wasn't speaking of taking only Georgia children. Some states have no facilities at all."

Abigail frowned. P.H. was right. She needed to be very diligent in learning to teach the blind. And the other teachers should learn as well. She glanced at Trent, who focused on his meal. But at least he didn't say no again.

Chapter 18

Harsh, cold wind sneaked its way down the back of Trent's neck in spite of his heavy jacket. Wishing he'd worn gloves and a wool scarf, he yanked his collar up and shivered, urging Warrior into a gallop. The norther had come up during the night, dusting the grass and trees with a light frost. Only the second week in November, it was early for a cold front in South Georgia.

He'd had a slow week at his office at Mimosa Junction this week and hoped it would remain the same. He hadn't been to the school in several days, and anyway, Abigail had been so busy lately learning and teaching, he'd hardly had a chance to speak to her.

On the other hand, he'd spent most of his time at the school with P.H. They'd discovered many interests in common, and he admired her business astuteness and insight. He chuckled. She had slowly won him over to the possibility of adding more students. If it proved true that there was a need they could fulfill, then come spring he'd start searching for more teachers.

He slowed Warrior to a trot when he reached the gate and leaned over to lift the wooden latch. Albert was nowhere in sight when he pulled up to the barn, so he led Warrior into his stall and removed the saddle and bridle.

Albert came rushing in. "Sorry, Dr. Trent. Just finished up my breakfast. Shore is a cold, frosty day."

"Yes it is. If you plan to be out here today, you need to stoke that stove up more. I wouldn't want you to get sick."

"More important not to let the livestock get too hot. I'll be fine. You know I don't get sick." He twisted his mouth and squinted his eyes in thought. "But I reckon I got a little rheumatiz' in that arm I broke."

"That's very likely. Use the liniment I gave you." Trent waved and headed for the house, hoping since it was Saturday Abigail might have a few minutes to talk to him.

The murmur of female voices drew him to the parlor. Virgie, Helen, P.H., and Abigail were ensconced on the chairs and sofas. Bright-colored fabric covered their laps, spilling over onto the floor. All eyes turned on him as he stood, feeling helplessly out of place. A pretty shade of pink washed over Abigail's cheeks.

"Dr. Trent!" P.H. bolted out of her chair, fabric tumbling onto the floor. "Just the man I wanted to see. I have a job for you." She sailed across the room and took his arm, leading him into the foyer.

Trent glanced back, but Abigail ducked her head and gazed intently at the red satin on her lap.

"I needed an excuse to escape. Never was much for creating things with a needle and thread." She laughed. "Now I'll have to find something for you to do so I won't be guilty of lying."

"What are they making? Everything is red and green."

"Costumes for the Christmas concert."

"We're having a Christmas concert? Whose idea was that? They usually do a nativity play."

"They'll still have the play. The concert is extra." She smiled. "It was Abigail's idea. And I agree."

"But all the children are deaf except for Lily Ann. How will they sing?"

"You'll be amazed. Just wait." She tapped a finger against her lips for a moment; then her eyes brightened. "I know. We'll tour the third floor."

Puzzled, Trent gazed at her in confusion. "What on earth for? The third floor has been closed since the family lived here. It's only used for storage. The maids dust and air the rooms out every few weeks, but that's all."

"Yes, but we'll need it when we have more students. Let's take a look and see what can be done with it."

Trent shrugged. "All right, you're the director."

She stopped and turned her eyes full on him, a smile parting her lips. "You do realize my trial period is over. If you want me to leave, now is the time to say so."

He gave her a look of surprise. "I'd forgotten all about that, P.H. I think you're an excellent director. If you want the position, it's yours."

"Good." She looped her arm through his. "Let's go look at that third floor, shall we?"

Trent hadn't even seen the third-floor rooms since he brought some boxes down last Christmas. He sneezed as P.H. stopped on the landing. "Seems like it might be time to dust again."

She laughed. "A little dust never hurt anyone." She glanced to their left then to the right. The hallway stretched the width of the house in both directions then turned. "How many rooms are on this floor?"

"Let's see." Trent thought for a moment. "The old nursery is to the right. It consists of a parlor/playroom, a classroom, two large bedrooms, and the nanny's room. To the right there are three rooms which Virgie once told me were occupied by overflow guests when the house was full. Around the bend, in both wings are more rooms. They've been used for storage for as long as I can remember. I don't know what their use was originally. Perhaps they were occupied by house servants."

"Well, let's look at the nursery quarters first." She led the way and threw open double doors into a huge, empty room. "The playroom?"

"Yes, this was the playroom, and the schoolroom was just beyond. Although, it's hard to tell with all the furniture gone."

"And where might that be?" The eagerness in her voice awoke something in him. This was his heritage. His father and aunts must have spent their childhoods in these rooms.

"I suppose in the attic or perhaps stored in some of the other rooms. I'll ask Virgie."

They wandered from room to room, actually finding some nice

pieces of furniture in a few, but mostly they were either empty or filled with trunks and boxes.

P.H. opened a door in one of the rear halls and gave a gasp. "Look, bed frames. Dressers. Nightstands. Just standing here."

"There must be mattresses somewhere," Trent mused, running his hand across an oak headboard.

"Probably not in great condition after all these years. We'll need to have new ones made or purchase ready-made ones."

Trent frowned. "You're pretty sure the school is going to grow."

"I know it is. I feel it in my bones." She smiled. "And besides, didn't you tell me the St. Louis school was overcrowded?" She perched on the edge of a straight chair.

"Yes, but they're getting ready to build on."

"But if they are overcrowded, that indicates a need. We have to be ready to meet the need, Trent."

He tapped his fingers on the top of a small nightstand. "All right, P.H. We'll start getting the rooms ready with what we have in storage. But I'm not going to buy a lot of extra furniture and equipment until we're sure we'll need them."

"Perhaps we should move the school to the third floor and use all the second-floor rooms for bedrooms."

Trent threw his hands up and laughed. "Maybe we need to call a meeting with the entire staff and get some ideas before we do anything."

She snapped her fingers. "You're absolutely right. We should get some input. I'll schedule a meeting right away. Which day will work best for you?"

"I'm a doctor. Remember? Just set your day and time, and I'll be there if I possibly can. How's that?"

She frowned. "Not great, but I suppose it will have to do."

They checked the attic and found mostly broken pieces of furniture and old trunks. Trent couldn't help wondering what the trunks held and determined to check for himself someday. But for now, he planned to escape from P.H. and her plans and try to get Abigail alone for a few moments.

❧

Never had sewing seemed such a chore. Abigail concentrated on her stitches, determined to do a good job on the costumes in spite of her turmoil. She barely heard a word of Helen's chattering. Virgie wasn't saying much either. Could she be concerned about Trent and P.H. as well?

Oh for goodness' sake. Why should she be? And why should Abigail be concerned? It was none of her business if Trent had fallen for the director. But they'd been upstairs for over an hour. For what possible reason did they go up there?

That was it. She refused to sit here, a captive of her own foolish thoughts. She stuck her needle in a pincushion and stood, laying the costume on her chair. "Who wants a cup of tea?"

"I'd love one." Helen started to rise. "I'll help."

"No, no. I can get it. Virgie? How about you?"

"No thank you. Don't want anything." She smoothed out the skirt she was working on, gazing at it with a critical eye. "This seam look straight to you?"

Abigail was crossing the foyer with the tea tray when Trent and P.H. came down the stairs. P.H.'s head was thrown back, and her laughter preceded her down the stairway.

They reached the foyer, and Trent stepped over to Abigail and took the tray from her. "Let me carry this in for you."

"Thank you, Dr. Quincy."

He gave her a surprised glance. "Why so formal?"

"Very well, Dr. Trent." She pressed her lips together and headed for her chair.

"Abigail, I wonder if I might speak with you when you're not busy."

She glanced at him, searching his face. "Yes, of course. We'll be stopping for the midday meal soon. Do you want to talk to me before or after dinner?"

"After, if that's convenient. It may take awhile."

P.H. frowned. "I was going to schedule the meeting with the staff after dinner."

Trent threw her a quick glance. "Surely the meeting can wait. I'd think perhaps after school one day. After all, it is the weekend." He turned back to Abigail.

P.H. slapped her forehead. "Forgive me. My zeal overcomes my common sense sometimes."

Trent laughed. "Your zeal is the result of a good heart. So I think it can be forgiven."

Abigail pushed back the pang of jealousy that stabbed at her. Trent was right. P.H. was a good-hearted woman as well as a wonderful director. She deserved the praise.

Abigail forced her attention back to her sewing as Trent left.

P.H. sat and picked up the fabric she'd been working on earlier. "He's such a delight to be around, and now that he's decided I'm not the big bad wolf, he's been very open to some of my ideas about the school." She gave Abigail a curious look. "However, the man needs a wife to smooth out the rough edges."

Dismay washed over Abigail. Had P.H. designated herself as the wife Trent needed?

"When are you going to be kind to the good doctor and let him know you return his affections?"

Startled, Abigail looked at P.H. "Excuse me?"

"Oh come now, Abigail. Anyone can see that Trent is enamored of you and that you return the feeling. That is, everyone knows it but you and Trent."

The smile started in Abigail's heart, spread to her lips, and set her eyes glowing. Warmth in her cheeks was a pretty good sign her face was red for everyone to see. She must have been wrong about Trent and P.H.

"That's what I been telling them both, but they don't pay no attention to me." Virgie, who'd been silent most of the morning, broke in now with her droll sense of humor.

Abigail couldn't help the giggle that emitted from her. "Nonsense. You're both imagining things."

"Uh-huh!" Helen grinned. "Well, if you let that man get away, it won't be our fault."

"All right. That's enough from all of you. We'd better pay attention to these costumes if we want our concert to be a success."

They worked until the gong called them to the dining room. Abigail's appetite had surprisingly returned, and she enjoyed the stuffed pork roast and baked sweet potatoes.

Her friends' words rang warm inside her when she went for a walk with Trent after dinner. The sun had come out, and the wind had calmed to a pleasant cool breeze.

They strolled down the lane to the bench beneath the magnolia tree.

"P.H. told me we'll have a concert to enjoy this Christmas." Trent leaned slightly forward and looked into her eyes.

"Oh yes. We'll start practices the week after Thanksgiving. All the children will sing. And Lily Ann will have a solo." Her eyes lit up as she spoke about the event. "She'll also have a special surprise for everyone if we can accomplish it in time."

"Oh? And what is that?" Trent smiled and took her hand.

She started to pull away then changed her mind and let her hand rest in his. "If I tell you, it won't be a surprise, silly. You'll have to wait like everyone else."

He laughed. "I'm sure it will be worth waiting for."

"Yes, it will. But what is our director's staff meeting about? She seems quite excited."

"Oh, she is. And since this isn't a surprise, I don't mind telling you."

Abigail listened intently as Trent told her about their plans to expand the school, opening it up for more students.

"Why, that's wonderful, Trent. Last week she mentioned her desire to do that, and I'm so happy you agree with her."

"It may be quite a lot of work for everyone. Especially you. If we do admit more blind children, we'll need teachers trained to teach braille."

"I don't mind helping. Charles and Helen are already learning with me. And I can hardly believe the progress we've made this past month." She looked closely at him. "P.H is very encouraging."

"Yes, she's a fine director, although quite opinionated in some areas. But, in spite of that, I rather like her." He laughed. "She reminds me of Carrie in a lot of ways."

Relief washed over Abigail. Carrie was his childhood friend. So what he felt for P.H. must be friendship, too. Abigail gave a little laugh.

"What? Did I say something funny?"

"No, I just had a happy thought." A very welcome happy thought. "I'm glad you hired her." And she knew she meant it.

"So am I." He gazed deeply into her eyes. "Abigail, there's something I have to say."

Her heart throbbed, and she lowered her lashes.

"Look at me, please, Abigail."

She looked full into his deep blue eyes, her lips trembling, and waited.

"I know we've only known each other a few months. But I've grown to admire the wonderful, kind, and thoughtful person you are."

Her eyes flooded with sudden tears, and she blinked rapidly.

"I love you." He spoke the words almost in a whisper, and yet strong and firm. There was no doubt he meant them.

Joy rushed over her like ocean waves.

"Oh Trent. I didn't dare to think— Oh! I love you, too. With all my heart."

A smile spread across his face, and he lifted her hand to his lips. Then he looked once more into her eyes.

"And you'll do me the honor of marrying me?"

She nodded. "I will be so happy and proud to be your wife."

His arms enveloped her, and she lifted her lips to meet his in their first wonderful kiss.

When the tender moment was over, she nestled at his side, lifting a silent prayer of thanks up to God.

"How soon?" he asked. "Can we marry soon?"

She laughed. "It depends on what you mean by soon. My parents will need to be here. I don't think my mother and father would be very pleased if they weren't invited to their only daughter's wedding."

"I'd hoped we could spend Christmas together as man and wife."

She sat up and faced him, her eyes wide. "This Christmas?"

"Can we? Is that too soon?" His eyes had taken on a boyish pleading.

"Oh dear." She put both hands to her cheeks. "But next week is Thanksgiving. Christmas is only a little over a month away."

"We can send a telegram to your parents to see if they can come that soon." He hesitated. "Or do you hate the idea of such a short engagement?"

"No. Not at all." She gave a little laugh. "Very well. If my parents can come. But not on Christmas Day."

Trent's eyes lit up. "How about the day of the Christmas program? We could get married directly afterward."

She puckered her brow in thought. "That might work. Let me talk to Virgie and Helen and P.H. They can help decorate."

"There used to be a grand hall. But it's divided up now. We could decorate the foyer and dining room."

"And the staircase. I can come down the stairs on my father's arm." She wondered if the starry feeling in her heart was reproduced as stars in her eyes.

"I'll take you to town to send that telegram first thing Monday morning."

Hand in hand they walked back to the house to share their good news.

Chapter 19

Trent stepped into the dining room, already festive for the Christmas celebrations in less than two weeks. He knew the women were scrambling madly to have everything ready to decorate for the wedding next week.

He'd been busy treating sick people all week, but having found himself free for the moment, had decided to sneak into the rehearsal.

A temporary stage had been built at the back of the dining room. If Trent didn't know better, he'd think it was a permanent structure.

A dark blue curtain covered with silver stars hung on the back wall of the platform, and a makeshift stable stood in front of it.

Molly as Mary and Sonny as Joseph crossed the stage.

"They'll have a real live donkey for the play." Trent turned at the whisper and smiled at Abigail. She tiptoed around and sat beside him.

After a wonderful portrayal of the nativity, they cleared the stage; then all nine children filed back out. The five tallest, ranging in age from ten to fourteen, made a straight line in back with the four youngest in front.

The piano had been moved from the parlor and stood at the far side of the stage. Helen stepped through a side door and sat on the stool.

Trent stood amazed as the children, deaf except for Lily Ann, sang "O Little Town of Bethlehem," "Joy to the World," and "Silent Night." Helen played each note firmly. The children's melody was off some, but the beauty of their voices and the worshipful look in their eyes was the most moving thing Trent had ever seen or heard. His eyes filled with moisture. This had to be a miracle.

"How do they do that when they can't hear."

Abigail slipped her hand in his. "Partly vibrations. And some of them can hear a little, you know." They sat and listened in silence until the children filed out.

"During the actual program, they'll remain where they are and Lily Ann will step forward. This is the moment when she'll have her special part."

"Hmmm. And you still aren't going to tell me what it is."

"No sir." Her eyes sparkled. "But as I said before, it will be worth waiting for."

"I can't wait. But to be honest, I'm more interested in the event that comes afterward." He ran his thumb across her hand and put his forehead against hers.

"Behave yourself, Trent." She smacked him lightly on his arm. "The children will see."

He grinned. "They won't mind."

She burst out laughing and stood. "I have work to do. Will you be here for supper?"

"I plan to if I'm not called away." He stood and gave her a peck on the cheek. "There. That was harmless."

She shook her head. "I'm leaving. I have to be in my classroom in ten minutes."

"I'll walk with you. I'm supposed to be helping Albert and Solomon work on the third-floor rooms."

"Howard is going to help today, too."

"Good. We can use the extra hands." The project was proving to be more difficult than originally thought. The floors all had to be revarnished. And some of the windows needed replacing. But the furniture was the biggest problem. A lot of the pieces they'd originally thought could be used were in need of repair. They also needed more desks.

P.H. and Trent had both made inquiries, and they'd already received plenty of indication that there were indeed children in a number of states waiting for a place to open up in a school. The parents of one deaf-blind child had heard of Quincy and had written to Trent.

Could they help the child? Trent wasn't sure, but thoughts of Piper wouldn't allow him to say no, although P.H. thought it was unwise to take the little boy, whose name was Davy.

Trent saw Abigail to her classroom and went up to the third floor, where the three men were already working with P.H. directing.

She came over to him. "It's going to be a glorious venture, Trent. With this floor for the school, we'll have more than enough room on the second floor to convert it into bedrooms."

He nodded. "I believe you're right."

"Have you seen your bride-to-be today? She's glowing like a lantern."

"Yes, I watched the rehearsal with her. I don't suppose you know what Lily Ann's special part of the program is, do you?"

"Of course I do." She swatted his arm with a rolled up paper she carried in her hands. "But I happen to know Lily Ann and Abigail want to surprise you, so don't try to play your tricks on me."

He laughed and went over to help Albert move a wardrobe out of one of the bedrooms. "Where is this going?"

"In storage for now. But P.H. say it's gonna end up in a bedroom on the second floor. Looks kinda big to go in a young'uns room. Don't you think?" He scratched his head and furrows appeared between his eyes. "Maybe she better think that over."

"I heard that." P.H. appeared as if out of nowhere. "Don't be silly. This wardrobe is going into one of the maid's rooms. But for now, into the back room on the east wing."

They hauled the heavy piece down the hall and around the corner. By the time they reached the back room, they were both huffing and puffing.

They both leaned against the door to catch their breath.

"So, you gonna be an old married man in a few days." He clapped Trent on the back. "I was startin' to think you ain't never gonna have a wife and children."

"I was beginning to think the same thing, Albert. But I was waiting for the right girl to come along." He yanked out a handkerchief and swiped it across his forehead.

"Well, you couldn't have done better than Miss Abigail. I had her pegged to marry you the first time I saw her."

"You did, huh?" Trent chuckled.

"Yes sir. I shore did." Albert smiled. "Miss Abigail ain't just pretty as a picture. She kind and good hearted. She make a good wife for a fine doctor like you."

"Thanks, Albert. I appreciate that. I respect you, too, you know."

"Shore, I know that. Ain't I been lookin' out for you since you been knee high to a grasshopper?"

"You have, Albert."

"And Virgie, too." He sighed. "I should of married that gal when we was younger."

Trent nodded. "I always wondered why you didn't."

"She married Thomas when she was just fifteen. After he died, she grieved so. Wouldn't look at no man." Sadness crossed the old man's face for a minute. "Besides, I figured she was too good for the likes of me. Her being the refined lady she always been. Your grandma took her under her wing when she was a little girl and trained her up herself."

Coldness washed over Trent like someone had poured ice-cold water over him, and he drew in a sharp breath. "Are you saying Virgie was a slave?"

"She was until your grandmother freed her. Just like me and my mama and daddy." He glanced at Trent in astonishment. "What did you think?"

Nausea hit him. "I thought my father hired her when he married Mother."

"Well, he did. After she was freed, she worked for your grandmother for wages. And then went to work for your mama and daddy. But she born a slave into your grandfather's family. That's just a fact, Dr. Trent."

"Carrie?"

Albert's eyes gentled, and he placed his hand on Trent's shoulder. "Carrie born free. So was Solomon. Don't be grieving, Trent. We's all free now."

ᚱ

Trent swallowed. "Thank you for telling me, Albert. I must have had my eyes closed not to know."

He worked quietly the rest of the morning. When he went downstairs, he found Virgie in the infirmary scolding Sally May for not cleaning the floor well enough. He stepped inside and placed his arms around her and hugged her tightly.

ᚱ

Abigail sat between her mother and Trent as the curtain came up and revealed a bearded Sonny leading the donkey that carried Molly through the streets of the little town of Bethlehem. They stopped at an inn then turned away, dejected, and went to the next. Finally an embarrassed innkeeper played by Donald Atwood, motioned toward the back of the inn. The curtain came down for a short intermission.

When it was pulled back up by Solomon and Charles, the stable stood. Inside were Mary, Joseph, and a doll baby Jesus. Lily Ann and the other angels did their parts, and two little shepherds stood aside as the wise men offered gifts.

The curtain fell again, and when it rose, the actors and actresses had been transformed into a Christmas choir. They stood in front of the stable and sang their heavenly songs. And while they sang, they signed each word, a few of them fumbling, others confidently. All with proud expressions on their faces.

Abigail heard Trent's intake of breath. The signing of the songs had been another surprise for him. When the last note was sung, Lily Ann stepped in front, carrying a small handmade book.

As she ran her hands over the page, she read aloud. "'For unto us a child is born, unto us a son is given.' Isaiah nine, verse six."

She stepped back and the entire choir finished the verse.

Then they all bowed their heads and the curtain came down.

Applause broke out in the dining room as parents, grand-parents, and family friends showed their delight and their support.

Abigail heard Trent take another deep breath. When he looked down at her, she gave him a radiant smile, not even trying to hold back the tears. "Worth the wait?"

"It was more than worth the wait." He narrowed his eyes and grinned. "That was very fast learning for a child her age. Did she really read it, or was it memorized?"

She held back the giggle that threatened to come up. "Maybe a little bit of both. But just wait until next year."

"Next year." He smiled and squeezed her hand.

She stood, slipping her hand from his. "I'll see you in a little while." She turned to her mother, and they walked out together into the foyer.

A large pine tree stood in the corner, decorated with strands of popped corn and dried berries. Ornaments sparkled from every branch, including many the children had made through the years. Brightly wrapped packages waited underneath. Some were the presents the children had made and would give to their parents after the wedding and Christmas feast.

"Abby darling. That was amazing." Susan James, coiffed and dressed to the hilt as befitted the mother of the bride, smiled sweetly.

"They worked so hard, Mother. They're wonderful." They started up the broad staircase. Butterflies had begun to dance in her stomach now that the play was over. In just a little while she'd be coming back down these stairs to meet the man she'd spend the rest of her life with.

"Yes, they are indeed wonderful. And I think your young man is fairly wonderful, too."

"Oh Mother, he is. I know you're going to love him."

Helen waited upstairs. They stepped into Abigail's bedroom. Her mother's wedding gown, which was now Abigail's, was spread out in all its glory on the bed. Pearls glistened on the bodice and lace fell from the sleeves and neck.

Her mother and Helen helped Abigail into the billowing dress and buttoned her up the back. When the gown was perfectly in order, her mother picked up the veil that would now adorn the head of the third generation. The fine old lace rested perfectly on Abigail's auburn curls.

"It seems like only yesterday I was wearing this dress, and your granny was arranging the veil for me." She sighed. "Someday it will be your daughter's turn."

Abigail's stomach jumped at the thought. "And you'll be here with us, Mother."

She glanced around the room. So much had happened in the six months since she'd first entered this room. She'd been so nervous and yet so overconfident at the same time. But with God's help, some of the things she'd aspired to accomplish had come to pass. Important things such as the sign language classes and braille for Lily Ann. And now that it was established, they'd be able to help more children in the future.

Her mother and Helen went downstairs. Abigail started down the stairway, between polished rails decorated with evergreens and red berries. Her father was waiting at the bottom of the stairs. She placed her hand on his arm, and as the music began, they walked through the lovely arched double doors into the dining room that had been so transformed. Petals carpeted the aisle where Lily Ann had scattered them for her. She walked slowly, her eyes on the face of her bridegroom.

The minister from their church stood in front of the stage, which was now hung with a beautiful red velvet curtain.

Trent stepped forward and took her hand. He promised to love and cherish her always. Abigail promised to love and obey her husband. Then the minister spoke the words that declared them one forever.

As their lips met in their first kiss as husband and wife, Abigail knew that this moment was only the beginning of a wonderful future together.

The Scent of Magnolia

Chapter 1

Georgia, February 1892

Helen Edwards flung the gown, for she couldn't rightly call the ruffled silk expanse of elegance a dress, into the growing pile on the floor of the cluttered third-floor storage room. At least, it was a storage room now, whatever it might have been in the Quincy family past. Bending, she pulled another sheet-wrapped gown from the ancient trunk, releasing a fragrance of spices and mothballs. Her breath caught in her throat as she shook out the lovely blue silk and held it in front of her.

She bit her lip as she gazed into the oval French mirror that stood in the corner. If only her hair was blond or black or even red. Her brown locks pulled up in a severe bun, appeared mousy against the shining blue fabric. She sighed and focused on the dress. Should she try it on? How embarrassing if anyone should walk in and catch her, the proper, spinsterish school teacher, primping in who-knew-how-many-decades-old fancy clothing. She cocked an ear. Hammering and other noises from the west wing assured her that Albert and his helpers were busy with the third-floor renovations. The Cecilia Quincy School for the Deaf would soon be moving their classrooms from the second floor of the old renovated mansion to the third with its much needed space.

Quickly she spread the gown across the trunk. Unbuttoning her sensible, dark brown garment, Helen lifted it over her head and laid it across a straight-back chair.

A moment later, the sky-blue silk slid down her small frame. She closed her eyes for a moment and ran her hands across the smooth, billowing yards and yards of the skirt. Then taking a deep breath, she opened her eyes. Her breath caught. Why, she looked young. Nowhere near her thirty-two years.

A gasp from the doorway was the only warning that she wasn't alone.

"Oh! Miss Edwards. You're so beautiful. You look just like a princess."

Her cheeks blazing and heart thumping, she turned to the ten-year-old girl standing in the doorway, her blue eyes enormous.

"Please shut the door, Molly." She was careful to enunciate and look straight at Molly so the child could read her lips.

Molly Flannigan hastened to obey and then stepped over to Helen. Her hand reached out. She jerked it back. "May I touch it?"

Helen gave a nervous laugh. "Of course you may. Then I have to change back into my own dress before someone else comes in here. By the way, what are you doing up here?"

"Miss Wellington sent me to find you. She wants to talk to you about something."

"Very well. Would you like to help me put these things away? Then we'll go downstairs together."

Molly chattered in her slightly high voice and clipped off words as she helped return the garments to the huge trunk. She exclaimed over each one. "But who do they belong to?"

"I'm not sure. They're very old, so their owners must be long dead by now. I suppose they belong to Dr. Trent." Helen smiled, wondering what Dr. Trent Quincy's new bride, Abigail, would think of them. Helen couldn't wait to show her. It would be like Abigail to cut them all down into dresses for the little girls and fancy vests for the boys.

Helen wrapped the blue gown in its old white sheet and placed it on top of the others. Sighing, she closed the lid with a thunk then walked down the hall with Molly.

"I sure wish I knew who owned those dresses. They must have been awfully rich." Molly shook her head in emphasis, causing her long black braids to wave from side to side.

"I suppose they were," Helen said. "It's my understanding the school's original benefactress, who was our own Dr. Trent's grandmother, was quite wealthy."

"Is she the one who freed all her slaves?" Molly turned her eyes up to her teacher.

"That's right." Helen nodded and gave the girl's hand a gentle squeeze. "I'm pleased you remember the facts you've learned about the history of our school."

Molly's eyes danced. "Mrs. Alexandra Quincy, widow of Mr. George Quincy, freed all her slaves ten years before the Civil War began. She gave them all land and a cabin and the opportunity to work for wages if they wished. Soon afterward, she moved into a small house on her property and told her son, Thomas, to make the big house into a school in memory of her youngest daughter, Cecilia, who was deaf"—her expression sobered—"completely deaf like me. And they named it the Cecilia Quincy School for the Deaf."

"Excellent, Miss Flannigan. Perhaps you can recite those facts during the end-of-the-year program."

"Really?" She giggled as they rounded the corner to the main hallway.

"Yes, really." Helen gave a gentle pull to one of Molly's braids.

"Miss Edwards?"

"Yes?"

"I won't tell anyone you tried on the dress."

Warmth rushed over Helen's cheeks. "Thank you. It would be rather embarrassing if anyone knew."

Molly nodded her head. "You want to know a secret?"

"Only if it's yours to tell and you want to."

"It is." She swallowed. "I used to try on Mama's dresses. You know, after she went to heaven."

Helen's heart lurched, and she paused at the head of the stairway, blinking back tears. "Oh sweetheart. I understand. It must have made you feel close to her."

Molly swallowed again then nodded. "Pa walked in one day and saw me. He hugged me really tight. But when I went home again at the end of school, they were all gone. And so was her picture."

Helen put her hand on Molly's shoulder. "I'm sure your father thought that was best for you."

"I know. He said we had to move on. But we'd see Mama again some day." Her lips quivered. "Do you think that's true? Will I ever see my mama again?"

Gathering the girl into her arms, Helen sent a silent prayer for the right words.

"Your mother knew Jesus and so do you. Yes, I believe someday you'll see her again."

A sigh of relief escaped from Molly's lips. "I believe so, too. It's just sometimes it seems so long. And. . .I can't remember exactly what she looked like anymore."

The conversation remained with Helen as she went about her Saturday chores. She wondered if Molly's father knew what his daughter was going through inside. Probably not. He'd seemed distracted ever since his wife had passed away two years before.

❧

Patrick Flannigan, with a grin he couldn't hold back, drove his buggy down the street toward home. He couldn't recall the name or the words to the tune he whistled, but its jolly rhythm matched the satisfaction he felt inside. Who would have thought his small leather shop would gain so much popularity. The last year he'd seen a steady increase, but in the past four months business had boomed. He'd need to hire more hands soon.

He stopped in front of the white frame house he'd called home since he and Maureen had married fifteen years ago. She'd have loved the improvements he'd made, especially the additions to the kitchen and the screened-in back porch.

But he knew, if she could see what was transpiring down here on earth, she'd be thrilled that he'd be bringing their little Molly back home soon. The school had been good for her. It had helped keep her from grieving too much. And she'd continued to learn things that would be helpful to her as she grew up. Her lip reading had improved and her speech was much better. He'd been tickled when she came home for Christmas and showed him the sign language she'd learned.

But it was time for her to come back home and live with him. Now that he could afford to hire more help he wouldn't have to work such long hours. And he could pay someone to care for her when he was away at work.

Hurrying inside, he picked up the clutter around the house then changed his clothes and packed a small bag. An hour later, he'd left his horse and buggy at the livery near the train station and was on the train headed out of Atlanta.

He sank onto a cushioned seat near the back of the car, grateful that the railroad now went through Mimosa Junction, a small town near Molly's school. Otherwise he'd be driving his buggy or a wagon all the way. Contentment washed over him at the anticipation of his little girl's joy when he told her the news.

૨*

Scuffling sounded through the room as the children entered and began to settle at their desks. Tommy Findlay pretended to trip and fell into his seat. A smattering of giggles greeted his comedic acting talent.

Helen, who stood next to her desk, decided to ignore Tommy's attempt to get attention.

"Boys and girls, please get settled and take out your history books."

All obeyed except Tommy, who hadn't been watching her lips. When he noticed everyone else, he hastened to remove his own book from his desk and look at the blackboard to find the page number. He darted a look at Helen, and relief washed over his face as he saw her indulgent smile.

When the books were opened, the children turned their

attention to Helen's lips, waiting for further instruction.

"I'd like for you to read pages 102 through 107 and answer the questions on page 108. If you need help, please raise"—a knock on the door interrupted her—"your hand. You may begin now."

She stepped to the door and opened it to find one of the maids with her hand raised as if to knock again.

"Yes, Sally May?"

"Miz Wellington ast me to ast you to send Molly to her office right now." She gave a quick curtsy then added, "If you please, ma'am. I'm s'pose to walk with her."

"Very well, just a moment please."

Helen walked over to Molly's desk where the girl was already reading her assignment. She touched the girl on the shoulder.

"Yes ma'am?" Curiosity filled Molly's eyes.

"Miss Wellington would like for you to come to her office, please. Sally May is here to escort you."

Molly's eyes widened. "Am I in trouble? I haven't done anything naughty, Miss Edwards. Truly, I haven't."

"Of course you haven't. I'm sure it's nothing to worry about. Put your things away, please, and go with Sally May." Helen patted Molly on the shoulder and waited for her to get her things in order then walked her to the door.

Helen's eyes followed the two down the hall. When they started down the stairs, she shut the door and returned to her desk.

A little twinge of worry tickled at her as she went about her duties and helped the children who needed her. It wasn't like their director to call the child out from her studies. Helen only hoped there was nothing amiss. Molly didn't need another tragedy in her life.

Molly didn't return, but soon Sally May tapped on the door again, this time with a note from P.H. Wellington, informing Helen that Molly was spending the afternoon with her father and asking her to come to the office at the close of the school day.

When she dismissed the children at three, Helen slipped into her room for a moment to freshen up. She poured water into the washbowl and dabbed the cool liquid on her face. A glance in the mirror assured her all her brown curls were tamed and secured in the bun at the back of her head. She smoothed her skirt then walked downstairs to the director's office and tapped before opening the door.

P.H. Wellington stood at a window gazing out across the side yard. She turned when Helen entered. Her drawn face sent a wave of dread through Helen.

"Please have a seat, Helen." She sat in her chair behind the desk and sighed.

"You're frightening me, P.H. What in the world is wrong?" She frowned. "Not another death in the child's family?"

"No, no. Nothing like that. Although it may very well be the death of Molly's future."

Helen sat with her hands tightly clasped in her lap and waited.

P.H. slapped her hand on the desk. "Patrick Flannigan is removing Molly from the school."

"What?" Helen sat up straight. "But why? Does he have complaints about our curriculum or something else?"

"No." The fiftyish woman reached over and patted Helen's hand. "He had nothing but praise for Molly's training and education."

"Then why take her out?"

"It seems Mr. Flannigan's business has prospered and now that he can take care of his daughter's needs—including a nanny, it seems—he believes she should live at home with him." She gave Helen a sympathetic glance. "I know you've grown fond of Molly. I've only been here a few short months and I care about her. And she's thrived under your tutelage. But he seems to have his mind made up. I imagine he misses her and feels guilty for leaving her here as long as he has."

"But he visits often and she goes home during the summer and on holidays."

"I know. But apparently his mind is made up." She paused for a moment. "Perhaps you should try reasoning with him. After all, you've been Molly's teacher for more than two years."

"What is that, compared with being her father for nearly eleven?" She bit her lip. "Oh P.H., Molly is such a bright child. And she's even shown an interest in teaching when she's older."

"Children often have dreams at her age that don't last."

"I know that. But at least she has dreams. I hate to see them dashed because of a lack of education." She sat up straight. "Where are they now?"

"He took her for a drive in his rented carriage. He promised to be back by suppertime."

Helen stood. "Pray, P.H. Surely one of us can make him see reason. At least we have to try."

"I'll pray, but I'm afraid I've already said all that I can to the man. I'll have to leave any reasoning to you, my dear."

As Helen sat in the parlor and waited, she lifted her heart to God. There must be a way to make him understand how important education was to a deaf child. Surely he would see. She'd make him see.

"Now what are you pining about, Miss Helen?"

She raised her head to see Virgie, long-time retainer, who had been born into slavery but now ruled the household staff with iron tempered with the gentility of love.

"Oh Virgie. Molly's father wants to take her home with him for good. How can I convince him he's wrong?"

Virgie eased her thin body down next to Helen on the settee. Her soft brown hand patted Helen's. "Have you asked the Lord?"

"Yes, I was praying before you got here."

"Did you ask Him the same thing you asked me?"

"Well, yes. Of course."

"What makes you so sure that's what's best for our Molly girl? Maybe the good Lord has a different plan. Maybe not. But you might ask Him what He wants instead of what you wants for that child."

Chapter 2

Where in the world were they? They'd been gone all afternoon. Helen paced her second-floor bedroom. Laughter floated up the stairs and in through her open bedroom door. She hurried out the door and glanced down the open staircase. Sissy, a young maid, had the newly hired Flora in tow. They disappeared down the first-floor hallway leading to the kitchen.

She turned to go back to her room but paused at the sound of carriage wheels. She stepped back out of sight and waited until the front door opened. Relief surged through her when Molly walked in followed by her smiling father.

Helen smoothed her skirt and patted her hair then started down the stairs. She arrived at the bottom just as Molly and Mr. Flannigan turned from hanging their coats on the coat rack.

"Miss Edwards!" Molly, with one braid loose and her black curls flying, hurried across to her and grabbed her hand. "We drove the carriage really fast. It was so much fun."

"That sounds like fun, Molly. Why don't you run upstairs and straighten your hair and clothing while I talk to your father."

"Can we take Papa up to the third floor and show him where the new classrooms are going to be?"

"If he'd like to see it, I'm certain we can."

"Oh no." Molly snapped her fingers. "I promised Lily Ann I'd help her with her arithmetic."

"Perhaps someone else wouldn't mind helping her," Helen suggested with a smile.

Molly's eyes brightened momentarily then her shoulders slumped. "No. I promised. Would you show Papa around while I help Lily Ann?"

"Now, Molly"—Mr. Flannigan gave an embarrassed laugh—"I'm sure Miss Edwards has things to do."

Helen hesitated. Perhaps this was her opportunity to speak to Molly's father uninterrupted. She threw him a brief smile. "Actually, I'm free until supper. I'd be happy to give you a tour of Quincy School's latest project."

"Thank you!" Molly threw her arms around her father's waist. "I'll see you in a little while." She hurried up the stairs.

Helen watched Mr. Flannigan as his eyes followed Molly. She could only call his expression adoring. There was no doubt in her mind that he loved Molly.

When he turned to look at her, his smile was almost boyish and his green eyes sparkled. Apparently, Molly got her deep blue eyes from her mother.

"Well Mr. Flannigan, shall we go up, too?" Helen gave a nod toward the stairs.

"It would be my pleasure, ma'am." His smile broadened as he offered his arm.

The third floor was quiet for a change, except for the echoing sound of a hammer from the end of the west wing. Helen guided her guest to the double doors in front of them and they entered a large room with a stage on one end.

Mr. Flannigan whistled. "An auditorium, no doubt."

"Yes. Converted from the former ballroom." She motioned toward the stage. "This, of course, is an addition. Albert, our groundskeeper and stableman, designed it himself and built it with some hired labor and a lot of volunteers. We were totally amazed to discover he had all these talents. Well, Virgie wasn't surprised, but they've been friends all their lives."

"Will you be adding permanent seating?"

"No, Dr. Trent ordered chairs that can be easily removed if we wish to utilize the room for other purposes, such as parties or indoor activities on rainy days. They should arrive any day now."

They walked down the hall and turned onto the east wing. "Our younger children will be on this wing." She turned into the first room on the right. "This will be a combined playroom and nap room for the five- through seven-year-olds. It was converted from part of the old nursery."

Helen showed him the classrooms on that hall, avoiding the storage room with the trunk full of ball gowns.

Mr. Flannigan nodded politely but didn't seem very interested. Perhaps the tour had been a mistake.

Helen hesitated when they arrived back at the stairway, uncertain whether to continue to the west wing. Suddenly she pressed her lips together and straightened her back. This was her opportunity to show Molly's father what he would be taking her from.

She continued walking. She turned into the west hallway, passed up the first room, and entered the second. The walls were filled with bright paintings, and tables and cases stood around the room, waiting for science projects and specimens.

"This will be Mr. Waverly's science class. Molly's favorite. She'll miss it very much."

He gave her a startled look then frowned but didn't say anything when Helen led him down the hall to the other rooms. His eyes brightened. "Molly is doing well with sign language, isn't she?"

Hope rose in Helen at his question. "Yes, she's doing very well. She shows so much promise. It would be a shame if she had to stop learning now."

Annoyance shadowed his eyes. "I appreciate your showing me around. When will you be moving the classrooms to this floor?"

"Very soon. Maybe as soon as next week." Although he hadn't replied to her comment about Molly leaving, Helen couldn't help the hope that remained in her heart.

But for now, she'd leave it alone. Perhaps she could talk to him after supper.

As they reached the second floor, Molly and seven-year-old Lily Ann came out of the girls' dormitory. The girls stopped in the doorway, signing into each other's hands.

Mr. Flannigan's brow furrowed. "What are they doing?"

"Lily Ann has hearing, but she's completely blind. When we added sign language to the curriculum, she insisted on learning it, too. She signs to the deaf children, and they sign in her hand."

"That is amazing." He whispered the words, and Helen wasn't sure he intended them for her.

Molly noticed them standing at the stairs. "Oh Lily Ann, it's my papa and Miss Edwards."

The girls hurried to join them.

"Papa, did you like our new schoolrooms? Aren't they nice?" Molly grabbed her father's hand, and they walked down the stairs together. Helen and Lily Ann followed.

Molly didn't seem to know she was leaving the school. Had Patrick Flannigan not mentioned it yet? Was it possible his mind wasn't completely made up?

"Papa, is it all right if I play outside with Lily Ann until supper-time?" Molly's long black lashes fluttered as she looked up at her father's lips.

"I suppose so. Perhaps Miss Edwards will consent to sit on the porch and visit with me while you girls play in the yard."

Helen threw him a surprised glance. She wasn't about to pass up the chance to talk to him more. She nodded and slipped through the door he held open. The screen door closed behind them, and Helen motioned to the wicker chairs and tables grouped at one end of the wide porch.

When they were seated, he turned to Helen. "I didn't realize you teach blind students, too."

"Well, officially, we haven't up till now." Helen glanced at the girls. "Lily Ann's parents are friends of Dr. Trent's. They didn't want to send her away to a school for the blind, so Dr. Trent agreed to take her as a student on a trial basis. She's been here two years now—since she was five—and learns quickly."

"But how do you teach her? Orally?" Amazement filled his voice.

"Yes, until recently that was our only method for teaching her. But we added braille to her course of studies a few months ago. She loves being able to read some of the simple stories for herself."

He shook his head. "You and your colleagues are doing wonderful things here."

"Thank you, Mr. Flannigan. We only do what we can to make their lives better." *So please don't tie our hands where Molly is concerned.*

"Mr. Flannigan, would you consider changing your mind about taking Molly away?"

"You make me sound like some kind of ogre. Of course I'm going to take her home with me. She's my child." He snapped the words then added in a softer tone, "I appreciate all you've done for Molly. Her time here has given her a chance at a much better life than she would have had otherwise."

"But don't you see? There's so much more for her to learn! Please don't cut her education short." Helen paused for breath. "Think about her future!"

"Her future is with her father!" He rose. "How can you think she's better off away from me? She's learned all she needs to."

"No she hasn't." She noticed Molly glance that way and lowered her voice. "There is so much more for her to learn. Why can't you see that? Stop being so stubborn."

"Stubborn? Because I think my child belongs at home with me? This subject of conversation has ended, Miss Edwards." He turned and motioned to Molly.

"What, Papa?" Molly ran up the porch steps.

"Get your coat. You're coming with me."

Helen gasped. "But it's almost suppertime."

His eyes were hard as they gazed into hers. "Miss Edwards, I'm quite capable of feeding my daughter."

❧

Patrick tried to focus on Molly, who sat next to him in the carriage. But his thoughts kept going to that infuriating woman with her ridiculous ideas. How dare she treat him as though he were doing something evil when he was only trying to be a good father to Molly.

Why, she actually raised her voice to him. And those eyes. Those strange blue eyes the shade of a spring sky that he'd thought so pretty had been clouded with anger when she shouted at him.

Well, he'd show her. He'd take good care of his daughter. Maybe he could find someone in Atlanta to teach her more of that sign language. He bit his lip. He didn't think that was likely.

"Papa, look." Molly pointed out the window at a dog chasing a black cat.

"Would you like to have a dog, Molly?" He patted her hand and waited for an excited reply. When she didn't answer, he realized she hadn't read his lips. He touched her shoulder to get her attention, and she looked up.

"Would you like a dog, Molly?" he repeated.

Her eyes lit up. "We have six dogs, Papa. We have a collie named Goldie, who lives in the barn. And she has five puppies. They're so cute."

He bit his lip and tried again. "Well, what about a kitten?"

"Oh Papa. We have the cutest kittens. Nellie Sue, the mouser, just had seven of them." She giggled. "Virgie said not a mouse in the country would dare show its face around Quincy School."

He nodded. "That's very nice, Molly. I'm glad the school has pets."

He stopped the horse in front of the hotel. He lifted Molly down from the carriage and tossed the reins to the boy who stood waiting.

"Is this your hotel, Papa?"

"Yes, and it has a fine restaurant. I thought you might enjoy eating here tonight instead of the school."

"Sure. That'll be fun. I hope they have good things to eat like Cook does." She tossed him a big smile.

"Well, I'm sure they'll have almost anything you'd like." He guided her to the restaurant door, where they were seated at a table set with crystal and silver.

They ordered fried chicken with mashed potatoes and gravy, sweet potatoes, and fried okra. Molly wrinkled her nose at the okra but ate the rest with pleasure.

"Well, what do you think? As good as Cook's?" Patrick eyed his daughter and grinned.

She took another bite of her drumstick and closed her eyes in thought. "Well, it's very good, Papa. And almost as good as Cook's. But don't tell her I said so. It might hurt her feelings."

Patrick laughed and made a buttoning motion on his lips.

Molly giggled. "You're funny, Papa."

They finished with chocolate cake and ice cream. Molly's eyes widened when she saw the enormous dessert in front of her.

After they'd eaten, they sat in the lobby and watched the people coming and going. They laughed behind their hands at a portly woman's wide-brimmed hat topped by a large blue bird.

"Papa, did you see my new classrooms?"

He hesitated. "Yes, I saw the classrooms. They look quite efficient."

"I know. Especially the science room. Mr. Waverly says we can go on more nature walks because we have more room to keep the insects and leaves."

Patrick watched her eyes grow bright with excitement as she talked about the anticipated new projects.

"You like your school, don't you?" Sadness ripped through him.

"Oh yes, Papa. It's the best school in the world. Did I tell you we have a new sign language teacher?"

"Yes, I believe you did. A Miss Wilson?"

"Yes, she's just out of college. And Virgie says if she's half as good a teacher as Miss Abigail was, she'll be wonderful." She paused to take a breath then giggled. "I mean Mrs. Quincy, 'cause she's not Miss Abigail any more."

She loved these people. He could see it in her eyes, hear it in her voice. But she was his child. She needed to live with him. That's what Maureen would want, wasn't it? He sighed. Maybe he needed to at least think about this before he did something he'd regret. He'd send a telegram to his assistant tomorrow and let him know he wouldn't be back as soon as he'd said he would.

❧

Helen yanked the thread from the dress she was mending for the third time. She rethreaded the needle and tied a knot. Why had she spoken so rashly? What if she didn't even get a chance to say good-bye to Molly?

Forgive me, Father. Virgie was right. I didn't ask You what Your will is for Molly's life. I'm so sorry.

Helen started at the rattle of harness and the sound of carriage wheels. She waited until she heard Molly's voice and then the sound of her feet running up the stairs.

She rose and laid the dress on her chair then went to the foyer. Patrick Flannigan stood still, his face a myriad of emotions as he watched Molly fly up the stairs.

Helen cleared her throat, and he looked her way. "Mr. Flannigan, I spoke out of turn. Can you forgive me?"

"I will, if you'll forgive me. I wasn't very nice." He ran his hand around the band of his hat. "And perhaps you were right. At least you've given me something to think about. Good night, Miss Edwards."

"Good night, Mr. Flannigan." She closed the door behind him and started up the stairs, overcome with the goodness of God.

Chapter 3

The chalk screeched across the blackboard, sending a shiver down Helen's spine. She finished writing the homework assignment then turned to her class.

Her students sat with heads darting from the board to their tablets. Helen smiled at the diverse expressions on their faces—from Molly, who bit her lip as she concentrated with furrowed brow, to Sonny, whose bored expression and darting glances betrayed his restlessness.

One by one, they closed their tablets and raised their heads to look at her lips, waiting for instruction.

"Boys and girls, I know you're all excited about the chili supper at the church tomorrow night."

Phoebe Martin's hand shot up. The seven-year-old's eyes sparkled.

"Yes, Phoebe?"

"Do we get to help Miz Selma with the baking?" Hope filled her eyes.

"I think Cook said the older girls could help out this afternoon, Phoebe." Helen frowned at the giggles that rippled through the room.

"But I'm seven." Phoebe's lips trembled. "Isn't that old enough?"

"Ordinarily it is, Phoebe. You know Cook often lets you and Lily Ann help her. But today she needs the girls who are over ten and have been helping her awhile." Helen smiled at the child. "But there will be other times when you can help."

The bell rang to signal the teachers it was time to dismiss. Helen's quick glance at the door alerted the other children, who looked expectantly at Helen.

"All right, boys and girls. As you know, there will be no classes this afternoon as some of the teachers and older students are helping with preparations for tomorrow. Be sure to do your

175

homework. You may line up at the door."

Papers rattled and shoes scuffled against the hardwood floors as the children lined up at the door.

"Stop that!"

Helen jerked her head toward the line of students just in time to see thirteen-year-old Jeremiah jerk his hand back and stare at Helen. Sonny had grabbed onto the student in front of him to catch his balance.

"Jeremiah! Return to your desk." Helen gave him a severe look that broached no back talk.

"Boys and girls, you are dismissed." She gave a little wave then shut the door behind them and walked over to Jeremiah.

"We've had this discussion about picking on other students before, haven't we?" She tapped her hand on the edge of his desk.

"Yek mem." His broken, almost unintelligible speech aroused Helen's sympathy. Jeremiah had only enrolled at midterm and had very little training until he came to Quincy School. She straightened her back. She couldn't let her sympathy enable him to pick on the other children—especially the young ones like Donald and Sonny, who seemed to be his favorite targets.

He looked closely at her lips through narrowed eyes. Apparently he'd learned lip reading on his own and was very good at it.

"Jeremiah, I don't like punishment. But your mistreatment of the younger boys has to stop. I want you to clean the blackboard." She paused.

Relief washed over his face at what he apparently thought was his full punishment.

"I also would like for you to read Matthew 7:12 and write a half-page essay on what the verse means."

"A hak page?" Dismay filled his voice. "But. . ."

"No 'buts,' Jeremiah." She knew it would be a struggle for him because he could only print and still had trouble even with that, but it was necessary for him to learn not to bully.

"Yek ma'am." He rose and walked to the blackboard.

When he'd finished, Helen patted him on the shoulder. "Thank you, Jeremiah. Now hurry and get washed up for dinner. I hope you enjoy the chili supper tomorrow night."

A small grin tilted his mouth as left the classroom.

Helen gathered her things together and went to her room to freshen up. When she came downstairs, Dr. Trent stood in the foyer visiting with Mr. Flannigan. Molly held her father's hand with a look of delight on her face. The same look she'd had ever since he'd arrived.

She nodded a greeting.

"Helen. There you are." Dr. Trent smiled in her direction. "We were just about to go in to dinner. I can smell Selma's good Georgia gumbo and I can't wait much longer."

"I agree completely," Helen said. "Will you and Abigail be at the chili supper tomorrow night?"

"Unless I have a medical emergency. I hear they'll be using Virgie's chili recipe and her spices."

Helen laughed. "Yes, Cook mixed up the secret spice mix yesterday, and Albert took it to Ezra Bines." When Virgie had stepped down as cook a few years ago to take over as head housekeeper, she'd given all her recipes to Selma, who'd been her assistant cook for years. Ezra traditionally made the community chili once a year in an enormous iron pot over a roaring outdoor wood fire. Although Virgie had given him her basic recipe, the spices remained a secret.

Mr. Flannigan held his free arm out to Helen. "Miss Edwards, may I escort you in to dinner?"

Heat warmed her cheek, but she placed her hand on the proffered arm.

Dr. Trent chuckled. "Well all right. I know when I've been snubbed."

Molly dropped her father's arm and stepped over to the doctor. "You may escort me in, Dr. Trent."

The doctor bowed. "It would be my pleasure, Miss Flannigan."

Mr. Flannigan held Helen's chair then took a chair between P.H. and Howard Owens, the boys' dorm parent, at the other end of the table.

Helen smiled to see Dr. Trent at the head of the table. He wasn't here for meals often since his wedding. He gave thanks and asked the blessing on the food.

Sissy and the new server came in and began to dish up the soup. The smell of Georgia gumbo wafted across the room.

"Thank you, Sissy, it smells wonderful." Helen dipped her spoon into the savory stew. She'd had Louisiana-style gumbo before and loved it. Since coming to the school, she'd acquired a taste for the Georgia version. Chunks of okra, shrimp, crab, smoked sausage, and rice swam in a liquid of tomato sauce and delicious spices. The onion and various peppers tingled on the tongue.

The gumbo alone could have been a complete meal in Helen's opinion, but before long the servers removed the bowls and began filling their plates with tender pieces of steak in brown gravy, potatoes, and green beans.

When the meal had ended, Molly and two other girls helped to clear away the dishes. Helen smiled at their eagerness to help in the kitchen today.

Helen was in the foyer talking to Virgie when Mr. Flannigan walked out of the dining room.

He removed his hat from the rack and held it in his hands, running his fingers around the band. "Miss Edwards, I wonder if I might have a few words with you."

Helen tensed. Was this the moment he would tell her he had decided definitely to take Molly home?

ᘒ

Patrick stood beside Helen on the wide, white framed porch. He hesitated, uncertain what to do. "Would you like to sit over there?" He indicated the wicker chairs at the end of the porch.

"I think I'd prefer to walk down the lane, if you don't mind." Her smile was tremulous, and she motioned toward the gate.

"I don't mind at all." He offered his arm, but she didn't seem to notice. She gathered her shawl around her and walked down the steps.

"It's a nice day, isn't it?" Her hand waved, seemingly to the air in general.

"Yes. One of the reasons I love the South. Who would think early February could be so mild?" He glanced over. A soft brown curl had come loose and hung around her face. He wondered what it would be like to brush it back. He jerked his head around and looked forward just as she glanced his way. He didn't need to be having a thought like that about his daughter's teacher. They reached the gate and he opened it so she could pass though.

"So you're not from the South originally?" She waited while he closed the gate then continued down the lane.

"No, I grew up in Pennsylvania. I came to Atlanta to start a business with a friend." He realized he was still holding his hat and plopped it on his head. "He didn't care for Georgia, so after a year he sold me his share of the business and went back home."

"But you apparently like it here." She smiled.

"Love it. Still do." He paused then continued, "Besides, I'd married Maureen by then and didn't really care where I lived so long as she was with me."

Helen stopped beneath a live oak tree and looked into his eyes. "Maureen was your wife," she said softly.

"Yes." He swallowed past the sudden lump in his throat. "And that brings me to what I wish to talk to you about."

She stiffened for a moment then took a deep breath. "You're taking Molly from the school?"

"I'm still not sure." He shook his head, hating his seeming inability to make a decision. "Part of me thinks Maureen would want me to take our daughter home, but then I watch her with her teachers and the other children here. I see them conversing with sign language. She's happy here. When we went to dinner last night, all she could talk about was Miss Wilson, her new signing teacher, and how nice it would be when the school moves to the third floor. She's happy because she gets to move from the dorm and share a room with one other girl."

"Yes, now that we'll have more room, only the small children will sleep in the dorm. The older ones are very excited."

"There's something else." Familiar pain and frustration gripped him. "Communication is difficult between Molly and me. Sometimes I forget to look directly at her when I speak or enunciate clearly."

Helen nodded. "Yes, I can see that would be a problem. You could learn to sign, you know."

Hope rose in him. That was the very thing that had been niggling at his mind. "Do you think I could?"

"Of course." Her blue eyes flashed with excitement. "Anyone can learn sign language."

Without thinking, he grabbed her hands. "Could you teach me?"

Pink washed over her cheeks, and he realized he was clutching both her hands. Quickly he released them. "Please forgive me, Miss Edwards. I meant no disrespect."

A gentle smile touched her lips. "I know you didn't and I'm not offended."

"Would you consider teaching me?"

"That would depend on how long you plan to be here, Mr. Flannigan." She bit her lip.

"I can only stay a week. I have to get back to my shop." He frowned. There was no way he could stay away longer.

"I can teach you some basic signs in that time," she said. "And we have a book you can take with you when you go."

"Wonderful! When can we begin?"

She held both hands up and looped her little fingers together. "This is the sign for 'friend.'"

Hopeful, but feeling a little foolish, he made the sign. "Is that right?"

Her lips tilted and her eyes sparkled. She leaned back against the tree. "Perfect." The smile faded. "Of course Molly will be with you to help you learn when you go home."

Suddenly the solution came to him. At least a temporary one. "Miss Edwards, I think I should let Molly stay in school until the end of the term. In the meantime, I'll be learning sign language. Then I'll make a decision about next year."

Relief washed over her face. "I think that's a wonderful idea, Mr. Flannigan."

"I know you're busy, but could we get together for a short while every day until I leave? That way, maybe the book won't scare me to death."

A rippling laugh proceeded from her throat. "That won't be a problem. And since tomorrow is Saturday, would you prefer morning or afternoon for your lesson?"

"I promised Molly I'd take her to the river for a picnic tomorrow. Perhaps we could have the lesson afterward?"

"Of course." She pushed away from the tree. "And now I think I should get back and see if there's anything I can do to help Selma."

"Oh yes. The chili supper is tomorrow evening." Eagerness rose up in him. "Would you care to share a table with Molly and me?"

"I'd be delighted, Mr. Flannigan," she said. "Perhaps Molly and I can teach you some signs for the food and utensils."

"In that case, Teacher, perhaps you could drop the mister and call me Patrick."

A startled look came on her face. "I suppose that would be all right." She lifted her chin. "And you may call me Helen."

৵

Helen sat in front of P.H.'s desk. "Patrick Flannigan has decided to leave Molly here until the end of the term."

"Ha!" P.H.'s eyes shone. "I knew you'd get to him."

"What do you mean?" Helen hoped her voice was as shocked

as she felt. "Why, I had nothing to do with it. He decided on his own."

"Uh huh." P.H. grinned. "I'm only teasing, Helen. Don't get all riled up."

"Well that wasn't nice, P.H." Helen bit her lip. Their director needed to grow up, even if she was fifty years old. "Apparently, it's obvious to him that Molly loves it here. He also realized he needs to learn sign language so they can communicate better."

"Bravo for him. He's a father who puts his child first. That's refreshing." P.H. frowned. "But why did he plan to take her out of school in the first place?"

Helen hesitated. "I believe he thought his late wife would want him to bring their child home."

"Hmmm." P.H. tapped a pencil against her desk. "How long ago did his wife pass away?"

"It's been a little over two years. Molly still grieves for her mother sometimes."

P.H. nodded. "I've often found that after a while the memory starts to fade and people feel a little guilty. So they put restrictions on themselves that their loves one would have never wanted."

"You could be right," Helen said. "Molly told me she can't always remember what her mother looked like. Mr. Flannigan may be going through something similar."

"So what is the plan? Do we give him a book to take home with him?"

"Yes. And I've agreed to teach him a few basics before he leaves next week."

Amusement crossed P.H.'s face. "You? Why not the sign language teacher?"

Helen gasped. "Oh dear. When he asked me to teach him, it never crossed my mind to suggest Hannah."

"Oh well, she has enough right now anyway, learning the school and getting used to all the children. Perhaps it is best for you to do it, if you don't mind." She grinned.

"Stop looking at me like that." Helen stood. "I'm only trying to be helpful. For Molly's sake. I have to go see if Cook needs my help in the kitchen."

P.H.'s laughter followed Helen down the hall.

Chapter 4

Children's laughter rang out across the schoolyard. Games of tag and hide-and-seek were already in full swing. The late afternoon sun cast shadows, and although it was a warm day, Helen, who sat on the top step of the church, shivered when a gust of air passed over her skin.

"Mmm, that chili smells wonderful." At the sound of Abigail's cheerful voice, Helen turned.

"It sure does. You missed the chili supper last year, didn't you?" Helen looked up from the step at her friend.

Abigail laughed. "Yes, by a good while. I can hardly believe it's only been eight months since I arrived here." She gathered her skirts around her and settled next to Helen.

"You know we're going to be right in the way of folks going in and out of the building." Helen made the observation but made no move to rise.

"I know, but it's the perfect spot to see everything." Abigail wrapped her shawl across her stomach, leaving her hand there for a moment.

Something about the protective movement sent a rush of excitement through Helen. "Abigail! Are you expecting?" Her excitement was reflected in her whispered words.

"Shhh. Yes. How did you know? Am I showing?"

"No, silly. You can't be more than a couple of months along. It was the way you laid your hand over your stomach." She noticed the redness cross her friend's cheeks and felt warmth in her own. "Forgive me, Abigail. I shouldn't have been so outspoken."

Abigail giggled and flicked her wrist at Helen. "Oh, it's all right. But I'd better be careful or the whole community will know before I tell Trent."

Helen gasped. "Oh my. You haven't told him yet?"

"I wanted to wait awhile to make sure." She cut her glance at Helen.

"But you are sure, aren't you?" Helen grinned.

"Yes. I'm going to tell him tonight." Abigail gave a little shake of her finger in Helen's direction. "Don't you dare say anything. He has to think he's the first to know."

"I promise." She stood and held her hand out. "You'd best get up from there. Let's go inside."

Abigail waved her hand away. "Don't coddle me. People will notice."

"All right. Let's see if we can bring the silverware out to the tables." Helen stepped up onto the porch, keeping an eye on her friend.

Baskets of desserts and breads sat on a table at the back of the church. Odds and ends of forks, spoons, and knives, donated by the ladies of the community from time to time, lay in a bucket waiting to be taken outside.

Virgie and Selma stood giving directions.

Helen laid a hand on Virgie's wrinkled brown arm. "What can we do to help? Is the silverware ready to go out?"

"Yes, but grab that stack of tablecloths to put over the tables. Them boys been scrubbing them down, but I don't want to take a chance they missed a spot of bird droppings."

Helen heard something like a cough or gag from behind her. She grabbed the tablecloths and shoved them into Abigail's hands. "I'll be right behind you with the utensils."

She grabbed the bucket and followed Abigail outside and down the steps.

Abigail bent over, making choking sounds.

Helen put her arm around her. "Honey, are you all right? Should I get Trent?"

Abigail stood up straight and looked at Helen, her face contorted, then emitted a loud guffaw.

Helen stepped back. "You're laughing. I though you were nauseated because of what Virgie said."

Abigail grabbed Helen's arm to steady herself. "I'm sorry. I couldn't help it. The thought of covering up bird droppings with Virgie's spotless white tablecloths was too much."

Laughter bubbled up in Helen and exploded. She linked arms with Abigail and they walked over to the line of tables, still laughing.

"Well ladies, are you going to share the joke?"

Helen gasped and looked up to see Patrick walking toward them, a smile on his face.

"Oh Mr. Flannigan. It was nothing." Helen took a deep breath to regain control. "But please come meet my friend Abigail, Dr. Trent's wife."

Abigail offered her hand, and Patrick took it and gave a gentle shake. "I'm very pleased to meet you, Mrs. Quincy."

"And I'm delighted to meet our sweet Molly's father at last." Abigail looked from Patrick back to Helen. "I'd better get these cloths on the tables so we can get the dessert table set up."

She began shaking out the cloths and smoothing them down on the long board tables.

Helen darted a glance at Patrick and found him giving her a very admiring look. She blushed. "If you'll excuse me, Patrick, I need to help Abigail."

"Of course. I'll just go see if I can help stir chili or something." He grinned.

"Ezra will run you off if you come near his chili. But I think I saw Dr. Trent getting the boys together for a game of kickball." She glanced toward the back of the church. "Yes, there they are. He could probably use another man to help keep order."

"I'm your man. I'll go see what I can do." A red lock fell across his forehead, nearly reaching his eye.

She'd never noticed how handsome he was before. Well, maybe she had, at that. She watched him walk away.

"Come on, Miss Lovelorn. I could use some help here." Abigail's laughter rang out again.

Humph. Abigail had been laughing a lot lately. She must

really like married life. But why did she have the idea Helen was lovelorn? She felt herself blushing again. It seemed she was blushing as much as Abigail was laughing.

She turned and grabbed an end of the cloth Abigail was trying to get onto the table evenly. "I'm not lovelorn. Don't be silly."

"You don't like Mr. Flannigan?"

"Well, yes, I like him. He's a very nice man. But not the way you are implying." She blew a lock of hair out of her eyes and frowned at her friend. "The very idea. I hardly know him."

Contrition crossed Abigail's face. "Forgive me, Helen. I shouldn't be teasing you. I remember how I felt when people would tease me about Trent. Before I even knew I loved him."

Helen gave her friend a suspicious look. "Well, don't think I'm in love with Patrick Flannigan. Because I'm not."

"Oh no. I was only talking about me. And Trent." Abigail bit her lip then cleared her throat. "We'd best get the rest of the cloths on the tables. I see some ladies coming with baskets of food."

"Yes, and from the way the chili smells, I'd say that it's almost ready, too." Helen helped smooth the last cloth just in time. She and Abigail helped get the bowls and plates set up on one end of the table. They laid out spoons, forks, and knives in separate piles. Soon the breads and desserts covered one of the tables. And little bowls with chopped onions and chopped peppers were placed around the tables.

Reverend Shepherd stood on a tree stump and called out for everyone to hear. "Let's gather around now and say grace, brothers and sisters." The crowd flocked around, and after thanks had been given, they lined up with their bowls.

Patrick appeared at Helen's side. "Molly is saving three seats at the second table. We already have our chili and corn bread and she sent me to fetch you."

⁊

Patrick couldn't remember the last time he'd enjoyed himself so much. From the delicious food to Molly's giggles when he made a mistake signing the word for one of the utensils. Helen's delight when he got them right made him work harder just so he could see her eyes sparkle and her soft pink-tinged lips tip into a smile.

"Papa!" Molly tugged on his sleeve. "Why are you staring at Miss Edwards?"

"Uh. . ." He laughed. "Well, she's a mighty pretty lady, don't you think?"

"Oh Papa, 'course she's pretty."

Helen's face flamed. "Well, thank you both, but could we talk about something besides my appearance?"

What had he been thinking? That was the problem. He hadn't been thinking. "I'm sorry, Helen. It just sort of blurted out. I didn't mean to embarrass you."

"That's quite all right. I realize you were being polite." Her face still flushed, but at least it wasn't beet red anymore.

"Okay, Molly, you didn't show me the sign for knife." He hoped Molly would follow his lead and change the subject.

The men brought out lanterns, hanging them in the trees and standing them on the tables and the porch as dusk started to fall.

Some of the younger children were nodding off to sleep, so their mothers began to gather up platters and leftovers to take home.

Helen rose. "I need to help clear away."

"Will you ride with us, Miss Edwards?" Molly pleaded.

"Well. . ."

"I was about to invite you myself." And he regretted that Molly had beaten him to it. He enjoyed Helen's company and wasn't quite sure why. Of course, she was a very kind and gentle woman and was obviously Molly's favorite teacher. So naturally, he liked being around her.

"That was so much fun, wasn't it, Papa? And that chili was as good as Cook's. Didn't you think so, Miss Edwards?" Molly continued to chatter practically nonstop on the ride back to school.

Patrick grinned. He suspected his daughter was talking to stay awake. "I'll take you to the hotel for lunch tomorrow, Molly girl. How does that sound?"

"Fried chicken?" She leaned her head on his shoulder and patted a yawn.

"Fried chicken it is." He glanced down, but her eyes had closed. He glanced over at Helen and smiled.

"I think she's off to dreamland," Helen said. "She's had a busy day."

"Thank you for spending your time with us tonight. It meant a lot to Molly." The reins hung loosely in his hands, and he let the horses go at their own pace.

"It was my pleasure. She's very dear to me."

"To be honest, it meant a lot to me as well." He cleared his throat. "I haven't had the pleasure of a lady's company very much since my wife passed away. I'd forgotten how nice it was."

She was silent and he could have kicked himself. He seemed to be speaking out of turn a lot lately.

"Thank you, Patrick. I enjoyed the evening, too." She patted back a yawn. "Oh, excuse me. It must be catching."

He laughed. "Nothing to excuse. I'm a little drowsy myself. So are you still willing to give me a sign language lesson tomorrow afternoon?"

"Yes, of course. And Miss Wilson has put some things together for you to take home with you when you go. A sign language book and a book about life for the deaf. She thought it might help you when you take Molly home."

"That's very kind of her. I'll be sure to thank her." He turned into the dark tree-lined lane leading to the school.

Helen was silent, and he glanced over to see if she'd joined Molly in her slumberland. A moonbeam made its way through the branches and bathed her hair and skin with pale gold. His breath caught in his throat and she looked up at him with a question in her eyes. "Did you say something?"

"No, no. Just a hiccup." Well, that was brilliant. What in the world was wrong with him tonight? He'd allowed moonlight to affect his brain.

He stopped the carriage at the front porch. He came around and helped Helen out of the carriage then lifted a groggy Molly down.

Helen put an arm around her. "Why don't you let me take her inside and help her get to bed."

"If you're sure." He bent over and kissed Molly on the cheek then looked at Helen. "I'll be here to get Molly around eleven in the morning."

"I'll make sure she's ready."

"Good night, Papa." Molly yawned then leaned against Helen as they walked up the porch steps.

Patrick watched them go. A strange longing shot through him and his eyes misted. Spinning on his heels, he got back into the carriage and drove down the lane.

❧

Helen took Molly to her dorm and left her in the girl's dorm mother Felicity's tender care, even though what she really wanted to do was tuck the child into bed and sit by her side until she went back to sleep. She'd been warned all through her training to care about her charges but not get attached. How did one not get attached to a child?

All right, she had to admit she wasn't as close to the other students as she was to Molly. There had been a special bond between them from the day Molly had arrived. Her heart had gone out to the little girl who had so recently lost her mother. But as time went on, her attachment to Molly had nothing to do with sympathy over the girl's grief. She loved the child for herself. And she should have guarded against that. Guarded her own heart and Molly's, too.

She couldn't fool herself. Patrick loved Molly and missed her. That was obvious. And although he'd been wise enough to see he wasn't ready to take her with him, Helen knew he would do whatever was necessary to get ready. He would have his daughter with him and soon.

With a need to escape her own thoughts, Helen went downstairs in search of someone or something to distract her. She heard voices in the parlor and relief washed over her.

Virgie and P.H. sat with cups of steaming tea. Suddenly there was nothing Helen wanted more than a cup of tea.

She sank into one of the overstuffed chairs. "Is there anything left in the pot?"

"Half full and still piping hot." Virgie reached for the extra cup and saucer on the tray. "Thought you'd be needing this when you got here."

"Thanks, Virgie. You're an angel."

Virgie chuckled. "I'm no such thing. The good Lord created angels and the good Lord created people. Take another look."

Helen couldn't help the giggle that came up from deep inside. "Oh Virgie, what would I do without you? You're a breath of joy."

Virgie handed over the steaming cup. " 'The joy of the Lord is your strength.' Just like the good book say it is."

Helen let Virgie's soft, soothing voice wash over her.

P.H. sat straight up and stared at Helen. "What's wrong with you, Helen?"

"I'm just tired. It's been a long day." She took a sip from her cup and let the hot liquid flow down her throat.

P.H. frowned. "Today has had the same length of time as any other day. Maybe it was just a little more filled up than most."

Helen leaned back and listened to P.H. talk about moving the classrooms up to the third floor in two weeks. She tried to let the words push out the thoughts of Molly and Patrick. But the thought that came to her in response to P.H.'s words was that Patrick would be gone the following weekend. And Helen didn't like the thought at all.

Chapter 5

Patrick watched the screen door shut behind Helen. She had said her farewell and left him and Molly to say good-bye in private. He hoped Helen hadn't gone far. Molly would need her teacher's comfort when he drove away.

He lifted his daughter's chin and mouthed the words *I love you.* Then he made the sign for it, and Molly's mouth dropped open.

"Papa! When did you learn that?" Molly's deep blue eyes sparkled with excitement mixed with her tears.

"Miss Edwards taught me yesterday." He smiled and flicked Molly's braid. "She thought we might need it."

"Oh Papa." Molly flung her arms around his waist and squeezed. "I wish you didn't have to leave."

A twinge of sadness shot through him that she hadn't said *I wish I could go with you.* Apparently, it hadn't even crossed her mind that she might. He sighed. He was glad he'd never mentioned his earlier intentions to her.

"I'll be back next month," he reminded her.

"You promise?" She stared up into his face.

"I do." In fact he might not wait a month, but he didn't wish to build her hopes up until he knew he could get away from the shop sooner.

She nodded. "All right, Papa. But you'll write me letters?"

"I will. In fact, I'll write to you on the train and mail it when I get to Atlanta." He stroked her hair back, glad it hung loose today. She had the same black curls and deep blue eyes as her mother.

"And you'll tell me all about the train ride?" Her lips trembled, but she pressed them together and held her chin up.

"Every single thing. I'll even eat in the dining car so I can tell you about the food." He grinned.

"There's a dining room on the train?" Her voice rose with incredulity.

"There sure is. I saw a little girl eating one of those new ice cream cones I told you about."

"You sure you aren't making that up just to tease me? Do they really serve ice cream in cones made out of cookies?"

"Well, not exactly cookies but something similar. I'll take you to the candy store in Atlanta this summer and prove it to you." Anything to get those tears from her eyes.

She nodded and rubbed the toe of her shoe against the ground. "Summer's a long time away." Her mournful tone stabbed at his heart.

"Not really so very long, sweetheart. Time will pass quickly for you with all the excitement of moving the school's classrooms. And don't forget you'll have a new bedroom soon and just one girl to share it with."

A sigh escaped her lips, but she nodded. He could still hear the sigh when he drove down the lane and headed for Mimosa Junction.

❧

Helen awoke to a sunshiny Saturday. She yawned and stretched lazily then glanced at the little clock on her bedside table. Six thirty! She needed to hurry or she wouldn't have time before breakfast for her morning devotions. And heaven only knew if she'd have time later in the day; she'd be so busy helping with the move. After hastily washing up, she dressed then picked up her Bible and sat in the rocking chair by her window.

A cardinal flew past the window with a flash of red that reminded her of Patrick's curls. He'd been gone nearly two weeks and she couldn't believe how much she missed him. With a guilty start, she opened her Bible. *Forgive me, Lord, for letting a foolish thought keep me from Your Word.*

She had finished 2 Timothy yesterday, so she opened to the first chapter of Titus and began reading Paul's instructions concerning the appointment of bishops. She gasped when she came to verse six.

Of course the rule about only one wife referred to a mono-gamous relationship and Maureen was no longer living. Still, it appeared Patrick was still very much in love with his deceased wife. One more reason for Helen to banish any stray thoughts of romance from her mind. Even if she cared for him in that way—which she certainly didn't—he would never see her as more than Molly's teacher or even a friend.

A sudden sound of shuffling feet and muffled giggles startled her from her thoughts. Oh no. It was time for breakfast and she'd not finished her Bible reading. With another quick apology to God, she arose, smoothed her skirt then followed the children and their dorm parents downstairs.

P.H. was practically bouncing as she came from her downstairs apartment. "Helen! This is the day."

Helen laughed. "Yes it is. And I suppose everyone is here and ready to get busy."

"Well, no. But I told them all to eat a good breakfast first. Dr. Quincy and Abigail won't arrive until midmorning as he had a patient to visit first." She linked her arm through Helen's and they walked into the dining room together.

The children were almost too excited to eat and had to be reminded several times to settle down. By the time the meal was over, several volunteers had arrived to begin moving furniture. Felicity and Howard sent the children outside to play. The two neighbor girls who volunteered from time to time promised to keep a close eye on them while the adults worked.

Helen had already packed up most of her classroom books and supplies but headed to the second floor after breakfast to finish up. She went into Abigail's classroom, which hadn't been in use since last semester. She smiled as she walked over to the small table and chair near Abigail's desk where Lily Ann had sat and worked while Abigail taught the deaf children English and spelling. After Abigail's wedding, Lily Ann's braille instruc-tions had stopped temporarily. Helen and Charles Waverly, the science teacher, were learning the written language for the blind. In the meantime, they both taught the child orally as they had before braille had been added to the curriculum.

Abigail had planned to teach the little girl for a while after her honeymoon, but now with the baby on the way that wasn't likely. Helen sighed. Abigail had allowed herself to become attached to Lily Ann just as Helen had to Molly. It made things more difficult when circumstances changed. Should she pull back a little from Molly? A knot formed in her stomach, and she shook her head. Not yet. If Patrick really did remove Molly from the school, she'd just have to cross that bridge when she came to it.

A sound of laughter drew her attention to the window. Stepping over, she looked out over the yard and saw Albert driving Dr. Trent's carriage into the barn. Oh good. Abigail was here.

Quickly, she finished packing the last box then went downstairs and into the parlor.

Abigail looked up and set her teacup on the table beside her chair. "Helen! This is so exciting. Come have a cup of tea with me and tell me what I can do."

"Just talk to me for a while. We haven't had a chance to visit since the chili supper." Helen leaned over and gave her friend a hug.

"But surely I can help pack up school supplies or something." She frowned.

Helen laughed. "Sorry. Too late. I'm all done. And so are the other teachers." She sat on the settee by Abigail and accepted a cup of tea. "Don't worry. There will be plenty to do next Saturday when we move the children into their different rooms."

"What happens to the dormitories?" Abigail took a sip of tea and then threw Helen a questioning look.

"They plan to convert the girls' dormitory into a bedroom and sitting room for Felicity. I believe Howard has chosen to have one large bedroom with a corner for a desk, so the boys' dorm will be converted into a large bedroom for him and a small utility room."

Abigail nodded. "And the former classrooms will be converted into bedrooms for the students."

"Yes, and they are so excited." Helen put her cup down on the table and leaned back.

Abigail sighed. "I'd wanted to explore the third floor before they started remodeling, but I missed my chance."

Helen sat up. She'd almost forgotten. "Abigail, you'll never believe what I found in one of the storage rooms."

Abigail's eyes filled with curiosity. "Well, tell me, please. Not a dead rat or something else nasty, I hope."

"Ewww, no." Helen cringed. "I wouldn't be sharing that with you. I found an old trunk full of absolutely gorgeous ball gowns."

"Where in the world did they come from?"

"They're very old. I would say they've been there since before the War." Helen picked up her cup and took another sip.

"Really! They must have belonged to Trent's grandmother and aunts." Abigail's eyes brightened. "What shape are they in?"

"That's the surprising part. They were wrapped in sheets and seemed in fairly good shape."

"Hmm. They'd probably fall apart if anyone tried to put them on," Abigail said.

Helen squirmed for a minute then cleared her throat. "Well, actually, I tried one on." She grinned. "It held up quite well. I think they might be useful for making costumes."

"You mean for the end of school program?"

"Why not?" Helen shrugged. "Perhaps we could write a play based on those old days."

Abigail gasped. "We could have a reenactment of Mrs. Quincy's freeing of the slaves and the beginning of the school."

Helen nodded. "My thoughts exactly."

"Is the trunk still there?" Abigail jumped up. "Let's go look."

"I have a better idea," Helen said. "Why don't we ask a couple of the men to bring the trunk down here? That way you won't need to climb all those stairs."

Abigail heaved an irritated breath. "Please don't treat me like an invalid."

"I wouldn't dream of it." Helen chuckled and pulled her friend down beside her with a gentle tug on her arm. "But there are a lot of things up there you could trip over today."

"You're right." Abigail folded both hands on her stomach for just a moment. The expression on her face was one of wonder and awe. She let her hands slide onto her lap. "I'd never forgive myself if my baby came to harm because of my carelessness."

After lunch, Albert and one of the neighbor men brought the trunk down to the parlor. Helen motioned to Virgie, who was walking by the door.

"What you bring that old trunk down here for?" Her soft voice nevertheless held a hint of disapproval when she saw the bound luggage sitting in the middle of the parlor floor.

"It's full of fancy dresses." Helen lifted the hasp and opened the lid. "Do you recognize these?"

The old woman frowned and stepped over to the trunk. Her brown hand reached out and touched the blue silk gown that rested on top. "This here dress belong to Miss Cecilia."

Abigail's face paled. "You mean the deaf child for whom the school was named?"

Virgie nodded. "Sweetest little thing I ever knew. And kind she was."

Helen frowned. "But I thought she died when she was a child."

Virgie shrugged and nodded. "Miss Cecilia pass away when she was fifteen. But her mama let her go to the ball that year."

"Rather young," Abigail murmured.

The old lady nodded and sighed. "I reckon the old miss would have given that chile anything she wanted that year. They knew she was dying, you see."

"How sad." Tears pooled in Abigail's eyes.

Helen patted her arm. "Yes, very sad."

Abigail ran her hand over the silk. "I think I'd like to keep this one. I wouldn't like to cut it up." She lifted it from the trunk and laid it across a chair in the corner.

Virgie smiled at the next one. "This here belonged to Miss Claire. You should've seen her sashaying around like she the queen of Sheba, her golden curls bobbing up and down. She the only one of the children who didn't have black hair."

The tension in the room lifted as Virgie described Claire and Suzette, pointing out the dresses and where they wore each.

Helen breathed a sigh of relief. It would have been a shame to cancel the project of making the dresses over into costumes due to sentiment. Although Claire Quincy Bouvier had passed away years ago, Trent's Aunt Suzette still lived somewhere in France. An old lady now, Helen doubted she even remembered the gowns.

ॐ

Patrick gave final instructions to his assistant, Stu Collins. He took a deep breath, relishing the scent of leather and oil, then glanced around the shop, making sure he hadn't forgotten anything. He tossed a wave at Stu and walked out the door. He made a quick stop at home to retrieve his already packed bag. An hour later he was on the train to Mimosa Junction.

It had been three weeks since he'd left his daughter sobbing on the porch of Quincy School. He knew she'd be surprised to see him and as happy as he was that he could come back so soon.

He leaned back on the leather seat and glanced out the window at the countryside rolling by. He still wasn't sure what he was going to do about Molly. He wanted her home, but she was learning so much at the school. Would it really be fair to remove her from the program now? He sighed. Well, he had several months before he'd need to make a decision.

He dozed off and on, coming fully awake when the train pulled into Mimosa Junction. The sun was setting as he stepped onto the platform of the nearly empty station. He tipped his hat to a lady standing on the platform then headed for the livery.

A boy sat on a three-legged stool oiling a saddle. " 'Evenin', Mr. Flannigan. Good to see you back."

Patrick smiled. "Good to be back. Are the horse and carriage I rented last time available?"

"Yes sir." The boy jumped up, wiping his hands on his leather apron.

"No, I don't need them until morning. Just wanted to ask you to hold them for me. I'll need them for several days." After the arrangements were made, Patrick started toward the hotel. He walked down the dusty street. Most of the stores were closed already. Passing an empty building, he frowned. The sign said MILL'S GENERAL STORE. He was pretty sure it had been open for business three weeks ago. Pretty short time to shut down and empty out a store. A few doors down he noticed the hardware store was also empty. He continued on to the hotel and registered for a room. He left his luggage and came back downstairs, wondering if he should go back and get the rig and drive on out to the school. He glanced at his watch. No, definitely too late. He went into the dining room and ordered a meal.

When the waiter brought his food, Patrick said, "I noticed a couple of newly emptied buildings around town."

The waiter nodded. "Yes sir, Mill's General Store and Tom's hardware shut down. They took their families and moved to Atlanta."

"Both of them?"

The waiter shrugged. "They were brothers. They decided to go in business together in the city."

"Rather sudden, wasn't it?"

"Oh. No sir. They'd made their plans six months ago. A feller by the name of Watson bought the store. He's getting ready to remodel it before opening for business."

"What about the hardware store?"

The man shrugged. "No buyer as far as I know. Won't be the first time a building has stood deserted in this town."

Patrick thanked the man and turned his attention to the delicious meal, suddenly realizing he was hungry. He wished he'd left Atlanta earlier. He could have had dinner with Molly and Helen.

Now why had he included Helen in that thought? Come to think of it, he'd thought about her a lot lately. Well why not? She was Molly's teacher and seemed to care a lot for his daughter. Of course he'd think about her.

But why did he smile or grin like an idiot when those thoughts of her came? Shoving the question to the back of his mind, he wondered if she'd have some time for him while he was here. She could tell him how Molly was doing and perhaps teach him some more signs. He wasn't doing too well on his own.

Maybe she'd like to go for a drive with him so they could have a nice long talk.

The last time he'd seen her, her soft blue eyes had seemed sad. Could she have been sorry to see him go?

He sighed. *Don't be ridiculous, Patrick Flannigan.* He continued to chide himself throughout dinner.

Chapter 6

Helen braided her long hair and wrapped the braids around her head, fastening them with hairpins. She'd decided with the work she'd be doing today, helping to move the girls into their rooms, the braids would work better than putting her hair in a bun.

She glanced in the mirror, turning her head this way and that. Besides, she rather liked the effect. If she had time to mess with braids every morning she might just stick with the hairstyle.

She gave a little laugh and shook her head at her silliness. What difference did it make anyway?

With a final glance to make sure her simple housedress was straight, she opened her door and nearly bumped into Charles Waverly, who stood with his hand raised to knock.

"Oops. I nearly knocked you in the head." He grinned and stepped back, letting her catch her breath.

Helen laughed. "You startled me. That's almost as bad."

"Sorry. P.H. wants you and me to put our heads together and come up with a more practical classroom schedule, now that we have more students and teachers coming soon."

Helen frowned. "We only have two new students so far, with three more coming in the next few months. By then, the school year will be ending and we'll have the whole summer to think about scheduling. Why is she in such a big hurry?"

Charles shook his head. "You know P.H. When she gets an idea in her head, she wants it done yesterday."

"True." Impatience surged through Helen, but she gave a chuckle as they walked to the stairs side by side and started down. "Well, we can't do anything about it this weekend. Let's each give it some thought and discuss it next weekend. Is that all right with you?"

"That's fine." He gave her a sideways glance and his eyes

sparkled. "I like your new hairdo. It's very becoming."

Surprised, Helen felt heat surge over her cheeks. Charles wasn't one to hand out compliments. He generally tended to tease in the other direction. "Why thank you. I wanted to make sure my hair stays out of the way while I'm working today."

They entered the dining room to find everyone seated. P.H. darted a pointed look in their direction. "Ah, here you are at last. If you'll take your seats, Howard was just about to say grace."

Helen hastened to her seat with Charles right behind her. He held her chair then hurried around to his place on the other side of the table.

Helen could hear P.H.'s shoe tapping. *My goodness, P.H. We're not in that big a hurry. Calm down.* She kept the thought to herself and bowed her head as Howard asked God's blessing on the food and on their day's endeavors.

They were halfway through the meal when Helen heard voices in the foyer. It sounded like. . .could it be? She finished her breakfast, trying not to cast darting glances toward the door.

She waited while the children filed out after their house parents. They were going to be moving their own things to the bedrooms once the furniture was in place. Some of the neighborhood women had been kind enough to make new quilts for the beds and bright scarves for their dressers. In the meantime, the two volunteers, Becky and Amy, would take them outside to play until time for the noon meal.

The sight that met her eyes as she stepped into the foyer made her heart leap. Patrick looked down at Molly, whose arms were wound tightly around his waist. The sparkle in Patrick's eyes matched the one in his daughter's as she gazed adoringly upward.

"I wasn't expecting you today, Papa." Her voice quivered.

"I wasn't sure I could make it, sweetheart, and I didn't want to raise your hopes then have to dash them." His glance drifted to Helen and the sparkle brightened even more, if that were possible.

"Good morning, Helen." His smile sent a thrill through Helen.

"Good morning to you, Patrick." She hoped he didn't misconstrue the lilt in her voice and think she had a personal interest in his presence. Because, of course, she didn't. She was simply happy for Molly's sake.

Molly tugged on his sleeve. "You're just in time to help move the furniture to my new room."

"Yes, I was just speaking to Albert about that very thing. In fact, I think I'll help with the others, too." He pulled one of her braids. "Is that all right with you, Miss Flannigan?"

Molly giggled. "All right. But we'll do something together later?"

"I promise we will." He stooped and kissed her on the cheek.

"I'll see you when it's time to eat then." Her eyes were roving toward the door that had shut behind Amy.

"You can count on it." He grinned. "Now run along and join your friends, if you'd like."

After Molly ran outside, Patrick turned to Helen, grinning. "I'm assuming we won't be working together today?"

"Ummm. No." Helen laughed. "I'll be helping clean out the dormitories and then help the girls get settled in."

"Then, as Molly said, 'I'll see you when it's time to eat.'" He gave a slight bow and started up the stairs.

"The man is smitten."

Helen composed her expression before turning to face P.H. "Whatever do you mean?"

P.H. laughed. "Never mind. Did Charles speak to you about my request?"

"Yes, he did. We'll be thinking about it this coming week then get together next Saturday. Does that meet your approval?" Helen hoped the words didn't sound sarcastic, because she didn't intend them to be. At least, she didn't think so.

"Perfect! I have every confidence in the two of you to get this organized. Of course, you might want to get some input from Miss Wilson, as well, since she teaches two separate sign language classes."

"Yes, of course. You want the new schedule for next year?" Helen tried not to fidget, but she needed to get upstairs.

"Actually, I thought we'd go ahead and implement it as soon as the new teachers arrive." She looked down at her skirt and brushed at a nonexistent piece of lint.

Helen felt her mouth drop open and clamped it shut. She took a deep breath. "But that will be in late March. We'll be preparing for end-of-school testing and the program just weeks later."

P.H. patted Helen's arm. "I know, dear. But we really need to try out the new schedule, so if it doesn't work, we'll have the entire summer to fix it. Now I need to speak to Selma. I have every confidence in you and Charles." With a flutter of her fingers she charged toward the kitchen.

Helen sighed then shook her head and started up the stairs. P.H. could be trying at times, but she was an excellent director and most of her ideas worked perfectly. On the rare occasions they didn't, P.H. was the first to admit her mistake and start over again.

The morning passed swiftly, and although the work was tiring, Helen enjoyed visiting with Hannah Wilson, Felicity, and some of the neighbor ladies while she worked. She missed Abigail, who was usually right in the middle of any school work project, but she and Trent had gone to Atlanta on business.

Although they'd all taken periodic breaks, by the time Flora came upstairs banging on a cowbell to announce dinner was ready, the noon break was a welcome relief.

Laughter rang out through the dining room as they shared silly mishaps that occurred throughout the morning.

Helen had cringed when she'd heard the men teasing Patrick about his dandified looks in comparison with their work clothes. After all, Patrick hadn't known it was a work day, but she soon saw that he was a good sport and gave back as good as he got.

An hour later, refreshed and in good spirits, everyone was back at their tasks.

School had been held all week in the new third-floor classrooms so that Albert and a few neighbors could transform the former classrooms into dorm rooms. By late afternoon, the touch-up work had been finished on Felicity's and Howard's living quarters and all the student rooms and were now ready for occupancy.

Molly and her roommate, Trudy, one of the new students, stood in their room and looked around with awe. Molly turned and gave Trudy a big hug. "Isn't it beautiful? And it's all ours, Trudy. We won't even have to worry about the little girls getting into our things."

Helen glanced at Patrick, who stood in the doorway, and they exchanged a smile.

Trudy gasped and stepped over to the washstand. Her hand reached out to touch the rose that adorned the porcelain wash-bowl. "Oh Molly," she whispered. "We have our own pitcher and bowl, and they aren't even tin."

Helen choked back laughter. The tin pitchers and wash pans in the girls' dormitory had been what Felicity referred to as her bane of existence for years, and apparently the girls felt the same.

"All right, girls. As you can see, Sissy and Flora have filled the pitcher with warm water, so now would be a good time to clean up for supper. Sissy or Flora will empty them later and refill them in the morning. But you will be expected to clean up any splashed water. Can you manage that?"

"Yes, Miss Edwards." The girls echoed each other.

"Very well. You have twenty minutes before supper. We'll see you in the dining room."

She shut the door and waved at Patrick, who'd already headed for the stairs. She grinned as she went to freshen up. She'd bet he had no idea his red curls were dusted with plaster.

❧

When Helen came downstairs, Patrick stood in the foyer talking to Howard and Charles. Molly stood beside him, her hand in his. He'd donned his suit coat and his hair was free of dust. It seemed as if Mr. Flannigan had done some freshening up, too.

All eyes turned in her direction. Patrick took a step toward her, but before he could speak, Charles offered his arm. "May I escort you in to supper, Helen?"

Disappointment clouded Patrick's eyes for a moment but disappeared so quickly that Helen wondered if she'd imagined it.

Not wanting to be rude, she took Charles's arm. "And who will escort Miss Molly in, I wonder?"

"Papa and I are going to the hotel for dinner, and. . ." Molly stopped at a touch from her father's hand.

"Oh, I see." She'd hoped for an opportunity to speak with Patrick after supper and ask how his signing was coming along. "In that case, I'll see you when you get back, Molly."

She turned away before they could see the disappointment that surely showed in her eyes.

❧

Patrick tried to keep his attitude cheerful for Molly's sake, but the memory of Helen holding Charles Waverly's arm didn't make it easy.

Was Waverly simply being a gentleman or was he interested in Helen romantically? He couldn't blame the man if he was. After all, she was a beautiful woman as well as a kind and gracious lady. The real question was whether Helen returned the man's interest. If interest it was.

"Papa, you're not listening to me." Molly frowned and looked about to cry.

Contrite, Patrick pulled up in front of the hotel. "I'm sorry, angel. I guess my mind did wander a little."

He walked around and helped her down then proffered his arm.

A shy smile tipped her lips. "I like it when you treat me like I'm all grown up."

"Well, I'm practicing for when you become a grown-up young lady." He patted her hand. "But let's hold that off for a few years."

She giggled then pressed her lips together as they walked into the lobby and crossed to the dining room.

The waiter remembered Molly from the last time and delighted her by addressing her as Miss Flannigan.

Halfway through her chocolate cake, she yawned and sighed. "I'm sorry, Papa."

"Think nothing of it, sweetheart. We've had a busy day." He stretched his mouth open, covering it with his hand. "There, you see? I'm sleepy, too."

She laughed. "Oh Papa. You just pretended to yawn."

"You caught me." He grinned. "What do you say? Let's head back to the school so you can try out that new bedroom. I'll bet Trudy's lonely there all alone."

"Oh. You may be right." She folded her napkin and laid it on the table then stood.

Before they were out of town, her head sank onto Patrick's shoulder.

She roused enough to walk inside when they arrived at the school.

Helen met them at the door. "Ah, a sleepy girl, I see."

Molly yawned. "I slept all the way from the hotel, Miss Edwards."

Patrick returned Molly's hug. "See you in the morning. I'll drive you and Trudy to church, if you like."

"Oh yes. I'd better go tell her." She started to the stairs then turned. "Good night, Papa. Good night, Miss Edwards."

He glanced at Helen, surprised to see distress on her face.

"Is something wrong?" he asked.

"Patrick, you can't take someone else's child on a drive unless their parents have left written permission for you to do so." She bit her lip.

"Oh, it never occurred to me." What an idiot he was. "It should have. I know I wouldn't want Molly to leave the school with someone I hadn't met."

She nodded.

"I hate to disappoint the girls after I've promised." He glanced at her. "Do you think it would be all right, if a member of the staff went along?"

"I think so. You'd need to ask Miss Wellington." P.H. could be pretty strict where the children were concerned.

"Actually, I was going to ask you if you would ride with us anyway. That is, unless you've agreed to go with someone else." Like Waverly.

"Yes, I could go. I usually ride in the wagon with the children, but they have plenty of other adults riding with them." She lowered her lashes. "I wouldn't want to disappoint Molly and Trudy. That is, of course, if P.H. gives her approval."

Moonlight streamed through the door and touched her hair with gold. Patrick wanted to caress the silky braids that wound around her head.

"Like I said, I was going to ask you before. So please come with us even if Miss Wellington won't allow Trudy to go."

A blush tinged her cheeks and she smiled. "Then I'll see you in the morning, and I hope Trudy will be with us on the drive. Good night, Patrick."

He stood there for a moment after she'd closed the door. Happiness surged through him. And this time, it wasn't mixed with guilt. Somehow he knew Maureen wouldn't mind.

Chapter 7

The silence in the parlor had gone on too long. Helen opened her mouth to ask Charles to please repeat his last statement, but the sudden chiming of the clock gave her another precious moment of respite.

Charles sat across from her, the scheduling book on his lap. His face was flushed and seemed to grow redder by the moment.

Oh dear, she hadn't heard him wrong. He'd said his affection for her had transcended friendship sometime ago and could she possibly accept him as a suitor.

She swallowed past a sudden lump in her throat. How could she let him down without crushing his ego? She cleared her throat. "I'm not quite sure what to say, Charles. This is totally unexpected. Could you give me some time to think about it?"

Relief tinged with hope ran across his face and he smiled. "Of course. I realize it's rather sudden. After all, we've been friends and colleagues for years."

"Yes, yes, that's right." *Coward. Just tell him you don't think of him in any other way. Don't prolong his anxiety.*

"How long do you think you'll need to consider the idea?"

She dabbed the sudden moisture from her chin and forehead, hoping he didn't notice. "Well, I'm not sure. I'll let you know."

Charles frowned. Oh dear. His reaction was so unlike the happy-go-lucky jokester she knew who could make her laugh even when she didn't feel like it. She brightened. Maybe this was another of his jokes. She threw him a hopeful look; but no, he was serious. It was written all over his face.

She stood. "I believe we have the schedule all ready for P.H., don't you agree?"

He glanced at the schedule and nodded. His countenance was a picture of disappointment. "Yes, I think so." He rose. "I hope I haven't caused you distress, Helen."

"Oh no. No, I'm honored. Who wouldn't be? And you know I'm fond of you. But I need to think about it." She threw a rather weak smile in his general direction. "Now we'd better take this to P.H. and let her look it over."

"Yes, of course." He crossed to the door and held it open while she passed through.

After leaving the schedule with P.H., Helen murmured a quick good-bye to the director and Charles and scurried up to her room, almost dizzy from the encounter with Charles. At least he'd waited until the schedule was finished before blurting out the unwelcome revelation.

Helen eased into the rocking chair by her window and leaned back. She'd hoped Patrick might visit again this weekend, but now she was glad he hadn't. What if he'd noticed the glances Charles had begun to cast in her direction? She shut her eyes tightly. And what if he had? Patrick had never indicated by word or expression that he thought of her as anything but Molly's teacher.

She, on the other hand, couldn't deny her growing attraction to Patrick Flannigan. She sighed. Well, she could just get over it. There wouldn't have been any hope for the two of them even if he was interested in her. He lived and worked in Atlanta and her life work, the passion of her life, was right here at Quincy School. It was impossible.

Perhaps she should consider Charles's request. They had the same goals and interests in life. And she did care for him. He'd been a dear friend for years. It wasn't everyone who could make her laugh. And anyone could see he was quite handsome. So what if the sight of him didn't send her heart into double beats and turn her knees to jelly. Those feelings would likely come if they were married. She groaned. She wouldn't think about that now. She had more important things to consider. Like the new student who would arrive next week. She'd arrive just in time to try out for a part in the Easter cantata.

The cantata itself wouldn't require much thought on her part. Abigail would be in charge of that. She'd done such a wonderful job on the Christmas concert and play that her election as drama and concert director had been unanimous. And after the Christmas play, the magical moment came when Abigail and Trent had exchanged their wedding vows.

Moisture pooled in Helen's eyes. Would she ever experience the joy that had radiated from both bride and groom on that day? Their faces had glowed with it. She closed her eyes again and tried to picture herself walking down the aisle toward a beaming Charles, but the fantasy groom that stood there waiting for her had taken on the form and countenance of Patrick Flannigan.

Her eyes flew open. This was ridiculous. She might as well find something constructive to do if her rest was going to bombard her with romantic fantasies that would never come to pass. So much for the relaxing weekend she'd hoped for.

She went to her writing table and picked up a small stack of papers that still needed to be graded. She'd planned to do it here, but perhaps her classroom would help her keep her mind on sensible things.

She climbed the stairs to the third floor where the smell of new wood and fresh paint still permeated the air. She stepped inside her classroom and stood in the doorway, beholding with satisfaction the smooth oak cupboards that housed supplies and books. She wondered what old Mrs. Quincy would think of her school today. Six new desks had been added in anticipation of the new students that were expected and perhaps others who hadn't enrolled yet.

Next year would be different, all right. One of the students was a thirteen-year-old boy named Roger Brumley, who'd had no formal schooling. He had partial sight and very little hearing. She only hoped they could help him. The mother of a nine-year-old deaf-blind boy had applied only to change her mind and withdraw the application. Helen hoped she'd found another school and hadn't decided to keep him at home.

With a sigh, Helen sat at her desk and began to grade the history papers. As she took one from the stack, she noticed a stiff piece of braille paper. Lily Ann. Apparently she'd decided it was time to get back to work learning to write. Helen ran her hand over the dots the child had made with her stylus. She wanted to help Lily, but unfortunately the girl was further along in her braille studies than Helen.

"All right, Lily Ann," she whispered in the empty room. "I'll get the book out and do my best."

She finished grading the papers and stacked them neatly on her desk with a paperweight on top. She stood and picked up Lily Ann's paper and went to one of the cupboards. She took the braille instruction book out and headed for the door.

After lunch, she returned to her room and sat by the window. She had several hours to study the braille book. Helen hoped she'd learn some new words in that time.

She suddenly realized she hadn't thought of Patrick or Charles for hours.

A sigh escaped her lips. Unfortunately, the problem hadn't gone away. She had to decide what to do about Charles. And in all fairness to him, she shouldn't prolong the decision.

❧

Patrick gave the piece of luggage another swipe with a soft cloth and looked the enormous black bag over with a critical eye.

Philip Taney had ordered the bag specially made to hold all his belongings as he traveled through Europe on his year abroad.

"You see," the young man had explained, "I don't want to have to worry about handling two or three bags everywhere I go."

"But this one might get heavy, don't you think?" Patrick had eyed the lad with some amusement.

Philip had shrugged. "I'm strong. Besides, my valet will be with me."

Patrick chuckled now, thinking of the boy who'd spent a fairly large amount of money to get the bag exactly as he wanted it. It wouldn't surprise Patrick a bit if Taney ended up selling or discarding the magnificent piece for something more practical, valet or not. But that wasn't his business. The spoiled young man was used to getting what he thought he wanted, and his wealthy father didn't seem to mind footing the bill.

He placed the bag on a shelf behind the counter and glanced at his watch. He'd hoped to be finished early today so he could catch the early train to Mimosa Junction. He hadn't seen Molly in two weeks. He grinned as a pair of light blue eyes flashed into his mind instead of his daughter's dark blue ones.

He'd been careful not to make his attraction to Helen known to her just yet. For one thing, if she didn't return his interest, it could be awkward since she was Molly's teacher. However, he was afraid he might have been a little too distant the last few times he was there. Much to his chagrin, he'd noticed on his last visit that Charles Waverly acted a little too chummy with Helen. Of course, he'd also noticed she'd seemed uncomfortable with the man's attention. Perhaps it was time to try a little subtle attention of his own.

He was about to close up shop when Philip Taney charged in with a friend in tow.

"Hello, Patrick. This is my friend and soon-to-be fellow traveler, Ronald Simmons. Can you show him my bag?"

Patrick turned and took the bag off the shelf. "Here you go. All finished."

Philip took the bag and held it out for his friend's inspection. "See? What did I tell you?"

"That's perfect." The tall young man looked over at Patrick. "Can you make one just like it for me?"

"I'd be happy to. I'll start on it next week."

The boy's face fell. "But we're leaving Tuesday."

Patrick sighed. It wouldn't do to pass up business when his shop was just starting to flourish. But if he agreed, it would mean he'd have to skip his planned visit to the school.

"All right. If you can pay me ahead of time, I'll get started on it tomorrow."

The deal made, Taney took his bag and the two left Patrick standing there filled with dismay.

Perhaps he should have refused. The lad could have purchased another bag either at his store or elsewhere. But then, what sort of reputation would his shop have? He shook his head. No, he'd done the right thing. He needed to make sure his finances were secure for Molly's sake.

The next week crawled by, but at last he found himself getting off the train at Mimosa Junction. He noticed activity around the general store and a brand-new sign hanging above the door that said WATSON'S MERCANTILE. So the new owner was getting the store ready for business.

He wondered if the hardware store had a buyer yet. It would be just the right size for his leather shop. A thrill shot threw him at the thought. Now why would he think of something like that? He chuckled—a very nervous sounding chuckle. He had a thriving business in Atlanta. He wasn't looking for a change. Of course, if he was, Mimosa Junction wouldn't be a bad choice. The junction was just what its name implied, and customers came from miles away in three different directions. He gave another short laugh. But he wasn't considering a change in location, was he?

The next morning he arrived at the Cecilia Quincy School for the Deaf just in time to have breakfast with his daughter.

"Papa, what are we going to do today? Can we go for a drive in the carriage?" Molly's exuberance rang across the table.

"I should hope so. It's a beautiful spring day." March had indeed come in like a lamb, as the saying went.

"Trudy's parents signed a permission note so she can go with us." She darted a look at her friend and roommate.

Trudy blushed, but hope filled her warm brown eyes.

"If it's all right with the director, I think that's a mighty fine idea." Patrick winked at Molly then at Trudy. Both girls giggled.

After breakfast, Patrick waited in the foyer while the girls helped clear the table. Helen walked out, with Charles Waverly following closely behind.

"Miss Edwards?" Although they'd been on a first name basis for a while, he was reluctant to use her first name around the other teachers.

She smiled and stopped beside him. "Yes, Mr. Flannigan?"

Charles stood there as if unsure what to do. Patrick gave him a polite nod then turned to address Helen.

"I wondered if you'd agree to accompany the girls and me on our drive." Helen blushed and he hastened to say, "I mean, as a chaperone of sorts."

Charles stiffened. "Weren't we going to go over the schedule again, Helen?"

"P.H. seemed quite satisfied with the last version." Helen gave him a gentle smile. "I don't think it's necessary to change anything, do you?"

"I guess not." He glanced from Helen to Patrick. "Well then, I'll see you at noon."

Patrick watched the man walk away, wondering whether to feel pity or irritation.

"I'd be more than happy to go along as a chaperone." She cast a worried glance after Charles.

"I'm sorry if I caused a problem for you." Perhaps there was more between those two than he'd realized. The thought sent disappointment twisting through him.

Helen gave a sad smile. "No, the problem was already there, and I'm afraid it's my own fault for not taking care of it before now."

"I see." He didn't see at all but was relieved that she considered Waverly a problem that needed to be taken care of. "Here come the girls now."

"Papa! We're ready to go." Molly grabbed Helen's hand. "Will you come with us, Miss Edwards?"

Helen laughed. "Your father just asked me the same thing, and I said yes."

Both girls squealed with delight and grabbed her hands. The three of them went outside and down the stairs, their hands swinging between them as Patrick followed behind, feeling rather left out.

Patrick grinned when Molly and Trudy climbed into the backseat. Just what he had hoped they'd do.

The sun was shining brightly by the time they drove away. Patrick took every side road he came across in order to lengthen their drive.

"Papa, are you lost?" Molly's worried voice from the backseat brought him to his senses.

"No, sweetheart. Not at all." He turned and gave her a reassuring smile, knowing his assurances were true. "I'm heading back to the main road now."

"Well, I'm getting hungry. It must be almost dinnertime," Molly said. "Are you hungry, Trudy?"

"Well, yes." Trudy blushed.

"I'm hungry, too, girls." He grinned over his shoulder. "How about we go get something to eat at the hotel?"

"Fried chicken, Papa?" Molly asked.

"You mean the fried chicken that's almost as good as Cook's?"

Molly glanced at Trudy. "It's almost as good, but we mustn't tell Cook that, all right?"

"Okay. She'd probably never cook fried chicken for us again."

A choking sound came from Helen's direction. "Now, girls, you make Cook sound vain and she isn't at all."

"Yes ma'am." Molly nodded. "But she is a little bit vain about her fried chicken."

Helen threw her head back slightly and laughed again. Patrick's breath caught. Was anyone ever so lovely?

Chapter 8

Helen tapped on the director's door. When asked to come in, she opened the door and stepped into the office. The other teachers and both house parents were already seated, as was a tall and regal-appearing young girl who sat with chin up and ankles crossed.

Helen glanced at P.H., who gave her a tight smile and nodded to the chair next to the new student. "Miss Edwards, this is Margaret Long. Margaret, Miss Edwards is our English, history, and geography teacher."

Helen smiled and offered her hand, which the girl gripped and released as though it might bite.

Helen sat and turned to the girl, enunciating clearly. "I'm very pleased to welcome you to our school, Margaret. Do you go by Meg or Peggy?"

The girl lifted her chin more and peered down her nose at Helen. "Certainly not. You may call me Margaret." The girl's speech lacked the singsong tone often noticed in the speech of the deaf. But goodness, how did the child learn to be so haughty in only twelve years?

Helen leaned back and lifted her brow at Hannah, who ducked her head to hide a smile.

Goodness. The girl was only twelve?

P.H. cleared her throat. "It seems that Margaret is much more advanced than our other students, Miss Edwards. There may need to be some one-on-one teaching."

Margaret, who apparently had been following the conversation quite well, raised her hand.

"Yes, Margaret?" P.H.'s eyes weren't exactly narrowed, but Helen had seen that expression before. She could only wonder what had transpired before she arrived in the room.

"If your teachers aren't qualified to teach me, I'm quite capable of learning from books on my own."

Helen felt her mouth drop open and quickly pressed her lips together. The little rascal.

P.H. took a deep breath and let it out slowly. "Miss Long, the teachers at Quincy School are quite capable of teaching you anything you need to learn."

Margaret sniffed audibly and tossed her head. "Yes ma'am. If you say so."

"I do." P.H. glanced at Felicity. "Will you please get Margaret settled in and ask one of the other girls to show her around? She can meet the rest of the children at supper."

Felicity stood. "Of course. Come with me, dear. You'll feel right at home before long."

Margaret stood and sent the housemother a benevolent glance but remained silent and followed her out of the room.

The moment the door shut behind them, Charles turned to P.H. "Are you sure she's only twelve? How did she learn to be such a snob in twelve years?"

P.H. sighed. "She had a good teacher. You didn't meet the mother. You will next weekend. Then you can judge for yourself."

Howard shook his head. "I hope she doesn't have a brother headed our way."

Charles laughed and the two men walked out together.

"What do you think, Helen?" P.H. threw her a curious look.

"Well, it's a little too soon for me to tell." Helen bit her lip. "Perhaps her attitude is a covering for something that bothers her."

P.H. nodded. "Good. You're going for mercy instead of judgment. Somehow I knew I could count on you to do that." She turned to Hannah. "Take a lesson from Helen, my dear. She's a wonderful role model for any teacher."

Hannah who only recently finished her training and was teaching for the first time, smiled shyly. "Yes, I know."

"Oh you two. You're going to make me cry or else make me conceited." Helen laughed. "I'd better get upstairs and see how the other girls react to our newest addition."

She arrived at the top of the stairs to see Felicity leave one of the nicer bedrooms and shut the door behind her.

Felicity stopped when she saw Helen and whispered, "Her parents insisted that she have a private room. P.H. told her it would depend on how many students enroll. But for now, at least, Miss Long is ensconced in her private palace and holding suit."

"What do you mean?" Helen felt queasy.

Felicity motioned toward the door. "See for yourself." She walked away.

Helen tapped on the door and opened it.

Margaret sat in an overstuffed chair in the corner, while Trudy and Molly unpacked her trunk. She glanced at Helen then turned back to the girls.

"Be careful. That's my favorite dress. It needs to be hung on a hanger and smoothed down."

"What's going on here?" Helen stepped into the room and took the green velvet dress from Trudy.

"We're helping Margaret, Miss Edwards," Molly said. "She gets headaches when she travels."

"In that case, it might be best if you two return to your own room and let Margaret lie down and rest. She can unpack her trunk later."

The girls scurried out and Helen laid the dress back in the trunk. She couldn't help but notice all the dresses. "If you need help, Margaret, I'll send one of the maids up to help you when they're not busy. But you need to realize that we expect the students to take care of their own personal needs as much as possible."

The girl's eyes shot daggers at Helen and when she spoke her voice was scornful. "In my old school, I had my own personal maid."

"That may very well be, my dear." Helen kept her face pleasant. "But that's not the way we operate here."

"Fine, you may leave now. I want to rest." Margaret clamped her lips together and turned her back, but not before Helen noticed the tears that had filled her eyes.

Helen shook her head and left the room, shutting the door softly. She knew Margaret's parents had moved to Georgia from Alabama and hadn't wanted their daughter to be so far away from them. Was the girl simply spoiled or was she perhaps brokenhearted over leaving dear friends and beloved teachers?

Helen sighed. Time would tell. In the meantime, she had no intention of allowing Molly and Trudy to become the girl's slaves, willing or unwilling.

⁂

"Pat! Pat Flannigan!"

Patrick swung around and his heart leapt. Jane Fuller, a friend of Maureen's, waved from across the street. Her red hair hung in curls below a fashionable sapphire-blue hat.

He waited while she made her way across the busy street, closing his eyes when a boy on a bicycle dodged to miss her.

Laughing, she stepped up on the sidewalk and grabbed his arm. "Pat, it's so wonderful to see you."

"Jane, I thought that bike had you for sure. I see you're still taking crazy risks."

She giggled and dropped his arm. "Why haven't you been to see me, you naughty boy? It's been over a year."

Had it really been that long? He sighed. How could he tell her that the sight of her caused him to miss Maureen that much more?

"It's all right. I understand." She touched his arm. "But Pat, it's been more than two years. Maureen wouldn't want you to keep grieving."

"I know. And I'm not, really." He smiled. "I guess I'll always miss her. She was my childhood sweetheart, you know. Sometimes, I think that's what I remember the most."

"But she'd want you to get on with your life. Fall in love again. Get married." She paused and looked at him. "Uh oh. What's the red face about? There is someone?"

"Well, maybe. I'm not sure." He frowned and stumbled for words.

Jane tilted her head until she could look into his eyes. "Hmmm. This sounds very interesting. Too interesting to talk about in the middle of the sidewalk. Come to dinner tonight? Michael would love to see you."

"I'm sorry. I have an order that needs to be filled before tomorrow. I'll be working late." He hesitated then went on. "But I'm on my way to the café around the corner. Come eat lunch with me."

She tilted her head for a moment. "I think I will." She turned and motioned to her carriage driver to follow then took Patrick's arm.

A few minutes later, they were settled at a neat table, covered with a red-and-white tablecloth.

He tapped the table. "Not the fanciest place in town, but it's clean and the food is good."

"Never mind the food. I want to hear about the woman you're in love with." She leaned forward and looked intently across the table at him.

Patrick laughed. "Let's order first. I'm starving."

"Oh, all right." She flashed a smile at the waiter and ordered chicken salad and lemonade.

"Now, tell me." She folded her hands on the table.

Patrick shook his head. "There's not a lot to tell. I've fallen for one of the teachers at Molly's school."

"Really?" Surprise filled her eyes. "Well, does she feel the same about you?"

Their food arrived. After the waiter left, Jane bowed her head and Patrick prayed over the meal.

She took a bite of her salad then glanced up. "Well?"

"I've no idea." He took a bite of his roast beef.

"Oh Pat. Don't tell me you haven't spoken to her about it."

"All right, I won't tell you." He grinned.

Laughter pealed from her throat. "I've never known you to be shy."

"It's not shyness." He laid his fork on the plate and leaned back, suddenly without appetite.

"At first, you see, I felt guilty. Like I was betraying Maureen. But lately, I realize that, like you said, Maureen would want me to marry again."

"Then what's the problem?" Her eyes widened. "Do you doubt she'd be a good mother to Molly?"

"No, Molly adores her and she seems to feel the same way." He heaved a sigh. "I'm just not sure it would work. My business is here and she's dedicated to the children at the school."

"Oh, is that all?" She sipped her lemonade then grinned. "Ask her. If she cares about you, she'll leave that school in the blink of an eye."

"But would it be right for me to ask her to do that? It's obvious she loves her work."

"Well, she'll still have her work. She can teach Molly." Jane took another sip. "There you are. The perfect solution. Now you can tell her how you feel about her."

Later, as Patrick worked at his bench, his thoughts turned back to their conversation. He wasn't sure whether to be amused at Jane's simple assessment of the situation or be irritated at her lack of understanding. It didn't really matter, he supposed. The situation was still the same.

&

After thinking over Margaret's educational needs, P.H. determined that although she was so far ahead, she would continue with the other students in Helen's classroom for the rest of the year, with some additional reading and essays to keep her from becoming bored. She could work at her own level in Charles's mathematic and science classes. Over the summer, Helen and Hannah would work out Margaret's classroom schedule for the following year.

The week following Margaret's arrival went well. She was respectful to the teachers and made friends with all the other children.

Helen left her classroom on Friday with a breath of relief. They'd all misjudged the child. She'd probably been tired from traveling and that had caused her temporary behavior problem.

Over the weekend, she noticed Margaret, Molly, and Trudy with their heads together several times. They seemed to be establishing their own little circle of friends but were still friendly with the other children.

Helen went looking for Margaret after church on Sunday. She found her and the other girls talking beneath one of the magnolia trees in front of the house. Helen breathed in the lemony, sweet scent of the fresh blooms in appreciation. She loved the scent of magnolia.

The girls glanced up as she approached and for an instant Helen saw the look of animosity in Margaret's eyes; just as quickly, it was gone. Perhaps she'd imagined it.

"Were you looking for us, Miss Edwards?" Margaret flashed a sweet smile.

"As a matter of fact, I was looking for *you*, Margaret." She sank down on the soft green grass beside them and tucked her skirt underneath her leg. "Did Trudy and Molly mention the Easter cantata?"

"Why yes, they did." A flicker of something flashed in her eyes, but once again it was gone. "I think it's wonderful that Lily Ann is singing the lead part."

"Yes, our Lily has a beautiful voice. But so do the rest of the students." She smiled at Molly and Trudy then turned to Margaret. "Would you like to sing in the choir, dear?"

"Oh, could I?" Her voice lilted with excitement. "I'd really like that."

"Wonderful, we're having practice tomorrow afternoon at two." Helen rose from the soft ground and inhaled the fragrant air once more. "You girls need to get washed up for dinner. It won't be long now."

"Yes, Miss Edwards," they chorused. She smiled and went back inside. How nice to see them getting along so well. Margaret was more than a year older than the other two girls, but they were close enough in age to enjoy each other's company.

Lily Ann was sitting on a bench in the parlor, alone. Her home was nearby and she usually went home on the weekends, but this Sunday her parents were away. She glanced up. "Hello, Miss Edwards."

"Lily Ann, why are you sitting here by yourself? Don't you feel well?" Helen reached over and felt the child's forehead. "You don't seem to have a fever."

"I'm not sick. I'm just sitting here." She tapped her fingers on the bench.

"Would you like for me to read you a story, dear?" Lily Ann loved books and her braille skills weren't up to the level of the books she wanted to read.

She drew in a breath. "Oh yes, ma'am."

"All right. I think we'll have time for a story after dinner." She gave Lily a hug. "Your voice all fine-tuned for tomorrow's cantata practice?"

"I don't know." Lily whispered the words and her sightless eyes blinked fast.

"Lily, are you crying?" Helen peered closely, but no tears were visible.

"No, I'm not crying." Once again, her eyes began to blink. It seemed more a nervous reaction than tears.

"Are you sure something's not wrong, Lily?"

"Yes ma'am, I'm sure." She stood. "May I be excused? Sissy said I could help set the table."

"Yes, of course. And don't forget. We have a story-reading appointment right after dinner."

She watched the girl walk away toward the kitchen. She was

such a little slip of a child. And usually cheerful. It wasn't like her to appear melancholy. Helen scoffed at herself. Lily Ann most likely just missed her parents. And Helen needed to stop looking for trouble where there was none.

"Helen." At the sound of her name, Helen groaned as Charles walked across the foyer from the library. At least this was one problem she hadn't imagined.

"Charles, could we speak privately later? Perhaps after supper?"

"Yes, of course. Shall we take a stroll down the lane?" His eyes held both hope and dread.

After their walk, his eyes would only hold one emotion. It was time she stopped delaying the inevitable.

Dread filled Helen's heart all during supper. She only hoped Charles wouldn't be too hurt at what she had to say. When the meal was over, she and Charles walked down the lane together. When they stopped beneath one of the live oaks, she looked up into his eyes.

Charles sighed. "Your answer is no?"

"I wish it could be yes, but I don't feel that way about you, Charles. I consider you a dear friend and I hope we can remain so."

He smiled and, leaning forward, planted a kiss on top of her head. "We'll always be friends, Helen. I regret putting you in this position. Let's not mention it again."

At bedtime, as she sank into her soft mattress, she thanked the Lord for giving her the courage to at least set this one matter straight.

Chapter 9

Excitement rippled across the new auditorium and the children filed backstage, getting ready for the practice.

Helen stood in the doorway and glanced over the huge room, envisioning chairs lined up side by side in rows from back to front. She gave a little chuckle. More than likely there would be about ten rows for the school staff, including the teachers, the students, and their families.

Helen headed for the dozen or so chairs that had been brought in for those who wanted to watch the practice. She sat beside Abigail, who was glancing over a list of students who'd volunteered to be in the cantata. Worry was written all over her face.

"Is anything wrong?" Helen hoped not. They only had a short time to get the musical together.

Abigail looked up. She shook her head. "I'm not sure. Lily Ann withdrew from the cantata."

"What? But why?" The little girl loved to sing and had been looking forward to her solo as well as the acting itself.

"She said she didn't want to do it." Abigail tapped her pencil against the chair beside her. "Did she seem melancholy while I was away?"

Abigail and Lily Ann had grown very close during the time Abigail had taught the child. She'd been happy when Trent and Abigail married, but she missed her teacher very much.

"No, she seemed fine." Helen hesitated. "But come to think of it, she was behaving a little strangely yesterday. Especially when I asked her about practice."

"I see. . . . Well, no, I don't see." Abigail heaved a sigh. "I'm going to ask Beth to sing Lily Ann's part today, but I don't want to replace her just yet."

"I think that's a good idea." Helen nodded. Elizabeth Thompson, one of the older girls, had partial hearing and seemed to stay with the melody quite well. "And Beth won't be that disappointed if Lily Ann changes her mind."

Abigail smiled and glanced at the girl going up the side steps to the stage. "No, our Beth hasn't a competitive bone in her body."

"Have you met the new girl yet?"

"Margaret? Yes, she's going to sing before we begin the practice. I need to know where to place her."

At Abigail's signal, Felicity sat at the piano. She nodded toward the wings, and Margaret walked onto the stage.

Silence fell across the listeners as Margaret sang "Silent Night."

Helen listened in awe. The girl's voice was beautiful. She glanced at Abigail, who seemed as mesmerized as Helen.

Margaret sang the last note and stood waiting.

"Thank you, Margaret. I'm putting you in the soprano section for now."

The girl smiled and walked off the stage.

Abigail turned to Helen. "Well, if Lily Ann doesn't sing the lead, at least I know who'll take her place."

Helen caught her breath, feeling like she'd been punched in the stomach. "Oh no." Could Margaret have had something to do with Lily Ann withdrawing? Surely not. Helen closed her eyes. She was imagining things about the new girl again.

Abigail cast a sharp look in her direction. "What? Oh no, what?"

Should she say something? But what if she was being overly suspicious and Margaret was innocent?

"Nothing. I just had a thought." She turned as Beth took her place on stage while the others lined up behind her. Today they were practicing the songs only.

Helen couldn't keep her glance from drifting to Margaret, who stood with the other sopranos, a look of total sweetness on her face.

Finally, Abigail stood. "Very good. We'll need to practice at least three times a week. So let's plan on Mondays, Wednesdays, and Fridays at four."

"Yes, Miz Quincy." The voices chorused from off the stage.

"But remember, if you should fall behind in your school-work, you will be out of the cantata."

They filed off the stage—some to do homework they'd put off, others to play outside until supper.

Uneasiness bit at Helen as she said good-bye to Abigail and went to the parlor in search of Virgie.

Virgie sat in her favorite wing chair, brushing Lily Ann's hair. They both turned their heads as Helen entered and sat in a rocker across from them.

"We missed you at practice, Lily Ann."

Lily Ann tilted her head toward Virgie, who pressed her lips together and began braiding Lily Ann's silky brown hair. "You goin' to answer Miz Helen?"

Lily Ann hiccuped. "Excuse me." She lifted her chin resolutely. "I'm not going to be in the Easter cantata."

Helen nodded. "Yes, Miss Abigail told me. Is anything wrong?"

Panic seized her face, but she shook her head. "No ma'am."

Helen glanced at Virgie, who gave a shake of her head. Helen nodded. They'd talk later.

After supper, Helen made a beeline for the parlor where she found Virgie waiting for her.

"All right. What's going on?"

Virgie sighed. "I wish I knew. Something's got that little gal spooked."

"But she wouldn't tell you anything?"

"Not with words, she didn't." Pain crossed Virgie's thin brown face. "But something's bothering our Lily girl. So what are we going to do about it?"

Darkness enshrouded Helen's thoughts as anger rose like a thundercloud in her heart. Why would anyone wish to cause that precious child pain?

Helen jumped up. "I'm not sure what's going on, but I have a pretty good idea who might be behind it." Her fingers balled into fists.

Virgie stood and stepped over to her, worry filling her faded brown eyes. "Miz Helen, honey, don't let sin get aholt of you now. Lift Lily Ann and whatever's in your mind up to the Lord. He love that little angel more than we do." She placed both hands on Helen's shoulders and gave her a gentle shake. "And if someone's causing her grief, well, the Lord love them, too. And He knows how to make it all come out right."

Helen bit her lip and nodded. "Thank you, Virgie. I'm sure you're right. I think I need to go upstairs and try to calm down."

Calm, however, was the last thing Helen felt as she paced her room. She was almost certain Molly and Trudy knew what was going on, and she was tempted to charge into their room and demand they tell her. But something held her back, and she was pretty sure it was God. She knew in her heart Virgie was right, but so far Helen had been unable to calm the turmoil inside her.

She dropped into the rocking chair and put her face in her hands. "Lord, forgive me for this uncontrolled anger. Please calm me down and show me what You want me to do."

At first, she sensed no change, but gradually, as she stayed in God's presence, peace like a warm cloak fell upon her. She breathed in a deep, welcome breath of surrender and let it flow back out through her lips.

&

While her class studied their history chapter, Helen looked over papers the children had turned in at the beginning of class.

Thursdays were usually the worst day of the week, with the students tired and ready for their weekend to begin. But they'd been model students all day, without even one scuffle or argument.

She glanced up from her desk and scanned the room in case anyone needed help. Every head was bent over in study except for Trudy's and Molly's.

Helen stood and walked over to Trudy's desk. Her book was closed and she stared straight ahead. Helen touched her on the shoulder and Trudy glanced up. Fear clouded her eyes.

"Why aren't you working, Trudy?" Instead of speaking, the girl signed, "I don't want to."

What? She didn't want to? Perhaps Helen misunderstood.

"Are you having trouble with the reading?" She frowned as she questioned Trudy.

Trudy shook her head and darted a glance at Molly, who sat at the next desk.

With dread in her heart, Helen stepped over to Molly's desk and sighed. Molly's book was also closed.

Helen touched her hand to get her attention. When Molly looked up, her eyes pooled with tears.

Helen tried to keep her face composed. "You don't wish to study either?"

Molly shook her head.

"You realize we have an important test tomorrow?" Helen tapped her foot on the floor.

Molly nodded.

Helplessness washed over Helen. How could she handle something she didn't understand?

She walked over to Margaret's desk expecting a repeat of the disobedience. Margaret's book was open and she perused the page intently. She glanced up and smiled. Anyone would think she was totally innocent. Helen didn't believe that for a moment. Somehow she was controlling the other girls. But how?

Instructing Molly and Trudy to remain at their desks at the end of class, she returned to the papers she'd been grading.

She'd dealt with defiance before, but this was something different. *Lord, show me what to do and guide me as I speak to these girls.*

When the class filed out the door, Helen's glance happened to fall on Margaret just as she looked back at Molly and Trudy and her eyes sent a silent message. Helen clamped her lips together.

She motioned to the two girls to come up front and stand in front of her desk.

"All right, girls. This behavior isn't like you at all. I know something is wrong, and I don't believe it's your fault. Is someone bullying you in any way?"

Alarm sprung into both girls' eyes, and they both shook their heads vehemently.

"You can tell me. I won't let anyone harm you." She glanced from Molly to Trudy. "I promise. Please tell me what's going on."

Both girls stood silently, their faces pictures of misery.

Helen sighed. "Very well. I have no choice but to keep you in detention for an hour every day until you explain your conduct."

"But Miss Edwards"—Molly clamped her hands over her mouth and signed—"what about our homework?"

"What about it? You'll work on it during detention. If you can't complete it in that time you will still have an hour before supper."

"But, but"—Trudy caught herself and signed—"the cantata?"

"I suppose you'll both have to drop out since you can't get to practice." At the pain on their faces, Helen wanted to cry.

"All right, girls. Return to your desk. You have another half hour. I would suggest you study your history."

Helen sighed. She had no idea how to handle this situation. Ordinarily, she'd take the matter up with P.H., but the director had gone to New Orleans to meet with a family who was interested in the school for their son. Since she had family of her own there, P.H. had decided to stay and visit, so she wouldn't be back for at least a week. If Helen couldn't get the situation under control, she'd have to bring it to Trent Quincy's attention.

❧

Patrick looked around the dining room table. Although normal conversation went on amidst the teachers and students, the tension in the room was tangible. He glanced at Helen, who ate her breakfast in silence, only looking up when someone spoke directly to her.

Molly had run to him when she saw him in the foyer and thrown her arms around him. But instead of the bubbling over happiness that usually permeated her greeting, she'd burst into tears. She'd said she was crying because she was happy to see him, but that didn't ring true or even make sense.

Helen left the dining room while he was speaking with Howard. When he stepped into the foyer, he found her waiting for him. "Mr. Flannigan, could I have a word with you?"

"Yes, of course. I was going to ask you the same thing." He motioned toward the front porch. "Shall we go outside?"

"Yes, that's fine."

They'd just seated themselves when Molly charged out the door. "Papa!"

"He stood and motioned to his daughter. "I'm over here, Molly."

"I didn't know where you were." She twisted her hands together.

"Well, as you can see, here I am." He smiled. "I need a moment with Miss Edwards then we'll go for a drive, all right?"

Molly sent Helen an imploring glance then she turned to her father. "Can't I stay here with you?"

He gave her a puzzled look then glanced at Helen. "Does someone want to tell me what's going on?"

"I think Molly should answer that." Helen looked at Molly. "Do you want to tell your father what's wrong, since you won't tell me?"

Molly stood breathing hard. She moistened her lips and darted a glance toward the front door. "Papa, can we go somewhere? Just you and me, so I can tell you?"

He frowned and sent a questioning glance toward Helen.

Helen nodded. "I think that's a good idea, Patrick. You and I can talk later."

Molly grabbed his hand. "Hurry, Papa. Let's go now."

৵

As the carriage drove away, Helen sank back into the wicker rocker. She sent up a prayer that Molly would open up to Patrick and get her fears out into the open.

The front door flew open and Margaret stepped out on the porch. She spotted Helen. "Oh Miss Edwards. You startled me."

She glanced around. "Have you seen Molly?"

"Yes, you just missed her, dear. She went for a drive with her father." Helen peered at the girl to see her reaction.

Margaret's face paled. "Oh. Well, I'd better go back inside."

"Why don't you sit and visit with me for a while?"

"Oh thank you, but I need to go inside. I have things to do."

"Nevertheless, I'd like for you to stay. I think we need to have a little talk."

"Oh, very well." She flounced over and sat on the cushioned sofa.

"How was practice yesterday?" Helen rocked slowly back and forth.

"Why, it went very well." She threw an impatient look in Helen's direction.

"You have a lovely voice," Helen said. "Good enough for the lead part."

A pleased look washed over Margaret's face. "Yes. I always had the lead parts at my other school."

"Did you now?" She rocked steadily. "I was surprised when Lily Ann withdrew from the cantata. She has a lovely voice as well."

"Does she?" Margaret tossed her curls. "But she's just a little girl. She shouldn't have the lead anyway."

"Hmmm. You think not?" Helen stopped her chair. "Do you have any idea what's wrong with Molly and Trudy? They're not acting like themselves lately."

"No. They seem okay to me. Where did you say Molly and her father went?"

"Just for a drive." Helen paused before going on. "I believe Molly had something she wished to talk to her father about. Something important I believe."

Panic crossed the girl's face.

"Margaret, perhaps there's something you'd like to tell me before they get back."

"No. Why would you think that?" The panic—if indeed Helen hadn't been imagining it—was smoothed over by Margaret's usual sweet expression.

Chapter 10

Trent shook his head, looking almost dazed. "It appears the new student, that angelic-appearing little girl, has been terrorizing other children."

Helen flinched at the word *terrorizing*. What in the world had Margaret done? When Patrick and Molly had gotten back from their drive, his face had been set like stone. He'd asked Virgie to please send for Trent Quincy, since the director wasn't there.

Helen had paced the foyer while Patrick, Trent, Molly, and Trudy had been closeted in the director's office for fifteen minutes. Finally, Trent had opened the door and asked Helen to step inside.

She glanced at Molly and Trudy, who sat huddled up together next to Patrick on the small sofa. "Are you girls all right?"

Molly nodded. "Yes, Miss Edwards."

It was the first time Molly had spoken to her in days and she breathed a sigh of relief.

Trent stepped to the door and motioned to someone. A moment later, Virgie appeared.

"Virgie, would you please take Molly and Trudy to the kitchen and get them a glass of milk or something? That is"—he turned with a questioning glance at Patrick—"if it's all right with Mr. Flannigan."

"Yes, but please keep them away from the other children for now, Virgie." Patrick brushed the hair back from Molly's face. "You don't mind going with Miz Virgie, do you?"

Molly shook her head, and the girls stood and followed Virgie from the room. As soon as the door shut behind them, Helen jumped up. "Will someone please tell me what is going on? What has Margaret done?"

Patrick rose, too, and stood by the empty fireplace. "It seems, since the day she arrived, the young lady has been controlling both Molly and Trudy."

"Yes, I was afraid it was something like that. But how did she manage? Trudy is rather timid, but Molly is not a weak-willed girl."

"It seems she threatened if they didn't do everything she told them, she'd hurt Lily Ann."

Helen's stomach knotted. "But surely they wouldn't believe her? Why in the world didn't they tell someone?"

"Apparently she's a very persuasive young lady. She told them poppycock stories of atrocities she'd performed at her former school." Trent's lips clamped together and his face blazed with anger. "Of course, the stories were totally untrue. I spoke to the director of her former school before I approved her enrollment here. According to him, she'd been a model student."

"I wonder. . . ." Helen frowned. "Oh, not about the atrocities. I'm sure the director would have known if that were true. But she may not have been the model student he thought."

"What do you mean?" Patrick asked.

"I mean, bullies aren't always found out, because their victims don't usually tell." She bit her lip. "Molly and her father are close. She knew he'd believe her and she trusted him to make things right. But that's not always the case."

Trent nodded. "I see what you mean. Well, I suppose I need to contact her parents. We can't have a child here that terrorizes the other students."

That word again. "I wouldn't exactly call it terrorizing. More like bullying. But she must be troubled to do such a thing."

Patrick took a deep breath. "Are you suggesting she be allowed to stay?"

"No. It's not my place to do that. But I think she should have a chance to defend herself."

"Molly wouldn't lie about it!" Patrick protested. "I thought you knew her better than that."

"Of course I do." She laid her hand on his arm and then quickly dropped it. What had possessed her to do something so intimate? "But Margaret needs to speak for herself."

"Helen's right." Trent strode to the door and pulled a bell cord. When Sissy appeared, he instructed her to escort Margaret to the office.

The fear in Margaret's eyes and the ghastly paleness of her face as she walked into the room struck a chord of sympathy in Helen.

"Hello, Margaret." Trent motioned to a chair he'd placed in the middle of the room facing him, Patrick, and Helen. She sat on the edge of the seat and swallowed audibly.

"Margaret, it has come to our attention that you've been bullying some of the other students." Trent tapped his fingers on his knee.

"No I haven't," the child's voice shrilled.

"Young lady, it would be better to tell the truth. Lies always get found out in the end." After he'd spoken, Patrick sent Trent an apologetic glance.

She caught her bottom lip between her teeth, and a frown creased her forehead as her eyes filled with tears.

Helen's heart hurt for the child. What could have caused her to behave in such a way?

"I'm sorry." Margaret's whisper was almost inaudible.

Trent's expression softened. "Margaret, everyone does things at times they regret. I sincerely hope that's what you mean and that you aren't merely sorry you got caught."

A crimson blush rushed across her face, and she licked her lips. "I...I don't know. I'm just sorry. What are you going to do to me?"

Trent looked at the girl for a moment. "Why did you threaten Molly and Trudy and tell them untrue stories about your actions at your last school?"

"I don't know." She pressed her lips together and her breathing quickened.

Trent threw a helpless glance toward Helen. Apparently he'd never dealt with a serious disciplinary problem before. He turned his attention back to the girl. "I'm sorry. I can't accept that as an answer. Until we get to the bottom of this, you're confined to your room. I will, of course, notify your parents of your behavior."

Panic crossed Margaret's face and her hands tightened into a fists.

"That will be all for now. You're dismissed to your room."

"Please don't. . ." Margaret heaved a sigh. "Yes sir."

After the door closed behind her, Helen immediately turned to Trent. "Would you mind if I talk to Margaret and try to get to the bottom of this?"

"By all means." Trent took a handkerchief from his pocket and dabbed his forehead. "Let me know if you have any success."

Helen nodded and glanced at Patrick. "I know you're angry because of what she did to Molly, but try not to judge her too harshly until we find out more."

He nodded. "I'll try. After all, she's only a child. I wish you success."

&

Helen set the dinner tray on a small table outside Margaret's room, tapped lightly before opening the door, and walked in.

Margaret looked up from the window seat. "Miss Edwards. You brought my supper?"

Helen smiled. "You didn't think we'd let you go hungry, did you?" She glanced around and spotted a table in the corner. "Why don't you move that table over here for your tray and I'll visit with you while you eat."

Margaret jumped up and hurried to do as instructed. When she was seated again, she laid the snowy white napkin across her lap and lifted the dome lid from her plate. "Oh, ham and sweet potatoes. My favorite."

"Yes, and that little covered dish contains peach cobbler." She moved a glass of milk closer to Margaret. "Cook thought you'd like the cobbler."

Margaret put down her knife and fork and turned wide eyes upon Helen. "Why is everyone being so nice to me after what I've done?"

"Well, first of all, very few people know the details, and besides, we care about you, Margaret. And I, for one, would like to help, if you'll let me." She motioned to the tray. "Why don't you eat before your food gets cold? We can talk afterward."

Margaret ate slowly, finally pushing the tray away. She turned to Helen. "What do you want me to say?"

Surprised, Helen said, "The truth, of course. I'd like to know why you threatened to hurt Lily. Why you ordered the girls not to talk to me, and what this all has to do with Lily Ann. Because it does have something to do with her, doesn't it?"

Margaret's eyes widened and she ducked her head. "I always have the lead."

A knot formed in Helen's stomach. "What do you mean?"

"You see, my mother is very proud of my voice and she expects me to have the lead. Always." She bit her lip.

"But, sweetheart, I'm sure your mother understands that sometimes that's not going to happen. Lily Ann has a lovely voice, too. And she already had the part before you arrived."

"But I want my mother to be proud of me." Tears swam in her blue eyes and began to run down her cheeks. "She's so good at everything and all I can do is sing."

Helen closed her eyes for a moment and took a deep breath. "How did you get Lily Ann to withdraw from the cantata, Margaret?"

Shame washed over the child's face. "I—I..."

"Please tell me."

"I told her if she didn't, I would trip Mrs. Quincy and make her lose the baby."

Waves of nausea and shock washed over Helen. "You would have done that?"

"No, no,"—sobs broke out from Margaret—"no, I wouldn't have. Not really."

"But Lily Ann thought you would, so she did what you wanted."

"Yes." Margaret's voice broke as sob after sob racked her body.

"There's more, isn't there?" Helen laid her hand on Margaret's shoulder. "You might as well tell me all of it."

"I made Lily Ann promise not to tell anyone. But Trudy saw me talking to her, saw her crying. She told Molly, and they came and told me to leave Lily Ann alone."

"And that's when you threatened them?"

"Uh-huh. I was afraid they'd tell. So I told them they had to stay away from Lily Ann and if they told anyone about any of it, I'd hurt her." By now she seemed bent on telling all. "I made some stories up so they'd believe that I'd really do mean things."

"But why wouldn't they speak to me?"

"I was mad because you liked Molly so much." She gulped. "I guess that was just being mean. I told them they couldn't talk to you."

The memory of the episode in the classroom with Trudy and Molly ran through Helen's mind. "But you forgot to tell them not to sign."

"Miss Edwards. I don't know what got into me. I never did anything like this before. I promise."

"I believe you, Margaret." Helen reached over and tucked a stray hair back in the girl's ribbon. "Jealousy can be ugly and vicious. Just as other sins."

At the word *sin*, Margaret gasped. "I didn't know I was sinning. Is God mad at me?"

"Margaret, God loves us and sent Jesus to pay the price for our sins." She looked directly at the girl. "Have you accepted Jesus as your savior?"

Margaret nodded with tears flooding down her cheeks. "Yes ma'am. But I forgot about Him for a while. Does that mean I'm not a Christian anymore?"

Helen swallowed past the lump that formed in her throat. "Sweetheart, 1 John 1:9 tells us 'if we confess our sins, he is faithful and just to forgive us our sins, and to cleanse us from all unrighteousness.'"

"Can I do that now?" She slipped off the window seat and knelt by her bed. In a few minutes she rose. "I know He forgave me. But I have to tell Molly and Trudy and Lily Ann I'm sorry and ask them to forgive me, too."

"I'm sure they will, Margaret." Helen stood and picked up the tray. "If you need me for anything, ring for Sissy and she'll come get me."

"Thank you, Miss Edwards." Margaret opened the door for her. "I know how much you care for Molly. Thank you for not being mad at me."

Helen took the tray to the kitchen then went to have her own supper. Trudy and Lily Ann were subdued but the tension was gone. Molly had gone to the hotel to have supper with her father. Afterward, Helen stepped outside and sat, all the events of the day rushing through her mind. Trent would speak to Lily Ann and her parents after church on Sunday, but Helen needed to tell him what Margaret had confessed. Abigail also needed to know because of the situation with the cantata.

The sound of horse hooves and the jingle of the harness drifted up the lane and the carriage came into sight.

The welcome sound of Molly's giggle rang out. Patrick helped her down from the carriage. "Good night, Papa." She ran up the steps and went inside without seeing Helen.

"It sounds like we have our happy girl back."

Patrick started. "Helen. I didn't see you." He came up the steps and onto the porch then sat in the chair next to her.

Leaning back, he took a deep breath. "What a day."

"Yes, it was indeed." Helen smiled. "Margaret confessed to everything."

Relief crossed his face. "Why did she do those things?"

"Well, the surface reason, if you can believe this, is that she wanted to sing the lead in the cantata." Helen frowned. "But I believe there's a deeper reason behind it all."

"Well, I hate to see any child punished, but that young lady needs to learn a lesson so it doesn't happen again."

"Yes, of course she does. But I think she's truly sorry. We had a talk before supper."

Helen told him everything that had transpired with Margaret. "I believe she was sincere, Patrick."

He nodded. "I hope so. What action do you think Trent will take?"

"I don't know. He's planning to speak to her parents as soon as possible. But for now, she's confined to her room, except for school."

"I'm thankful Molly told me about it. There's no telling how long it would have gone on or what course it would have taken next."

Helen nodded. "Or it may not have lasted much longer. The fact that she caved in and confessed everything so readily makes me think her conscience was hurting her already."

He smiled and touched her hand. "You have a sweet soul, Helen Edwards. You always seem to see the good in people."

She blushed. "Thank you, Patrick. I'm afraid I'm not quite as good-hearted as you think. I struggle with ill thoughts toward people just as everyone does. It's a process, I guess. By God's grace, we grow in character."

"Yes, but some of us have prettier characters than others. I don't know anyone I'd rather spend time with." He touched her cheek. "There, I've embarrassed you. I didn't mean to do that."

"You didn't embarrass me." She turned her head. "Well, perhaps just a little. I enjoy your company, too."

"Helen."

Her pulse quickened as he looked deeply into her eyes. She caught her breath. She wasn't ready for this. Besides, nothing had changed. His life was in Atlanta. Hers was here. She jumped up. "I really need to check on Margaret. I'll see you at church in the morning."

Without giving him a chance to say anything more, she hurried inside.

Chapter 11

The rustle of starched dresses and scuffling of shoes joined the muffled laughter and conversation of neighbors and friends who hadn't seen one another for a week.

Helen helped usher the children to their seats on the long pews. She stepped into the row, but before she could sit, she felt a hand on her elbow. Her heart gave a little jump as she looked up into Patrick's smiling face.

She moved over so Molly could sit beside her with Patrick on the end. Flashing them both a smile, Helen straightened her spine and looked forward to where Silas Monroe, the song leader of the day, stood behind the pulpit, fanning through the pages of the hymnal.

Silas cleared his throat loudly, and the congregation gave him their attention. "Good morning, brothers and sisters. It's nice to see you all here on this fine, sunshiny Lord's day. The first song we're gonna sing reflects that nicely. Turn to page forty-seven."

Helen knew the lovely gospel song by heart, and she sang along with the other raised voices.

"Oh there's sunshine, blessed sunshine,
When the peaceful, happy moments roll;
When Jesus shows His smiling face,
There is sunshine in the soul."

To be honest, she wasn't feeling all that sunshiny this morning. The situation with Margaret still hung over them. Dr. Trent had decided to leave the matter in the director's hands since she was expected back the next day. So, until then, the girl was confined to her room except to attend church services.

But that wasn't the only thing weighing on her. She couldn't deny to herself any longer that her feelings for Patrick had grown beyond friendship. And if his actions were any indication, he felt the same toward her. She'd struggled most of the night with the conflict in her heart. Should she take the chance on falling in love and having to leave the school and the children who meant so much to her? If not, then could she harden her heart toward Patrick and prevent that from happening?

She started at a tug on her sleeve and realized everyone had stood. She gave Molly a smile and stood, her face blazing.

Patrick threw her a questioning lift of an eyebrow, and she pretended not to see but focused on the hymnal as they sang the last verse.

Reverend Shepherd's message was on hearing God's voice. Helen listened intently. How could she know she was doing God's will? Obviously His Word was His will, but some things couldn't be found in the Bible. What about finding God's will when the choices were both good ones? How did one know?

The reverend spoke of letting God guide you, of God's still, small voice and inner peace, but Helen couldn't quite wrap her mind around what he was saying. Of course, there had been times when she knew in her heart that she was or was not making a right decision. But many times, she continued to struggle. She sighed. One thing she was sure of—God's Word was truth and if she didn't understand then it wasn't God's fault.

As she stepped outside, the noonday sun hit her full in the face. Oh dear, a hot day for the beginning of April.

After she'd shaken Reverend Shepherd's hand, she started to walk toward the wagon.

"Helen."

She turned at the sound of Patrick's voice to find him and Molly with eager looks on their faces.

"Molly and I would be pleased if you'd go to dinner at the hotel with us." He ran his fingers around the brim of his hat and gave her a hopeful smile.

"I'm sorry. I'm Margaret's monitor today. I can't leave the

school." Gazing on their disappointed faces, she added, "But I wish I could accept your offer."

"Then perhaps we can go for a walk later."

"Perhaps. As long as we don't go far."

Helen watched them drive away and turned to help get the younger children into the wagon. Disappointment and relief battled inside her.

At the school, Selma had prepared a dinner of pork chops, sweet potatoes, stuffing, glazed carrots, and all the home-canned condiments for which she was famous. Helen barely tasted the delicious meal. She did, however, drink several glasses of sweet tea and had a small slice of caramel pecan cake. In spite of everything, she felt better afterward. She chuckled to herself. Perhaps sugar was a medicine.

After the girls had helped clear the table, Helen escorted Margaret to her room.

"Do I have to stay here all day again today? I need some air. Can't you take me outside for a little while?" She gave Helen a pleading look.

One thing that didn't work with Helen was cajoling. She'd been teaching far too long for that to sway her. "I'm very sorry, dear, but Dr. Trent was quite clear. Besides, you've just had a nice drive in the fresh air to the church and back."

Margaret sighed and flounced over to the window seat. "Oh all right. I know I deserve it."

"Miss Wellington will arrive tomorrow, dear." Just saying the words brought relief to Helen. P.H. could get on her nerves sometimes, but there was no denying that things went much more smoothly when she was here. "Then we'll get this whole thing straightened out."

"What do you think she'll do to me, Miss Edwards?" The girl's voice held a niggling of fear.

"She'll be fair. That's all I can say for certain." Helen gave an emphatic nod. "Miss Wellington is always fair."

Margaret sighed. "Any punishment she can think of would be fair. What I did wasn't nice at all."

Helen wished she could have allowed Margaret to speak to Molly, Trudy, and Lily Ann. Once Margaret made things right with them, things would be better. But without permission from Dr. Trent, who wasn't at church this morning, Helen couldn't give her permission.

"No, it wasn't nice at all, but God has forgiven you and I know the girls will, too. Would you like for me to bring you some more books?"

"No, thank you." Margaret gave her a pensive look. "I believe I'll write in my diary and draw a little."

"I'm very happy you have a diary. I've kept one since I was nine years old. And I'd love to see your drawings one day, if you wouldn't mind."

"I guess that would be all right." She stood and lifted the lid of the window seat.

Helen left and went to her own room. *Dear God, please let this work out for everyone's good.*

❧

Patrick tried to focus on Molly, but his mind kept drifting to Helen. Had she seemed a little distant today?

"Papa, did you hear what I said?" Molly put her fork on her plate and frowned.

"What? Oh Molly, I'm so sorry. I'm a little distracted today." He took a drink of tea.

She gave him a forgiving smile. "It's all right, Papa. I was just wondering if you think you'll ever get married again."

He coughed as the sweet tea went down wrong. He grabbed a napkin as he continued to cough while Molly pounded him on the back.

When he caught his breath again, he looked at Molly. "Why did you ask that?"

"Oh, I don't know. You're not really old, you know. And Trudy said you'd probably want to get married again someday."

"Oh she did, did she? What do you think of the idea?"

She looked up at the ceiling with a wise expression on her face. "Oh, I think it would depend on who you wanted to marry. She'd have to be nice and like children. Especially me."

He nodded. "Yes, I can see that would be a necessary requirement. Did you have someone in mind?"

She grabbed her fork and took a bite of apple pie. After swallowing, she nodded. "Miss Edwards is nice and she's not married yet. It would be a shame if she had to be an old maid all her life."

He pressed his lips together to hide a grin. "I suppose she seems old to you?"

"Well, sort of. But we wouldn't want some silly young girl to live with us, would we?"

"No, I guess not." He shook his head. The things the child came up with. "But perhaps Miss Edwards wouldn't like to be married to me."

Molly's lips curled up in a smile. "I think she likes you."

A pleasant jolt ran through him. "Why do you think so?"

"Oh Papa," she rolled her eyes and signed, "I'm not a baby. I see how she looks at you."

"How?" He held his breath.

"The same way you look at her when you don't think anyone sees you." She giggled.

Startled, he sent her an anxious glance. "You're imagining things."

She cut a glance his way and licked her fork. "I don't think so."

Patrick laughed. "Finish your pie, Miss See-all and Know-all. We need to get back to the school."

Well, it seemed he had his daughter's approval. Too bad it wasn't a practical idea.

As they drove out of town, she turned to him. "So are you going to?"

"Am I going to what, angel?"

An exaggerated sigh escaped her lips. "Propose marriage to Miss Edwards."

"Honey, it's not that simple. I couldn't ask Helen to give up the teaching position she loves. And my shop and our home are in Atlanta."

"Oh, that's no problem." She brushed a piece of lint off her skirt. "Move the shop here."

❧

Helen caught herself glancing out the door again. She simply had to stop that. They'd be here when they got here. And she had to stop caring. She spun on her heel and headed for the stairs. Perhaps she should go find something to work on.

In her room, she sat in the rocker by her window and picked up the pillowcase she was embroidering. After stabbing at the fabric and sticking her finger for the third time, she sighed. Maybe she'd take her embroidery out on the porch and work in the fresh air.

She stood and carried the pillowcase with her downstairs. The murmur of voices drifted from the parlor. She stepped to the parlor door and looked inside. Virgie and Felicity sat in matching rockers working on costumes.

"Mind if I join you?"

"You come right on in here and sit yourself down." Virgie motioned to a chair across from her. "There be a nice cool breeze coming through the window."

Helen grinned. What Virgie considered a nice cool breeze barely moved the lace curtain. But then, Virgie had lived in Georgia all her life.

After Helen was seated, she picked up a fan and moved it back and forth. "It feels like summer already."

"Uh uh, baby girl," Virgie shook her head, "you ought to know better than that. How many years you been here?"

"You're right. Come July, this would feel cool." Helen smoothed the pillowcase and began pulling the pale pink thread through

247

the material to form a flower petal.

"How that Margaret girl doing up there shut up in her room?"

"She's lonely, I think, but she'll be okay."

"Give her plenty of time to think about her ways." Virgie's soft voice soothed Helen's mind, relaxing her.

"I expect you're right," Felicity agreed. "She'll think twice before she pulls a trick like that again."

Helen held up her embroidery and peered at one of the stitches. Was it a little crooked? She pulled it out and redid it. "I believe she's truly sorry. And who knows the real root cause for what she did?"

Virgie gave her an approving smile. "I expect you'll be finding out."

"I certainly hope to." She wondered if there was any basis to Margaret's fear of her mother's disapproval. She had only spoken with the parents for a few moments when they brought Margaret to the school. The lady had seemed very nice, but of course, looks could be deceiving.

Virgie nodded. "How are the childrun liking their new classrooms?"

Helen threw her a look of thanks for changing the subject. "They are settling in very nicely. And they love the auditorium. It echoes."

Virgie gave a soft chuckle. "I expect it does. Big, old, hollow room like that. When it gets filled up with chairs and people, it won't echo so much."

Helen glanced at the green velvet Felicity was fashioning into knee-length breeches. She wondered which lady of the Quincy family had worn it and to what occasion.

The sound of a carriage out front drew her attention, and she glanced toward the door then quickly back. Virgie sent her a knowing smile.

"What?"

"I didn't say anything." But Virgie's smile grew bigger.

Felicity giggled. "Anyone can see you and Mr. Flannigan like each other."

Helen's face flamed. "Of course we like each other. As friends. Nothing else," she snapped.

Felicity nodded. "If you say so."

The screen door squeaked open and Helen shushed her. "Be quiet. He'll hear you."

"All right. All right." Felicity pressed her lips together and made a motion as if she were buttoning them.

"Oh you."

"Bye, Papa, I'll see you in a little while." Molly's voice rang out. "Don't forget what we talked about."

Her shoes tapped across the foyer and up the stairs.

"Someone better go see if that man need something. He just standing in the foyer."

Helen stood and laid her embroidery on the chair. "Oh all right. I'll go."

Patrick stood in the foyer looking around helplessly. Relief crossed his face when she stepped out of the parlor.

"I wasn't sure where to find you," he said.

"Oh, were you looking for me?"

"Yes, we talked earlier about going for a walk? I wondered if you're still interested."

"I think that would be fine. Let me put my sewing away."

She stepped into the parlor and picked up her embroidery. "I'm going to look in on Margaret then go for a walk."

Felicity grinned. "I can check on Margaret for you."

"No, thank you. I need to put my sewing away anyway. And get that smug look off your face, Felicity. We're just friends."

"If you say so."

Helen shook her head and went upstairs. Margaret was busy writing in her diary and didn't need anything, so Helen went to her room to put her things away. She straightened her dress and patted her hair. Should she change her blouse? No, of course not.

The one she was wearing was just fine even though rather plain.

She took a deep breath and changed into a pretty blue blouse with a lace-trimmed collar. She might as well look nice if she was going to stroll down the lane. After all, it was Sunday afternoon. You never knew who would come to visit. *Oh stop it, Helen,* she scolded herself. *You want to look nice for Patrick.*

She lifted her chin and went downstairs.

Chapter 12

The fragrance of magnolia blossoms saturated the air as Helen and Patrick strolled down the lane. The peach trees were just starting to blossom as well. Helen inhaled deeply. One of the things she loved most about Georgia. The fragrance from early spring and throughout the summer was almost enough to offset the heavy, humid heat, which was already making its discomfort known.

They stopped just before the gate and sat on the bench beneath the old live oak tree.

"It's so beautiful here in the spring." Helen glanced around. "Sometimes I sit here and imagine the Quincy family and their friends before the War. I can almost see them strolling on the lawns and gardens, the ladies in their wide hoopskirts and the men in their ruffled shirts."

Patrick grinned. "I'd say those ruffled shirts and hoopskirts weren't too comfortable in the summertime."

Helen smiled. "Probably not. The things we put up with for fashion."

"So you think you'd like to have lived in that period of time?" He pulled a piece of grass and tapped it against his palm.

"Heavens no! I could never have tolerated slavery. It must have been horrible for the slaves." A shudder went through her.

Patrick sighed. "Yes, it must have been. I wonder if their owners realized that."

"Some of them, perhaps. But I imagine, for those who were born and raised in that society, it was just part of life. It was the way things were."

"Are any of the servants here former slaves?"

Helen bit her lip and sadness washed over her face. She nodded. "Virgie and Albert. But I believe they were quite young when the late Mrs. Quincy set all the family slaves free."

"Set them free?"

"Yes, well before the War. As I understand it, her husband left everything to her when he passed away." Admiration for the brave woman washed over her as it did every time she thought about it. "She freed all the slaves and gave them each land and a cabin. The ones who wanted to continue to work for her received salaries. Most of the blacks around here are descendants of those same slaves."

Patrick shook his head. "You don't hear too many stories like that. She must have been a fine woman."

"Yes, but probably not too popular with her neighbors afterward."

A carriage came around the bend and stopped at the gate. The driver got down and opened it.

"Look. It's P.H. We weren't expecting her until tomorrow." Helen waved as the carriage rolled by them.

Patrick stood and tipped his hat as the director waved back then motioned for them to follow. "That's good. Perhaps we can get this thing with Margaret settled and I won't need to stay over."

Disappointment tugged at Helen, but she managed to keep a pleasant expression on her face.

"Not that I'm eager to go," Patrick said, "but I have a business to run."

"Yes, of course." And there it was again, glaring in Helen's face and bursting her enjoyment of the afternoon. His life was in Atlanta; hers was here. "I suppose we'd better get back to the house to welcome her back."

When they entered the house, the foyer was teeming with excited children surrounding P.H., each attempting to tell her hello. Helen grinned. P.H. could be firm in her speech sometimes, but she had a heart of gold and the children knew it.

Felicity and Howard finally managed to round the younger children up and take them to the mudroom to wash up for supper. The older students trailed behind. Enticing aromas drifted out the door from the kitchen area.

P.H. gave a little moan of delight. "I have sorely missed Selma's cooking."

"Miz Wellington, Selma is one right good cook." Virgie believed in giving credit where credit was due and never mentioned that she'd taught Cook everything she knew.

"Now, let me go freshen up. Miss Edwards, Miss Wilson, and Mr. Waverly, I'd like to see the three of you in my office after supper, if you please." She grew suddenly serious. "I need you to explain to me about the incident with our new student."

"How in the world did you find out about it?" Charles asked her.

"I received a telegram from Dr. Quincy, but he told me very little. So I finished my business affairs and took the first train I could get."

"Actually Helen is the one who knows the details." Charles glanced hopefully from P.H. to Helen. "The rest of us have heard very little of the matter. Perhaps she's the one you need to speak with."

"Very well. Now let me go. I'm hot from the sun, dusty from the train, and famished."

"Wait, Miss Wellington," Helen called after her. "I believe Mr. Flannigan should be included in our conversation. His daughter is involved in this, and he must return to Atlanta tomorrow."

"All right. Mr. Flannigan, too." P.H. fluttered the fingers of one hand over her shoulder without turning around.

Charles and Hannah headed toward the dining room.

Patrick glanced down at Helen. "Thank you for suggesting my presence at your meeting with the director."

"Of course, you should be there." She nodded. "I need to take a tray up to Margaret. I'll see you in a few minutes in the dining room."

Since the children were eating their supper upstairs, the teachers and director and Patrick had the dining room to themselves.

As much as Helen loved the students, the supper meal was her favorite of the day. The relaxing, casual conversation of adult friends and colleagues melted away the cares of the day.

She was pleased, if not a little embarrassed, when Patrick seated himself beside her.

Sissy served alone tonight since there were only a few dining. She dished up the soup and filled their glasses with either water or sweet tea then left the room with a soft swish of her skirts.

The main course was a cold chicken dish with vegetables on the side, followed by a rice pudding.

When the meal was over, Helen and Patrick followed P.H. to her office. After Patrick told her what Molly had revealed to him, Helen took over and talked about the meeting with Dr. Trent and Margaret's subsequent confession.

"Dr. Trent confined Margaret to her room until your return." Helen went on to tell her about Margaret's sorrow over what she'd done and her repentance to God. "She desires to apologize to Molly, Trudy, and Lily Ann, but of course I couldn't give her permission to approach them. I'll leave that up to you."

P.H. stood. "Thank you both. Helen, I'll speak with Margaret tomorrow. I'll also need to talk to the other three girls. And of course, I'll send a wire to Margaret's parents asking them to come. They need to know what's going on. Perhaps they'll have an idea of the root cause of her behavior." She frowned. "They may choose to remove her from the school."

❧

He should have taken the train last night for Atlanta, but until this situation with the girls was cleared up, he simply couldn't leave his daughter here without being nearby. Patrick left the hotel and walked toward the livery. To be honest, he hated the thought of leaving Helen as well.

As he passed the vacant hardware store, he paused and peered through the window. Plenty of space and it appeared to be clean. The niggling of an idea began to form. He did like the rural area.

But could he make a living here? He walked on, a wrinkle creasing his forehead as he thought. The thought of moving his business here hadn't even crossed his mind until Molly had suggested it.

He arrived at the livery and the owner called out from behind the counter. "Good morning, Mr. Flannigan. Will you need the carriage today?"

"No, just a horse." He would be making a quick trip to the school to speak to the director and say farewell to Molly and Helen. A horse would be faster.

He took notice of his surroundings as he rode the two miles to the school. Pink, red, white, and violet wildflowers dotted the green grass and many of the magnolias already had velvety white blossoms. It truly was beautiful and peaceful here.

He rode around the building to the barn. Albert glanced up and grinned, "Morning, Mist' Flannigan. A might fine day, wouldn't you say?"

"I sure would, Albert. Love the sunshine."

"Yes suh. Not a cloud in the sky." He reached for the reins. "You be stayin' long?"

"I'm not sure. It depends on. . ." He stopped. He supposed he shouldn't be discussing the matter with Albert. Even if he had been with the school forever.

"Depends on what Miz P.H. gonna do 'bout that chile?" He lifted his wrinkled brown hand and pulled a glossy five-pointed leaf off a sweet gum tree and stuck it between his teeth.

Patrick chuckled. "Is there anything that gets past you?" He patted the horse on the rump and turned to go.

"Not much, suh. Not much." Albert's cackle followed Patrick as he walked toward the house.

The foyer was empty except for one of the maids, who knelt beside a small table, polishing the surface with cedar oil. Patrick's nose twitched at the strong aroma.

"Mornin', Mistuh Flannigan." She nodded then turned back to her chore.

Miss Wellington came down the stairs, followed by Margaret. "Ah, Mister Flannigan. I'm glad you're here. She stepped onto the foyer floor and pulled Margaret beside her. "Well, child, here is the first one I believe you need to speak to."

Margaret's face was pale and tear-streaked. She lifted her eyes and looked at Patrick. Her lips quivered. "Mr. Flannigan, I am so sorry for what I did. Truly I am."

Patrick couldn't help but notice that Margaret's demeanor was much different from when he'd seen her last. Somehow she appeared older than her twelve years, as though she'd left childishness behind. Whereas her sorrow two days before was obviously more from getting caught, her countenance now held true repentance, just as Helen had said.

He reached out and took her hand. "I accept your apology, Margaret. I don't think you'll ever do anything like that again and I forgive you."

Her indrawn sob was followed by a torrent of tears. "Thank you, sir."

Patrick squeezed her hand before gently letting go. He glanced at Miss Wellington, who had a tender but firm look on her face.

The maid stood and, with a little curtsy, retreated into the kitchen area. Miss Wellington stepped over to the bell cord and gave a tug.

A moment later, one of the older maids appeared. "Yes ma'am?"

"Sally May, please fetch Molly and Trudy from Miss Wilson's class and Lily Ann from Miss Edwards's and ask them to come to my office. And tell both teachers I won't keep them long."

Sally May headed up the stairs and Miss Wellington turned to Patrick. "Mr. Flannigan, I'm having a meeting later today with the teachers. You are welcome to stay and join us if you can. If you need to get back to Atlanta, I assure you there will not be a repeat of this unfortunate incident."

Patrick glanced at Margaret, who said, "I promise, sir. I only hope Molly and Trudy will still want to be my friends. But I won't blame them if they don't."

"I believe you, Margaret." He turned to the director. "If you don't mind, I'll stay for the midday meal so I can say farewell to the teachers."

A hint of a smile graced Miss Wellington's lips and her eyes danced. "Absolutely you should stay. I'm sure the *teachers* will want to say good-bye to you as well."

At the emphasis on *teachers*, a hint of suspicion bit at Patrick and he peered at the director. However, her face was composed and her eyes as well. Perhaps he'd imagined the teasing tone in her voice."

❧

Helen stood on the porch watching Patrick ride away on the chestnut mare. His back was straight and the muscles in his shirt sleeves tightened over his biceps. A shiver ran across her shoulders as she imagined a knight of old on his trusted steed. A laugh escaped her lips. *Really, Helen Edwards. Get a grip on yourself and stop acting like a love-struck girl.*

She turned and went inside.

Virgie had just come out of the dining room, presumably inspecting it to make sure it was in perfect shape after the midday meal. She smiled at Helen. "You like that redheaded Irishman, now, don't you?"

Helen felt her face flame. Apparently Felicity wasn't the only one who'd uncovered her secret. "He's a very nice man. Of course I like him."

"Umm. Hmm. I think it's more than his nice ways you like."

Helen laughed. "All right, Virgie. I do like Patrick. But there's no sense in even thinking about it."

"And why's that? Can't you see the way that man look at you, honey?"

Helen sighed. She couldn't deny that. "But it's hopeless. His business is in Atlanta and I can't leave the school."

Surprise crossed the soft brown face. "Why do you think that?"

"Why, because I'm needed here. Especially now that the school is growing. More students will be enrolling next year." What was Virgie thinking?

"Land sake, child." Virgie touched her cheek. "You ain't the only one who can teach these young'uns. I expect there be a line of young gals just waiting for the chance."

Shock ran through Helen. How could Virgie say she wasn't needed? She swallowed past the sudden lump in her throat. "I need to grade some papers, Virgie. I'll see you at supper."

She rushed upstairs and into her empty classroom, happy that the children were in other classes this hour. It would be different next year. There would be so many they'd have to divide up the classes into groups.

She sat and placed her face in her hands. Could Virgie be right? Was she really not needed here? She knew there were other teachers who were just as qualified as she to teach deaf children, but she'd been working hard to learn braille so she could help Lily Ann. Now that Abigail was expecting a baby, it would be out of the question for her to do it as she'd planned.

Mixed emotions ran through her. She could marry Patrick, if he asked. But how could she bear to be away from these children? She'd taught some of them for years.

Well he likely wasn't going to ask anyway. So why get herself all stirred up over nothing. But what if he did? Could she bring herself to go away? Even if there were other qualified teachers would they love these precious children the way she did?

Helen sighed. The idea was too fresh in her mind. She wouldn't think about it right now. Besides, she had work to do.

Chapter 13

P.H. looked exhausted. Helen sympathized. The director had been gone for nearly a week and then returned to a problem that required a great deal of wisdom to resolve. Both windows in the office were open, but no air circulated and the late afternoon heat was oppressive. Helen's arms, in elbow-length sleeves, were too warm and her forearm clung to the leather chair's arm. The other teachers looked just as uncomfortable.

"I won't keep you long. I know you have things to do before supper." P.H. picked up a cardboard fan from her desk and moved it rapidly back and forth then returned it to its resting place. "I'm sure you're all aware of the incident with Margaret."

Charles cleared his throat. "Miss Wilson and I only know there was a problem concerning Margaret and some of the other children."

Hannah nodded. "All I really know is that Margaret is confined to her room."

P.H. nodded. "Margaret has been bullying three of the other girls. Not physically, but rather psychologically. I believe the girl is truly sorry for what she's done. She has even repented to God and apologized to the girls and to one of the parents."

"Well, that's good." Charles seemed a little confused. "Will she be returning to class soon?"

P.H. sighed and picked up the fan. She tapped it against the desk then laid it back down. "I'll go into Mimosa Junction in the morning and send a telegram to her parents. They need to know about this. Perhaps they'll have an idea of the root cause of her behavior.

"In the meantime, I would like to allow Margaret to return to her regular class schedule and take her meals in the dining room. As I said, she's repented of her actions and I don't believe we'll have any more trouble on that line. The other three girls have assured me they haven't discussed this with the other children so there shouldn't be any problem. I did, however, want you to be aware of the situation. Some disciplinary action is needed, so she will not be allowed to go outside during recess or after school until I hear from her parents. I would appreciate it if one or more of you would volunteer to take her outside for an hour of exercise and fresh air once a day."

Helen was about to offer to do it when Hannah spoke up. "I'd be happy to do that, Miss Wellington."

"Thank you, Miss Wilson. I was hoping you would volunteer." She smiled. "I know you have a younger sister near Margaret's age. And you're not that much older yourself." She chuckled.

Hannah blushed. "Yes ma'am. I'm happy to do it."

Helen flinched. But P.H. was right. Margaret probably needed someone young to help her through this time. Hannah Wilson was all of twenty-one. At thirty-two, Helen sometimes felt ancient. Most of the girls she'd gone to school with had been married for years and had children. *My, how time passed.*

She sighed. She needed to snap out of this melancholy before she started feeling sorry for herself. She didn't regret the years she'd spent teaching. She loved her work and the students. Still, she had to admit, sometimes her heart longed for a family of her own. A sudden picture of Molly's deep blue eyes and Patrick's sea green ones smiling at her in much the same way appeared in her mind.

She jumped up. "Yes, that's a wonderful idea, Hannah. And now, if we're finished, I have some essays to grade before I go to bed."

A loud boom reverberated through the room followed by a rolling of thunder that lasted several minutes. Helen placed her hand on her chest and gave a shaky laugh. "Whew! That was close."

"It sure was," Hannah said between gasps of breath.

Charles laughed. "Well we need rain to cool things off a bit.

Don't let a little thunder scare you, ladies."

P.H. frowned. "That first one sounded like something was hit."

Someone pounded on the door and Albert burst in. "Miz Wellington. The live oak tree by the gate been hit. It split plumb in two."

Within moments, they followed Albert down the lane. Half the tree lay across the lane, its shiny green leaves scattered everywhere. The bench she'd sat on with Patrick the day before was hidden beneath, more than likely shattered.

"Oh dear!" P.H. slapped her palm against one cheek. "What a mess."

"Yes ma'am." Albert stood shaking his head. "It is that. Reckon I best be gittin' the mules hitched up and yank that thing off the road."

"You need help, Albert," P.H. said. "And don't tell me you don't. Get a couple of the Hedley boys to give you a hand. They can cut the trunk into firewood. When they're finished, send them to my office and I'll pay them for their work."

"Yes'm. If you say so." Albert's face reflected his displeasure and he walked away mumbling. "Could do it myself though."

Helen grinned at P.H. "I think you've insulted him."

Charles chuckled. "The man thinks he's still a spring chicken. I wonder how old he is anyway." When no one answered, he gave a wave. "I have some things to do before supper. And I think I smelled apple cobbler when we came through the foyer. I'm famished."

Hannah nodded and followed.

P.H. glanced at Helen. "Do *you* have any idea how old Albert is?"

Helen thought for a moment, doing some mental calculations. "I'm not sure, but he's older than Virgie and she was an adult when old Mrs. Quincy freed the slaves. I'd say Albert is at least in his sixties. Maybe older."

P.H. nodded. "Ten years older than me or more. That settles it. I'm going to talk to Dr. Quincy about hiring another hand to help Albert with the work around here."

"I'm sure Dr. Trent will agree, but Albert's going to throw a fit," Helen said. "Is Margaret to have her supper with the other children tonight? Or should I take her a tray?"

"I think a tray tonight. I need to speak to Felicity and Howard before having her join them again. Also the girls who help out during the supper hour will need to know the rules concerning her discipline."

Another clap of thunder pealed through the air. Helen nearly jumped out of her skin and noticed that P.H. had started as well. Lightning flashed across the darkened sky. Helen grabbed her skirt as the wind whipped it around. Large drops of rain splattered on Helen's skin and on the lane leading to the house.

"Here it comes," P.H. yelled over the noise and took off running to the house.

Helen lifted her skirts and hurried after the director. Maybe the rain would cool things off, either that or make it more hot and humid. Either way, she didn't want to get caught in a downpour.

੩੦

Patrick sank into his seat just as the storm broke. He'd missed the earlier train, but it had given him a chance to meet with the man who was handling Tom Mill's property and make an appointment to see the building on Saturday.

He still wasn't sure why he'd done it. Why would he want to move a business that had just begun to prosper? Not to mention the fact that he owned a home in Atlanta. Molly might not want to leave the only home she'd known. Although, now that he thought of it, she was the one who'd put the idea of moving to Mimosa Junction into his head.

Well, it wouldn't hurt anything to look at the former hardware store. Just to satisfy his curiosity. Even though he had no real intention of moving from Atlanta, the memory of Helen's small hand on his arm the day before mocked his resolution.

He slid down in the seat and pulled his hat forward to cover his eyes. Maybe he could sleep on the way to Atlanta. Maybe he could escape the sight and scent of Helen while he slept.

❧

The storm raged outside Helen's window. Clap after clap of thunder shattered the air and rain poured down in torrents. Between the storm and thoughts of Patrick, she'd tossed and turned for the past two hours. Just as she began to drop off to sleep, a flash of lightning lit up her room and she sat straight up. With a sigh of exasperation, she got up. Who could sleep with all this going on?

She poured a glass of water and drank the contents, but it barely made a dent in her thirst. What she really needed was a glass of Selma's lemonade. She knew a pitcher of lemonade was most likely on the kitchen counter.

She slipped her feet into her slippers and threw on her robe, buttoning it up to her neck. Lighting a lamp, she then adjusted the wick. She eased her door open carefully so it wouldn't squeak and tiptoed down the stairs. Was that a light in the parlor?

Helen tiptoed to the half-open door.

Virgie sat with her feet up on a small stool. Blue velvet fabric from one of the old gowns overflowed her lap as she sewed. She glanced up as Helen slipped through the door. "Come right on in here, Miss Helen. Looks like you can't sleep either."

"I don't see how anyone can sleep with all the flashing and noise going on. You don't think we have a tornado in the vicinity, do you?" She set her lamp on the side table, sat on the settee, and leaned back.

"Don't think so." The elderly housekeeper slipped the needle and thread smoothly through the thick fabric. "Just a spring storm. Nothin' to worry your head about."

Helen gave a little shiver, remembering the close call they'd had the year before. Thanks to their former director, they'd all made it safely to the storm cellar. The only damage had been to the house, and Dr. Trent made sure repairs were made posthaste. "I'm sure you're right. Hope so."

"Got lots on your mind, don't you, honey girl?" Her soft cadence was almost enough to put Helen to sleep right there in her chair.

"No. Just the storm." She lowered her eyes at the half lie.

"Ummm hummm. Just the storm." Virgie rocked and sewed.

"Well, if you must know, I do have thoughts of Mr. Flannigan running through my head." She flashed a look at Virgie, half hoping for advice, half dreading it. When none was forthcoming, she stood. "I'm going to see if there's any lemonade. Would you like a glass?"

"Don't think you goin' to find any. Wasn't any left after supper." She rethreaded her needle and knotted the thread. "Now I could sure use a cup of tea though."

"Won't it just heat you up more?"

"Never too hot for tea. It always soothes."

"You're right. That's what I need, too. I'll put the kettle on." Helen picked up her lamp and went to the kitchen.

The large homey room enveloped her with scents of cinnamon and clove. Even the faint smell of lye soap couldn't detract from it.

Helen set the full kettle on the stove and stirred the still-hot coals. It wouldn't take long. She removed a tin of tea leaves from the pantry and put them in a brown porcelain teapot then prepared a tray with cups, saucers, and sugar. Within a few minutes the water was boiling and she poured it over the leaves. By the time she'd strained the tea into the cups and carried the tray to the parlor, her eyelids were getting heavy.

She handed Virgie a cup of the hot brew then sat back on the settee. She sipped and then yawned.

Virgie chuckled. "I think maybe you goin' sleep after all."

Helen smiled. "And I think you knew preparing the tea would make me sleepy."

"I told you tea always soothes. Sometimes before you even get it to your mouth."

"Thank you, Virgie." She took another sip. "I'll just take the cups back to the kitchen then I'm going to go back upstairs."

"No, you're not. You leave that cup right on the tray," Virgie said. "I'll put them away. Go on to sleep now. You got classes to teach in the morning."

Helen rose and stepping over to Virgie, she pressed a kiss on her cheek. "Good night, Virgie. And thank you."

But as sleepy as she was, once she lay on her bed and closed her eyes, dark red curls, sea green eyes, and a tilted smile haunted her thoughts and on into her dreams.

※

Patrick stared out his bedroom window as rain pelted the hedges around his house. The storm had followed him all the way to Atlanta and showed little sign of stopping anytime soon. If this continued much longer, the rivers could overflow their banks. He only hoped and prayed the deluge had slackened back at Quincy School. Thoughts of the river that flowed across the Quincy property filled him with dread. As far as he knew, the area hadn't flooded in years. But that didn't mean it couldn't happen.

Patrick had seen firsthand how fast river water could rise when he'd traveled to Rome, Georgia, on a business trip a few years earlier. As he'd watched out the window of his third-floor hotel room that day, he'd thought he was dreaming as a steamboat floated down Broad Street. Of course Rome was situated between three rivers, but each river had done its own damage.

Perhaps he should have stayed in Mimosa Junction. What would happen there if flooding should occur? Would they be able to evacuate the school in time? He determined to be on the first train to Mimosa Junction in the morning.

After a few hours of fitful sleep, Patrick awoke to sun shining through the window. He breathed a sigh of relief. One day of rain, even a hard rain, shouldn't be enough to bring a river's water levels up.

Patrick began his week finishing up the work on a handmade

saddle and shipping off some orders to mail-order customers. Then he turned to checking through his books to calculate how much of his business was mail order. Mail order business shouldn't be affected by a move. *If* he moved. He left instructions with his assistant and told him he'd be back Monday night.

Saturday, he arrived in Mimosa Junction in time for a leisurely lunch in the hotel dining room before his appointment at the hardware store.

An hour later, he walked out the door, a bill of sale and a ring of keys in his hand. And a curious mix of anxiety and excitement in his heart.

Chapter 14

Patrick flinched as rain pelted him from all sides. There hadn't been a cloud in the sky when he'd left town ten minutes ago. He urged his rented horse to a run, shielding his face as well as he could with his hat brim.

By the time he arrived at the school and turned the horse over to Albert, he was drenched from head to toe.

The squishing of his soaked boots as he entered the foyer caused him to cringe. Especially when Virgie walked out of the room to the left with a dusting cloth and stared at him.

With a sheepish, apologetic smile in her direction, he sighed. "I'm sorry about the floor."

A soft chuckle left her lips. "It's all right, Mr. Flannigan. Don't think anythin' about it. Can't be helped in this weather. Wait right there a minute though."

Dutifully he stood, trying not to move and shake more water onto the floor, until she returned with a thick braided rug, which she threw down on the floor by his feet.

"You slip off those boots and that hat and throw them on the rug. Then you can go into the infirmary and change into some dry clothes." She motioned to the room she'd just left.

"I have no dry clothes with me, Virgie." Patrick stared down at the water puddling around his feet.

"Don't you worry none. Dr. Trent always keep extras here for when he has to stay over with sick young'uns." She ran an eye over his form. "Just about the same size, I'd say."

A pattering of feet from the stairway drew Patrick's attention and horror filled him as Helen stopped on the first step and gaped at him.

"Looks like you got caught in the downpour." She pressed her lips together but not in time to hide the amused smile on her face.

He must look a sight.

Virgie scowled in her direction. "Don't you worry about it now. Just run along. I'm goin' to take care of Mr. Flannigan."

"Of course. I'm sorry to have stared." Her eyes danced and she didn't look very sorry. "I'll run up and tell Molly you're here. I don't believe she's expecting you and I know she'll be ecstatic." She spun and hurried up the stairs without another word.

"Don't pay her any mind, Mr. Flannigan." Virgie patted him on the arm. "I don't expect she'd look any better if she got caught in a downpour. Not that you look bad or anythin' of course. Because you don't."

"All right, Virgie. I get the idea. You don't need to worry about my feelings." Patrick slipped out of his boots and tossed his hat on the rug then headed for the infirmary door with the sweet, elderly retainer following behind.

She motioned him to a door in the side wall and he slipped through. She handed him a thick towel then retrieved clothing, including socks and underwear, from a chest in the corner. "Leave them wet clothes on the floor. I'll have one of the maids fetch them and hang them to dry behind the stove in the kitchen. Might take some time. Hope you planned on stayin' awhile." With a smile, she left him alone.

When he was dry and dressed, he ran a comb through his unruly curls, which would be more unruly as soon as they thoroughly dried. No wonder Helen had been amused. He probably looked like a redheaded sheepdog. Still, his heart hammered at the thought of the covert smile. It was quite attractive, even if her humor was directed at him. He headed for the door and went into the foyer again.

Molly ran into his arms with a scream of delight. "Papa! I'm so happy to see you. I didn't know you were coming."

"You didn't?" He pulled back and gave her a look of mock surprise. "I would have thought you'd have heard my heart beating with joy all the way here."

She giggled. "Don't be silly, Papa."

He laughed and glanced around. "Where did Miss Edwards run off to?"

"I think she went to the parlor to sew costumes. I think some of them are for the Easter cantata, you know."

"Oh yes, that's not very far off. I can't wait to see it. And to hear you sing." He tweaked her cheek and she ducked away.

"I only have two lines to sing solo. But I sing them after every verse." She smiled and glanced toward the stairs. "Margaret is to be allowed to sing in the choir, too. But Lily Ann has the lead."

"That's very nice. And I'm happy they are letting Margaret take part." He peered at his daughter. "No more threats?"

She shook her head. "Margaret is very nice, really. We're becoming quite good friends."

"That's good news to hear." He planted a kiss on her forehead. "And you're a very good girl, Molly. I'm very pleased with you. And I know Jesus is, too."

She blushed. "Thank you, Papa. Did you wish to speak with Miss Edwards? I can go get her."

"No. I don't want to intrude on her work. It was nothing. I just wanted to greet her."

"I knew it. You like her." She grinned. "You really like her."

He grinned and tugged at one of her braids. "Stop that, little rascal. What would you like to do this afternoon? I'd planned to take you for a ride on the horse, but the rain put a stop to that."

"Hmmm. It's almost dinnertime. After that we have our practice, although Mrs. Quincy probably won't be here unless it stops raining." She put her finger on her cheek and thought. "We could help Sissy and Flora set the table."

"Will they let us?"

"Sure. That's less work for them."

A laugh erupted from his throat. "All right with me. Lead the way."

❧

Silver clinked against china as Sissy and Flora served the chicken soup. Helen thanked Flora and focused on her bowl and spoon.

What she'd really been craving lately was chilled cucumber soup. But cucumbers wouldn't be up for a while, or any other fresh vegetables for that matter, although the hot Georgia climate made it possible to have them earlier than the northern states.

Why in the world was she thinking about garden vegetables? She dipped her spoon in the bowl a bit too forcefully, causing a drop to splash onto the tablecloth. Because she didn't want to think about the handsome Patrick Flannigan sitting across from her. That was why.

She lifted her head and glanced at him. His curls were still damp from the rain and one of them had curled over his forehead in a perfectly adorable way. She shouldn't have laughed at him. Well, she hadn't really laughed. But she almost had.

Sissy cleared her throat and Helen looked up. Oh dear, she hadn't even noticed when the girl had removed her soup plate. She leaned back slightly so Sissy could serve the main course.

She glanced across the table and met Patrick's eyes. He smiled a lazy smile then turned to his food.

Now why had he smiled like that? As though he had a secret and it involved her. The very idea.

He looked up again and this time she couldn't help return his smile. Her heart sped up. She wondered if she'd have a chance to speak with him today. About Molly's progress of course. The girl was a delight and always did so well. None of the teachers had complaints about her. Patrick must be very proud of her. It was sad that Molly had no mother to gush over her about her grades. Men seemed to take it for granted their children would do well. She sighed. If she had a child like Molly, she'd be about to burst her buttons with pride.

She pushed away her dessert plate. Well, she didn't have a child of any sort and probably never would.

Patrick was waiting when she stepped into the foyer a few minutes later. She smiled and nodded then started to walk past him.

"Helen." He stepped forward.

"Yes?" she asked, trying to control her breathing.

"Could we talk for a while?" His eyes gazed into hers.

She glanced toward the stairs. "Perhaps the upstairs parlor. It's seldom used except on parents' days."

He offered his arm and she rested her hand there, barely touching.

"Won't Molly be looking for you?"

"I told her I wanted to talk to you then I'd watch the practice." He glanced down at her. "She told me to ask you to come watch as well."

"Of course. I never miss the practices if I can help it." She averted her eyes as they walked up the stairs and turned toward the large sitting room.

When they were seated in matching wing chairs, Patrick turned to her. His eyes seemed to pierce hers, and she felt as though ocean waves would dart out and overcome her at any moment.

"Helen, I can't put this off any longer. I care for you deeply and it's high time you knew it." He took her hand as though afraid she might remove it as she'd done once before. "Is there a chance you might feel some affection for me?"

Her heart pounded hard and happiness washed over her, followed by dread. She lifted up a prayer for wisdom.

"I do care for you. But Patrick, you live in Atlanta and I don't know if I can leave the school."

He started to speak but stopped and looked at her as though searching her heart. "I know your teaching is very important to you."

She smiled a sad little smile. "As was pointed out to me recently, there are plenty of teachers and the school could do without me quite nicely."

"What? Someone actually said that to you?" His eyes flashed.

"No, no. They didn't mean it as an insult. Just assuring me that if I should decide to leave, the school would go on."

"I see. Then why did you say you couldn't leave the school?"

"It isn't the school, really. It's the children. I love them so much. I don't think I could bear to be away from them."

He blew a breath of air out. "Well, I can't blame you. I'm no match for the children here. I know that."

He dropped her hand and stood. "I appreciate all you are doing for Molly. Perhaps we'll remain friends."

"Wait. Don't you want to hear about Molly's progress this week?"

"Perhaps later. I promised I wouldn't miss her practice." He gave a slight bow and left the room.

But. . .she hadn't meant the children were more important than he was. Had she? But of course that's practically what she said. Was it true? Were they more important to her than Patrick? She clutched at her throat and swallowed deeply. If not, she'd just given up a chance for happiness with the only man she'd ever loved.

⁂

Well, that was that. Patrick was glad Helen hadn't gone to the practice. He wasn't ready to pretend everything was as it had been before. In spite of what he'd said about remaining friends, he wasn't sure if he could do that. His feelings for her were too strong to scale back now.

He'd come close to telling her that he was moving to the Junction. She'd still be near the children. Could even continue to teach some if she wanted to. But he couldn't. Maureen had always been first in his life and he in hers except for God. He couldn't even contemplate entering into a marriage where his wife would put others first.

He sighed and tried to focus on the practice. Mrs. Quincy had made it here after all, driving over with her husband in an enclosed carriage. Molly's voice was true and clear when she sang her solo lines. And Lily Ann sang like an angel, her sightless eyes lifted upward as if she could see into heaven itself and the One to whom she was singing.

The practice ended and Mrs. Quincy stood. "Good job, everyone. I think we're almost ready. Sonny, you were a little late coming in with your verse after Molly's. Try to work on that."

"Yes ma'am." The ten-year-old boy, who loved to clown, grinned and saluted. Mrs. Quincy shook her head and laughed.

Molly grabbed Patrick's hand and they walked from the auditorium together.

"I wonder why Miss Edwards didn't come to practice. She never misses one." Worry lines puckered the skin between her eyes.

"Something must have come up. You don't need to worry. I was with her an hour ago. She's fine."

Her lips tilted in a half smile. "I'm sure you're right. I'm disappointed she wasn't there. That's all."

The afternoon crawled by for Patrick. He wanted nothing more than to leave before he ran into Helen. He wasn't ready for that. But he didn't want to disappoint Molly and make her sad by leaving right away. Still, he had no intention of being seated across from Helen at supper.

"Papa, guess what we're having for supper?" The lilt in her voice would have told him even if he hadn't already smelled the chicken frying. But he couldn't resist teasing her a little.

"I couldn't guess in a million years. Why don't you tell me?"

She giggled. "Can't you smell that chicken? I've been smelling it for an hour now. It made my tummy growl. And Sally May said Cook made a caramel pecan cake—my favorite after chocolate."

"That sounds wonderful, sweetie, but since you'll be eating supper an hour sooner than the adults, I believe I might go ahead and leave while the rain has slowed down. I should really take the late train back to Atlanta."

"You mean you won't be here for church in the morning?" Disappointment clouded her beautiful blue eyes.

"Oh honey. I really need to leave. Does it mean that much to you?"

She nodded. "But it's okay, Papa. I understand if you need to leave tonight."

He groaned inwardly. "Well, maybe I'll wait until tomorrow. After church you and I will eat at the hotel and then I'll take you back to school. I'll take the later afternoon train."

She threw her arms around his neck. "Thank you, Papa. I love going to church with you."

He returned the horse to the livery and asked them to send a horse and carriage around to the hotel in the morning. The rain began again just as he entered the hotel. He glanced up at the sky. Concern ran through him. Maybe the danger of flooding was there after all. He'd see if the rain continued another day. Perhaps he wouldn't be leaving after all.

Chapter 15

By morning, the rain had slowed to a drizzle, but as Patrick stood at the hotel doorway waiting for the carriage, he noticed dark clouds hung low and heavy in the sky. The muddy street in front of the hotel was waterlogged to the point of deep puddles standing everywhere. He was relieved to see no sign that the river had crested, but that didn't mean it wouldn't.

The boy from the livery rode up on a palomino gelding, leading the mare Patrick had used the day before. Patrick pushed the door open and went outside, rain peppering him.

"Morning, Mr. Flannigan. Sorry about the carriage. Mr. Hays said it'd be sure to bog down in the mud."

"It's all right. I'd already thought of that. Planned to exchange the carriage for a horse anyway."

"She's all rested up and ready to go." He handed Patrick the mare's reins then whirled his own mount around and took off down the street.

Patrick stood in the muddy street trying to decide if he should ride to the school or go ahead and board the train for Atlanta. But no, he couldn't chance it. If the river overflowed its banks, the school would be at risk.

He mounted up and headed down the street. This time, he wore a rain slicker in case the drizzle turned into a downpour again.

As he passed his new place of business, he grinned. Molly would be tickled, but he wouldn't tell her yet. He didn't want it to get back to Helen that he was moving. If she decided to change her mind, he wanted it to be because she loved him. After all that was the main reason he'd bought the store and made plans to move his business. He loved her and wanted to spend his life with her in a place she'd be happy.

The thought ran through him that perhaps he should make it easier for her and tell her the truth. But stubbornness bit at him and he shoved the thought away.

Helen glanced toward the classroom window and breathed a breath of relief. It appeared they were in for a long, slow rain today rather than more storms as she'd feared. She lifted her hand to her lips and patted back a yawn. Between the storm outside and the storm within her own heart, she'd slept very little last night.

Had she done the right thing by refusing to form a relationship beyond friendship with Patrick? It seemed the only practical thing to do, at least at the time, but through the night her heart and thoughts had lashed at her. She'd given up her chance at love and marriage to the only man who'd touched her heart and soul.

But what else could she have done? Of course, another teacher could meet the children's educational needs. But emotionally she was tied to them and they to her, weren't they? She'd been with them for several years now. One by one their faces had drifted before her closed eyelids. Of course the three she was most concerned about were Molly, Lily Ann, and Margaret. She felt that she could help Margaret through whatever emotional trauma she was suffering.

She started as a snore sounded from the rear of the room. Jeremiah was sound asleep, his head lolling to the side. She shook her head and headed back to his desk. She touched his shoulder and he jerked, his eyes big and darting from side to side.

He looked up and relief crossed his face. "Sorry, Miz Edwards," he said, in broken English.

She nodded and smiled. "It's all right, Jeremiah. Didn't you sleep well last night?"

He shook his head.

"Neither did I." She gave him a pat. "But we'll both have to do the best we can to stay awake. Why don't you go get a drink of water and see if that helps?"

He nodded and went to the stand in the corner. She cringed as he slurped from the glass.

Helen gathered up the English papers and returned to her

desk. It would be dinnertime in a few minutes. She was glad she only had one class this afternoon. Perhaps she could find time for a nap. Probably not though. Virgie needed help finishing the costumes. Easter was only a couple of weeks away.

Most of the children wouldn't be going home for the holiday since it was a short one, but many of the parents came to spend the day here with their children. The Easter program was always a big event for the school—and would be even more so now since Abigail had taken over the music and drama department.

When the class was finally over, she dismissed the children and went to her room to freshen up for the midday meal.

She washed her face at the basin and blotted it with a soft towel. Her eyes strayed longingly to her soft bed. She sighed and headed for the door.

When she entered the dining room she stopped short at the sight of Patrick seated between Molly and Howard. She hastened to her chair, her heart hammering wildly. Why hadn't he left for Atlanta?

During the meal, she tried to listen to Patrick's conversation with Howard, but Felicity and Hannah, who were seated near her, kept up a constant chatter about the weather and the upcoming holiday.

"I hope the rain lets up before Easter." Hannah took a sip of her tomato soup. "It would be a shame if some of the parents couldn't come."

"Oh, I'm sure it won't last that long." Felicity reached over and patted the young woman's hand. "Spring rains come and go this time of year. And storms can burst out at any moment. But they seldom last long."

Helen wasn't so sure. If the rains didn't slow down soon, the river could overflow its banks. And the school was in a valley. Flooding wasn't probable, but it was possible.

The children filed out of the dining room, following Charles and Hannah. Helen stepped to the door at the same moment as Patrick. He stood back and let her pass through the door. With misery nearly overwhelming her, she ducked her head and stepped into the foyer.

"Helen?"

At the sound of Patrick's voice, she turned. "Yes?"

"I know you need to get to your class and I'll be leaving for Atlanta later this afternoon, but I wanted to ask you to at least think about what we discussed."

The consternation in his eyes matched that in her heart, but a glimmer of hope rose inside her. Was there still a chance? Was there a way to work this out?

"Yes, Patrick. I will."

He reached for her hand and pressed his lips to her palm. "Thank you."

Her heart thumped wildly as she went upstairs. *Oh God, show me what to do. I love him so much. If there is a way for us, please show me.*

By midafternoon, the sun came out brightly and the temperature was a little cooler than before the rain. That was good. A month or so from now, rain would only make things hot and humid.

Helen stepped out onto the porch for a breath of fresh air, but the chairs were all damp so she went inside and gravitated to the parlor.

Virgie was half asleep in her rocking chair, her hands resting on the pile of fabric on her lap. She started awake as Helen sat across from her.

Virgie yawned and shook her head from side to side. "This weather making me sleepy as a bear in winter. Pourin' down rain one minute, sun streamin' down the next. Wish it would make up its mind."

"I hope the rain is over for a while."

"I do, too. Seems like everything in the house is damp. It isn't, but it sure do feel like it."

Helen retrieved the vest she'd worked on the day before from the basket by her chair. "I know. If it isn't rain in the spring, it's humidity in the summer."

Virgie chuckled the soft deep laugh Helen loved to hear. "Listen to us, complaining and jawin' about the weather like that's goin' to change anything."

Nodding, Helen sewed a button on the vest. "Do you have any idea of what Abigail has in mind for these costumes? They don't look much like Easter costumes to me. You'd think she'd want white and gold for the angels."

"The Easter costumes are already done." Virgie lifted an eyebrow. "These are for the end-of-school program."

Helen paused. "Maybe I just assumed they were for Easter because the Easter cantata is coming up. Perhaps she plans to do the end-of-school play we'd discussed about the Quincy family."

"Well, I s'pose we'll just have to wait and see." Virgie cast a glance at Helen. "You seem all out of sorts. What wrong with you?"

"Oh, I'm all right. Just struggling with some difficult decisions." Helen avoided Virgie's piercing glance and focused on sewing another button tightly in place.

"Would it be somethin' about a redheaded Irishman?"

"Maybe." Helen put down the vest and stood. "Oh, I'm not in the mood for sewing. I think I'll go for a walk."

"Mighty soggy out there. You likely to sink right down into the mud." Virgie pursed her lips and squinted her eyes as she threaded her needle again.

"Well then, maybe I'll go to my room and read for a while. I'll help sew tomorrow. If Abigail doesn't intend them for Easter, there's probably no hurry."

Instead of heading upstairs, she went outside. Virgie was right. The yard and lane looked like a bog. But at least the porch furniture was dry now. She settled onto one of the white wicker rockers and soon the rhythmic cadence of motion began to soothe her anxious thoughts.

The door opened and Margaret came out with Hannah. They

were so intent in their conversation they didn't notice her.

"Hmmm. I don't think we can go for a walk, Margaret." Hannah's cheerful voice carried across the porch. "It's much too muddy."

"Then let's sit out here on the porch." They turned. "Oh Miss Edwards." Disappointment was obvious in Margaret's voice as she stared at Helen.

Helen rose. "If you two need a quiet spot to visit, this is the very place. I was just going in."

"Thanks, Helen," Hannah said. "But you're welcome to join us if you like." The halfhearted tone belied her words.

Helen smiled. "Another time, perhaps. I have some letters I wish to write before supper."

She trudged upstairs to her room. It seemed as though Hannah was getting along quite well with Margaret. She hadn't seen the girl with such a big smile in a long time. Perhaps P.H. was right. Maybe a younger woman like Hannah was just what Margaret needed.

As she reached the second-floor landing, Molly and Patrick were coming down from the third floor.

"Miss Edwards, I've been showing Papa my new drawing." Molly's face glowed with pleasure. "And he loved it. Didn't you, Papa?"

"I sure did, sugar. It's one of the prettiest live oak trees I've ever seen."

Helen smiled. "Molly drew it from memory. I'm sure you recognized it."

"Of course. It was the tree by the gate." The look he gave her was tender. "I know I'll miss sitting in its shade."

Helen blushed at the memory of her hand snug and warm in his before she'd pulled it away. Yes, she'd miss the tree, too.

"P.H. is going to let us plant another one in the same spot."

"That's a good idea." His lips curved into a smile that also flashed in his eyes. "I wonder how long it takes a live oak tree to grow to the size of that one."

"At least twenty-five years, Papa," Molly said. "We looked it up in our science book."

He nodded. "That's much too long. We need to move the bench."

Helen burst out laughing. "We definitely need to move the bench."

"What's so funny about that?" Molly looked from Helen to Patrick, a confused look on her face. "Anyway, we've already moved the bench. It's under the magnolia tree on the other side of the gate."

"Oh yes, I think I did see the faithful bench when I rode up the lane this morning." He cut a glance at Helen. "Too bad it's so muddy down that way. We could try it out."

Helen bit her lip to keep from smiling. "Pay no attention to your father, Molly. I think he's being a little silly today."

Patrick's laughter rang out. She loved it when he seemed happy like he did today.

"I suppose you'll be leaving now that the rain has stopped. As you can see, we're perfectly all right."

"Yes, I hate to leave, but I do have a business to run." He turned his gaze fully on Helen. "I would like to talk to you about something before I go."

"Flannigan."

Patrick turned to look toward the caller.

"There you are." Dr. Trent came up the stairs, a serious look on his face. "I was wondering if you could do me a favor. It's rather an emergency."

"Of course. Glad to help any way I can."

"I need to check on one of the Blaine boys on the other side of Campville, but I also need to get some medicine to an elderly lady in Mimosa Junction." He shook his head. "Of course, these things happen sometimes, but since you're going there anyway, I was hoping perhaps you could drop the medicine off for me so I won't be so late getting home to Abigail."

Patrick darted a quick glance at Helen and a flash of disappointment shadowed his eyes, but he smiled as he replied. "Yes, of course I will, Dr. Trent."

Relief washed over Dr. Trent's face. "If you'll come to the infirmary with me, I'll get the bottle of medicine for you. I can't tell you how much I appreciate this."

"Please, don't give it another thought. I'm glad to help." He sent a smile of regret to Helen then opened his arms to his daughter, who flew into his embrace. "I'll try to come next weekend. But if not, then at least the one after that."

With a final kiss on Molly's cheek, Patrick headed down the stairs.

Helen put her arm around Molly and they stood together and watched him until he entered the infirmary.

At a sniffle from Molly, Helen drew her closer. "It's all right, sweetie. We'll find some way to make the time go by in a hurry. He'll be back before we know it."

But what had he wanted to talk to her about? Had he changed his mind about waiting for an answer? If he had, would she have been able to make a decision?

She patted Molly's shoulder. "At least it's not raining."

Chapter 16

I t was the final practice. Easter was tomorrow and the cantata would be held after dinner. Helen sat in the back of the auditorium. Abigail turned and gave her a questioning look. Helen held her clasped hands up in victory. The neighbors had all been invited, in addition to the families and the staff, so the room would be full. Abigail had been a little nervous about the children's voices carrying all the way to the rear of the room, but Helen could hear them just fine.

She kept darting glances toward the door behind her. Patrick hadn't come last weekend after all. He'd promised to be here this weekend, but Saturday was half over. Molly would be devastated if he wasn't here for the program. And to be honest, so would she. After searching her heart, she'd decided if he still wanted to court her, she would agree. Who knew? Maybe if they spent a lot of time together, they'd decide they didn't care as much for each other as they thought.

A short laugh escaped her lips. No chance of that on her part. She'd missed him so much these couple of weeks she'd had trouble keeping her thoughts on her teaching.

After watching Margaret develop an attachment to Hannah that bordered on hero worship and with Abigail spending more time with Lily Ann again, Helen realized the school would do fine without her if her relationship with Patrick developed that far. P.H. would make sure everything was always in tip-top shape, and Dr. Trent was always here whenever he was needed.

She would miss all the children and staff terribly, but she doubted they'd miss her much after the first few weeks. Life would go on for all of them. And perhaps she'd finally have a husband and child to love. For Molly was already like a daughter to her. And she was still young enough to have more children.

The doors creaked open and Patrick sat down beside her. Heat rushed to her face. Oh dear, she already had them married with children and he wasn't even courting her yet.

"Sorry to be so late," he whispered. "I had some things to tie up before I left Atlanta."

"You're just in time. The song they're getting ready to sing is the one with Molly's solos."

The choir started the song beautifully; then Molly stepped forward. Her glance surveyed the room, finally reaching the back. When she recognized her father, her eyes lit up for a moment then she began to sing the verse. Patrick applauded as she stepped back and the choir joined in the rest of the song.

Lily Ann was at home with a sore throat and instructions from Dr. Trent to gargle often and eat spoonsful of honey and lemon. Abigail and Helen were praying she wouldn't have to miss the cantata. But the child's health had to come first.

When practice was over and the children dismissed, Molly made a beeline for Patrick and threw her arms around him. "Papa, I was afraid you weren't coming."

He put his arm around her as they left the auditorium. "I said I'd be here, didn't I, princess?"

"Yes, but sometimes things happen beyond our control."

Patrick looked at his daughter with amazement then glanced at Helen. "I think my daughter is growing up."

"Yes, that happens." Helen laughed. "She's certainly wise for one so young."

Molly made a sound of exasperation. "You two don't have to talk about me as though I'm not here."

Patrick's eyes danced. "I beg your pardon, young lady, and to make up for my lack of manners, how would you like to go to the hotel for ice cream? I happen to know they have some today."

"Yes, I'd love some ice cream." Molly clapped her hands in very childlike fashion.

"And I'm sure you'd like for Miss Edwards to join us?" He flashed a grin in Helen's direction.

Before Helen could accept, Abigail joined them. "Helen, would you mind helping me this afternoon? I have some finishing touches on the sets to make and Trent was called away earlier."

Disappointment seared Helen to the point that she almost made an excuse to say no. But then shame washed over her. Abigail had worked so hard to make the program wonderful for them all. Even in her condition, she'd kept going. Helen couldn't be selfish.

"Yes, of course I will." She smiled at Patrick and Molly. "Can we make it another time?"

Patrick grinned. "Yes, we can. Could we talk later?"

Helen nodded. "After supper?"

"It's a date." He turned to Molly and offered his arm. "I guess it's you and me, milady."

Abigail's face was a picture of consternation as they walked away. "Oh Helen, I'm so sorry. You should have told me you had plans. Go on with them. I'll find someone else to help."

For a moment, Helen was tempted, but it would be a good thing for Molly and Patrick to spend some time alone. And the staff was busy. There might be no one to help Abigail.

"Nonsense, I didn't have plans really. Patrick was just being kind." She looped her arm through her friend's and walked with her back to the auditorium.

"How many parents are coming early?" Abigail stopped halfway to the stage, panting.

"Are you all right?" Concern ripped through Helen as she eyed her friend's moist forehead.

"Yes," Abigail gave a half-gasp, half-laugh. "I get winded a lot easier these days."

Helen ran her gaze down Abigail's still trim figure. "Are you wearing a corset?"

"Of course. I can't let the children see my big stomach."

"Abigail, that's not good for you. Does Dr. Trent know you're wearing that tight thing?"

"Actually this is the first time I've worn it and he left before I put it on." She bit her lip. "Mrs. Carey says every woman must wear them."

"Well, Mrs. Carey is a million years old and probably doesn't know what she's talking about."

Abigail frowned. "She used to be the midwife before there was a doctor around here. Some women still use her to deliver their babies."

"Some women don't know any better. But you do, and you know very well you shouldn't be wearing a corset when you're with child." Helen heaved a sigh. "That's medieval. Or old fashioned, anyway. Why don't you go in the back parlor and slip out of it. You can put it back on to go home."

"Oh all right."

When they reached the stairs, Abigail went to the parlor and changed.

She laughed as she rejoined Helen in the auditorium. "You were right of course. I feel much better."

Relief coursed through Helen. "I should think so. Now I'll answer your question. We're expecting five sets of parents here tonight. Virgie has the maids preparing rooms for them. The others will arrive in the morning, some before church and some afterward."

"Hmmm. If the school keeps growing, there won't be room for them to stay the night here in the future."

"Maybe. There are seven empty rooms on the second floor and we still have half a dozen unused ones on this floor. Although they aren't fixed up yet." Helen glanced around. "What do you need me to do now?"

❧

"Did you have fun, pumpkin?" Patrick patted Molly's hand where it rested on the carriage seat beside him.

"Yes, but it would have been nice if Miss Edwards could have come with us." Molly turned her hand over and clutched Patrick's.

"I know, sweetie. But there will be other times." At least, Patrick hoped so. The day had been full of frustrations. He'd hoped by now to have let her know about his purchase of the hardware store and his plans to relocate to Mimosa Junction. But every time he'd thought he would have a chance to talk to her, they were interrupted, just as they'd been the last time he was here. He sighed. Maybe tonight.

A sudden clap of thunder interrupted his thoughts and caused Molly to jump. She sat up straight and clutched his hand tighter as the thunder continued to rumble and roll. Lightning flashed in the distance.

Patrick snapped the reins and the horses broke into a run. Even with the top up he didn't want to get caught in a thunderstorm with Molly in the carriage.

The first drops fell as they pulled up in front of the school. He walked inside with Molly then drove the carriage to the barn.

Albert cast a worried glance up to the sky as he took the reins. "You may as well plan to stay the night, Mr. Flannigan. Road's already muddy. Can't take much more rain without flooding into the fields and bogging down all the carriage wheels. I plan to bed down in the back room here myself."

"I'll see how it goes, Albert. I might just ride one of the horses to town if it doesn't get too bad." The words were barely out of his mouth when the sky opened up. With a wave at Albert, he took off running to the house. He pushed through the door and stood dripping on the floor. Not again.

Sally May came ambling into the foyer, her eyes big. "Whoo-wee. You better stand there while I get some towels. And get them shoes off, Mr. Flannigan, before Virgie sees that puddle on her floor."

Patrick chuckled but did her bidding. A few minutes later he repeated the same actions as the last time, only with Sally May as his guide instead of Virgie.

When he stepped back into the foyer wearing Dr. Trent's clothing once again, Virgie stood there with a twinkle in her eyes.

"I see Sally May took good care of you." She gave a nod of approval.

"Yes, she did. But I think her main motive was to keep you from being upset over the floor." He grinned. "You must be a mean woman around here, Miz Virgie."

Virgie gave one of her soft velvety laughs. "I might be or maybe they just want me to be happy."

"I think the latter the most likely reason." He glanced toward the stairs as a middle-aged couple came down with one of the boys between them. His eyes were shining as he walked between them.

"Some of the parents are already here, I see," he said.

"All of them that's coming tonight. It's nice to see the children with their mamas and papas." Virgie smiled at the couple. "The dining room right through that door. You sit anywhere you like and Bobby can sit with you."

At the sound of footsteps on the stairs, Patrick glanced up again, eagerly hoping to see Helen.

"She be down in a minute." Virgie's look of amusement sent a heat wave to his face.

"Who?"

She chuckled. "Who, indeed? I might have meant Miss Molly, mightn't I?"

"You might have, but you didn't, did you?"

"Ain't no sense in being embarrassed about it. She a sweet lady and mighty pretty, too. And you a handsome, strappin' fellow." She looked him up and down. "Nothin' wrong with it at all. You marry that gal."

Laughter rose in Patrick's heart. She'd hit the nail on the head. "Trouble is I'm not sure she'll have me, Virgie."

Virgie gave a little snort. "She'll have you. Be crazy if she don't. And there she come now." She walked away toward the kitchen, humming.

Helen's face radiated a very attractive pink blush and her eyes shone a welcome. He could only hope he wasn't misreading her.

"Molly will be right down. And she said don't wait for her." Her upturned face glowed.

"In that case, shall we go on in? I'm suddenly very hungry. The ice cream didn't stay with me long." He held out his arm and tucked her small, soft hand in the crook of it. Somehow it felt like it belonged there.

He held her chair and then claimed the chair next to her. He didn't care who usually sat there.

She blushed and ducked her head but failed to hide the pretty smile that tilted her lips. "Poor Felicity. You've taken her chair."

"I'm sure she'll find another with no problem." He squeezed her hand and then released it before anyone could see. "I decided, with all the guests here tonight, I'd take my opportunity to sit where I like. Besides, I heard Virgie tell some parents to sit anywhere."

"Well, if Virgie said it, then it must be all right. She sets the rules in the household."

Molly appeared at his elbow. "Papa, will you please scoot over and let me sit between you and Miss Edwards?"

Patrick held back a sigh and heard Helen cough in an obvious attempt not to laugh. He moved over a seat and Molly scooted in.

"Thank you." She turned to Helen, excitement in her voice. "Isn't it fun having all the parents here?"

Helen nodded. "Yes, it certainly is. I'm so glad we opened up the third floor and made all the changes. Otherwise we wouldn't have had room."

Sissy and two other servers came in and served the soup.

Patrick listened to the murmur of voices around the table and wished the meal was over so he could be alone with Helen and tell her his news.

However, once more his plans were upset. After supper, it was pouring down rain outside and there were too many people inside to find a private place. Finally he settled down beside her in the front parlor and simply enjoyed being near her as they visited with Hannah and Charles. Virgie was too busy to join them, and Patrick rather missed the soft cadence of her voice and her gentle humor.

He told Helen good night on the second-floor landing then went up to the small room he'd been assigned at the end of the other wing.

He was happy to see a Bible on the nightstand as his was back at the hotel. He sat on a comfortable chair by the window and opened the small book. He found his way to the seventh chapter of Luke, where he'd left off the night before. He laid the Bible down and crawled between crisp sheets.

Lord, if You want me to marry this woman I love so much, please work it out. If not, please give me the peace to accept Your will.

He'd found her eyes resting on him more than once today. Hope rose in his heart. He was almost sure she felt the same way he did. And he knew he loved her very much.

Peace washed over him in spite of the rain that pelted the roof and hit against the windows.

One thing he knew. Tomorrow he'd do everything in his power to find a way to talk to her in private.

Chapter 17

The sound of rain beating against the window woke Helen from a sound sleep. Would it ever stop? And on Easter Sunday.

She jumped out of bed and ran to the window. She could barely make out the shape of the barn through the pounding rain. A clap of thunder rent the air, followed by a flash of lightning that seemed to light up the backyard and the woods beyond. Trees swayed and bent from the force of the wind. She backed away from the window.

She lit a lamp in the darkened room and picked up the watch from her side table. Six o'clock already. Quickly she washed her face and hands then dressed in one of her Sunday dresses. They wouldn't likely be going to church in the storm, but she still wanted to look her best.

She stood in front of the wood-framed mirror on a stand in the corner. She pulled and twisted her hair this way and that. Finally, she wound it into a loose chignon on the back of her neck and allowed tendrils of curls to hang down the sides of her face.

She gave herself a critical look and shrugged. She didn't have time to stand here primping. There were guests in the house. Perhaps they could hold some sort of service in the auditorium after breakfast.

She found a scattering of people in the dining room, including Charles and Patrick. Patrick stood at the buffet, filling a cup with hot coffee from the large silver urn.

He turned around and their eyes met. He smiled. She blushed and returned his smile then sat on the chair he held out for her. Right beside his.

"Good morning, Helen." Charles tossed her a bright smile. She never had understood how he could be so friendly after she'd turned him down. Perhaps he realized he wasn't that interested in having a relationship with her after all.

Sonny's parents came through the door, followed by all the others. Perhaps none of them had been sure about venturing in alone. After all, this was a first overnight stay for all of them.

"I wonder if the other parents will be able to get here?" The question had been buzzing around her mind since she'd seen the weather.

"I wouldn't count on that." Patrick shook his head. "I rode down the lane when I woke up to check it out. It appears the road is washed out in several places. And the low spots are flooded. I don't think anyone is coming in or going out."

Felicity, who had just entered and sat at the table, gasped. "Are you sure?"

"I'm afraid so."

"Oh no." Helen's brow furrowed. "The children will be so disappointed."

"Well, perhaps the big meal and the program will cheer them up a little," Howard said, "although I know that won't take the place of their parents being here."

Charles returned to the table after getting more coffee. "I don't think many more were coming anyway. A couple, maybe. The others live too far away to make the trip more than to pick up their children at Christmas and for summer break."

Helen clapped her hands to her face. "Oh no. This means Dr. Trent and Abigail can't come either. How will we have the cantata without Abigail?"

Felicity grinned. "Guess it's up to you. You've been with Abigail nearly every practice."

"But. . .I can't."

"Of course you can." P.H. stood in the doorway and had obviously heard every word. "I have every confidence in you."

"What about Lily Ann's solo?" Helen knew she was working herself into a panic. "They won't be able to come either."

"You'll just have to get someone else to sing her solo." P.H.

found a seat next to Sonny and his parents.

Sissy and two other servers brought covered dishes and set them on the buffet. The aroma of scrambled eggs, sausage, and ham made Helen realize how hungry she was. She waited and let the guests go first.

As soon as her filled plate was before her, she focused her attention on the delicious food while she pondered her problem. There was only one student who could do as well as Lily Ann on the solo—Margaret.

Helen glanced across the table at the director and then switched her vision to Margaret, who sat beside her parents. She wondered if P.H. had spoken to them yet. It would make the situation easier for her if Margaret could fill Lily Ann's spot.

After breakfast some of the men, including Patrick, went to check the water level at the river. Helen breathed a sigh of relief. She knew Patrick wanted to talk to her, and she was eager to let him know she'd decided to agree to the courtship. But today wasn't shaping up to be a good day for that.

She hurried down the hall to the director's office and tapped on the door.

When she was seated across from P.H., she took a deep breath.

P.H. smiled. "You want to know if Margaret can be in the cantata."

"Well, I don't want to go against any decision you might have made, of course, but it would be nice if we had her lovely voice in there, since Lily Ann won't be here." She cast an eager look in the director's direction.

"As a matter of fact, I've had a quite satisfactory meeting with Margaret and her parents. I'm convinced nothing like the former episode will happen again. I also believe Margaret is truly sorry and she's suffered enough." She smiled. "So if you'd like to ask her to be a stand-in if Lily Ann can't make it, you have my permission."

"Wonderful!" Helen jumped up. "I'll ask her now. She's probably with her parents somewhere."

"I believe they were going to look at the science exhibit from last fall. Charles has displayed it again for the parents that didn't get a chance to see it."

"Thank you, P.H. You're a wonderful woman and we're lucky to have you as our director."

"Oh, go along with you." She waved her hand toward the door. "I'm a mean tyrant and everyone knows it."

Helen laughed as she sailed out the door and went in search of Margaret and her parents.

❧

The rain had finally slowed down to a slight drizzle. As Patrick stood near the bank of the river with Charles and Howard, he heaved a breath of relief. The river hadn't crested, so if the rain stopped, they wouldn't need to worry about any major flooding. But the rain itself had been a real gully washer and the road was almost impassible in spots. As soon as the rain stopped and the sun came out they could start filling the holes in the lane with gravel. Until then the house guests would have to be patient and stay put.

They returned to the house. Patrick still held out some hope of talking to Helen. But if she had to be in charge of the Easter program, he wasn't sure if an opportunity would arise. Besides, with the house full of extra people it would be difficult to find a private place to talk. He went in search of Molly and found her and Trudy in their room in an animated conversation.

Both girls jumped up when they saw him.

"Mr. Flannigan, guess?" Trudy turned big brown eyes on him.

"Hmmm. You just found out you're really a long-lost princess from some never before heard of kingdom."

Trudy giggled. "No. Guess again."

"Oh Papa." Molly gave him a look of disdain which quickly changed into a smile and a giggle. "Margaret has been given her freedom."

"Yes. I know. Because her parents are here."

"No, not that. She's all the way free now. Even when her parents leave. But that's not all."

"Oh, there's more? I think that's pretty big news as it is." And he wasn't too sure how he felt about it. After all, the girl had terrorized his daughter. A twinge of guilt bit at him. He'd forgiven her for that.

"It is," Trudy said, "but there's more. Margaret gets to be in the cantata and she'll sing the solo if Lily Ann can't come because of the weather."

"Or because she may still be sick," Molly added.

"Okay, that's very nice for Margaret. Not too great for poor Lily Ann."

"But Papa. Lily Ann would want what's best for the cantata. And everyone knows Margaret has the best voice after Lily Ann."

"So how do you girls feel about Margaret not being punished anymore?" He thought he could tell what the answer would be. Molly and Trudy had apparently forgiven and forgotten and were quite ready to be friends with the girl again.

"We're happy, Papa." Molly smiled broadly. "Margaret is sorry for what she did and we're all best friends again."

Trudy nodded. "We missed her," she frowned, "but she'd better not ever threaten to hurt Lily Ann again. And we told her so."

Patrick blinked back sudden tears and coughed loudly. "I'm proud of you girls."

"Miss Shepherd says we should always forgive when someone trespasses against us." Trudy's face was suddenly solemn. "Because we all need forgiveness."

"Miss Shepherd sounds like a very wise woman. Just who is she, by the way?"

"Our Sunday school teacher, Papa. Remember, you met her a few weeks ago."

"Oh yes, the preacher's daughter. And I'm glad you took her words to heart." He reached over and gave one of Molly's braids a yank.

Molly nodded. "I wish we could have gone to church today. It doesn't seem right to miss. Especially on Easter Sunday."

"Well, next Sunday will be here before you know it."

Patrick left and ambled over to his room where he removed his wet shoes and dried them the best he could. He hung his socks in front of the stove and stretched out on the bed. He hoped the weather would be nice this week. He planned to get the shop ready this week and start bringing supplies over from the Atlanta store. He hoped to have everything moved and the other store cleared out within two or three weeks. Most everything would come by rail.

He drifted off to sleep with thoughts of Helen and the possible look on her face when he told her the news.

æ

Margaret's voice drifted across the auditorium with angelic tones. Helen couldn't keep the smile from her face. What a gift the child had received from God. The audience seemed mesmerized. When the solo was over and the choir joined in for the final song, Helen dabbed at her eyes with a lacy handkerchief.

She and the boys in the group stayed after everyone else had left the room to fold chairs and put them away. She didn't really need to stay, but it gave her a chance to reflect. The cantata had definitely been a success. Now that it was over, and she knew she'd given it her all, she could refocus her thoughts where they truly wanted to go.

Patrick. Would they finally get a chance to talk so she could tell him? She sighed. The possibility didn't look too promising. The house was still full of people. Perhaps tomorrow.

After a delicious supper which proved to be nearly as sumptuous as their Easter dinner had been, most of the guests retired to their rooms. A few, however, joined the teaching staff in the large parlor for music where Hannah played the piano and the others joined in singing hymns. The evening flew by, and all too soon it was time to say good night.

Classes wouldn't resume until Tuesday, so the children had been allowed to stay up longer than usual in honor of their parents' visit.

Helen could only hope the roads would be passable by Tuesday. She couldn't imagine trying to hold classes if the guests were still here. The children would never be able to concentrate knowing their parents were downstairs.

As she stepped into the foyer, she found Patrick waiting. Everyone else had already disappeared up the stairs.

"Helen. I thought we'd never have a chance to say hello without dozens of people around." He took her hand tentatively as though he wasn't sure if he'd be allowed to keep it in his.

Helen smiled and let her hand remain in his. She could feel the calluses on his palm and was surprised to find the sensation rather pleasant. "I've been wanting to talk to you, too, Patrick, but I only have a moment. It's very late."

"I know. Besides, it wouldn't do to have anyone misunderstand. So for now, let me merely say, I have a great deal of admiration for you and hope we can let our friendship grow into something more. I have some news for you, but it will keep until a more opportune time."

"I have something important to say to you as well. But I don't want to wait. Let me just say that my answer to your earlier question is yes. I'd be honored to consider our friendship to be a courtship."

Light filled his eyes and the grin on his face spoke volumes. He opened his mouth to say something, but she pressed two fingers against his lips.

"Good night, Patrick. We'll talk tomorrow." She turned and ran up the stairs and into her room.

Oh dear. Had she been too bold? She stood against the closed door, her breath coming in excited little pants. What if he'd changed his mind? But he certainly didn't look like he had, with that big old Cheshire cat grin on his face.

A little giggle escaped through her lips. It seemed everytime she was near him she giggled about something. She hadn't done that for years.

Suddenly she noticed how stuffy the room was. She'd closed the window earlier to keep out the rain, but now she flung it open wide and breathed deeply of the clean, fresh air. A cow mooed from nearby. Albert had probably opened the barn door for the same reason she'd flung the window wide. Nothing smelled like rain-washed air. Maybe the storms were over. Probably not though. It was still early April. She wondered what Atlanta was like this time of year. Could she be happy living there? Being so used to country sounds and sights and smells? A vision of tight, dark red curls and sea green eyes drifted through her thoughts. And a smile that curled her toes. Oh yes, she could be happy in Timbuktu or the jungles of Africa, as long as Patrick Flannigan was by her side. She smiled. *And a sweet daughter like Molly*. She would take good care of her adopted daughter and teach her everything she would need to make her life as easy as possible. A home in Atlanta would be just fine.

She undressed in the moonlight and changed into her night-gown. She crawled into bed between crisp, cool sheets and sank her head into her soft feather pillow.

Chapter 18

Patrick whistled an old Irish tune as he shoveled sand into holes in the lane leading to the school. He hoped the gravel could be filled in before the next rain or the sand would all be washed away. But it was at least a temporary solution and would allow the parents to return home. All he'd thought about most of the night and all morning was his anticipated meeting with Helen. Her morning classes would be over soon and he only hoped she was free this afternoon, because he absolutely had to get the new building ready and get back to Atlanta to finish up there.

He finished filling two more holes then headed for the house. He was glad that so many men in the neighborhood had volunteered to help.

He washed up in the infirmary and changed into his own clothing, which Sissy had handed him as he'd walked in.

He entered the dining room and found Helen already seated. Her eyes lit up when she saw him. He took the chair next to hers. "Can we talk after dinner?"

"Yes, I'm free all afternoon." Her voice had a little lilt and his heart sped up. Even though she didn't know she wouldn't have to leave the area, she was willing to go with him. He was glad she wouldn't have to make that sacrifice.

Good. Now if they could find a private place to talk. He glanced around. One of the couples had already left for their home. He was pretty sure the rest would leave after the meal, now that the lane was passable.

For the first time in days, he actually enjoyed food. Amazing, the difference a few words from Helen had made. The gumbo was delicious and a fresh garden salad tingled on his palate. Fried ham and buttered sweet potatoes followed, with green beans that he would call fried. However they were prepared, they were delicious. The ever-present sweet tea refreshed him after the hard work of the morning. And Selma's peach cobbler with sweet cream whipped into soft peaks topped off the meal.

After the meal, he said his farewells to Molly, promising a surprise the following week, which curbed her tears.

A half hour later, the children had all returned to their classrooms and the parents had made their exits, among a lot of relieved laughter. Most said they had a wonderful time in spite of it all, but they hoped their return trip in May would be uneventful.

Patrick stood on the porch with Helen. "Shall we sit here or walk down the lane to the bench?"

"Oh. Let's walk down. I haven't had a chance to rest there since the other tree was removed."

"Fine with me. Let's see if the magnolia has as much shade as the live oak did."

The magnolia proved to have a great deal more shade than the live oak. One could have almost hidden on the bench beneath the blossom-laden branches. This was fine with Patrick because two men were working on the lane just a short distance farther along.

He waited while Helen smoothed her skirt then seated himself beside her on the bench. "It's been a disturbing couple of days, hasn't it?" Oh, that was brilliant. After waiting so long for this opportunity, he wasted it making small talk.

"Yes, it's been dreadful." She fanned her hand in front of her face and tapped her fingers on the wooden bench. "I certainly hope the storms are over."

"So do I." He reached over and took her hand. "Helen, there's something I need to tell you."

Her face paled and she inhaled sharply. "It's quite all right, Patrick. I understand if you've changed your mind about wanting to go beyond friendship." Misery and embarrassment were written all over her face.

"What?" Shocked, he lifted her chin and looked into her eyes. "Not at all. Why would you think that?"

"Well, I was afraid you'd think I was being too bold by saying what I said to you last night."

"No, of course not. You were enchanting. I've thought of nothing else since."

"Really?" A faint blush tinged her cheek.

Didn't she have any idea how he felt about her? He sighed. How could she? They'd talked very little about anything other than the school and how Molly was getting along. "Helen, I didn't intend to be so abrupt. I wanted to give you a proper courtship, but the truth of the matter is I'm in love with you and it's time you knew it. I want to marry you, if you'll have me."

She smiled. A joyful smile that sent his heart racing. "I love you, too, Patrick. And I want you to know that I will gladly go with you to Atlanta or anywhere else you wish to go. I don't care where I live, so long as I'm with you and Molly."

He pressed her hand to his lips. "Well, you won't have to. Because that's what I wanted to tell you. I'm moving to Mimosa Junction. I've already purchased a building for my shop and plan to start moving things here this week."

Wonder crossed her face. "You would do that for me? But Patrick, you don't have to. I know your business is already established in Atlanta."

"And it will be just as established in Mimosa Junction. To be honest, when I first started thinking about the idea, it was mainly because of you. But the more time I've spent in this area, the more I like it." He kissed her fingers again. "Besides, this way Molly can stay in school and you can continue to teach if you wish."

"You don't mind if I keep my job?"

"Well, for now at least. I hope perhaps in the future. . ." He stopped. Better not talk about babies. She was blushing enough already. "Well, you may teach as long as you like."

He slipped down onto the grass, glad it had dried, although he could still feel damp earth underneath the grass. "Helen, will you marry me?"

Tears pooled in her eyes and she nodded. "Yes, Patrick. I'd be honored to be your wife."

He quickly reclaimed his place beside her and took her into his arms. The first touch of their lips made his head reel. "Helen," he whispered, "can we make it soon?"

❧

Helen gazed up into Patrick's eyes, hardly able to believe she wasn't dreaming. She'd dared to dream about this moment, but the reality was so much more wonderful than her dreams. "How soon do you mean?"

"Of course I want you to have a proper engagement period, and I'll need to get moved and start looking for some land for a house. I wouldn't ask you to live in the rooms over the store."

"I wouldn't mind," she said then wondered again if her words were too bold.

"But I'd mind for you." He peered into her eyes. "I don't even know if you have family to consider."

She shook her head. "My father died when I was thirteen, and my mother passed away five years ago. I was an only child. Do you have family other than Molly?"

"No, what family members I have left are in Ireland."

She reached up and smoothed back the lock of hair that had fallen across his eye. "I love your hair."

He laughed. "You like this carrot-colored thicket?"

"It isn't carrot colored. It's a beautiful deep, dark red and it goes perfectly with your eyes."

"Well my darling, I only hope our children look like you. That's all I've got to say."

She bit her lip, fighting off embarrassment, then laughed. "I guess that must be a compliment."

"Very much so. You're beautiful, Helen. Don't you know that?" His eyes spoke even more than his words.

"Well, thank you. I'm glad you think so." She thought a minute. "I'll ask Molly to be my bridesmaid."

"She'll love that." His tender look caused butterflies to come alive in her stomach.

"I wouldn't want anyone else."

"Would the end of summer be too soon?" His hopeful look almost persuaded her.

"I'd sort of like an autumn wedding, if you don't mind. It's my favorite time of year." Although Georgia autumns didn't have the lovely colors and crisp days she'd grown up with. Still . . .the thought of walking down the aisle in a wedding dress in the sweltering heat of a Georgia August was totally unbearable. Imagine if her face should perspire and she couldn't even blot it with a handkerchief.

"Then autumn it is. You set the date and make the arrangements you like. Don't worry about the expense. I'll take care of it."

"You'll do no such thing," she retorted. "My parents left me with a tidy little dowry of sorts. It will do nicely to pay for the wedding and then some."

He laughed. "Are you always this stubborn?"

She threw him a teasing smile. "Oh no, sometimes I'm much worse. Want to call off the wedding?"

"Not a chance." He grinned. "I like stubborn women."

"Sometimes I'm very easy to get along with." She smiled, wondering what he'd say next. Not really caring, just wanting to hear his voice.

"I know." He tweaked her chin. "I like you that way even better."

The afternoon flew by. Helen felt as though they were the only two people on earth. Then they heard Albert coming up the lane, singing an old gospel hymn.

Helen gasped. "They must be stopping for the day. Have we been out here that long?"

"Doesn't seem that long." Patrick sighed and rose, helping her to her feet. "I think we'd better tell Molly the news before I go, don't you?"

"Of course. You don't think I can keep this secret until next weekend, do you?"

They strolled up the lane hand in hand until Helen gently pulled hers away.

They waited until after supper to tell Molly. They went out on the front porch, and surrounded by the sound of chirping birds and blossom-scented air, they told her the news.

"Oh Papa. Oh Miss Edwards. I've been praying you'd fall in love and get married." She took a deep breath. "Does this mean you'll be my mother?"

"Molly," Helen heard her own voice tremble, "I know you had a wonderful mother and I would never try to take her place, but I do want to be a mother to you. If you want me to."

Molly threw her arms around Helen. "I do. I really do." She pulled back and looked up into Helen's face. "Will I still have to call you Miss Edwards?"

Helen gave a shaky little laugh. "Well, you'll have to call me Miss Edwards until the wedding. After that, you'll call me Mrs. Flannigan in school and you can decide what you want to call me at home."

"Can I think about it?"

Patrick gave Molly a hug. "Yes, you have plenty of time to think about it. Do you think you can keep it a secret for a little while? Just until we get a chance to announce it?"

The stricken look on Molly's face told the answer very clearly. "Can't you announce it now? So I can tell Trudy and Margaret?"

Helen glanced at Patrick and met his waiting eyes. He grinned. "I guess there's no getting around it."

Helen laughed. "Let's tell P.H. and Hannah and Charles anyway. Oh, and Howard and Felicity. So they won't hear the news from the children."

They found Hannah and Felicity in the parlor with Virgie and told them the news. Virgie didn't say I told you so, but the smile on her face spoke volumes.

After they'd shared the news with the others, Molly kissed her father good night and went upstairs.

Helen followed Patrick out to the porch. Their tender farewell left Helen in tears.

"Please don't cry, sweetheart. I'll be back soon."

"They're happy tears. I promise. I'll be fine."

She stood there while he went for his horse then watched him ride away. But this time, she knew he'd be coming back, not just to Molly but to her.

Her prayers that night were mingled with laughter and tears. *Thank you, Lord. You've given me my heart's desire.*

❧

Patrick stepped into his new building. The previous owner had left it clean and in good repair. There really wasn't too much he'd need to do to ready it for its transformation into a leather shop. He missed the smell of oiled leather, and his hand, mind, and heart were eager to get back to their trade. Well, his mind and heart were more focused on Helen right now, but he was determined to build the business up. A man couldn't be truly happy unless he provided for his family. And he intended to do just that.

He worked until midnight, getting the existing shelves into the position he wanted them. The glass-doored cabinets were a bonus, since the ones he used for display in the Atlanta shop were built in. So this was one expense he'd not have.

He went upstairs and took another look at the living quarters. There were three small rooms. He didn't want to crowd Molly and Helen into such a small space, but it would be fine for him while he was looking for a homeplace.

❧

The Atlanta house looked small and forlorn with all its furniture and pretty knickknacks sold or packed away. He'd gotten rid of all the furniture. He couldn't expect Helen to live among Maureen's things. He'd already bought a few pieces of furniture for his rooms above the shop and he'd buy more for the new house whenever he had one.

He'd saved some things for Molly, including the clock that

had belonged to Maureen's family and the linens and china she'd brought from Ireland. Molly would want those when she was a grown-up woman. Just for a moment the familiar twinge bit at him. But quickly he shoved it aside. His grief was gone. At most, what he'd just felt was nostalgia. Maureen was his first love and always would be. But the love he felt for Helen, though different, was just as strong, perhaps stronger in its own way.

He ran his hand over the mantel he'd built the year they'd arrived here. He spoke, slipping back into the brogue he'd tried so hard to leave behind. "I'll be leavin' ya now, lass. But I'll be seein' you again someday. And you'll meet Helen, too, and I know you'll be lovin' her. Just you wait and see."

Turning his back on the place where he'd loved and lost Maureen, he shut the door behind him and got on his horse to head for the train station for the last time.

Chapter 19

December 1892

Helen jumped out of bed and hurried to turn the page on the huge calendar that hung behind her washstand. The first day of December. Just two weeks and two days until her wedding day. Butterflies banged against her stomach. She giggled. She did a lot of that lately. But why shouldn't a woman giggle when her wedding approached. Even if she had turned thirty-three last month.

She ran her finger down the calendar. The children would be dismissed for the Christmas break on the sixteenth. She pressed her fingers against her lips and then allowed her fingers to rest on the eighteenth. She was so glad her wedding fell on a Sunday. They planned to have the wedding at the church at two o'clock. She had no idea where they'd spend the night. Patrick said he wanted to surprise her. They'd leave for Savannah the next morning for a short honeymoon and be back the Friday before Christmas. Their first Christmas as a family. Molly was so delighted she didn't mind staying at the school while they were away. The teachers and other students would all be gone. But Felicity and Virgie would take good care of her and Selma had promised to let her help bake cookies and pies for the remaining staff's Christmas holiday. And of course, Virgie's small grandson would be there a lot as always.

She did her morning ablutions and got dressed. After tucking her hair into a bun, she grabbed the stack of graded essays from her writing desk. She'd take them upstairs to her classroom before going down to breakfast.

She arrived at the dining room door just as Sissy arrived with a fresh urn of hot coffee. The girl smiled and motioned with her head for Helen to precede her through the open doorway.

The buffet was already set with breakfast foods, including Helen's favorites—ham, fried eggs, and grits dripping in butter. She added a biscuit to her plate for good measure and sat down. Sissy brought her a cup of coffee.

"Thank you. I could have gotten that."

"Yes miss." She pressed her lips together then grinned. "But you already sittin' down and I was up. Anyway, you goin' be pourin' enough coffee once you is married to that Irishman."

Friendly laughter rippled across the table. Everyone seemed to think it was funny that the prim and proper Helen was marrying the wild-haired Irishman. Well, she'd show them.

"Actually, Sissy, I thought I'd turn all the domestic duties over to Patrick."

This time, after a shocked instance of silence, uproarious laughter burst out, followed by Molly's dismayed voice. "You mean Papa is going to do the cooking?"

Uh oh, she may have gone too far. "No, of course not, Molly. I was only teasing. I promise I'll cook and clean and do laundry."

Molly blew a breath of air out. "Oh, good, but you won't have to clean or do laundry. Papa is going to hire a maid." She clapped a hand over his mouth. "Oh no. That was supposed to be a surprise."

"Don't worry, I won't let on that I know." Helen glanced around the room and placed a finger to her lips. "No one else will tell either."

That wasn't the only secret. Patrick had found them land with a small but nicely built house already on it. He'd been working on it for the last three months, and Helen hadn't been allowed to see whatever improvements he'd made. She had a sneaky hunch he might be adding a room but wasn't sure. Ordinarily, curiosity would be getting intense, but with the excitement of planning for the wedding and the birth of Abigail's baby daughter, there hadn't been a lot of time to dwell on it.

Baby Celeste had been born in early October and had quickly stolen everyone's heart. Abigail looked nearly as trim as she had at her wedding. She had agreed to be Helen's matron of honor.

After breakfast, Helen went to her classroom. Within a few minutes her first-hour students filed in.

Lily Ann took her desk near the front, so Helen could help her with braille in between her other teaching duties. Abigail had decided not to return to teaching and Helen didn't blame her. P.H. was looking for a braille instructor since they were expecting two more blind students the following year, including an eleven-year-old deaf-blind boy.

The thought of living with a double handicap like that was overwhelming to Helen, and she had no idea how anyone could teach him. But on the other hand, who would have thought a blind child like Lily Ann could have learned sign language, which she insisted on doing? The deaf children signed in her hand or finger spelled and it worked quite well. It had opened more communication between Lily Ann and the other children. But of course, Lily Ann also had her hearing.

A ripple of excitement ran through her at the thought of helping more students. Of course, if she and Patrick had children of their own, she would need to retire from teaching, at least until they were older.

"Miss Edwards!" Phoebe's broken speech brought her back to the present. She was having a little trouble focusing today.

"Yes, Phoebe?" She stepped over to the child's desk.

"Bobby and Sonny keep pulling my hair." She was nearly in tears.

Helen glanced at Bobby, who sat behind Phoebe, and Sonny, who sat beside Bobby. Both had guilty but gleeful looks on their faces. She motioned for them both to follow her and led them out the door and into the hallway.

"All right, boys." She spoke while she signed. The little rascals wouldn't be able to say they didn't hear her. They were both proficient in sign and lip reading. "I know those long blond braids are tempting to pull. It's probably a lot of fun."

They both gave vigorous nods.

"But did it ever cross your minds that those braids are attached to Phoebe's scalp and it hurts when you yank on them?"

They looked at each other then looked away.

Bobby spoke first. "I didn't think about that. I won't do it anymore, Miss Edwards. I promise."

"I won't either." Sonny made a crossing motion in the general vicinity of his heart.

"I think you need to both apologize to Phoebe."

Dread crossed their faces.

"In front of everbody?" Bobby's eyes widened.

"Right now would be a good time." She tapped her foot and gave them a stern look.

"Yes ma'am," they chorused.

The boys shuffled into the classroom and marched back to Phoebe's desk. After apologizing they took their seats.

"Do you forgive them, Phoebe?" Helen asked the frowning little girl.

"Yes, I forgive them." The frown lines became deeper. "But aren't they going to get a whipping?"

Helen bit her lip. Apparently Phoebe needed a little teaching on forgiveness.

"I don't think that's necessary." She tossed a warning glance at both boys. "But if they ever do it again, they'll go to the director's office and I don't know what Miss Wellington might decide to do."

Helen returned to her seat, hoping the rest of the day would be uneventful. She couldn't wait until suppertime. Patrick would be here.

❧

Patrick stood back and surveyed the house. He hoped Helen would love it as much as he did. He'd finally had to face the fact that he wasn't a good enough carpenter to do what he wanted and get it done in time, especially since he also had to run his business. So he'd hired several carpenters to do most of the work for him

A wide porch stretched across the front of the white frame house wrapping around one side where it met the L from the added room. There was plenty of space to add more rooms if they needed them. Or they could even add a second floor. But for now, he thought it was just about perfect.

He'd already brought in the furniture he and Helen had picked out. And he'd placed the heirloom clock on the mantel in Molly's room. He'd let her decide which of Maureen's other things she wanted to display. He hoped she'd keep them in the cedar chest at the end of her bed until her own wedding.

He mounted the midnight-black gelding he'd recently purchased. The new carriage and two carriage horses were housed in the barn along with a milk cow. It was a hassle to come out here twice a day to take care of the livestock, but he had found some very good deals which he hadn't wanted to pass up.

He rode into town and went to his rooms above the shop. His employee, Jim Porter, would move in there this weekend, when Patrick planned to take up residence in the new house.

He changed and headed for the school. He couldn't wait to see Helen and Molly. Soon, they'd all be together—a family in their own home.

&

Helen couldn't breathe. She gasped. Panic took over and she looked around wildly.

Abigail gave her a worried look. "Be still and breathe in slowly, then let it out slowly. Now do it again. That's good. You're fine. Just a case of nerves."

Helen concentrated on slow breathing while Abigail adjusted her veil, drawing it down over her face. "You didn't fall apart at your wedding."

Abigail laughed. "That's what you think. But I had my mother there and that helped. Just pretend I'm your mother."

Helen giggled. "How can I pretend that? You're five years younger than I am."

"There, you have your laughter back. You'll be fine. Especially when you start down the aisle and see Patrick looking at you all lovey-dovey eyed."

"Lovey-dovey eyed?" Helen wailed. "Now I'm going to think of that when I look at him. If I start laughing while walking down the aisle, you're a dead goose."

"I promise you won't think about anything but Patrick." She patted the veil. "There, you're ready. And I hear the music. We need to go to the door to the vestibule so we can see Molly walk in."

They peeked in and watched Molly step through the door to the sanctuary. She walked down the aisle in perfect step to the music. Abigail patted Helen on the shoulder and stepped away.

She took a deep breath. She wondered how long it would take Abigail to walk down the aisle.

The music got louder and she heard her cue. She stepped on the red carpet and started down the aisle. Lifting her eyes, she looked toward the front of the church. The reverend was at the front and Dr. Trent stood by Patrick's side. As she looked directly at Patrick, her heart almost stopped. The expression on his face showed adoration and eternal love. She was about to be joined to her dream man. No, better than that. The godly man the Lord had brought into her life. He stepped forward and took her hand. She felt numb and yet tingling with life at the same time. She heard the reading of the vows. She heard herself answer and then Patrick.

Then loudly and clearly the reverend said, "I now pronounce you man and wife. You may kiss the bride."

Patrick gently lifted her veil and bent his lips to hers and she melted into his embrace.

A roar of noise brought her back to reality as their friends clapped.

The reception didn't last long and soon Helen was kissing Molly. "Sweetie, we'll see you in a few days. I'll miss you."

"I'll miss you, too, Mama."

Electricity ran down Helen's entire body. Molly had called her *mama*. She winked back tears and hugged Molly tightly. "I love you, Molly."

Then she was swept past the crowd and into the carriage. She leaned her head on Patrick's shoulder as they drove away.

Patrick slipped his arm around her. "I love you, Mrs. Flannigan."

"Oh. I love that name. And I love you, Mr. Flannigan." She looked up into his eyes. "Where are we going?"

"We're almost there. Close your eyes."

She laughed as joy came flooding up. "Oh, all right." She shut her eyes tightly.

The carriage turned and a few minutes later stopped.

"You can open your eyes now."

Her lashes fluttered up and she looked at their house. But was it the same house? It was magnificent. She drew her breath in. "Oh Patrick. It's beautiful. I love our new home. The porch is wonderful."

He hopped out and came around to lift her down. Instead of putting her on the ground he carried her up the porch steps and opened the door. Her heart thumped as he carried her over the threshold of their home.

When he set her on her feet, she swayed, and he caught her, drawing her closely to him. He pressed his lips to hers, gently at first, then deeper. "Welcome home, Helen."

"Oh Patrick, my darling. I was home the moment we were pronounced man and wife. But here, in this wonderful place, we can start our life together."

And then his lips claimed hers again.

Frances L. Devine grew up in the great state of Texas, where she wrote her first story at the age of nine. She moved to Southwest Missouri more than twenty years ago and fell in love with the hills, the fall colors, and Silver Dollar City. Frances has always loved to read, especially cozy mysteries, and considers herself blessed to have the opportunity to write in her favorite genre. She is the mother of seven adult children and has fourteen wonderful grandchildren.

If You Liked This Book, You'll Also Like...

Love's Story
by Dianne Christner

Venture into this classic historical romance set in California from bestselling author Dianne Christner. As a female journalist, Meredith has something to prove with her big story on forest conservation. But when her heart becomes entangled, will she risk her career? Also includes a bonus story, *Strong as the Redwood* by Kristin Billerbeck.
Paperback / 978-1-63409-901-1 / $9.99

The Lilac Year
by Janet Spaeth

Travel to the northern prairie wilderness where this historical romance from author Janet Spaeth is set. Mariah is searching for her nephew and a quick way to leave the frontier when she meets homesteader Ben Harris. Also includes the bonus sequel, *Rose Kelly*.
Paperback / 978-1-63409-908-0 / $9.99

Wildflower Harvest
by Colleen L. Reece

Enjoy an inspiring historical romance set in Wyoming territory from author Colleen L. Reece. Dr. Adam Birchfield risks losing love in order to keep searching for his brother. Also includes the bonus story, *Desert Rose* in which a woman falls in love with a man through his letters.
Paperback / 978-1-63409-907-3 / $9.99

JOIN US ONLINE!

Christian Fiction for Women

Christian Fiction for Women is your online home for the latest in Christian fiction.

Check us out online for:

- Giveaways
- Recipes
- Info about Upcoming Releases
- Book Trailers
- News and More!

Find Christian Fiction for Women at Your Favorite Social Media Site:

 Search "Christian Fiction for Women"

 @fictionforwomen